A Moment's Surrender

For anyone who's "loved and been loved, and made a mess of it," John Burt's suspenseful, sharply observed debut novel captures the messy intense nature of love, rivalry, simmering secrets and fractured friendship. Paul Bishop, the former friend of a famous poet, grapples with old and new betrayals when his ex-friend and ex-lover both burst back into his stalled life. A sudden murder forces hesitant Paul into action as he wrangles his feelings for two very different women, all three characters gripped by a complicated love for the darkly charismatic poet. Burt offers a witty, entertaining portrait of literary academia while at the same time delving deeply into the tangled emotions of his vividly drawn characters. True readers will happily surrender to *A Moment's Surrender.*
Elizabeth Searle
(author of *The Drama Room* and screenwriter of *I'll Show You Mine*)

Praise for *A Moment's Surrender*

Riveting and rich, this is a novel that takes on the complexities of love with deep compassion. It is a gorgeous exploration of grief, the connections that sustain and break us, and the surprising grace that can unfold as we die and as we heal. It makes you ponder human existence and the stories in our own lives that are not over. It is a book that is nothing short of a gift to its reader.
Marjan Kamali
(author of *The Stationery Shop* and *The Lion Women of Tehran*)

A Moment's Surrender is a rigorous examination of four people who learn the painfully high cost of trifling with love. John Burt's emotionally rich and psychologically complex novel pulls the reader into a tangled web of relationships that slowly unravels in the aftermath of a senseless murder. With its vividly rendered settings and insightful intelligence, this splendidly written book casts a spell as its characters lurch toward redemption.
Stephen McCauley
(author of *My Ex-Life* and *You Only Call When You're in Trouble*)

The mystery at the core of John Burt's psychologically rich and emotionally satisfying debut is not only what killed famed poet Tom Corbin; it's how Fate—in its ravenous appetite for trouble—has undone and will ultimately remake the man, women, and child in his immediate orbit. *A Moment's Surrender* shimmers with intelligence and with astute insight into the many ways we all possess to destroy and save each other.
Christopher Castellani
(author of *Leading Men*)

A Moment's Surrender

John Burt

Hollywood Books International
the fiction imprint of Press Americana

Published by
Hollywood Books International
An Imprint of Press Americana
americanpopularculture.com

Cover Art: Albert Bierstadt, *Among the Sierra Nevada, California, 1869*
Cover Design: Press Americana

Library of Congress Cataloging-in-Publication Data
Names: Burt, John, 1955- author
Title: A moment's surrender / John Burt.
Description: Hollywood : Hollywood Books International, the fiction imprint of Press Americana, 2025. | Summary: "A Moment's Surrender follows freshman writing instructor Paul Bishop in the aftermath of the murder of his former best friend, the renowned poet Tom Corbin. Haunted by guilt and bound by a devastating secret, Paul takes it upon himself to care for Tom's terminally ill widow, Susan. But the truth he withholds - that Tom had planned to leave Susan for another woman, Paul's own long-ago lover Rachel Lake - draws Paul into a painful triangle of loyalty, betrayal, and unresolved desire. Caught between the two women, Paul must navigate a web of grief and deception that threatens to undo them all"- Provided by publisher.
Identifiers: LCCN 2025030106 | ISBN 9781735360188 paperback
Subjects: LCGFT: Fiction | Novels
Classification: LCC PS3552.U767 M66 2025
LC record available at https://lccn.loc.gov/2025030106 [lccn.loc.gov]

The awful daring of a moment's surrender
Which an age of prudence can never retract
By this, and this only, we have existed
Which is not to be found in our obituaries
Or in memories draped by the beneficent spider
Or under seals broken by the lean solicitor
In our empty rooms
—*T. S. Eliot, "The Waste Land"*

1

THE TWO RENO POLICEMEN—TO WHOM PAUL BISHOP HAD AL-
ready lied before he had made up his mind about lying—were friendly
enough, though not so friendly as to put him at ease with them, especially
since they kept calling him "sir," a term from which they did not try
to polish away the oblique menace. One of the policemen, Southern,
appeared to be a teenager, down to the acne moonscape on his face.
The other, Trask, might have been the teenager's wheezy, chain-smoking
grandfather.

Bishop had offered them seats around his dinette table, cluttered with
three sections worth of freshman composition papers and the remains
of his sandwich. Classes had just ended, and he, an adjunct instructor
still after eight years, was spending Tuesday at home with his grading.
It seemed silly to apologize for the mess, but he wished he had emptied
the dirty Club Cal-Neva ashtray, filled with the wreckage of an entire
pack of Lucky Strikes, into the kitchen trashcan before they came. As the
instructor turned off the radio among the greasy plates on the kitchen
counter, President Carter was announcing plans to provide for the Cuban
refugees who were arriving at Key West by boat every day from the port
of Mariel.

Although Bishop knew the policemen would be expecting him to
meet their eyes, he kept stealing glances at the dead grass and sand of
the ruined courtyard through his apartment window. The instructor
looked into old Trask's seamed face just long enough to get off his lie. But
Trask gazed blearily at Bishop as if he had not heard him. Before Bishop
looked away, he noticed the network of broken vessels in the whites of
the policeman's eyes.

"So, it was Friday morning around eight when your friend left for
home?" asked Southern, just checking the details, a touch of deference
in his tone.

The instructor turned to him, smiling, glad to be of help. "Yes, Friday. After breakfast. Around eight." He brushed the spilled ashes from the ungraded papers into his palm. Then, not knowing where to put them, he shook them onto the floor.

"His wife, Susan," Trask added, glancing coldly down at his notes to check the name, "didn't call in about him until Monday night."

"Because he missed his Monday classes. That wouldn't have been like him." Still holding his smile, the instructor was sure that he had explained it all.

The old man instantly looked up at him, his eyes coming alive. "So not coming home all weekend, that wasn't a strange thing for him to do?"

No. Bishop thought, the smile draining from his face. *She must have been used to that. She knew what kind of man he was.*

Bishop didn't like where this was going. But what he said was, "I don't know anything about that. All I know is that he told me he was headed home to Riverside when he left."

He wished he had been less testy about what he said.

This is why Bishop had lied: he knew that when Tom Corbin, who had once been his closest friend, had left Reno on Friday morning after giving his Thursday poetry reading at the university where Bishop, since dropping out of graduate school, had taught expository writing, he was not headed back down to Riverside, to his wife and small son, but over to Reseda, where his girlfriend, with whom he had planned to move in, waited for him.

The poet had told his friend that he had mixed feelings about leaving his family, and mixed feelings also about the woman he was leaving them for, but he had made up his mind. By confiding in Bishop about it, the missing man had made his friend part of it, whether he wanted to be or not. This situation was further tangled by the fact that, back in graduate school, they both had had a complicated history with the girlfriend. She had once, almost ten years earlier, been an issue between them, and Bishop had dropped out over her. That was why, Bishop knew, Corbin had felt he had to tell his friend the plan. *He wanted me to give my God-damned permission to live with her. And I had to give it.*

Bishop was so ashamed about having anything to do with his friend's affairs that when the two policemen asked him whether he knew where Corbin had been going when he disappeared, the instructor had lied to them instinctively. He didn't want anything to do with Corbin's mess.

It was not his business who Corbin was fucking now. Really. But it never occurred to Bishop to doubt where Corbin was. He was with *her*. And he hadn't had the decency to call his wife.

Hadn't had the decency to tell his wife he was leaving her? No. It isn't that he doesn't care about hurting her. Because he does care. Christ, he even still loves her. It's that he's too ambivalent about what he's doing to tell her about it to her face. He's just a coward like me. But I'm not going to hurt her by doing Corbin's dirty work for him. And I'm not letting these cops do it either.

Bishop had told the same lie—that her husband was on his way home to her—to Corbin's wife when she had called on Saturday morning after the poet had not turned up. That she had called looking for her husband was another thing Bishop didn't tell the policemen. It would have meant explaining too many things he didn't even want to face, never mind explain. As Trask continued to look through him, Bishop thought, remembering the tremble of the woman's voice on the phone, *It doesn't seem possible to tell just one lie.*

Bishop had not been able to stop thinking about Corbin's wife since the poet had shown him her photograph and told him the plan. Seeing the hint of a quaver beneath her embarrassed smile, the instructor had instantly felt a wave of guilt, as if he were the one who would make her suffer, not his friend, her husband. When he heard that same quaver in her voice on the phone—she was new to him—that photograph kept coming back. Bishop's flash of feeling for her did not stop him from lying. In fact, the flash of feeling was among the reasons for his lie. He hated himself for hurting her. But hurting her, he knew, was all he would wind up doing, whatever he did.

Before Bishop could say anything to her, while his first lie to her had still not fully formed itself in his mind, Corbin's wife had already begun apologizing to him, as if it were wrong of her to intrude on him. That she felt the need to do this only made it harder for him to tell her something he knew would cause her pain. It was obvious from that apology that this wasn't the first time she didn't know where Corbin was. She was used to being lied to, and used to having to accept the lies. But this time Corbin wasn't just off on another spree with some girl he'd picked up at a poetry reading. Bishop could not face wounding her, but whatever he did, whether he told her the truth or lied to her, he still played the same part in Corbin's betrayal of her. Either way, Corbin was making his friend do something ugly to his wife, something Corbin had no right to expect from him.

Honesty just doesn't come easily to me, he had thought, listening over the phone to her soft breathing as she took in his lie. But he saw at once that his thought was wrong. *Because every lie I have ever told began exactly the way this one did, with a flinch at a crucial moment. I've never had the nerve to be boldly dishonest, or boldly anything. So it's facing reality, not telling the truth, that doesn't come easily to me.*

Then Corbin's wife had told him that she had only bothered him because something had happened to her that she had to talk with her husband about, something that couldn't wait, though she wouldn't tell Bishop what it was when (because he couldn't stop himself) he had asked her what was the matter. Whatever it was about, it must have been really bad, bad enough that she couldn't keep the urgency out of her voice, bad enough that with a rudeness that had to be out of character she was willing to brush aside Bishop's pretense that he didn't know where her husband was, because she really had to reach him right now. But Bishop saw that she couldn't press him about where Corbin had gone off to unless she told him about what had happened to her, and she couldn't bring herself to tell him that. So she let the issue drop.

Bishop's question, however sympathetically he had meant it, had made her catch herself and stop short. She hadn't meant to tell him that she was in trouble, but it had slipped out, and it was too late now. He knew she was trying to keep him from hearing how afraid she was. And she was really afraid. So when she, trying to back pedal, had said to him that she was sure it would be all right, and her husband would straighten it all out when he finally got home, Bishop felt a pang, because what she said was so obviously false; it wasn't going to be all right—she wouldn't have had to nerve herself to make the call in the first place if it were—but she couldn't burden someone she barely knew with her problem. And Bishop knew Corbin was not coming home to take care of her.

The lesson that nobody should count on Bishop for help, that his nerve would always fail him when it counted, was something he thought he had learned almost a decade before, from the very woman Corbin was leaving his wife for. Bishop still quailed, remembering what he had done to her, and then what she had done to him. At least he had learned then what he was, once and for all. Every story he would ever be a part of was already over.

It was much easier for the instructor to lie to the two policemen than to Corbin's wife. But years of practice had not made him perfect as a liar, and he knew the two officers had sensed right away that he had been holding something back from them. And they, he guessed, were also holding back something from him, hoping to catch him in his mendacity.

After the third trip around the same set of questions, asked more and more pointedly by the increasingly ungrandfatherly Trask—Had there been any trouble on Corbin's mind that Bishop had noticed? Did Corbin seem afraid or worried? What could Bishop tell them about his own relationship with Corbin?—Southern told the instructor that Corbin's stabbed body had been discovered earlier that morning just south of Lone Pine, and that his driver's license had been found in the brush nearby, but that there was no sign of his car. Both officers looked at Bishop from faces with no trace of expression, although he knew they were observing him closely to see whether what they told him was really a surprise.

Bishop was sure the policemen were taking note of his reaction, but he didn't care. He did feel grief, plenty of grief, and he was ashamed that he didn't feel even more of it. But he had also earned the guilt he was sure Southern and Trask saw on his face, because it had never crossed Bishop's mind that Corbin might actually be in trouble, and now the instructor felt shame about how badly he had served his friend. Bishop had been angry and resentful about how all through the three days of his visit the poet had put his greater success in life in Bishop's face.

Since Corbin had left Bishop's apartment on Friday, the instructor had been rehearsing the speeches he would make when he saw Corbin the next time—knowing that when it came to it the poet would charm Bishop again out of making them, as usual. All the while, Corbin had been dead, so there would be no making up with him now. *What an idiot I am,* Bishop thought. It was as if his own ugly feelings against his friend, not whoever actually did it, had tracked Corbin down on Route 395 and stabbed him to death.

But Bishop stuck to his story.

As the policemen were exchanging looks, Grandfather Trask got a call on his walkie-talkie. Bishop gathered that a drifter had tried to use Corbin's credit card in Bakersfield. The clerk in the liquor store in Bakersfield had been suspicious about the card, since drifters don't normally have gold cards, so he had called the police. The police in Bakersfield learned that a missing person report had gone out earlier that day about the owner of the credit card. Shortly after that, Corbin's Firebird had turned up not far from the liquor store. The drifter was also wearing Corbin's windbreaker.

After this call, the officers lost their interest in Bishop. Southern told the instructor that he was sorry to have had to tell him about his friend's death. It must be a terrible shock. Bishop wondered whether Trask, who said nothing but was impatient to go, was ashamed about having treated him as a possible suspect. *No,* Bishop thought, *he's just ashamed about thinking I might ever have had the stuff to stab anyone.*

As the officers were leaving, Bishop understood that the lie he had told them was safe. It maybe wasn't even a lie. If Corbin had died in Lone Pine, he had not yet turned off the road that would have taken him home to Susan—for the first time, with a little thrill, Bishop used her name. Corbin had still been on the road to Riverside and his family; he had not yet passed Inyokern where he would have turned onto Route 14 to Reseda and his other life.

Susan need never know that the last thing her husband had done before he died was to betray her. Bishop promised that he would keep what Corbin was going to do from her. Bishop would make up for his lie to her—even if it meant telling her other lies. He would protect her as she bore her grief. And as she faced whatever it was she had been afraid to tell him, he would find a way to help her. Whatever that meant.

6

2

*W*HEN PAUL BISHOP FIRST HEARD A FAMILIAR VOICE IN THE HALL-way of Frandsen and came out of the office he shared with four other instructors, he saw that something must have happened to Corbin. He was an out-of-focus picture of himself. He had none of that bluff, lumberjack air that Bishop thought was second nature to Corbin, the one that put him in charge of every situation. Corbin himself must have been aware that he was off because he apologized to the Chair of the English Department about being tired from his long drive. But Bishop saw instantly that Corbin was like a man who was holding back bad news a doctor had told him.

Corbin had been invited by the department to give two poetry workshops for its creative writing students, followed by a public reading, followed by dinner at a restaurant on Fourth street, the Depression Deli, a name, Bishop told him, that purposely left it unclear whether it referred to the decor inside or the state of mind of the patrons. The poet had become a very big shot, having made a name for himself as a fiery opponent of the war in Vietnam and, more recently, of the US role in the ongoing civil war in Nicaragua. He was certainly too big a shot to give a reading at short notice, especially during the last week of classes without any chance to promote the event as it deserved.

But the plan of Corbin coming to read in Reno had been broached by the poet himself, who had called Bishop only two weeks before with the idea and had proposed to charge only the most nominal of honoraria. The instructor tried not to flatter himself that the point of the reading was to visit him, but it was hard to see the proposal any other way. On the phone, Corbin had been unsettled about something, but he held back from telling his friend what it was, falling back on academic gossip. Bishop wondered what was going on.

Corbin had said that he had gotten used to his poetry workshops in

Riverside over the years. "Oh, and, by the way, how are you doing? Will you be able to stay on where you are next year?"

"Yes, I think I can stay on in Reno," Bishop laughed, "so long as I don't ask for anything. There will always be freshmen who can't write."

"Is it really true that freshmen are becoming worse and worse writers every year?" Corbin asked, "Or is it only their poetry that keeps getting worse?"

"I think they're still just eighteen years old, like always."

"Were we that dumb when we were eighteen?"

"Maybe, being eighteen," Bishop sighed with mock resignation, "we didn't think to ask that."

Corbin was to drive up from Riverside on Wednesday, give his workshops and reading on Thursday, followed by dinner. Such events in Reno always had to be on Thursdays; Fridays were for basketball. To everyone's further surprise, he rejected a stay at the Mapes Hotel, a historic, once-elegant venue where the department usually put up its guests, and insisted on staying with Bishop in his little apartment in the Northeast of town.

Bishop lived in the dusty wasteland between Reno and Sparks, near the State Fair grounds. His building appeared to have been converted from a prior incarnation as a motel, with three two-story concrete blocks of apartments around a courtyard of sand and dead grass. There was a twenty-four-hour grocery store a few hundred yards away, surrounded by a parking lot so large it was hard to imagine it ever becoming full. But between the store and the university was a decrepit rendering plant, which at least once a day, usually as Bishop was walking home, would fill the neighborhood with the stench of decaying offal. Just the place to impress a recent winner of the Lamont Poetry Prize.

Corbin had started his drive up from Riverside before dawn and planned to arrive in the late afternoon at the department offices where Sharon Curtis, the student editor of the literary magazine, *Brushfire,* would pick him up to drive him thirty-five miles north of town to visit Pyramid Lake. Now Corbin would have at that point already driven eight hours through desert scenery, coming up as he did on the direct route through the Owens Valley. But Pyramid Lake was a spot to which the department had traditionally taken its visitors, so Sharon, who had taken two other visiting poets to Pyramid earlier in the year, was deputized to bring her car and drive him north.

Corbin was eager for Bishop to accompany him on this trip because "they had a lot of catching up to do." Bishop's Chair encouraged him to go along for the ride because of unspoken nervousness about leaving poor Sharon alone in the car with a man of Corbin's reputation. Corbin was a lawsuit waiting to happen. Everyone knew that.

After the preliminaries were over, Corbin allowed Sharon to steer them over to the student parking lot where he settled passively into the passenger seat of her freshly swept out Maverick. She looked across at him as she put her car in gear, obviously wondering how to break the ice. But Corbin didn't even look at her. Bishop sat warily in the back seat, behind Corbin, unsettled by the poet's mood, watching Sharon as she set her jaw as she reversed out of her space.

In ten minutes, they had crossed over to Sparks; in another five minutes, they were out in the sagebrush hills for the sprint to Sutcliffe, the Paiute town on the lake shore. As they drove on in silence, Corbin took the ballpoint out of his shirt pocket and begin to click the button in an idle tattoo with his thumb. Bishop knew that his friend had something to say but couldn't say it in front of a student.

Sharon, who had read Corbin's poems—indeed had brushed up on them for the occasion, although she had told Bishop that she found them too egocentric and declamatory for her taste—tried to interest the poet in conversation about the other writers who had given readings over the last couple of years. When William Stafford had visited in November, she said, he had made difficult ideas very accessible. "Yes, some of his best poems *are* just moralized anecdotes," Sharon went on. "But they have real power." She described how he had read aloud "Traveling Through the Dark." When the speaker accidentally hits a doe with his car at night on a mountain road, Sharon explained, he has to face down his guilty confrontation with a nonhuman life the driver can kill but never understand. It was a particularly poignant moment, Sharon said, and worth the whole poem, when the speaker discovered that the killed doe was pregnant, and that with cruel charity he would have no choice but to kill the unborn fawn that was still alive inside her.

"Accessible," Corbin said, and broke off. He had been about to say, "God save me from ever writing accessible poems," but stopped himself. It was too late to blunt the rudeness of his remark, however, and Sharon fell silent for a few moments. Bishop pretended not to have heard. In the mirror, he saw Sharon's wireframes flash in the afternoon blaze as she flung her golden hair out of her face. Bishop might have thought of it as just an automatic gesture, had he not noticed that she gripped the wheel more tightly and focused her attention more closely on the empty road ahead. Corbin's remark unsettled Bishop also, because he knew that Corbin was mostly rude only when it was strategic to be rude, and being rude to smart, attractive young women who had come there to look up to him was not like him. Something was off.

It is not always embarrassing to discover that one is being handled tactfully, Bishop thought, *but it is always embarrassing to be caught in the act of being tactful.* Corbin was too wrapped up in his own mood, however, to notice when Sharon brought to bear what Bishop thought were, under the circumstances, remarkable reserves of tact. She was also a film student, she said brightly, and *The Misfits,* the last film with Marilyn Monroe and Clark Gable, had been filmed in the desert just around here. Coming to her rescue, Bishop picked up the thread, "Yes, I loved that film too, a great film despite all the tragedies involved in its making."

"Let's keep an eye out," Sharon said, "we might see some of the wild horses that film was about."

Bishop pretended to scan the horizon. It was the very end of April—in fact, the last week of classes—and there was a green wash of new growth on the dusty hills. Bishop knew that if you stepped outside and looked down, there were tiny flowers everywhere. Through it all, Corbin was looking down at his hands, folded as if casually in his lap, still clicking the ballpoint.

On the outskirts of Sutcliffe, Sharon saw the flashing lights behind them. "I'm really sorry," she said, "It's the Tribal Police. I must have been speeding. I'm really, really sorry." Bishop knew that the Tribal Police were not going to arrest Sharon, and would probably not even ticket her, but they would certainly make it clear that they didn't like strange white people to behave as if the speed limits on the reservation didn't apply to them.

Sharon's shoulders tensed, and she looked rigidly ahead, sure that her day had been ruined, sure that the whole visit had been ruined, sure that she had brought lasting disgrace on the university.

The officer walked very slowly up to the car to allow the perpetrators to marinate in their anxiety. Sharon had rolled down the window with difficulty before the officer could tap on it. "I'm sorry!" she said, before he had even drawn in his breath to speak.

Corbin raised his head and stared into the officer's face. Then he raised his palm. "How!" he said.

The officer said nothing. Sharon flashed Bishop a panic-stricken glance over the seat back. The officer looked at his pad and wrote something on it.

"Jesus, Tom," said Bishop, "don't you have any sense? Do you want him to put us in jail?"

"Safest place for me," Corbin said. The officer looked hard at him for a moment as he spoke, but then Corbin uncharacteristically turned his eyes away, and the officer returned his attention to Sharon who was fumbling in her purse for her license. "Better than going home," Corbin added, to nobody.

"Officer," said Bishop, "We're sorry. This man is our guest. He's a stranger here, and he doesn't know anything. He's visiting us at the university."

Corbin was looking out the opposite window. Sharon held herself still, the license in her hand, but tears had begun to run down her face.

"He'd spend tonight in jail if it were totally up to me," the officer said, taking the license and returning his attention to his pad. "But my business is with this young lady, and not with him." Then, looking evenly at Bishop, "And not with you either."

Sharon took off her wireframes and rubbed them in a fold of her blouse. Bishop watched her and knew that as long as she concentrated on this task, she did not have to meet the policeman's gaze. As Sharon sniffled over her glasses, the officer softened. "Are you safe with these men?"

"Yes, I'm safe." She turned to look up into his eyes with a tear-streamed face. "The man in the back is my professor. The other is a guest. I'm supposed to show them the lake."

"I see," the officer said, and then stopped short. Sharon was gasping, trying to catch her breath.

"No point in getting you in more trouble with your teachers," he said at length.

"Thank you, officer, thank you," she said.

"But I'm going to write you a ticket."

"Thank you, officer, thank you."

"Keep better company next time."

"Thank you, officer, thank you."

Through all this interaction, Bishop watched Corbin who continued to gaze out of the passenger side window.

Somehow, they all felt they had to go through the motions of finishing the expedition. Sutcliffe seemed abandoned by the time they got there, although there was the inevitable pickup at the convenience store, and the rusting bike toppled alongside a trailer. Atop the hillside above them, a brown water tower with a conical roof squatted on concrete blocks. Sharon guided the car cautiously down the street, as if afraid of setting off an alarm, and nosed the car to the deserted beach. She parked, got out, but didn't know what to do next. Bishop jumped out of the back seat and opened the door of the passenger seat for Corbin whose mind still seemed to be elsewhere.

As they stood on the beach, the wind began to stir. The naked mountainsides plunged steeply down to the water on all sides, each slope black and gray and sere, an implacable place where every tattered human fragment wore to nothing. The lake, which ran for fifteen miles to their north and was perhaps ten miles wide, was an opaque, turquoise color. It didn't look like water at all. It could have been a lake of ammonia on one of the moons of Jupiter. The rising breeze seemed to be combing it into white streaks, and little waves glittered in the sharp sunlight. At their feet, brown foam swept in and out with the skittering waves. Before them, the great pyramid rock rose up, the one certain thing in a world where nothing mattered but that rock. They looked at it, but it did not look at them. They looked at it and looked at it. At length, they looked away.

A cloudburst would be coming in from the west in an hour. In advance of it, suddenly, the fresh perfume of wet sage washed over them. *That scent,* Bishop thought, *like nothing else in the world, the scent of possibility, and the scent of missed chances.*

3

*L*YING ON THE COUCH IN HIS LIVING ROOM THAT NIGHT—HE HAD given Corbin his bedroom—Bishop was shocked at the change in Corbin since graduate school, or even in just the year or two since he had last seen him. The instructor wondered whether the poet had been equally shocked at what Bishop had become. *No, he wouldn't be shocked. Nothing I do shocks anyone. He wouldn't even be disappointed because none of it would be a surprise.*

In graduate school back in Storrs, before they both crashed out of the program—Bishop because he failed his orals and Corbin because he decided, he said, that he would prefer to write poetry than write about other people's poetry—they had been very close. And it was Bishop then who had been the adventurous one, the ambitious one, or at least the one who had ideas about how in the poetic symbol the universal incarnates itself in the concrete, which imbues everyday things with a radiance that lifts them out of the quotidian and opens to the soul some new way of Being (Bishop did not always resist the habit of capitalizing that last word), or about how only through the bodily experience of rhythm do we experience language not as a mere third-person report of our sense experiences but as a first-person flash of the absolute spirit. (This last he said as if it were obvious to everyone what he meant.)

They had lived together since they had met on campus on Admitted Students Day. After several hours of sitting in on classes, there was a reception with the advanced students at which Bishop—over squares of different kinds of cheese or olives dried out on toothpicks—made awkward conversation about literary theorists he had only read snippets of at Central or had heard his professors mention in offhand ways. After a year spent teaching tenth grade in New Britain—where as a senior he had done his student teaching—Bishop had been unlucky enough to be drafted but lucky enough to spend his two-year enlistment as an air traffic controller at Fort Bragg rather than being sent to Vietnam. So his recollections on these subjects were shaky. He found himself next to another, slightly younger incoming student, whom Bishop seriously described to himself as "dashing," and who was also fresh from Italy after graduating from Wesleyan. They found themselves confessing to each other about their shared embarrassments and immediately felt as though they had known each other for their whole lives.

It was reassuring that the other young man, who introduced himself as Tom Corbin, was as bewildered about it all as he was. But Bishop was struck by how relaxed the young man seemed to be about all the things he was not in the know about. The young man supposed he would get the hang of it sooner or later. "Nobody's born knowing that stuff," he insisted, "so they must have picked it up somewhere, and if they can, so can we."

Bishop was a little less sure; it all seemed to him like some kind of mystic handshake the advanced students had kept among themselves to separate the experts from the amateurs. Corbin scoffed at the idea that anybody in that room could really be much of an expert on anything. "If you don't get it," Bishop laughed to him, "it's less of a problem that I don't."

"Don't let them scare you," Corbin had said to him about the advanced students by whose conversation Bishop had been intimidated. "All they want is to get ahead. But when you talk about poetry you actually mean what you say. So you've had to work it all out for yourself. It doesn't mean anything that you can't talk about it as glibly as they do," Corbin added. *Whether that's true or not,* Bishop had thought, *I will be your friend forever.*

Later, they went to the housing office to sort through the deck of index cards on which apartments were listed. They rented the first floor of Mrs. Coelho's house on Maple Avenue in Willimantic who preferred to rent to graduate students because, she believed, they were quieter than the college students were and wouldn't keep her sick husband awake while she was taking a double shift at the hospital at Mansfield Training School.

They didn't keep Mr. Coelho up, but they did keep late hours, many of them spent grading the stacks of papers that came in every Monday and had to be returned every Friday. Bishop, not having had such things beaten out of him yet, sometimes regaled Corbin with choice ironic marginal remarks from the papers he was grading, proof that at least in English 102 in the year of our Lord 1968 civilization was being upheld: "Archeologists finding this paper would begin to advance new theories about what brought down the American republic."

In his freshman writing class, Corbin would write two sentences on the board that, to first appearances, meant the same thing. He would spend the class having students tease out the differences between them, which always turned on far deeper issues than the students might have expected. ("Hawks and Chickadees are equally birds." "Americans and Vietnamese are equally human.") He had tried out many pairs of sentences this way, always running them past Bishop first.

They also tried out paragraphs from their own essays on each other, not so much testing out the arguments as trying to see who could come closest to the edge of nonsense without falling over. Corbin wrote: "To Quentin those muddy drawers were not just Caddy's innocence or her daring or her vitality but everything his world had had at stake and lost, something to be brandished in the face of the outsiders like the Bloody Shirt." Bishop wrote: "Ultimately Iago teaches Othello the bleak lesson, the only lesson tragedy has to teach, which is that you must empty your mind and learn to eat Time." Long after, Bishop understood that they had been more serious about what they said than they let on; it was exciting to believe that their views might somehow matter, a belief that the intervening years had taken from them.

Maybe it was for the best, Bishop was later to think, that it had all seemed so consequential to them since, otherwise, the crush of work might have been hard to bear.

There would be potluck suppers every Friday on Maple Avenue with some four or five others. People brought tureens of lentils with little disks of kielbasa or maybe a vegetable lasagna with spinach or something involving kasha and roasted Brussels sprouts from a mimeographed vegetarian cookbook (from a restaurant in Ithaca) that was going the rounds hand to hand. Bishop would always make a pie and thought, if he said so himself, that he kept getting better at it. He had hoped it might be an unorthodox way of making a hit with girls, and it might have been, among the kind of girls he knew. But there was wine too, good stuff, not the Boone's Farm the college students drank or the Gallo their parents did (their workers were on strike, you weren't supposed to drink that).

On these occasions, there would be something to read, and over the wine they would talk about it. They draped themselves over the couch and armchairs Corbin and Bishop had inherited from earlier tenants of the two-family on Maple Avenue, or gathered around the stove under the fluorescent circle in the kitchen, where the remains of the pie would sit on the cold burner, and the refrigerator shuddered every time Bishop clicked the latch handle to bring out another bottle.

Corbin and Bishop always played different roles in these conversations. They had grown to depend on each other, to feel that they needed to sharpen their ideas against each other if they were to have anything to say. Corbin had a poster of Raphael's *The School of Athens* over his desk. In its center was Plato, bearded and balding, with the face of Leonardo da Vinci, sternly pointing his finger at the heavens, at an absolute reality known only to the mind, of which the world known to our senses is an imperfect copy. Plato was glaring into the eyes of the younger, dark-bearded, abundantly masculine Aristotle, who was mildly returning Plato's gaze, but firmly holding his spread hand out before him, opposing Plato's gesture, drawing notice to this world, the only world we actually know, the one we love and suffer in.

Naming each after a friend, Corbin had written little captions over the heads of all of Raphael's philosophers. He had written Bishop's name over Plato's head, which Bishop felt was not intended entirely as a compliment. Although Bishop took on Plato's part in their ongoing debate every Friday night, Bishop was not quite sure he wanted to be seen as so otherworldly since the imputation carried with it the idea that he somehow couldn't manage in this one. But he did relish the idea of seeing himself as someone who might feel his way into a world past illusion. And since Corbin had written his own name over Aristotle's head, partly as a challenge to his friend, Bishop could argue that Corbin's resolute this-worldliness, what he called his nominalism, made claims to a superior *savoir faire* that might just be unearned and led to a stoicism that seemed to him more like despair than like bracing up. They were happy not settling this argument; they had enough delicacy not to drive each other completely to the wall, and, besides, keeping up the dispute did help life go on. In fact, they depended on each other and couldn't quite be themselves without the challenge of the other. Their classmates joked that they were a married couple.

They thought these weekly colloquies made them better scholars too—although scholar is rather too dry a word for what they were hoping to become, although not—Bishop long afterwards conceded—a dry enough word for what they actually became.

In the "Methods of Literary Study" class they took that first semester, Bishop had first read Coleridge's *Biographia Literaria*. Unaware then that the ideas that excited him in the book had long been seen in academic circles as beyond dated, he felt as though a new star had swum into his ken. Poetry was not just about feelings. It was not just a representation of something in the world, or an argument, or a short narrative told in heightened language, or a decorated moral proposition. It was an occasion to know something through the poem that you can't know in any other way. (He put a touch of emphasis on the word *know*. Whatever that word *know* meant, it didn't mean anything easily summarized. That he didn't know exactly what it finally meant was part of the point: it was a call to a new way of holding a whole world in your hand, a world that would always refuse to hold still.) But what kind of knowledge is poetic knowledge? And here he would quote Coleridge's famous sentence about the imagination, repeating it, turning it over and over, weighing each word: *the primary imagination is the repetition in the finite mind of the eternal act of creation of the infinite I AM.* He had said this with a straight face then, and it grieved him now that years of mocking that sentence had given him nothing that had replaced its charm.

During that year, he had followed the idea back to its origins in Kant, which had led him to Emerson, for whom the radiant moment of knowing, the moment of symmetry between *what it is* and *what it means*, between fact and value, between this-worldly sign and other-worldly symbol, is always fleeting, and always instantly falsified as soon as one grasps

18

it too strongly. Finally, it led him to the brilliant but distorting mirror of Emily Dickinson, who teased him and evaded him, who mystified him and made him feel like a beginner, but who also never disappointed him.

When at the end of his third year, he failed his orals, his advisor had told him that he was far better at thinking about poetry in general than at actually reading particular poems and that every poem provoked from him the same ecstatic leap in the dark, the same hyperbole, the same inexpressible and ultimately private experience. Was that experience a spiritual one, or just an emotional one expressed in spiritual language? (It took Bishop a few seconds to see that the question was a devastating one.) Weeks later, when his humiliation had if not cleared at least lifted enough for him to give himself some account of it, he persuaded himself that his advisor had been right, that the role of poetry oracle, even if he did have the work ethic and the discipline for it (which his advisor doubted), was something he didn't have the daring to pull off. And the world didn't need to know what he thought about "My Life had stood—a Loaded Gun—," and "I heard a Fly Buzz—when I died—." He couldn't settle what he thought about those poems, anyway. But he still needed to make a living, and what he knew how to do was to teach freshmen how to write essays. By then, he did indeed know how to teach freshmen how to write essays even if he was wrong about why he had failed his oral exams.

Over the years of licking his wounds in Reno, having failed at love and having failed at poetry, Bishop came to believe that Dickinson had been beyond him from the beginning. Whatever poetry had meant to her, he was not smart enough for. And whatever love had meant to her, he was not strong enough for either.

Corbin had believed less, Bishop kept telling himself, *or perhaps he had better hardened himself in advance to his disappointments.* "Poetry emerges from *this* world," Corbin had told him, "and reflects it, and poets play a role in this world, but not often the role they think they play. They serve their interests, but they don't know those interests except in mystified ways." Corbin imagined he could see through them, given enough discipline and enough refusal to be fooled. All you can know honestly, he would say, is how little you know when you think you are in the know.

At Wesleyan, Corbin had been introduced to Sir Thomas Wyatt, whose skepticism and self-knowledge hit him, he told Bishop, like cold water thrown suddenly in the face. Wyatt had known from the first moment that loving Anne Boleyn would make a fool of him and possibly get him killed. But he also knew that for all that self-knowledge he still could not resist her, could not win her, could not leave off loving her, nor leave off hating her either. That perfect knowledge, matched with the perfect impotence of that knowledge, seemed, Corbin said, to be the center of a habit of life that at least had love of the truth to recommend it.

But Bishop never said, though he always felt, that Corbin was wrong about what drove him to Wyatt's poetry; what brought him to it was the presence of something tremblingly human that kept breaking through. (The same things, the things he loved him for, kept breaking through, Bishop thought, in Corbin himself.) Maybe Corbin would not have liked to admit this; it would have seemed idealized, something more in Bishop's line than in his. But there it was.

Corbin kept returning to how in "They Flee from Me That Some Time Did Me Seek" Wyatt sees with such clarity, and barely contained erotic excitement, his beloved's naked foot stalking into his chamber in the dead of night. And when, slipping up to the poet's bed, "in thin array after a pleasant guise," her loose gown falling from her shoulders, she takes the poet in her arms and asks, "Dear heart, how like you this?" Corbin knew, he had told his friend, that here the beloved speaks for herself as she almost never gets to speak in any lover's poems, and that she is worth everything, worth even every lie, whether his or hers.

Ultimately, though, Corbin put Wyatt behind him, seeking, first in one contemporary poet then in another, a poet whose worldliness might enable him to see through and denounce the lies around which our world is organized without merely substituting for those lies a new set of lies originating from some different quarter. Bishop knew, after Corbin had become famous and he himself had dropped out, that Corbin could infallibly smell out those lies. He had made a career of it. But Bishop also knew that Corbin had lost confidence about finding the truth and even wondered whether it mattered whether he did, so long as he caught the lies. Bishop knew that it had never occurred to Corbin to wonder what he had lost in making this transition since he saw that loss not as a loss of humanity but as a rejection of sentimentality. "Don't you know that the personal life is dead, and so is the poem of personal life? What is the *poet of feeling*"—he said this to Bishop with a derisive lift to his voice—"but a poet who places his own sensibilities before his duty to the world?"

Corbin might not have mourned this loss, Bishop thought, *even had he understood it more clearly.*

Who had to be Thales and who got to be Heraclitus in the allegory above Corbin's desk was something Bishop did not remember although he assumed that Corbin basically had them accurately assigned since, unlike himself, Corbin was a passable judge of people. But who was Zeno did matter, and this was Rachel, whose surname was Lake, but Corbin (Tom) and Bishop (Paul) always called her by her first name as they called each other by their surnames, except in anger.

She had not come to their Friday evening salons for the first few weeks. And she had not volunteered much in the classes they had in common either, though she paid close attention, her watchful eyes glittering, but also so cold that people involuntarily looked down when their eyes would happen to meet hers. She gazed at the other students like a sly haunted panther.

Over the leftover peach pie and Almaden on her first Friday night in the two-family on Maple Avenue, she wanted to know what made either of them so certain they were right, whether it was really possible, as she said Bishop intended, "to swallow the Paraclete feathers and all," or whether it was really quite fair to say, as Corbin was wont to have it, that poetry is little more than a record of something the poet wants and can't have. "A fantasy to fill a lack," Rachel had grandly pronounced. Her voice was dark and whispery, a smoker's voice, a voice that promised something you had better be sure you were ready for before you took it up. Hearing her voice made you want to feel her breathe on your ear.

"Why do you think the poets want anything for themselves?" she challenged Corbin. "I would think that what poets want is to get so far away from themselves that they can never find themselves again."

"If poetry means anything," Corbin replied, "it means it in the here and now. And, of course, I want something out of it. I want a better

21

world out of it."

Corbin might have been offended by the way Rachel jumped straight down his throat. But Bishop saw he was excited by it, even turned on. Bishop knew his own turn was next.

"How do you know," she asked Bishop, "whether what you call poetic knowledge isn't just a kind of intoxication, something that happens to your brain when you climb up to where the oxygen is thin?" There had to be something more to it than that, she maintained, but she wouldn't be pinned down about what that thing was, except that she was sure that it was not something in every way positive.

"What's your idea about it?" Bishop retorted.

"Poetry is how words give shape to the silence at their center," she said, "Poetry demands silence, but it needs just enough in the way of words to mark where silence begins. The words draw the line from beyond which nothing returns."

"And how is that silence different from plain emptiness?" Bishop pushed back.

"Because it sets the world on fire, but nothing seems to change, except that everything is different. When you feel it even the shadows hold their breath. And when you stop, you know exactly how death will feel." Those moments, when a poem would seem to follow her in the dark, when it would lift the hair at the back of her head, were, she said, what poetry was for her. That thought, she admitted, gave her a thrill which she knew she should hold at arm's length.

For beauty is nothing but the beginning of terror which we are barely able to endure, and it amazes us so because it serenely disdains to destroy us. Rachel would often quote these lines from the *Duino Elegies* proudly, but to Bishop she was like someone who had walked to the brink of a cliff in her sleep. He knew, however, that she could draw him on wherever she chose.

Corbin and Bishop would speculate about which of their hearts she would break. "Admit it," Bishop would say to Corbin, "when you imagine someone capable of saying, 'Dear Heart, how like you *this*?' it can only be Rachel you are imagining."

"I'd be careful about her," Corbin would reply, laughing, "*her hair is long, her foot is light, and her eyes are wild.*" But to the surprise of all three it was with Bishop she ultimately had a year-long relationship. And also to everyone's surprise, it was her heart that had wound up being broken in the weeks before Bishop's ill-fated oral exam.

Some years afterwards, moving into his little apartment between Reno and Sparks, he came across the parts of the journal—the one he had kept since junior high school—that dealt with these months. In it, he found he had had a great deal to say about Emily Dickinson's anguish and not a word about his own—and not a word about Rachel except quotations of her *bon mots*. He never wrote another entry. *If you can't be honest with yourself in your own journal, then why keep one at all?*

But even now (although that morning, knowing that Corbin was coming to visit, he had hidden it away in a drawer) he had a small photo of Rachel on his dresser. In the picture, she is perched on the edge of a chair in Bishop's living room, her body turned to the left, but looking up eagerly at something out of the frame to the right, her straight black hair falling on both sides of her marble-pale, strongly marked face, in a cascade to her waist. She is wearing a man's white button-down shirt and a black skirt. Her mouth is open in a guarded smile, but from her posture it is clear that whatever it is she has noticed out of the frame it is something that surprises and delights her. She seems about to leap up out of her chair and also out of the guardedness of her smile. Bishop took the photo himself, but he had forgotten what had delighted her, although he knew it was not himself. You don't see that look many times in life, and you have to come back to it once you have seen it. Sometimes, he still picks up the picture and wonders about that look.

When he walked late at night in the roads that led north into the sagebrush, it was Rachel to whom, in silent colloquy, he was trying to explain himself. And when he woke in the middle of the night in his tangled bed, it was the pressure of her body that he felt.

4

$\mathcal{B}$ISHOP HAD THREE SECTIONS TO TEACH OVER THE MORNING AND early afternoon, so, in fact, he saw very little of Corbin before the reading. That semester Bishop was teaching two sections of Rhetoric and Expository Writing and one of Developmental Writing, the latter a course whose very name had about it the odor of failure, and whose students stood at best a ten percent chance of graduation.

Between classes, in the office he shared with four graduate students, Bishop met with a succession of students who had come to contest the grades he had given on his most recent paper assignment. They were always students from the Expository Writing class; the students in the Developmental Writing class took their failure for granted and never came to office hours even when he asked them to. Each of the other instructors had a similar line of students seeking "help," some of whom they actually did.

Typically, the grade-contesting students demanded, in the tone people use when they are about to ask to speak to a supervisor in the customer service department, that he justify every point he had taken from them on their papers from the theoretical 100 they assumed was actually their due. Furthermore, they argued, it was Bishop's duty to design a prompt that specified the problem in enough detail that the students could write perfect papers by mechanically working through the prompt. Any failure of imagination in their papers was Bishop's fault because he had failed to make clear exactly what he wanted. Since the burden of proof, in any case, was on the instructor, because the students were the reason for the University's existence "and I pay your salary," these students usually assumed that it would be easy to get Bishop on his back foot, particularly if they came at him with special aggression.

Over the years, Bishop had resorted to telling the disgruntled students that if they were to write something so ill-considered on the job, they could not tell their supervisor that everything "was just a matter of opinion"—or, worse yet, "just a value-judgment"—so their opinions should count as much as anyone else's. Knowing that these students would shortly become the kind of people who, making much more money than he did, would enjoy putting little people like him in their place, Bishop frequently felt moments of *schadenfreude* as he held his ground.

He couldn't say with a straight face to other people that he felt his work mattered. But he also didn't think what he did was as small or stupid or meaningless as he assumed most other people thought it to be (and as he himself described it to other people as being when they asked him what he did). His work did matter to him, though he could never say so. In fact, by the end of the term, most of his students did write somewhat better papers although Bishop felt that that was probably more the result of their growing a little older and of their becoming a little more accustomed to hearing others form and develop their views than it was the result of any instruction he gave.

𝒯om Corbin was unnerved by what he had done at Pyramid Lake. What was he thinking? Being arrested in Sutcliffe wouldn't have gotten him off the hook. It was beneath him, a coward's trick. And it was too late: by now the only way out was through, as Marcus Aurelius said. It was all his doing anyway, and he had it coming to him, however it played out. When the time came, he would have no choice but to face the music. Which he'd better do like a man.

He gave himself a great deal of credit, though, for how well-behaved he was in the two poetry writing workshops he visited, in which he nodded appreciatively as the students read their poems aloud and told them he was very impressed by the effort they had put into their poems, which was not quite the same thing as saying he thought they were good poems, something which even in his apologetic state he could not bring himself to say.

One thin, high-voiced young man read an unexpectedly explicit poem about an erotic experience, which made some of the students look at each other furtively, and made the more sensitive among them discover that they needed to pay close attention to something on the desks in front of them. Corbin remarked kindly that every generation, his own included, seems to believe that it was the first to experience sexual climax. This made the awkward moment pass but didn't get the young man, who was—Corbin suspected—still a virgin, out of the hot seat.

A severe young woman, a senior from whom the class had clearly learned to expect such things, read, in a raised voice, a poem in conscious imitation but unconscious parody of Corbin's own style, about the assassination of Archbishop Romero in El Salvador, which had just been in the news. Corbin praised her for the power of her convictions— "Convictions that I am sure you know I share"—but he said nothing about anything she had actually done in her poem, a fact that she didn't notice in her pleasure at being praised by a poet she admired.

One student—only after she had started reading did Corbin notice it was Sharon Curtis—described how, hiking alone in the Stillwater refuge at dawn, she had surprised a colony of white-faced ibises, picking their way through the shallow marshland, living a life she could wonder at but not share. Corbin told her he thought that poem was fine, very fine. And he did think it was fine, for what it was. *You will never tell lies about nature,* he had said. But it wasn't clear that she believed he really meant what he said. Or rather it was indeed clear that she knew he had praised the poem's execution, but thought the poem's ambitions were small-bore. He noticed that she was downcast after his praise, but by then it was too late to change tack. He was proud anyway of how well he had behaved, and he only wished Bishop, who at that moment was walking his second class through George Orwell's essay "Shooting an Elephant," were there to notice.

*B*ishop *was* there to notice at the reading Corbin gave during the late afternoon in a lecture hall in the Jot Travis building. The setting might have seemed too academic for the poetry Corbin usually read although the truth is that most of Corbin's admirers had something to do with academia, but the Chair had wanted to choose a room that could hold the crowd he expected. Perched in seats that swung out from rows of permanent Formica tables under the fluorescent lights, the audience seemed more like delegates at a congress than like readers of poetry. But they paid careful attention, without the rustling of papers or undercurrent of whispers to be heard when Anthropology of Religion had been taught in that room earlier that afternoon. Both the faculty and the students thought the reading went very well, and since they had come prepared to enjoy it, they did. The students, Bishop knew, thought that being at the reading distinguished them, and they looked forward to talking about it among themselves that evening and with their regular instructors, who also felt burnished by the event, during the next class. He heard the faculty telling each other afterward that they had expected Corbin to be more of a showman and that they had expected perhaps even to be a bit embarrassed by him. They were surprised by how reasonable and intelligent he seemed to be. One even said he had not expected Corbin's poetry to be so accessible. Bishop knew that there was something very wrong.

Bishop had heard Corbin read his poetry many times since their first semester at UConn. Corbin had begun to develop his characteristic style during his first few months, and poems of his began to appear in *Prairie Schooner* and in *Poetry Northwest* in his first winter. *Lament of Saint Stephen*, the book that made him famous, and made him decide to quit graduate school, was accepted for publication by Atheneum in April 1972, a little more than a year after Bishop had dropped out of UConn, and published that December, leading to Corbin's first appointment at Riverside the next summer.

Corbin embraced neither the scruffy Bohemianism of the Beat poets, nor the anguished, guilty liberalism of Robert Lowell. Since the end of the Vietnam War, his interest had also turned to the destruction of the natural world by capitalist exploiters, making himself a name with his 1975 volume *With Usura*. In the later 1970s, inspired in part by the example of Daniel Berrigan, but even more by Dorothy Day and Pablo Neruda, Corbin began to embrace an ardent, liberation-theology-oriented Catholicism, convictions about which solidified his commitments to radical social reforms in Central America as well as in the United States.

At readings, Corbin was in the habit of calling out the complicity of the universities in the outrages of the Vietnam War and calling out as well the silent assent of any number of other famous poets. His denunciation of the poetics, and it would seem also of the characters, of the poets Richard Wilbur and Anthony Hecht, had given Corbin a reputation for formidability that his enthusiasts took to be a reputation for integrity. In the question periods after each reading, he had always shown particular interest in the questions asked by eager young women from the audience, and there had long been stories about what would follow although the truth of those stories was something about which nobody could vouch.

He had developed a fierce, declamatory style, full of glittering sharp edges, owing something to Blake's prophecies and to the biblical Isaiah. Corbin recited not in the singsong irregularly interrupted monotone chant that poets typically adopt but in a loud clear baritone that sounded more like singing than shouting. But at the reading in Reno, he didn't sound that way at all. The most intense passages, which Bishop had heard Corbin recite before at the top of his voice, he read instead in an angry whisper, and the passages of testimony that Bishop had heard so many times as a radiant *credo in unum deum*, Corbin read in a tone of quiet regret.

On reflection, Bishop may have preferred the more subdued Corbin he heard that afternoon to the poet everyone knew from previous years. The instructor heard in it a note Corbin had never sounded before, the still sad music, the tears of things. Had it always been there, and Bishop had been too dull to pick it out? He wondered whether he had really ever understood Corbin's poetry at all.

One feature of Corbin's reading especially gave Bishop something to wonder about. Without introducing it, except to the extent of saying that it was a poem by a new poet he much admired, he read a poem by Paula Kyriakos, whose first book, *An Obol for the Boatman*, had come out from Atheneum the previous autumn. Now it had never been Corbin's habit to foreground other poets at his readings. And if anyone were to imagine a poet he would quote in a reading, it certainly would not have been Paula Kyriakos, whose book had made a splash in feminist circles, and whose gorgeous formal lyricism and saturation in the history of poetry was as far from Corbin's poetry as it was possible to be. The magnetic attraction of her book was heightened by her extreme reclusiveness.

28

In the poem Corbin read, the shade of Clytemnestra, thinking only of her grief for Iphigenia, the daughter her husband had sacrificed to beg favorable winds to bring his army to Troy, seeks atonement and reconciliation with the shade of Cassandra, whom Clytemnestra herself had murdered, having in death come to realize that Cassandra, her husband's hostage and mistress, had suffered at the hands of the same man who had murdered Iphigenia. Corbin's choice could not have been more unexpected had he chosen to read poems from *Diving into the Wreck*—Adrienne Rich herself having written a harsh review of Corbin's own most recent book *The Mind-Forged Manacles*.

Hearing Corbin read from *An Obol for the Boatman* made Bishop wish he had read the book earlier. He had bought a copy the previous winter at Sundance Books, after reading Helen Vendler's review in *The New Yorker*, but had put it aside for the end of the term.

Corbin ended the reading as he ended every reading, with his sonnet "Lullabye." Bishop remembered when, early in their friendship, Corbin had written the poem, and during those first years Bishop had looked forward to the sonnet whenever he heard Corbin read. In the poem, Mary, nursing the infant Jesus, wonders at how during her pregnancy her child had ridden at her heart like any other baby, dreaming in the wordless rush of his mother's pulse. Even now he clings to her like any newborn: vulnerable, precious, speechless, bewildered, loving. The terrifying angel had told her she would bear the Son of God, whom earth and heaven will flee when he comes to reign, but the infant at her breast is a baby like any other. Why would the Son of God choose to be needy and dependent, when he could rule the world? Then she understood: what he wanted was to know what it is to be weak, to need love so deeply that he would die for lack of it, to have to rely utterly upon another person, to be a mother's child, to know a mother's love. What he wanted was to fear death and never to be free of the thought of death. What he wanted was to be mortal and to love as mortals love, knowing they have only the here and now to love in. What Mary had given him was the two things gods can't have, the mysterious experience of death, the mysterious immortality of love.

When he first read the poem Bishop felt that it showed that his friend did not actually believe what he had maintained in all their Friday night debates, that the poet cannot claim truth but only will to power, that the poem serves only worldly need and ambition and worldly ideology, not otherworldly poetic knowledge. "Lullabye" showed that Corbin was of Bishop's party without knowing it. The poem's Mariolatry also showed to Bishop that the Catholic flavor of his poetry was not just a way of packaging his political convictions to make them more persuasive, but that those convictions were themselves rooted in a sensibility deeper than anything he argued in public.

Over the years, however, Corbin's sonnet had come to serve another purpose, one that Bishop was ashamed to acknowledge: more than any of Corbin's other poems it had drawn young woman after young woman into his orbit and into his arms, had convinced them that he understood them, had convinced them that they were safe with him, although in fact whatever sympathy he professed for them was completely in the service of his predatory desire. Was that sympathy entirely a pretense? Maybe it was worse if he really felt the sympathy, since it only made the young women more vulnerable to him, made him more successful at sympathizing them into bed. What is more debasing than recruiting what's best about you to the service of what's worst? Bishop wondered whether it was clear to Corbin that this use of his poem had corrupted his art and corrupted his nature. It just had to be clear to him, didn't it? Corbin wasn't stupid enough not to see that. And he wasn't stupid enough not to see that what he did would come at a price.

But at the reading in Reno that last night, hearing Corbin recite the poem in that tone haunted with the tears of things that had so newly sounded in Corbin's voice, Bishop was sure again that his first impression of the poem had been right, and that Corbin, before his eyes, was trying to fight his way back to something in his poetry he had lost sight of, even betrayed. What Bishop heard in Corbin's voice as he read the poem felt like a culmination of the unease he had sensed in Corbin from the first moment he had laid eyes on him in the Frandsen hallway the previous day.

Because Corbin had only picked at his dinner that evening, the Chair caught Bishop's eye, wondering whether their choice of restaurant was the right one. Corbin did not even go so far as to get slightly buzzed with them, an experience they had hoped would give him a lasting impression of the University of Nevada at Reno as a nice place to visit. And he and Bishop left, pleading sleepiness, before the bluegrass band, the evening's entertainment, began to tune up. The Chair wondered if they should choose a more upscale venue for the next guest.

5

*W*HEN CORBIN CAME, FULLY DRESSED, OUT OF THE BEDROOM that Bishop had given up for him, he had already gathered up his backpack and his briefcase, and he went to put them in the back seat of his Firebird before doing anything else. Bishop, still sprawled under a sleeping bag on his couch, knew that Corbin, watching one old mystery after another—it was film noir week on KCRL—had passed a restless night. Bishop, himself, had been restless, finally dropping off to sleep after two. By the time Corbin returned from the parking lot, Bishop had roused himself, and, still in pajamas from graduate school, had rinsed out the frying pan in the sink and was getting ready to scramble eggs.

That Bishop had been listening for the other shoe to drop since Wednesday afternoon did not make it any easier for him to get Corbin's drift once he got around to it, which Corbin finally did as they were on their second cup of coffee. Corbin was leaving his wife, it turned out, and his just-about-six-year-old son Jack, the center of his life.

"Lots of men hurt their sons that way," Bishop said. "They still grow up."

Corbin gave Bishop a look. He wouldn't let Bishop dismiss what he was about to do to the son he said he loved. "Let me show him to you." Corbin took out of his wallet a photo of a little blond boy, pudgy and radiantly happy, on a swing. The boy had clearly just had a wild ride, and Bishop could almost hear his "Higher, Dad! Higher!" But it wasn't just the boy's joy that got to him. He saw in the boy's eyes a look of wholehearted love.

Out of nowhere Bishop felt a flash of anger. *Corbin will take that look from him. He may love him as deeply as he says. But he will still take that look from him because he wants something for himself more than he wants his boy's happiness.* Bishop shifted impatiently in his seat, and he saw that Corbin noticed it, but his expression did not change.

Bishop was shocked by his own reaction. He didn't even know the boy. But that thought didn't help him at all. Corbin was still staring as if Bishop had not just glared at the poet. Bishop knew that, hard as he had tried to keep Corbin from noticing this flash of temper, Corbin had known exactly what had gone through the instructor's mind. The poet had not only expected Bishop's response, but had desired it.

"And here is Susan, while I'm at it. I don't think you've ever seen her." Corbin casually put a photograph of her on the table next to the unfinished plate of scrambled eggs and toast. This moment was the one when something tectonically shifted in Bishop's nature. It would be a long time before he could work out whether it was something hindered and locked up finally breaking out into freedom or something in the foundations giving way.

"Her med school graduation photo, from four years ago," Corbin said, as Bishop picked up the photo. A slight young woman, younger looking than Bishop was expecting, in a graduation gown with the green hood of the medical school of Loma Linda University. *This is the woman he is going to hurt,* he thought. *And there's nothing I can do about it.*

She was very blonde, holding her soft cap on with one hand and, despite the suggestion of dark circles under her eyes, smiling with embarrassed amusement as the wind disordered her hair. But there was also a tremulous undertone, a sense that she was keeping her chin up with an effort. *She loves him. And she's happy.* He had to take another look. *No. She's hoping to be happy.*

Bishop examined the photo with as neutral an air as he could manage, but he was still quietly looking when Corbin gestured to have it back. After another second (Corbin had to gesture again), Bishop put the photo back on the table where he could still see it. He was disappointed when Corbin put the photo back in his wallet.

"She seems nice. Why are you jumping ship?" the instructor asked.

Corbin couldn't explain it. He was long past doing stupid things like falling in love. Didn't he, of all people, see through this stuff? That was why the actual experience of love, six months of abject, dark, all-demanding love, after he had thought he knew all about the subject, shocked him. And what he was going to do to his wife stung him. Which is not to say that he wasn't completely resolved on going through with leaving her. "I have no complaint against Susan at all. I want to be clear about that. I even still love her, whatever that means. Honestly, I'm not really worthy of her. She should love somebody who's better for her."

"You don't have to make me feel sorry for you," Bishop said, "I know how these things go. Nobody has to explain." Corbin looked closely at him, clearly wanting something from him. It took Bishop a second to see that what Corbin wanted had not actually been sympathy.

He realized that Corbin was used to hurting her. He was ashamed about it, and that was why he had never showed him his wife's photo, because he knew how Bishop would judge him. But now Bishop saw that for some reason Corbin wanted him to judge him.

"You are angry with me about this."

"I've never met your wife. Why should I be angry?" Bishop asked.

"But you are, aren't you?"

"It's not my right to be angry." But Bishop was still at a boil, and Corbin saw it.

"I'm angry with myself too. Not that it does any good. When other people do something like this you just put it down to human nature and sigh about it, but it's different when it's you that's doing it."

"Then why do it?" Bishop asked.

"Because I have it coming to me."

"Because you've earned this other woman?"

"You sound as though I'm talking about a prize. She knows me too well to give me any prizes. That's why I have to have her."

"Why go through with it if it isn't a good thing? Because there's no going back?"

"I don't think there's anything I could possibly do that Susan couldn't bring herself to forgive. She's good. She's good through and through."

"You mean she *would* forgive you, but she shouldn't."

"She doesn't know the first thing."

"Because she's good?"

"All right, have it your way. You think when I say *good* I really just mean *stupid about life.*"

"Don't you?"

34

"No. What do you think I am? But the fact is that when somebody forgives you even the forgiveness comes between you."

Bishop scoffed. And he didn't care whether Corbin heard it. The instructor saw that the poet was not fazed by what he had heard, but had expected it. He had wanted it.

"So this other woman, the one you're going to hurt your wife and son for, the one you're ashamed about loving, is she worth it?"

"No. Absolutely not." Corbin said this as if it should have been obvious. "She's a damaged person. But so am I. In just the same way. That's why she's right for me. It's a little scary isn't it, that that's what makes someone right for you? But when you're tired of all your own bullshit, it's actually thrilling. Because she sees right through me and won't stand for excuses. And I'm as tired of the excuses as I am of the bullshit. Even being tired of the bullshit seems like bullshit to me, something I'm only doing to prove that I'm the good guy after all, something that just entangles me in a deeper lie."

"I don't understand. If you're ashamed of how you've treated Susan, why don't you just go back to her? You've just told me you're sure she'd forgive you."

"I don't want to make any excuses to you," Corbin said, "because I already don't believe them, and I don't expect you to. And I don't want to make another promise to myself that I'll break the way I've broken every other promise I've made. I can't persuade myself that I really mean it even when I blame myself for my lies. I manipulate my own conscience as badly as I manipulate Susan. I'm tired of repenting and seeing through the repentance even as I make it. I've told so many lies that all I want now is to have to face up to the truth. At least this time I'll be with someone who sees me exactly as I am and won't put up with lies."

"That sounds like a recipe for a happy home."

For Corbin, the idea that his relationship or any relationship might be happy was naïve beyond words. He gave Bishop a look as if to say: *Come on. Whatever love is, it's certainly not the promise of happiness.*

Then Bishop remembered the question he had been on the verge of asking since the conversation had begun: "Why are you asking me about this? People leave their wives every day and the world doesn't end. Why do you have to ask my permission to leave a woman I don't know?" He didn't add, *And why does this matter so much to me?*

"Because you do know the 'other woman.' It's Rachel Lake."

"You're kidding."

"I need to know if you still have feelings for her."

"She's nothing to me," Bishop said quickly. "Nothing at all. It was all over nine years ago. I don't think about her." Bishop was looking out the window at the dead courtyard as he said this. He didn't have to acknowledge, even by merely exchanging a glance, that he knew Corbin had caught him in a lie.

Corbin let him hang, and both were at a loss about the next step.

Finally, Bishop turned to look the poet in the face, "Do you mean you'd give her up if I asked you to?"

"I wanted to be able to promise that. I really did," said Corbin, after a moment, acknowledging Bishop's glare, then shifting his gaze over Bishop's head so as not to be brought to a stop by him. "In fact, it's what I came here to ask you to do. It would have clarified everything. Especially since she's no good for me. But as soon as I got here, I realized I wouldn't be able to. That's the funny thing about doing something really stupid. Everybody keeps telling you how stupid the thing you're doing is. But you knew that from the beginning so that advice doesn't help you at all because it doesn't stop you from wanting it."

"So, what have you decided to do?" Bishop was still glaring.

But by now Corbin was ready to meet the instructor's gaze again. "She lives in Los Angeles, Reseda, now—believe it or not, she's a fifth-grade teacher in a parochial school—and when I leave here, I'm driving straight to her house, not to my house, what was my house," the poet explained.

That Rachel Lake would become a parochial school teacher was the last thing Bishop might have imagined. It was even stranger than that Corbin might leave his wife for her. *What on earth does she think she's doing? And what do those nuns make of her? They can't possibly know her.*

But Corbin wasn't finished with his revelations. He looked closely at the instructor and said, "Susan doesn't know at all what's coming."

"Because you can't face her about what you are going to do to her?

As if that would spare her anything?"

Corbin smiled, taking Bishop's point. "I would spare her if I knew how."

"You want to spare her?" This was more than Bishop could take. "Your wife must be really something."

Now it was Corbin's turn to look out at the ruined courtyard. "Yes, she really is something. That's why I was looking for a way to spare her. But I know I won't spare her."

"So after a lifetime of casually using women," Bishop was surprised by his bluntness, but this bluntness was what Corbin wanted from him. "You want Rachel to make you pay it up in full. But you'll be making Susan pay too. And she hasn't done anything the whole time except put up with you and promise to forgive you when you are ready to be forgiven."

"Yes," Corbin replied, "and that's what I'm freeing her from. Susan will never be free of me until I break her heart, and bad as that will be it will at least be a clean break, and better for both of us than my continuing to pretend I will ever be different from how I am."

"You won't save her at all," Bishop said. "All you're going to do is hurt her forever."

But Tom was ready for this: "I'll hurt her worse by lying with her for the rest of her life. As long as I am with Susan I don't know what I really am, because I don't know whether I am even capable of being honest. I tell myself I want to be a better kind of person. But what really happens is that I just *want* to want to be a better kind of person. And what I really want underneath it all is still the same. I want to be a kind of person I also know I can never be. And I keep trying to trick myself into meaning fully what I can only half mean. At least with Rachel I unambiguously know what I am, even if what I am is an unredeemable liar."

He's been playing chicken with the truth about himself, Bishop thought, *the way a junkie plays chicken with an overdose. And just like that junkie, when his game of chicken goes to smash, he will face it with a kind of relief.*

This thought brought Bishop to a full stop. Finally he had to ask, "If you changed your mind about asking my approval about Rachel, why did you bring it up at all?" Bishop asked.

"I wanted to get right with you. I felt I owed it to you, considering." Suddenly, Corbin smiled again.

Bishop was taken aback by this response and didn't know what to think. That Corbin might leave his wife, whoever she was, was not a surprise. That he would leave his wife for Rachel Lake was a surprise. But that Corbin would feel he had to explain it all to Bishop was beyond surprising.

"How did you even run into her again?" Bishop asked.

"She read *An Obol for the Boatman* and figured out that I had written it, and in November she called me in the office to tell me so."

"Because she loved it so much she had to sleep with the author?"

"Because she was mad at me."

"How'd she know it was you? And what made her so mad?"

"I'm not telling you. It's not that I don't trust you, but I'm not telling you."

Bishop regretted he had not yet read the book. "So, it was her anger that lit her desire. Just like it always has."

"That's beneath you, Paul. And unfair to her."

For the first time in the conversation, Corbin was offended. Bishop knew that there was nothing he could say to Corbin's face that he had not also said to himself a million times. Bishop had known since they were students that Corbin knew himself better than Bishop knew him. In fact, that understated but unmistakable air of self-contempt Corbin always adopted when he talked about himself was part of the magnetism that had drawn Bishop to him from the beginning and that drew Bishop to him still, even in anger. But for Bishop to criticize Rachel was very different. Corbin didn't have to defend himself; he didn't even want to. But Rachel, Corbin had to defend.

And with that Bishop suddenly understood why Corbin felt he had to come to Bishop to ask his permission to live with Rachel. It wasn't that he was afraid he might hurt Bishop's feelings by doing it. It was that he felt he owed Bishop something.

Because he had kept his jealous rage over Rachel a secret not only from Corbin, but from Rachel herself, Bishop had not been sure that either knew why his affair with Rachel had come to grief. After the abortion, and after the failed flight to California, in which he had left her to face down her demons by herself, Bishop had been too ashamed, and also too proud, to confront her.

He had behaved badly after the procedure, though she had weathered her trouble anyway, however barely; if the relationship continued after that it was by her sufferance, and he had to watch himself, having learned now what he was. But the alarm had gone off in the back of his mind, and he couldn't ignore it. He couldn't face it either. He would feel too much like a fool if he turned out to be wrong about whether she was unfaithful to him. And there'd be no going back, with Rachel, once he accused her. Even if he weren't wrong, even if she had betrayed him as flagrantly as his horrified fantasy kept insisting for him in pornographic detail, a scene of self-righteous frenzy was still something he could not bring off. Because he knew what he'd done to her. Who was he to confront her about anything, after that?

Why did he think she was betraying him? Because she had asked him to do something shocking in bed. He knew, he just knew, that something was going on. Which is to say he didn't actually know anything at all. And it was just sick, totally sick, he told himself, even to have the thought. But that didn't keep that thought from coming back and coming back.

Sometimes he imagined that she was trying to relight the fire under their relationship, strained as it had been by the abortion and everything else. *Why don't you just enjoy me?* he pictured her saying, without even having to add *while you can.* This frightened him.

Then he wondered whether what she was doing in bed was something she had learned from someone else, someone new. He had to know. But he could not figure what sort of thing would be evidence that would confirm or disprove his suspicions. And maybe it was all just the echo of his own guilt about how he had behaved after the abortion coming back to him in the form of jealousy. There just was no embroidered handkerchief. The shame he felt about being betrayed was evenly balanced by the shame of possibly making a wrong accusation. But both of those were nothing to the humiliation of finding himself in a false position either way because he couldn't bear not knowing, and he couldn't bear finding out. So he said nothing, did nothing, he thought, although, in fact, he became more and more absent, more and more detached. And Rachel became only the more desperate in bed.

"No. Not so softly. Do it like you mean it," she commanded.

But he didn't mean it. What she asked of him scared him. Couldn't she read that in his face?

"Go on. It's not wrong if I ask you to do it."

But it was still all wrong for him. It was. But then anyway he did what he was told. She looked up into his face, her eyes blazing, locked on his, the red mark he had left rising in her cheek.

"Back the other way too, with the back of your hand. And just as hard."

Do people really do this? Then what happens to them?

This had started in January. Bishop was humiliated but afraid to say no. By February, she would reach her fingers into his hair and make a fist. "Take my hair like this when you pull," she said, looking him squarely in the face. "And pull as hard as you can."

Ultimately, he was reduced to slipping into the bathroom of the house she shared with three other women on Hanks Hill Road and checking whether the birth control supplies she kept in her medicine cabinet had been used. He could never tell whether anything was missing. The third or fourth time he did this, he caught a glimpse of his face in the bathroom mirror and thought that this was the look of someone who will always be made a fool of by his feelings, always made a fool of by his lust, and always made a fool of by other people. A coward's look.

What he decided to do, which he told himself would save him from Rachel if he was right, and would save Rachel from him if he was wrong, was to disappear without a trace. Without saying anything at all to Rachel, and leaving only a note on an index card to Corbin to the effect that he had gone back to his parents' house to study more intensely for his orals, then only three weeks away, taking only a backpack of clothes and a box of books, he slipped out to his parents' ranch house in Windsor Locks. He told them that they mustn't call him to the phone when somebody called, but just take a message and tell the caller that he would call back when he could.

He would study all day in his childhood bedroom, with the gray model battleship (USS *Arizona*) on top of the dresser, and the see-through P-51, its engine visible through the cowling and its cannons visible in the wings, hanging from the ceiling light. He didn't leave his room even when his mother left to make her swing shift at Pratt and Whitney, nor even when his father came home to change his clothes and shower the plaster dust out of his hair. Just at 6:30 pm, Bishop would take out the dinner his mother had left warming for them in the oven, and they would eat it on trays in the living room silently watching David Brinkley bitterly deliver the headlines, followed by the local news on Channel 30. When a story about student protests at UConn would come up, his father would mutter, "Jesus Christ. Time for Meskill to clean that place out. And fuck every one of them." But Bishop did not have the energy to rise to the challenge. Afterwards, before retreating again to his room to study, Bishop would leave the dirty dishes in the sink for his mother to wash when she came home after midnight.

Rachel called every morning, the messages she had left with his mother being at first bright and encouraging: "I hope those books you are having to read too quickly are still as great for you as they ever were," she said. "Don't blast through them so quickly you don't enjoy them." She called every day for three days, and her messages became a little more edgy every day. Finally, the message notes from his mother simply read that Rachel called and that he really should call her back as soon as he could. He wondered whether she had any idea what was the matter.

At the end of the week, he got what, to judge from the envelope, was a long letter from her. He had had long letters from her before, and he knew that if he read it, he would give in to her. He would believe everything. He would never face reality again, and it would no longer matter to him whether he did. He threw the letter into the trash unread. But even then he had to keep himself from rescuing it and opening it and letting it do its work on him. Finally, just a day before his orals, he got another brief note from her, which he also threw in the trash without opening.

On the day of his orals, he drove to the examination room in Arjona Hall straight from his parents' house and knew that he had failed before the first half hour was over. At the end of the exam, after only the briefest of discussions with his advisor—"Yes, I understand. Thank you for offering me another chance. Can I have a few days to think about scheduling it again?"—he drove to his apartment, packed his typewriter and his books into his trunk, and returned to his parents' house. Corbin did not happen to be at home when he got to the apartment, and Bishop left no note for him when he left. A week later, he got in the mail a note from Corbin expressing sympathy with him about his exam and telling him that Rachel had herself left Storrs for home in California the previous day.

*S*itting in the dirty kitchenette in Reno, it became clear to Bishop that at least now he finally knew that he had been right that Rachel had been betraying him. She—how stupid he had been not to see this since in retrospect it was perfectly obvious, but he had loved Corbin too much to believe it—had been sleeping with Corbin after the abortion, which is why he felt he had to ask Bishop's permission to take up with her again.

For almost ten years, Bishop had wondered whether Rachel actually had been unfaithful to him at all, or whether he had been so cruel to her just out of his own craziness. At bad moments, he had been certain that his suspicion of her was just his way of evading responsibility for what he had done to her. It was almost a relief to know what she had done. And her throwing him over for Corbin made sense to him, too, because it was a response to his failure to stand up for her when she needed it. Not that Corbin had stood up for her then about anything. Maybe she just thought she had to even the score with Bishop. She was scary. And maybe now she was evening the score with Corbin. That's how Corbin himself seemed to see it.

"All right," Bishop said, "You say I'm unfair to her? I'll stop being unfair to her. It's been a long time, and I don't have a right to say anything about it anyway. The only thing for me to do is to wish you every happiness."

"I didn't think you would take it this hard." Corbin looked away.

"I'm not taking it hard. I'm just taking it. It's a fact in the world, like the boiling point of water."

"I really am so sorry," Corbin said.

"As I said, no hard feelings."

42

"All right, no hard feelings."

There were a few more awkward moments. Neither of them wanted to end the visit on this note.

"Look," Bishop said, standing up, "We all do foolish things where our feelings are concerned. I think we can face that without making worse fools of ourselves than we have to." *Damn that Rachel Lake. Damn her. Just damn her. Everything she ever felt for me was a lie.*

"Thanks," Corbin said, as he got out of his chair. He smiled more warmly than he might have seemed capable of smiling, even with his oldest friend. Bishop could not figure out what he had said that had made Corbin so happy. "But I have many miles to go before I sleep," Corbin finally said, "I think it's time for me to find my way to Highway 395."

As Corbin opened the door, Bishop thought that Rachel had been right about him, and right about Corbin. But what she was doing to Corbin's wife was another thing entirely. Susan deserved none of it, from any of them. How could any of them put right what they were doing to her? Then, just as he thought this, Corbin suddenly smiled back at him, still standing in the doorway. Bishop was still brooding when Corbin returned from the door and gave him a quick, embarrassed hug. Startled by this gesture—when had Corbin ever done this before—Bishop snapped out of his revery, his anger draining from him, but Corbin had already passed through the door and it was too late to return it.

Pulling out of the driveway of the apartment complex in his red Firebird, Corbin turned back to Bishop, who by then was standing in his doorway, and waved to him through the car window, smiling. To his surprise, Bishop found himself waving back, also smiling. Then Corbin steered onto the street, towards whatever was about to happen, believing, Bishop thought later, that Bishop had accepted his friend with all his flaws and had forgiven what Corbin had not actually confessed to him.

6

ALL PAUL BISHOP COULD SAY, NOW THAT IT HAD BEEN OVER WITH for almost ten years, was that the notion that Rachel Lake and he had ever been lovers seemed very unlikely. And that she should leave him for Corbin seemed entirely in the course of nature.

When, in the tenth grade, he had dutifully, and under pressure from his mother, gone to a dance at school, and had not once nerved himself to the point of asking any of the girls to dance, his mother had assured him that there was a lid for every pot. At her most charitable, Bishop's mother could never have imagined that it would be someone like Rachel who would be standing in a corner like a loaded gun, waiting for Bishop to identify her and carry her away.

Somehow it had to do with Emily Dickinson, whom Bishop had felt himself not up to. Partway through their second year in graduate school, they had taken "American Poetry of the Nineteenth Century" together. They disagreed about Whitman, in whose poems Bishop thought he saw a world in which there was room for every person and every kind of experience. Rachel thought Whitman's poems sounded bombastic and vaporous, and she didn't believe all his professions about his caring for the *you* as much as for the *me myself*. *"What I assume you shall assume* sounds more like an order than like a promise to me," she said. "It's as if Schiller had said *All men shall be brothers, or else!*"

But they agreed about Dickinson, or, truth to say, disagreed agreeably. They fell into the habit of meeting at the house Rachel shared over on Hanks Hill Road to see what sense they could make of what had been discussed in class. It was exciting, and a new experience for both of them, to find American poetry mystifying. Both of them had thought American poetry amateurish and shallow, and they thought they had learned everything they needed to know about Dickinson's poetry in junior high school, for the Dickinson they thought they knew was a pathetic nightingale dressed only in white who shut herself in her room and felt sorry for herself.

When they saw Dickinson's poems in a form closer to how she had written them they learned that they had been wrong about her. They had always read versions of her poems edited by Thomas Wentworth Higginson and Mabel Loomis Todd, or by Martha Dickinson Bianchi, versions that squared off Dickinson's rhymes and smoothed out her rhythms and punctuated them in something like the way most people punctuate what they write, versions that, most of all, made the feelings involved easier to untangle and easier to bear. But they saw in Thomas Johnson's edition for the first time a very different poet.

In class, that day in February 1970, they had discussed her poem "My Life had stood—a Loaded Gun—." But Rachel felt they had left a lot unsaid about it because all the class had wanted to talk about was her biography as if she were a patient rather than a poet.

"That's what they always do when the poet's a woman," said Bishop, so they went over it again while sitting in her living room.

Rachel said, "This is a poem about sex. But her sense of what sex is is masculine."

"Why do you say that?" Bishop couldn't say why, but he felt implicated.

"Because she imagines herself as a gun, for one thing, and she sees sexual climax as a kind of explosion, not as a kind of dissolution. And when she imagines sex she compares it to killing things for pleasure. Look how much she enjoys (being a gun, after all) describing sexual pleasure in aggressive terms. Love and death run together all the time, since half of literature connects them, but it's more in the feminine mode to see one's self as the one who dies," Rachel explained.

"Then what about the Lorelei?" Bishop asked. "I would say the score is about even as far as demon lovers are concerned."

"But the point is, the speaker in Dickinson's poem is one of the killers, not one of those being killed. It's usually the speaker who gets killed by dark lover, not the speaker who does the killing at the dark lover's behest."

Bishop felt defensive. "I'm not signing up to do either thing."

"I'm sure you're not," she said, impudently. Bishop laughed. She was always teasing him that he was one of those guys who feel they have to apologize for their whole sex. They keep hoping that might win them the right kind of girl, she used to say. "Someone they could take home to mother," she would add, rolling her eyes.

Bishop was fascinated by the speaker's claim that as a gun she had "stood in corners" till her *Owner* "identified" her and—literally more than figuratively—"carried her away." "How do you 'identify' as yours somebody you've never seen before? It must have something to do with discovering the person who in all the world is the one who is the most right for you," Bishop argued.

"He may 'identify' her, may claim her as his, may even give her her identity, but it's she who calls him her Owner," Rachel said. "She's the one who gives him the name and defines the situation. He takes possession of her—that's what love is here, taking possession, the way one takes possession of a gun you found in a corner—but she takes possession of him too, by making him what he is, by taking possession of that fantasy of being his rifle and coercing him into inhabiting it with her. So who is possessing whom?"

"If any girl calls me her 'owner,' I'm running as far away as I can," Bishop interjected.

"Falling in love," said Rachel, not paying any attention, "means discovering the object of an obsession you've long entertained but never understood. It's finding that someone for whom you want to suffer love, that someone for whom you'll transcend yourself, even if you have to destroy yourself to do it."

In class, they had spent a fruitless half an hour trying to figure out who the poem was about. Was it about Charles Wadsworth? Or Samuel Bowles? Or maybe Susan Dickinson?

"It wasn't any of those people she loved anyway. Nobody ever loves another real person," Rachel said, "they only love their own demon lover in someone else, the person who is designed to make them unhappy in their own special way. With the person you love you are sure each was created only with each other in mind. Each is the destiny and the fate of the other. Next to that person nobody else matters. Your own self doesn't even matter, except in relation to that person. You have identity only to the extent that you are willing to transcend it in fire with the beloved, burning up the whole world in the process."

"That may have been true in poetry," Bishop rejoined, "But nobody believes something like that about themselves, because if they did, they would never risk loving. We can only say that sort of thing about other people. When we speak for ourselves, we always see ourselves as wanting to do our best for the person we love."

Rachel laughed, "Wanting to do the best you can for the person you love is just the most effective way to put them under your thumb. You help them and serve them until you master them. You make yourself necessary to them, and from then on they're just a bit player in your heroic fantasy about taking care of them."

Bishop was wounded by this remark, and looked down into his lap, but Rachel went on: "Everyone in love imagines they are rescuing the person they love. But there isn't very much difference between rescuing someone and capturing them."

Everything Bishop thought to reply to what Rachel said sounded naïve, but he also couldn't let what Rachel had just said go unanswered. "I think the only thing that saves us from getting lost in the world is love. We don't know the first thing about who we are until we know what it is to love someone else, to put someone else first."

Rachel was ready for this. "Nobody sets out to do all the bad stuff they do in love. If you thought that was what you were doing, you couldn't bring yourself to do it. But love is a dark secret that nobody understands and everybody is driven by. That's why love will always 'build a hell in heaven's despite,' as Blake says."

"If you really believed that you couldn't live with yourself," Bishop said, "because, like everyone else, you too need to love and be loved. Without that you die a little inside, and then you die for real. I don't care that there is darkness in love. And I know just as much about that subject as you do. But I know that love also lights the way through that dark."

They went back and forth about this for a few minutes, but then to their own surprise—neither of them remembered who started it, which must mean that it didn't matter—they reached that point about which Dante's Francesca da Rimini says "that afternoon, we read no further."

*I*n the second week of November, coming back in Bishop's car from seeing a student production of *Lysistrata*, Rachel announced to Bishop that she was pregnant. Before he could tell her that he would stand by her whatever she decided to do, and fulfill his responsibilities completely, whatever they were, indeed, before he could even say a word, she told him that she had arranged to go to an abortion clinic in Portland, Maine, and she wanted him to come with her to drive her back from the appointment.

The doctor had been recommended to her by an older student who, in those days before *Roe*, had had to avail herself of his services. She had been told to call the number she had been given from a pay phone and leave the number of the pay phone there, specifying the time when she could be called at that number, presumably from a pay phone in Portland. The doctor, in his other life a gastroenterologist, was said to do his work safely and painlessly. But he also demanded to be paid in cash upfront— mailed to the post office box address he gave Rachel on the phone at the end of their first conversation—before even scheduling the procedure.

Bishop immediately sold the used car his parents had given him after his college graduation to pay part of the expenses of the procedure. Rachel was very unwilling to accept any money from Bishop for this. But she also had no way of coming up with the money herself, and grudgingly had to accept his gift, which she insisted upon treating as a loan, but never repaid.

The old man also demanded a great deal of information about Rachel, apparently eager to find out whether she was a police agent or a blackmailer. His voice was so cold and so suspicious over the long-distance telephone that Rachel told Bishop she wondered whether she would be safe in his hands. But her friend told her not to worry, and she tried not to. Bishop told her not to worry too, although he didn't really know whether she ought to be worried or not.

This resolution not to worry did not survive their first few minutes at the appointment. They both, in unspoken ways, were glad that the weather on that late November day they drove to Portland was misty and drizzly. It seemed right to them that the weather should be as uncertain as their feelings. And such weather might make it easier, Bishop said—he had written the address down on one of his index cards—for them to slip inconspicuously in and out —"unseen even by God," Rachel added. But they felt very conspicuous, even when they were still on the interstate.

Following their instructions, they had gotten off route 295 just beyond the airport and had found themselves, after crossing the Veterans Bridge, in a neighborhood of plumbing supply warehouses and seafood processing factories abutting a railroad spur. "This can't be the place," Rachel said, "there aren't clinics here." But as they inched up the street, scrutinizing the addresses, they came among some isolated patches of triple-decker houses. Passing a body shop and a luncheonette, they at last came upon a strip mall on their left, where, between a pawn shop and a laundromat, they found what announced itself as a gastroenterology practice.

Despite the long drive from Storrs in Rachel's white Toyota, they arrived that Saturday morning half an hour early. They worried that a couple sitting in a car for a long time in the parking lot of the strip mall might be noticed, especially since they assumed that it was an open secret in the neighborhood what went on at that office. But it was also a neighborhood in which it was easy to be anonymous.

The front door was locked when they finally edged up to it, and the shade was down over the window, but a handwritten sign on the doorframe told them to ring the bell to enter. The doctor, a thin, goatlike old man, the farmer with the pitchfork in *American Gothic*, having moved the shade aside enough to have a brief glance at them, answered the door himself, and told them to sit in the anteroom while he made everything ready.

They sat down on the two folding chairs in front of the unused desk, assuming that there would be paperwork to fill out, or at least some kind of medical history interview. There was dust on the desk and grit on the floor.

As the doctor busied himself in the treatment room wiping down the examination table, laying out sealed paper packets of tools on a metal tray, adjusting a light on a movable arm, and finally washing his hands at the sink, Bishop and Rachel whispered about how seedy the waiting room was. Bishop was ready to back out and ready to think of backing out as somehow a plan of rescue. When all was prepared, and Rachel was called to the inner room, Bishop insisted on taking her hand and going to the door with her. Glancing into the examining room, he noticed a small brown smear of dried blood on the green tile of the wall, at about waist height. "Rachel?" he said.

"Yes, I see it too."

"Do you want to stay?"

"Consider your duty done, Paul," she said, a little coldly, "I'll take it from here."

Then she entered the room, closing the door behind her.

Rachel had barely recovered from the procedure—in fact, she was still bleeding a little—when it became time for her to fly to her parents' home in Riverside, California, for Thanksgiving. It was not normal for her to fly such a long distance for such a short holiday, but she told her parents she wasn't feeling well, and they, from what must have been long experience of worrying about her, bought her a ticket from Bradley Field to LAX.

Bishop was desperate to do something for her, anything. Finally, she told him—she had kept this back—she wasn't going home for just a few days, but would need to stay with her parents for a few weeks, indeed to the end of winter break in early January. Would he cover for her for her last week of classes after the Thanksgiving break? And send her students' finals and papers to her in the mail at the end of the term? He was relieved to have something useful to do. He had thought what they had been through together might draw them closer. But, in fact, Rachel had barely agreed to see him and had kept her thoughts to herself.

When the time came for her to depart, Bishop volunteered to drive her the thirty-five miles to Bradley Field in Corbin's Chevy Nova—his own car having been sacrificed the previous week. He hadn't been alone with her since their silent return from Portland and hoped he could use the forty minutes in the car—*please, let Corbin not insist on coming along to say good bye!*—to get things straight with her. But she wouldn't hear of it and had already booked a seat on the bus UConn had chartered to the airport for Wednesday morning although she agreed to let him say goodbye to her, with one chaste kiss, at the door of the bus.

On Christmas Eve, after a month of her not replying to his letters, he received a long letter from her. "Dearest Paul," she began. She hadn't used that phrase before, and he did not know whether or not to be on guard. "I have been wondering about the life we have been living. You probably have also been wondering about the same things. Before you start to worry, having read that last sentence, I want you to know that whatever we have been through I haven't stopped loving you. But we both still have to face how little either of us knew about life when we met each other, and we also have to face the fact that life is still a painful mystery you and I are very unlikely to solve.

"What I have mostly felt since that day in Portland, felt so powerfully that it has squeezed even my love for you into a corner, is blankness. I would call it despair if I felt I had a right to the word. I don't feel as though I have a right to any words, particularly those words that are full of meaning, however dark that meaning may be. I'd want any darkness, any suffering, so long as I could be sure that it would give me some sense of its own reality. I would hold broken glass tightly in my hand if I could be certain of actually feeling the pain.

"Once, when I was walking through the woods near Hanks Hill, I came across a snake that had half-swallowed a frog. Neither was struggling. The snake would lie still for a few minutes, as if it were not even alive, but every now and again would open its jaws and try to force the frog further in. The frog too seemed completely impassive, not trying to free itself, not even moving, its body as motionless as if it were waiting to seize a fly rather than trying to free itself from the snake's jaws. But it was breathing. I could see that it was breathing. The passivity of it, even the indifference to death that I saw in both the snake and the frog, fascinated and horrified me. How could such a moment of life and death struggle seem also to be a moment of complete blankness? I could not stay to watch the end of the story. But now I have to watch the end of my own, and I face it with the same emptiness I saw in both of them. Pain really does have an element of blank in it, a formal feeling like the chill and stupor people feel when they are freezing to death.

"Please don't believe that what I am feeling has anything to do with guilt over what we did, whether that day or any day before that. I think I am grown up enough to face facts as they are without extenuation or pretense. I don't think I could have done otherwise, and it would be not only false but useless for me to say anything different.

"Darling, what we've learned is that the ground under our feet is thin, and that at any moment it might give way, and who knows how far we will keep falling once it does? Will we hit a world at every plunge? Will we fall until we too finish knowing? I have always hoped that love was the bulwark against death, against nature, against all of the meaningless chances that can break us. But it's love itself that breaks us, isn't it? And it's not really true that love and death are always opposites. We imagine we are choosing for ourselves, making plans, coming to a sense of how the world works. But life has us in its power, and what life wants is to push through in its own way straight into death.

"For the last couple of weeks I have been haunting St. Francis de Sales, the parish I was raised in. It's always cool and bright in the sanctuary, and nobody remembers me there. Some days I will sit there in the pews all afternoon. Most days I light a candle. Sometimes I look over at the confessionals, remembering what it was like to be in them as a high-schooler. But that door is closed for me now. I know what things are beyond me to do, and it won't help me to confess what I'm not ashamed of.

"But I remember also what St. Francis de Sales said, when he too, as a young man, thought that he was beyond redemption, when he felt that even his longing for God's love was a kind of trick God was playing on him, to sharpen and redouble the suffering he knew he deserved all of and more. Maybe he suspected as well that his inner drama of guilt and extenuation was also a trick he played on himself, and his guilt and shame were not calls to repentance but only further complications of the original crime of pride, incitements to another round of mock remorse and mock redemption. It's hopeless to expect God to be impressed by our Kabuki.

"Then in the midst of all that the thought came to him that God is Love. Everybody says that phrase, and everybody imagines they know what it means. But it's a phrase that has worn out its meaning. Francis knew that if we are sick in the world, we are sick in our wills; we just can't get ourselves right again by willing it so, because everything we do we will always do for the wrong reasons, or in a tangle of contradictory feelings and aims it will always be beyond us to sort out. How do you will your way out of the thickets of your willing? But that's what Francis meant by 'God is Love.' It's a way out of all of the double binds of our own willing into a gentler and less self-defeating kind of love.

"Gentler, less self-defeating love? How can I believe such a preposterous thing? I'm sure you are asking that because I am asking the same question myself. That kind of belief seems to be something I would have thought I was just not capable of, like continuing to wait for Santa Claus. I always imagined that if I came to faith I would do it in some way that testifies that even the mercy of the Lord burns. But can't I at least hope that St. Francis de Sales is right? I just don't know. I can't think it through. I can touch it, but I can't grab hold of it. I hope to God he is right. I hope to God I can get there too.

"Please do this with me. Come to me here. I can do it if I do it with you. But I don't know how to ask it. Come to me here. I don't know any other thing to do. Please please please please do this with me."

Bishop did not know what to make of Rachel's letter. Was it a demand that he convert to the faith she herself wasn't even sure she had anymore? He was Catholic, or rather ex-Catholic, too. Or was it some sort of suicide note, or worse, an invitation to a suicide pact? For all her dark charisma, and all her air of mastery over life, he had known—he couldn't say how he knew this, but he had no doubt about it—that she was always fighting that temptation down. Even ten years later, he was still wondering whether it was that death-hauntedness, that never-ending struggle and never-ending flirtation with annihilation, that gave her her sexual electricity. He looked that idea in the face then closed the door on it. But it stayed there behind the door.

Whatever was driving her, it was something she was determined to keep Bishop at arm's length about. All through Christmas Day, while he went through the motions with his parents, he turned his thoughts over and over. After a sleepless night, at 7 am, having waited as long as he could bear to make the call, he called Corbin at his parents' home in Whitneyville, and was told by his annoyed mother that he had driven back to UConn the previous afternoon.

After his own mother had dropped him off in Willimantic later that day—so he could make some headway on his late paper grading, he said—Bishop did not know how much of what was on his mind he could tell Corbin about. He wasn't going to tell him about Rachel's pregnancy, believing, then anyway, that if anyone were to tell that story it was Rachel's to tell. He had to tell Corbin, however, about the religious conversion part even though, without the abortion part of the story, it might seem implausible since up to this point Rachel had been much more of a skeptic than an enthusiast. He didn't tell Corbin what Rachel might do. But he was terrified that she might do it before he could get there to stop it. What he really wanted was to get out to California right away and get a sense of the situation. He was trying to picture himself hitchhiking, but that was something he had no idea how to do.

He knew Corbin would be surprised by Rachel's religious turn and might well take a dim view of it, seeing it as some kind of impulsive mania—"Girls are sure strange, aren't they?"—or, worse yet, as some kind of manipulative design to keep Bishop under her thumb. Corbin had been down on her to Bishop for weeks though he and she met more and more frequently to look over her poems.

Bishop was all the more resolved to keep the abortion part of the story to himself because he knew how Corbin might take it were he to hear. He knew that Corbin would instantly take that fact as the key to all of her behavior since Thanksgiving, her avoidance of them, her religious conversion, her insistence that Bishop share it, and her ultimatum to him about it. Bishop felt that his reticence was a matter of loyalty to Rachel; he knew the view Corbin would take of it, and he couldn't stand to think of him doing so.

When Bishop first said that he just had to get to Rachel in California but had no idea how, Corbin immediately suggested they drive out together. Corbin still had a car although Bishop had just had to sell his own. Bishop was so glad of this chance that he did not pause to think of asking himself why Corbin had so generously volunteered to go on such a long trip.

Bishop knew that Corbin would feel that it was too mawkish to say that he was driving all the way across the United States and back just for friendship, just because his friend was in a jam and needed someone to see him through it. What Corbin said was that he had just had a terrible quarrel with his father over the war in Vietnam, a quarrel he thought might come between them forever, and that he would be willing to do anything, even to drive to California and back, to get it off his mind. But that was not, Bishop was later to discover, why he had volunteered for the drive.

Things had been tense between Corbin and his father, Bishop knew, since the Tet Offensive, but when Lieutenant Calley, whose company had massacred Vietnamese civilians at My Lai in 1968, was brought up for trial in November 1970, they reached a breaking point.

Corbin's father was not so foolish as to defend Calley, but he did argue that civilians often get killed in the fog of war and that the Vietcong also had massacred civilians when they held Hue during the Tet Offensive. "I hope you are ready," he said, "for how many people the Reds are going to start killing once they take over."

Corbin had replied, "Some of those people they are about to kill have it coming."

That was the last straw. "You call me complicit in genocide? Look to yourself, boy." Corbin had taken a step further than he had planned to, but he had been stampeded by his father's callousness. And his father would not let him retrace that step, because it gave him every advantage he would ever need. Everything was over between them but the shouting.

By noon Corbin was back on the Wilbur Cross Parkway in his Nova, driving seventy-five miles an hour, on his way back to Willimantic.

7

ON NEW YEAR'S EVE, AT THE END OF FIVE DAYS OF DRIVING, Bishop, who was taking his turn at the wheel, steered Corbin's Nova onto an exit ramp in Gallup, New Mexico. Crossing the railroad tracks, they found themselves on the old Route 66, passing the Historic El Rancho Hotel and several smaller motels from the heyday of that road in the 1930s, dispersed amid the red dust and the thin, scrubby trees. Passing beyond a lot full of heavy construction equipment, Bishop turned off the main road into a neighborhood of small, pink stucco houses. Finally, he saw ahead, up a small rise, a rose brick tower and cupola. "That will do," he said.

"What will do?" asked Corbin.

"You can wait here if you want. I won't be long."

"It's freezing out here. I'm coming with you," Corbin replied.

On the steps of the Sacred Heart Cathedral, before the leftmost of the three tall, arched doors, Bishop found a stunned little bird.

"It's dead. Come on." Corbin moved toward the door.

"Oh no it's not. Just look—it's breathing." Bishop kneeled.

Bending over where his friend knelt, Corbin saw the bird's beak working with effort as it strained to breathe. "Let's go. It's dying anyway," Corbin insisted.

"We don't know that. It might be hurt, that's all," Bishop said, "And it'll freeze if we just leave it here."

"Okay, Saint Francis," Corbin said. "We'll build a sparrow hospital right here and injured birdies will come from every state for you to fix their little bodies up."

"Let's get it warm and see if it survives." Whatever new quest Bishop had just launched himself on, Corbin saw he was not going to be diverted from it easily.

"Oh, for God's sake."

"Why not?" Bishop seemed to have no idea that it might be strange to imagine that God had called him to rescue a freezing bird.

"It's foolishness," Corbin sighed. "Besides, I thought you had some things to do. Why are we stopping here? What does this place have to do with us?" But Corbin knew he had already lost the tug of war.

Bishop was back at the car and had popped the tailgate up. He rummaged in the trunk and pushed aside a sleeping bag, a pack, one black Converse, and a wiffle ball. Then he found the shoebox with the new loafers Corbin's parents had just given him for Christmas. The tissue they were wrapped in sailed away, swirling and flapping down the frozen street.

Corbin plopped down on the Cathedral stairs. He shook his head, then locked his skinny arms around his knees till Bishop trotted back, his breath condensing like a steam train's exhaust.

"Wait. Don't just shovel him," Corbin laughed to see that his friend was squeamish about touching the bird with his hands.

Bishop knelt there, at a loss.

"You'll have to pick it up. With your hands. Some saint you are," Corbin shook his head.

Bishop laughed too. Corbin had called him St. Paul Bishop, Patron Saint of Lost Causes and Confused Maidens since they had first left Willimantic.

"You'll have to practice now. Wash beggars' feet. Kiss lepers. Raise the dead." Corbin laughed.

"Okay. Enough." After a moment's hesitation, Bishop raised the bird gingerly in numb unsteady hands. "I feel it breathing."

The box had fallen over in the wind. Corbin caught it before it blew away. "Alright," he said. "You should have kept that paper. Be sure to wash your hands when you go in. Being a saint might not protect you from getting whatever that bird might have."

Bishop placed the bird in the shoebox and carried it to the big front door which, they should have known, was locked, but at the side entrance up a concrete ramp at the left side of the church a little signboard on a metal stand said "Daily Masses: 9 am and 12 pm."

"I can light a candle anyway," Bishop said.

"Then go ahead. For the repose of birds."

"I sure could use a bit of that repose."

Hearing this, Corbin had to lay down his exasperation with his friend. "Don't let me stop you. Just don't be too long. Our Rachel is waiting for us. She just has to know whether you've been spiritually transformed."

"Oh no, she doesn't even know I'm coming."

"Sweet Jesus. She tells you to convert or die, or, anyway, convert or go away and never see her smiling face again, and just like that you're roaring across the continent. You're in earnest, anyway, for sure, whether she is or isn't."

"I'm going in. You don't have to come with me. Maybe you shouldn't," Bishop said.

Corbin turned and walked almost back to the car, a little bit taken aback by Bishop's surprising tone, then stopped himself. "It's too damn cold out here. Wait up!"

But the door had closed between them.

When Corbin caught up, entering the sanctuary from the side halfway towards the altar, he was brought to a halt by how the winter desert sun threw down pools of blue and green from stained glass windows along the nave. The brickwork behind the altar had a Navajo linked-diamond pattern, and the center aisle of the nave was tiled with red and turquoise chevrons like a Navajo blanket. Bright, cylindrical lights hung from the ceiling high above, marching in order towards the altar. The walls were rose-red like a canyon wall. But all the pews were blond and polished bright, and rank on rank of bright wooden arches spanned the nave.

At last Corbin saw his friend, shoebox in hand, pausing at the altar, staring up at the great crucifix before him, the thin face of Jesus looking not out at the pews, but disconsolately down at the floor before him. Bishop had to shift the box to cross himself, but then turned his gaze up to the rose window, at the other end of the nave, and watched the dust-motes pirouette in light. It was not the glass that Bishop gazed at, just the dust that sifted in and out of slanting, colored shafts. Corbin took a step, then stopped himself as Bishop paused before the first station of the cross, then moved on to the next one, muttering.

The church was empty, and Bishop took his time. Corbin watched him, stock-still, as Bishop worked his way along the wall. From far off, Corbin listened to the traffic passing, the squealing of a bus, a crying child. They were the pale thin ghosts of sounds, of lives.

When Bishop had worked completely around the church, he touched a knee down by the altar rail and crossed down to the rack where four or five candles burned in little red glass jars. He shifted the shoebox first then stepped away and put it on the floor between the pews.

Fumbling in one pocket, then the next, he found, in his handkerchief, a wadded bill, which he folded for the slot. Predictably, the candle wouldn't light. Corbin took a step to help him, but just then the wick flared up, and Bishop set it down.

"I'm ready now," said Bishop, turning back to where he'd put the shoebox down. And then, just as he touched the shoebox, out it flurried, the sparrow, and shot straight for the far end of the nave. "Jesus!"

"I guess it *was* alive," said Corbin.

"Oh no, look!" Bishop pointed as it flew round and round, trapped, beating from one end of the cathedral to the other, frantic. "We'd better save it."

"You've done that once too often."

"I'll get the sexton," Bishop exclaimed, and out he ran, through the little door behind the altar.

The sparrow struck a clerestory, faltered, then flew at the rose window at full tilt. When Corbin got there, he found on the stones a little puff of feathers, a smear of blood.

As Corbin squatted there, he saw Bishop come in, but pause just inside the door, unable to move. Bishop stared at him, his mouth open, for a few seconds, and then all of the expression dropped from his features. He looked blankly over Corbin's head, at the rose window, as if he had lost the power to do anything else.

Then the red-faced sexton pushed past him. "Are you boys making trouble? This is God's house, damn it! I've just called the cops and you'd better be out of here before they get here!"

After he closed the door of the car, Corbin asked, "Now tell me, which one is the sign of God's intent, the sparrow coming suddenly to life, or its beating out its brains against the glass?"

"God doesn't leave messages in code," Bishop said, with a bitterness that took Corbin aback.

Bishop started the Nova. "Let's go back home," he said, making a U-turn in the street.

8

As Bishop had said to Corbin, he had not actually told Rachel that he was rushing across the country to California to her side. For the entire ten days it took the two of them to drive from Willimantic to Gallup and back, in fact, he did not attempt to contact Rachel at all. For the first five days, he didn't want her to tell him not to come. This last fear might not seem rational, inasmuch as it was Rachel herself who had all but demanded in her letter that he come. But Bishop knew Rachel, and he knew that it was possible that by the time he got to Riverside she may have come to the conclusion that his arrival at her house would make a fool of her. For the second five days, he could not bear the idea of having to tell Rachel the story of how, he thought, God had made a fool of him in the cathedral in Gallup, and he had left her to do whatever it was he was afraid she might do.

When he had seen Corbin squatting by the dead sparrow, Bishop had suddenly felt completely empty and could not move. He was cold through and through like a body abandoned in a winter field. He wasn't even defeated because he wasn't anything.

All the way back to Connecticut, preoccupied with his failure of nerve, Bishop didn't give himself the opportunity to think about what his next step with Rachel would be. Or if there would even be a next step at all. Because he had heard the temptation of suicide in Rachel's letter, and, now that it was too late, he knew that whether she actually killed herself or not, he had left her to face down that temptation alone.

But two days after Corbin and Bishop pulled back into Willimantic, on the Wednesday before classes began, just as Bishop was typing the syllabus for his Developmental Writing course onto ditto masters, Rachel presented herself at his doorstep. While he stood there open-mouthed, she silently pushed past him through the door and pulled it closed behind them.

"Is Tom here?"

Bishop had been worried about how to nerve himself up to approach her. But there she was, and her impatience—she must have just arrived from her red-eye flight to Bradley Field that very morning—had swept away the problem of how he would bring himself to face her. She shifted from foot to foot as he collected himself. For the moment, all he had to do was to answer her question.

"He's at the library. He probably won't be home until dinner."

He saw the relief instantly rise in her face as if she had taken a deep breath. And it wasn't just that she was glad they were alone. Something she had feared had not happened.

"Good!" she said.

As quickly as it had come, though, the rush of reprieve passed, and she stood there fidgeting with the buttons of her parka, her downcast face flushed with cold. She didn't stamp off the snow that began to melt from her shoes. Bishop had never seen Rachel so abashed, so at a loss about what to do next.

She wasn't waiting for him to explain himself. And she didn't want to explain herself. She wanted something else from him, but he didn't know what it was. He wondered whether he had just been wrong about what Rachel had been going through in California. He had assumed that how he had failed her would be the first thing she would want to put to him. Maybe the idea that she was in danger was just his hysterical fantasy? But it was more likely, he decided, that she had come through it somehow and didn't want to talk about it, didn't want to think about it, wanted to pretend none of it had ever happened. A long moment passed, and she was still fidgeting, not meeting his gaze. The few flakes of snow that had been in her hair when she came in the door melted.

"Thanks for covering my class," she said.

Bishop could not fathom why it was, but the smile she gave him as she said this was an uneasy one. What was on her mind? Not the favor he had done for her six weeks ago. But why was she ill at ease? Why was *she* worried about what *he* might think? He knew that he had done to her something that he would never live down. But Rachel was also uneasy and couldn't meet his eye. *Could she think her letter crossed a line with me? Might she be embarrassed about what she wanted from me?*

They stood there together, both at a loss, in the front hall, as if each carried something that might go off.

"Um, I hope you're all right." This was as close as Bishop could come to what he had been thinking about.

"Do you have the spring bulletin?" Rachel said, "I don't know where my 103 will be tomorrow."

This question was obviously not what she had come from Storrs to Willimantic to ask him. He looked at her. She looked down at her feet.

"I guess I'm okay," she said at last, to her feet.

"You seem different. Did you put it right with God?" Bishop worried that he had asked this tactlessly. But, in response, she suddenly looked up at him and kissed him aggressively, as she had never done before, so aggressively that he was disoriented. After the first involuntary rush of pleasure, and his equally involuntary response, he felt under both a slight galvanic tingle of fear.

"No," Rachel said, "I've decided to accept love as it is, not as I want it to be."

Again, she kissed him aggressively. "And I haven't lost my faith in God. I've just lost my faith in salvation." This time he returned her kiss although he had no idea what either of the things she had said meant. As soon as she felt his kiss, she pushed him down on the floor, still wet with the snow from her shoes, and straddled his hips.

*A*fter, as she was straightening her skirt, Bishop said, "It's already getting dark. We're lucky Tom didn't walk in on us."

She looked at him with her eyes blazing. "Don't you tell him I was even here." Then she strode out the door without another word. Bishop walked back to the darkening kitchen and sat down at the table, mystified by what Rachel had done. He knew what had happened had been what she had come there to do, however hesitant she may have been about making the first move. Bishop was also mystified by why she spoke harshly about Corbin.

Bishop picked up the salt shaker and shook out a few grains on the kitchen table in front of him. He moved the little pile of salt crystals back and forth as he thought. He felt soiled, as if what he had done with Rachel were something to be ashamed of, as if it had revealed him to be a different kind of person from the one he thought he was. Never, since the first days of puberty, had he felt so dirty, but he could not understand why he felt that way. It was that she had been desperate with him, he thought, and he had been turned on by it. But what could making love to *him* have to do with desperation? Since when had anyone felt desperate desire for him? It was as if she were trying to make something up to him. No. It was more than that. It was as if she were holding on for dear life, like the drowning person who clutches and drowns her rescuer.

He swept up the salt into his hand, poured it into the sink, then washed his hands. He had never felt filthier.

As he had promised Rachel, Bishop did not mention this incident to Corbin. But Bishop did ultimately tell Corbin the story of the abortion, on the phone, when Corbin, having sublet his old room in the apartment on Maple Street, had called him about sending him his security deposit, several weeks after Bishop had failed his oral examinations, after Rachel herself had fled Storrs for good.

After hearing the story, Corbin said that perhaps he should have put two and two together about why Rachel was demanding that Bishop do something so out of character as to rush across the country on a religious quest. Corbin also said he was surprised he had not already heard that story from Rachel herself. As Corbin said this, for just a moment, Bishop thought he heard an undertone of woundedness in his friend's voice.

9

*W*HEN BISHOP HEARD HER CATCH A NERVOUS BREATH AS SHE answered the phone, like somebody who was bracing for even more bad news, the awareness that it was actually Susan who was at the other end of the line came over him so strongly that he had to close his eyes for a moment. He was shaken by the trace of fear he heard in her voice: *After what had happened,* he knew she was thinking, *it could be anything.*

His own voice sounded as though it belonged to somebody else. Both what he wanted to say to her and what he wanted to keep from her brought him up short. *I can't actually help her,* Bishop thought, *I've lied to her already. I can only hurt her worse, or lie to her more.*

But when he told her who he was he heard her exhale in relief: she knew him. And at least it wasn't the police again. He didn't have to explain why he was calling; of course, she knew the police had been with him, retracing her husband's last steps. She already knew that they had found Corbin's body in Lone Pine. "Tom told me how much you meant to him," Susan said.

Bishop too exhaled in relief. Suddenly he pictured her leaning her head softly into the receiver as she stood by the phone on the wall outside her kitchen, her free hand trying to brush away the hair that kept falling into her eyes. Her face would still be flushed, her eyes still swollen, but she had composed herself enough to be at ease with him.

Susan had given Bishop something, her belief that they had the same grief, that it bound them together. But he knew he hadn't earned that gift because all he could think of was how angry he had been about what Corbin had been about to do to her when he was killed.

Please let me know how to help her, Bishop thought. *Don't let me wind up hurting her despite myself.*

When Susan had called on Saturday, looking for her husband, Corbin had actually been dead, not settling into a new life with Rachel Lake, as

Bishop had thought. But what he had told Susan—that Corbin was on his way home to her—was still a lie, and his lie had put her through three days of anguish before she finally nerved herself to report Corbin missing after he had not shown up at his final classes of the semester on Monday, yesterday afternoon. Until then she must have assumed that her husband was just off on a spree with some girl as he usually was when he couldn't be found; she must have believed he would turn up again at her door when he was tired of his escapade.

"I can only imagine what you are going through now," Bishop said.

"It's all still unreal to me," Susan went on, "I know it will be worse later, when I've had a chance to think about it." This she said with a touch of friendly self-deprecation, sure of being understood. He heard the scrape of a chair; he pictured her at her dinette table, in no hurry to get off the phone, as if she had spoken to him a hundred times before, as if they had long known how to go through trouble together. Bishop almost forgot that they didn't know each other at all.

"I called to see whether there is any help I can offer you."

"I feel a little beyond help right now," she said. What she said sounded not like a rejection of his offer but like an apology for not having a request at her fingertips. Then she made another apology as if for imposing the disorder of her grief on him. "I can't organize my thoughts to figure out what I have to do next."

After a second, she gave him another gift: "It's kind of you to think of me."

"It doesn't have to be now. I'll be ready whenever you ask."

She thought a moment, weighing his offer. "That's very generous of you. And I will ask. But don't let me ask for more than you've bargained for."

Her self-control made him want to cry.

"Thank you, Mr. Bishop."

"You can call me Paul," he said.

"Then call me Susan."

Paul sat there, bracing himself, ashamed, after her courtesy, of what he was about to say. She didn't really know him, but she trusted him completely. Corbin may not have told Paul much about her over the years, but he clearly had told Susan a great deal about Paul. If he were a decent person, Paul told himself, he would have left it there. He'd already done the only thing he could do for her, offering his sympathy, and asking what help he could be. But he couldn't leave it there. Because he knew she wouldn't call him, wouldn't think of him when she needed help. Who was he, anyway? But the thought of hanging up and turning back to his own life was too much for him. *Her husband has just been murdered, and I'm the one who's needy, trying to push my way into her grief.*

"I'm sorry to break in like this, but I've just learned something I should tell you, something that might be better for you to hear from me than from the police."

She already knew that Corbin's body had been found, but she didn't know that his killer had just been arrested, which Paul himself had learned almost the moment it happened. When the Reno police had left his apartment, he had, assuming he would know how best to break this news to her, immediately dialed the number Susan had left with him when she had called on Saturday. But as soon as he opened his mouth to tell her what he had learned, he realized that there was no way to do this that would not have been every bit as brutal coming from him as it would have been coming from the police. By then he had already gone too far to keep from telling her what he had learned.

Every syllable he said must have hurt her in a new way. He stopped himself just short of adding that the killer had been wearing Corbin's windbreaker when he was apprehended. He heard her catch another breath and then stifle herself down. *And you pretend you want to help her. Some help you are,* Paul thought.

He knew that her posture would have stiffened in her seat, as she sat up straight and pressed the receiver tightly to her ear. In his mind's eye, he saw that her mouth was open in her straining face, her free hand clenched in the hair behind her neck. Paul waited, hoping his thoughts would clear enough for him to know what he should say next.

Then, after a few seconds silence, he heard her carefully inhale: she had regained control of herself. "Tom always picked up hitchhikers," she said. "They told him their stories. He was always somebody people told their stories to."

It's this memory of Corbin that is steadying her, Paul thought. Susan must have believed this memory would help him too. This memory of Corbin, whom she loved. But who hadn't loved her enough. This memory of Corbin, whom she thought they both loved in the same way.

"I remember," Paul said, gently, "Sometimes those stories went into his poems."

"Those were the ones I liked best," she said, brightening at their common understanding, "better even than the famous ones. Because he really heard people. When you had his attention, nothing mattered more than you did, whoever you were."

As she warmed to her recollection of her husband's poems, Paul thought, *What she wants now is to talk about Tom with someone who loved him. That's how she'll keep herself from drowning.* Those were the poems he liked best, too, he told her, dramatic monologues spoken by real people they knew, by Mrs. Coelho, their landlady, a night-shift nurse at the Knight Hospital, where the most debilitated inmates of the Mansfield Training School waited out their lives, or by Terry Caserta, who held court from the cash register at Amalfi Pizza, whom every student at UConn seemed to know, and who knew all their business.

Susan is right about him, Paul thought. *He did know those people. And it really was true that when you had his attention, nothing mattered more than you did.* Paul himself had felt that from Corbin, from the first moment, more than a decade ago, and on the other side of the continent, when Corbin had unexpectedly praised him on Admitted Students Day, and made common cause with him against the world he had been intimidated by. Paul had never stopped feeling that alliance, even during those last days in Reno, when Corbin had been behaving so badly to everyone.

But Paul couldn't stop himself from adding: *that's also why women were drawn to him.* Corbin knew how to make them feel they mattered; he knew how to listen to them. That's how he kept listening them into bed. Then a thought nagged him: *Still, that can't be what drew him and Rachel back together. Because Rachel would not be vulnerable to that now. Whatever went on between him and Rachel was different from all the rest. That's why Susan shouldn't know about it.*

While Paul was wondering about these things, Susan went on, "Tom would even have heard *him*, if he had given him the chance. Even now, he would have wanted to know that man's story."

It took Paul a second to understand what she was getting at: even the story of the man who killed him was something Corbin would have wanted to lift into the light. So even in how he died there was something she could love Corbin for. And his death happened because of what she loved best in him. *Why in the world would anyone want to leave someone who loved him enough to say that about him?*

"Tom was curious about people," he said. *Is this the best I can manage? Jesus Christ.*

"Tom knew everyone down to the ground." She paused for a second, gathering herself for something. "Did he show you *An Obol for the Boatman?*"

"He told me he wrote that book himself, that he was Olga Kyriakos. But you already knew that." Paul remembered that this was the book that had reignited Corbin's affair with Rachel Lake. But to Susan that book meant something else, something that urgently drew her to Corbin as well.

"That book was him down to the ground, what nobody else knew," she said, simply. "I knew Tom, and I also knew what everybody thought about him. They didn't know what really mattered about him."

She paused a second and then burst out: "He knew *me* down to the ground, anyway." She tried to choke back the flash of grief, but it again got the better of her. After a moment, she was able to finish her sentence though she had not yet caught her breath. "That made me love him despite everything."

Paul heard her testimonial, but he also heard her "despite everything," with its note of defiance. He wasn't sure whom she was defying. She was sure Paul would side with her against everyone else who knew Corbin. Because she thought he loved Corbin the way she did. Because she knew Corbin had loved him, something Paul himself was less sure about.

"Yes, there was nobody like him," he said. While Paul knew that wasn't a lie, he was angry with Corbin, and he became angrier with him as Susan praised him. *Why did you mess this up this way?* Paul wanted to ask Tom. *What could possibly have made it worth it to do what you did to her? Because you did love her, even if that didn't stop you. And you knew how good she is. Why couldn't you just have been happy that she loved you and took you as you are?*

"I know you had to bear with him too," said Susan, "and he wasn't easy. You must have felt what I felt in him. What made me just pour myself out for him, like everyone else."

Paul wondered why she thought it was safe for her to tell him this. They hadn't met, but she was sure he knew all about her, because she knew all about him, that Paul too had been hurt by Corbin and loved him anyway, just as she did, that he was already on her side. And she was right: he *was* on her side. And he loved Corbin even in anger. *But she doesn't know that I'm a filthy fucking liar.* He had to pause. *Please help me to do the right thing by her. Don't let me fuck this up like I fuck up everything.* After a moment he got ahold of himself.

"Yes, I felt that too," he said, "Despite everything."

"He had a way of drawing people to him. It always got him in trouble, and made him hate himself, that way with people," Susan said, "but it also made him matter. It's what I loved him for. Even if it was also what made him hurt me."

So Susan knew the kind of husband Corbin had been. And she wanted me to know that. Paul heard her breathing softly over the phone as she waited for him to respond to what she had said. But Paul had been brought to an impasse.

Whether Corbin really wanted to know people down to the ground, Paul did not know. He asked himself whether Corbin knew those girls he picked up at readings down to the ground. They would have thought they were safe with him because he made them believe they were special. Maybe he did think they were special. Maybe he thought they were safe with him too until he got tired of them.

But he couldn't think Susan was just wrong to love him the way she did. *It's a gift, to be able to love someone that way. It couldn't have all been just a waste, could it?* Paul wondered. *Whatever Corbin was, it couldn't be meaningless that she loved him. It just couldn't be. That would be too painful to consider.*

Paul knew that Susan had taken a risk with him, that he had to ac-

70

knowledge her confession. But his thoughts were still flurried, and he continued to leave her hanging while he pondered.

There seem to be two kinds of people in the world, Paul thought. *There are the kind of people who think that when you really know someone what you know is the special kind of dirt that makes them themselves, what they can't live down and can't get past. Then there are the kind of people who believe that when you really know someone what you know is what it is that they never completely betray so long as they continue to struggle with themselves. No matter how far gone they are you have to find some way that isn't a lie to love them anyway. Whatever love really is, it only begins after it has faced down disappointment.*

I know which type Susan is. And I'm afraid of finding out what type I am.

Susan had been waiting for him, but it was she who broke the impasse: "I was just about to say all I wanted was to love him, and I didn't care about anything else." She waited for him to agree.

"Yes." *I'd like to say that. But I didn't love him enough.* Paul had to catch a breath. *Not the way you do.*

"But now Tom and I will never get it right between us."

"It's not all over." Paul didn't know why he said this.

"When someone dies, what happens to your love for them? Does it still mean something?"

Susan's strange question was more than Paul could answer. What did he know about this kind of question? "I don't know. If you loved someone you just keep doing it," he finally replied.

"You do keep loving them. It doesn't seem possible to do anything else," Susan conceded, "but it doesn't help you. A memory can't light your way through the confusion because it's only the living person who can help you work out the next step when there's no way forward. It's the living person, not just the memory, that you want to be with you when you have to face the music."

He knew that she meant something by this last point that she wasn't going to tell him about.

"I don't think it's futile to keep loving." Somehow, Paul found himself almost pleading with her. "Maybe it teaches you to love other people, to love the world."

Susan paused to think about this.

"I think when you love," she said, "you love a person, some one person you've given yourself to completely, not the world, and no other person is the one you loved."

Paul felt he had taken a step too far. But she was telling him things it was strange to tell someone you have only just met. Because she knew they had Corbin in common.

"That you loved somebody," Paul said, "just has to keep mattering, whatever happens."

He wanted to believe that. But he couldn't say how it might matter. How would he even know? Had Corbin, had he himself, ever loved anybody in a wholehearted way? But Susan had. She had loved Corbin completely. So completely that she didn't care what he did. Paul envied her that, that gift of loving completely, despite everything, even if it was Corbin she loved, even if the whole thing was hopeless, and came to nothing. And suddenly, Paul knew what he wanted, and couldn't have. It was to love just the way Susan did, recklessly and without ambivalence and with everything. Without his flinch. Without his cowardice. It was to love *Susan* that way, the way she loved Corbin.

And then he knew exactly what he would do. He would keep Corbin from breaking Susan's heart from beyond the grave. He would keep her love for him safe, that love she had given herself so fully to that it made her what she was, that love that drew Paul himself to her although he couldn't have any part of it because it was love for somebody else, for somebody who hadn't loved her enough.

"After we die, if we know anything then," she said, not noticing that he had again fallen silent, "we will finally make sense of love, after all the confusion."

Let's hope so, Paul thought, *though I doubt even God will ever make sense of love.*

She paused a second. "And if we know nothing then, then we won't suffer, because we won't be there to suffer. If I felt he didn't love me, I think I'd look forward to death. Because there's nothing more painful than the thought that the one person who knows you best in all the world

72

doesn't want you, and that thought dies when you do."

Paul winced, glad she couldn't see him over the phone. She knew Corbin cheated on her. And she had managed to live with that. But she didn't know he was leaving her. That was a different story.

"I think it's for us, the people who are still alive," Paul said, "to do the loving. While we can."

He wanted to head off her dark thought. Not that he had the power to do it. Or even the right.

"I suppose so," Susan said, "And all our lives we don't keep that in focus. Until it's too late." Then, after a beat, "He thought a lot of you. Particularly these last few weeks. You were on his mind. He wanted to know what you thought. No, more than that. He *had* to know what you thought."

"What I thought of *An Obol for the Boatman*?" Paul smote himself for the stupidity of this question before it was even out. But he knew what it was that Corbin wanted to know what he thought about and that was the last thing he was going to tell her.

"No, more than that. I don't know what more. But something important. Something he really needed to talk with you about. Something from long ago. But also something that had to do with both of us, you and me, somehow. And with that book too. Because that's what got it started, that book. But I don't know what it was."

This is why she's so open with me, he thought. *She knows he was troubled about something important, something he wanted to see me about. She hopes I know what was on his mind. And I do.*

"I really wish I knew," he said, plausibly. *God, I hate myself.* Paul paused for a beat, disoriented for a moment by the spontaneity of yet another lie.

"It's strange," she said, making common cause with Paul as someone who, like her, had loved Corbin, but not enough to save him, as if he had died out of some failure of their love. "You never know when will be the last moment you ever lay eyes on someone you love. You think whatever you have to get straight can wait until he comes home. And then he doesn't come home." She paused a second to nerve herself up for what she was about to say. "He was unhappy. I don't know why. Not that he was ever really happy. But for at least the last six months, maybe since last November, it was much worse. I don't know what it was all about. I was hoping he would tell you what it was. But he didn't. And I don't think I'll ever know now."

"You shouldn't blame yourself about that." But she was too caught up in her thought to listen.

"The morning he left to drive up to Reno, it was about 4:30 am, when he left. I got up to make him coffee, fill a thermos for the road, and make a couple of sandwiches. And he went to wake up Jack. I thought, *Why do that? Why bother him? All it will do is make him sad to see you drive off.* But he hugged Jack until he woke up. Jack was groggy and crabby. And Tom hugged him and stroked his hair until he was fully awake. 'Dad, what are you doing?' Jack asked. 'I'm just giving you love, Jack. I want to take this hug with me to Reno.' 'That's just silly, Dad,' Jack said. And Tom laughed and let him go back to sleep. Then he hugged me really hard, and for a long time, until I said, 'Tom, come on. You're hurting me.' And that was the last time I ever touched him. Breaking that long hug was the last thing I ever did with him."

Paul knew that Susan had no idea why her husband had hugged her that way. But she was still full of her last thought.

"When I lie down in bed, the pillow still smells like his shampoo." Susan couldn't go on. She had to stop to collect herself.

All Paul could muster was, "I'm sorry."

"I haven't even told Jack yet. I don't know what I'm going to do when he gets back from school today. It's going to be so hard for him." Susan choked up.

"It's you he turns to when he's hurt."

"It will feel like I'm the one who's hurting him." She sighed.

"He knows you'll stand by him."

She was thinking. Her mind had rushed on to something else.

"And there was something I had to tell Tom, but I put it off. I thought, Why make him worry all through his trip? It will be hard enough to deal with when he gets back. Why not give him these three days? Now I'll never tell him."

"What was it?" Paul asked.

Then she closed a door between them. "Something I needed his help with. Something important. But it doesn't matter now."

"Something you still need help with? Something you mentioned when you called me on Saturday?" Paul persisted.

"I can't talk about it now." Then, changing her tone, she asked, "What will happen next with the killer? What's the next step?"

"In a day or so, probably on Thursday, there'll be an arraignment. The police told you that they found Tom's body in Lone Pine, in Inyo County, so it may be at the Superior Court in the county seat, some place called Independence. The killer will appear in court to be charged. Then the judge will consider setting bail."

"I want to be there. I want to see him."

Paul was wondering. He took the receiver from his ear for a moment and looked at the ceiling.

"Tom would have been able to hear him, what he is," she said, "It was his way. I want to see whether I can do the same."

"That will be hard."

"To take him as a human being?" Susan asked.

"Even to be in the same room with him. I couldn't do it," Paul said.

"We are called to love our enemies," she said as if that sentence settled the question.

Paul did not know what more to say. She insisted on making a moral demand of herself that he could not imagine anyone fulfilling. Something Corbin would never have asked of her. But when he heard her, he was drawn into it too. *I don't care how impossible this is. I want to be part of it.* "I guess there will be a lot of hard things you have to do," Paul said.

"More than you know. But I know about hard things. Did Tom tell you about me?"

"He showed me your graduation picture," Paul said.

"I'm an oncologist. Or, I will be. I'm a fourth-year resident. I try to make people well by making them feel sicker than they've ever felt before," she explained.

"It's a good thing they have you with them."

"I don't know that. But I'm the one they have. Mostly what I do is comfort the patient while nature takes its course. If it comes to it, I help them get used to the idea of dying. When my patients run out of hope, I can at least try to see them as the person they have always been, not just as the face of their disease."

"Not everyone can do that," Paul said.

"Now I'm the one without hope. So I have to do what Tom would have done. So I can still be who I think I am, not just a useless lump of grief."

Hearing that last phrase, Paul had to take a breath. "People do live with grief," he said, "They go on living, and it's no betrayal of the dead for them to live. We can't imagine that the dead would want those they left behind to die for them."

"Yes, I'm sure that's right. We have to think that the people we loved would want us to go on living. What life they will continue to have will somehow be through us, so we have to live. Even when we don't want to. Tom would have wanted me to be at the arraignment. It's a kind of test for me." She paused, thinking. "But I need someone to come with me. I don't have anyone else. And Jack will need help too."

"Yes, Susan," he said, as if it were the most natural thing in the world, "I'll come with you."

10

On Wednesday morning, the seventh of May, Paul Bishop picked up his final papers from the mailbox in his office and told the department administrator that he would be away for a few days, but he planned to return in time to give his final exam on the coming Monday. By mid-afternoon, he was driving down the Owens Valley, the very route his friend had driven only a week before.

Passing through the dusty, sunstruck desert south of Lone Pine, he wondered about where Corbin had stopped to pick up the hitchhiker who killed him. Was it just after Lone Pine? Or had Corbin picked him up earlier, further north, so that the hitchhiker had actually ridden with him, even talked with him, and then killed the man he had been chatting with? *No,* Bishop thought, *the killer would have wanted to do it right away, for fear of losing his nerve and not doing it at all.*

He pictured Corbin pulling over as he noticed the hitchhiker ahead. Did he look Tom in the eye as he climbed into the car, or did he avoid his gaze? Did Corbin smile at him and ask how he was holding up in the hot weather? Did the hitchhiker tell Tom where he was bound, or where he had started? Or did he only grunt in response to the poet's questions, and not make eye contact at all, perhaps because he didn't want to lose his focus on what he was planning to do, or perhaps just because he was drunk?

Bishop imagined the odor of sweat and dust he must have brought with him into the car, the filthy olive-green canvas backpack he may have lowered into the foot well of the passenger seat. Corbin would have tried to make conversation with him, would have tried one way after another of drawing him out. Paul imagined the hitchhiker sitting sullenly, not wanting to engage with the man he was about to kill. Bishop guessed that they must have driven together for only a few minutes. Since each moment would have brought the hitchhiker a new risk, he probably waited only long enough for the car to have driven out of sight of town, perhaps to somewhere he could force Corbin to a spot where his car could not be seen from the road.

When Bishop tried to picture anything beyond the moment when the hitchhiker first drew out his knife, he quailed, but his imagination ran on ahead of him. Corbin had probably driven into the brush calmly, figuring that the hitchhiker would merely take his money, and had gotten out of the car when the hitchhiker demanded it, figuring that the hitchhiker would take the Firebird and go off, leaving him to find his way on foot back to Lone Pine. Bishop knew Corbin had been mugged before, so he would know how to keep his head. But the moment when it became clear to Tom that the hitchhiker intended to kill him was something Bishop did not want to picture. He did not want to know whether Corbin had struggled, whether the hitchhiker had slashed him before he finally brought him down. But the picture rose in his mind anyway. Tom had always struck Paul as brave, and he hoped that this bravery had not failed Corbin at the last moment. Bishop wondered how his own bravery might have fared had it all happened to him.

Paul pulled off the highway, across from an RV park, where a gravel road bent off, through a cluster of trailers, towards the mountains, and started to cry for his friend, who had wanted something from him that Paul had withheld. Only at this moment did he grasp that Corbin had been asking him to find a way back for him to the arms of his wife.

Paul had not seen it because he had been so angry at discovering Corbin's long-ago affair with Rachel Lake. Now the instructor could see how ambivalent the poet's feelings were about leaving Susan for Rachel. Paul had missed the moment, as he always did, because it had never occurred to him that Corbin would ask for help.

11

*J*ACK CORBIN HAD BEEN AFRAID AS LONG AS HE COULD REMEMBER, but only in the last few months did he understand why. What terrified him wasn't the invisible stranger in his room who wasn't there whenever his mother, Susan, turned the lights on. And it wasn't the shower drain that might someday suck him down into nothing. Sometime before Thanksgiving, he noticed how often his father, Tom, for no reason, would hold him, stroke the back of his head, and kiss him on the forehead. When he was much smaller, when his mother was in medical school, or in the first years of her residency, it was his father who had mostly taken care of him. But lately, after her internship year was over, his mother had taken the lead. This warmth from his father struck him at first as no more than his father picking up where he had left off. But there was a pressure about it now that set Jack on edge. *Who would be needing all this saved-up love, his father? Or himself?* Both thoughts scared him.

After Christmas vacation, Jack never knew who was going to pick him up at after-school. Usually his father would pick him up at the after-school at about 4 pm. But every couple of weeks, then almost every week, and a few times more than once a week, Jack would find himself there late, even past 6 pm, after all of the other children had been picked up. One of the teachers would have to stay with him until his mother arrived from the hospital. When his mother came, she told the teacher that her husband had to work late and had forgotten to tell her to pick up their son. She was very sorry about it. The teacher who had to stay was angry with her, and his mother apologized to her and told her it would never happen again. But the teacher didn't believe her since it had happened before.

Jack was ashamed. It must have been his fault. When they got to the car, he cried again with relief, and his mother was stung by his tears. Holding him after she had buckled him into his seat, his mother asked him if he had really thought she might not come to pick him up at all. She promised she would care for him always. But that wasn't why he was upset. He was afraid for her because he knew she was lost, but he couldn't tell her, and he couldn't help her. Once they got inside the house she took him onto her lap on the lumpy orange couch while he closed his eyes and sucked his thumb. She didn't even rebuke him about it.

Every time his father didn't come home, his mother had to throw something together out of the freezer for dinner since his father usually did the cooking. Jack and his mom sat together at the dinette table quietly. She asked what he did at recess, but Jack didn't want to talk about it. He wanted to know when his father was coming home even though that question upset his mother.

On nights like these, Jack's father was never home by reading time. His father had always done the reading aloud because he was so good at the voices. But tonight, his mother would have to pick some other book for reading time because she couldn't do the voices as well. Sitting in his mother's lap as she held their book, Jack showed her that he could actually sound out the words by himself. *This would make her proud,* he thought. And she said she was proud of him. But he could not stop her from being sad. Sometimes he would recite the book from memory. His mother told Jack that it was nice to have him all to herself sometimes, but she kept listening for a car in the driveway.

There was a struggle at bedtime because he wanted to wait up for his father to get home. They would wait together on his bed with the lights out if he wanted. But he wasn't going to stay up. "That's how it's going to be, so don't fight me about it," she said.

He always planned to run to the door as soon as he heard it open, but he fell asleep quickly, exhausted from worry. No matter how long he waited, even if his mother had fallen asleep beside him on the bed before he did, he never managed to wake up when his father finally got back home.

Sometimes Jack's father was away at work for an entire weekend. His mother pretended she had known that was going to happen, but Jack knew that wasn't true. She didn't tell him, didn't want to tell him, how she was feeling about it, but he knew anyway. He wanted to comfort her, but it wasn't any use.

His father continued to be very warm to him, but he never said a word about where he had been. Jack knew that something was coming apart between his parents and that he could not stop it.

One night, Jack saw that his mother was worried about the same thing he had been worried about all along. The fact that she was pretending, that she for a long time had to pretend she wasn't worried, only made him more afraid. Lying alone in his bed after she thought he had fallen asleep, he wondered whether it would be easier to let the invisible man in his room snatch him.

On the Friday afternoon his father was in Reno, he suddenly felt a new and different fear. He knew his mother was going to be a little late picking him up at school because she had an appointment with her doctor. "Why do doctors need to have doctors?" he had asked at breakfast. His mother had smiled but hadn't answered him. At pick-up time, he ran to the glass wall of the classroom where a construction paper window frame had been taped to the glass to make a window for the preschoolers to wave goodbye. He wanted to see whether his mother's red Dart was turning into the parking lot. He saw her before she saw him, before she could put on a face for him. She had just stopped crying and was trying to control herself, but he could see that she was still gasping.

As soon as she stepped through the classroom door he saw, through the smile she had put on when she noticed he was watching, how death-pale she was. And when he ran to her, she lifted him up and, still in the doorway, held him to her tightly, and turned around and around with him, holding him so long that the teacher who all this time had been holding the door open for them gave her a look. It couldn't be just because his father was late, because he wasn't late, at least not yet. But she was afraid, and she was floundering. All he could do about it was to love her, and he knew that wouldn't help her at all.

His father did not come home that Friday night, although he was supposed to. This time when Jack melted down about it she cried too, which terrified him, because that wasn't like her.

She was so sorry, she said, when he saw how unnerved he was by her tears. *It must scare you to see me cry.* Yes, something was the matter, but that was as far as she would go. His father would help her figure it out when he came home. *He'll know what to do*, she said, and tried to smile, *He always knows how to help me. He'll get me through this.* She held Jack in her lap and rocked him silently, until, despite his resistance, she soothed him into relaxing, and he surrendered to sleep and she carried him to his bedroom.

Later that night, when he awoke in fear as he so often did, he slipped into her room, knowing that she would be annoyed with him for getting out of bed, but also hoping that she might lie back down with him in his room to lull him back to sleep. When he tried to awaken her, she was already awake, but lost to him in her thoughts, and her face was wet.

He put his face against her wet cheek. "Mommy, what's the matter?" She held him to her. "Mommy, are you sad?" She lay there, just breathing in and out for a second. "Mommy, let me care for you."

Slowly she sat up, shifting Jack into her lap. "No, darling, it's my job to care for you."

12

*B*ECAUSE PAUL BISHOP KNEW THAT ONLY AFTER SUSAN HAD picked up her son from school on Tuesday could she have told him about his father's murder, and about the arraignment they all would have to go to, Paul had arranged to stay Wednesday and Thursday night at the Motel 6 on University Avenue. He had no business that night in that grieving household, however much he wanted to help them. But he lay awake in his room, knowing that something painful was going on that he could do nothing about. He knew he was an intruder, and that what they were feeling was beyond his ability to console: *who am I anyway?*

But whatever he could or couldn't do, Susan had asked him to drive them to Independence, and that he could do even if he did not know how to face their grief. He hoped he wouldn't make things worse than they were. *How typical that it's about me, about whether I'll measure up, that I'm worried. I just can't keep me me out of it.*

Paul had brought to the bare room in the Motel 6 two paper cups of cold coffee and a jelly doughnut to eat in the morning since he expected there would be no breakfast at Susan's house. Naturally, he woke at four in the morning, after ninety minutes of sleep, and, with the volume turned off, watched the early morning weather and news on the television in his darkened room until the hour approached seven. The American hostages were still being held in Tehran. An editorial criticized the failed rescue attempt that President Carter had launched the previous week.

Susan's little house, on Massachusetts Avenue, just north of the University, was only a couple of miles away. She lived in a tan stucco ranch across from a junior high school on a modest arrow-straight street that seemed bare despite being lined with tall palms. The house was nearly obscured by a bedraggled pine tree, which had strewn the crabgrass yard with needles. A narrow concrete porch ran across the front of the house. Through the picture window in the living room, Paul could see an orange couch on one side of the room and a television set on the other. He glimpsed the galley window that opened into the kitchen and a dinette. The lights were still on in the two bedroom windows to his right. Susan's dark red Dart was parked in the driveway when Paul pulled his Datsun in alongside.

When he knocked on her door, he heard her sing out: "Come in! Come in! The door's unlocked. I'm so glad you're early!" Cheerful—as if they didn't know the mission.

He found Susan in the dark, cramped kitchen at the back of the house, putting a stack of ham sandwiches into a plastic bread bag, and filling a plaid thermos from a percolator of coffee. She then poured apple juice in a small green thermos for Jack.

She shook his hand and smiled at him. "It's good to actually see you. I've had to imagine you from Tom's description. And you look just how I thought you might when I heard you on the phone." Her voice was bright, which almost kept Paul from noticing how weary she was.

Despite how hard she worked at smiling for him, Paul could not help noticing the dark circles under her eyes. Her eyelids were still red, still swollen. He guessed that she had been up all night. Paul wanted to tell her she didn't have to put on a face for him. But he saw that she had to do it for Jack.

Susan and Jack, he knew, would have managed to go through the tasks that morning with the silent industry of the women who clear the rubble from the street after a night of bombing. She wasn't going to show Paul a thing. He wondered how much that self-control took out of her, what reservoirs of life it must have been steadily depleting. Has she mastered her grief, he wondered, or merely throttled it? *One way or the other it will always be waiting for her.*

As he watched her briskly organizing things at the counter that divided the kitchen from the living room, Paul noticed that she was quite a bit shorter, and quite a bit slighter, than he had expected her to be from the photograph Corbin had shown him in Reno. Her blonde hair, loose and alive under the soft octagonal academic cap in the graduation photo Paul had seen, was pulled back tightly in a ponytail that gave her the appearance of being younger than she actually was.

Dressing more formally for the day in court than he thought she would for the clinic, Susan wore a long, dark blue, open-throated dress that buttoned down to the belted waist. On her feet, she wore the crepe-soled flats he imagined she used for the long days of walking the rounds of the oncology floor. As she swept up the crumbs from the counter, he saw that she had chewed her nails to the quick.

"Would you like something to eat?" she asked.

"Oh, no thanks, I ate at the motel."

"I only have Trix anyway. Tom and I never have time for breakfast for ourselves." For a second, she sounded as though Corbin had just stepped out of town for the day, that they were about to go pick him up, perhaps at the airport.

"Let me go get Jack. He's in the bathroom, brushing his teeth."

Paul waited by the dinette where Jack had eaten a bowl of Trix and left a small puddle of milk around the bowl. The boy had stayed in the bathroom during Paul's conversation with Susan.

When Susan led a reluctant Jack back to the dinette, Paul thought the child looked pudgy in army pants, a plaid shirt, and cowboy boots. He was also wary and unhappy and exhausted.

Susan tried to introduce him to Paul, but the boy looked down at his empty bowl the whole time, and he didn't want to shake that man's hand. Paul saw the muscles of Jack's shoulders tighten when Susan told her son that he would be with his father's friend from Reno all day while she went into the courtroom by herself.

"Why do you have to go in by yourself?" Jack asked.

"Because it's not a place for children."

"But why take me then?"

"Because I need you with me all day."

Paul knew that the boy had seen through what his mother had said. The boy didn't at all want to go to wherever it was they had to go, and having a stranger with him wouldn't make it any easier. He just wanted to go back to bed and cry.

"Can't we just stay here? Can't you just stay with me here, and let *him* go to and talk to the judge?" Jack looked away from her and set his shoulders.

Before he could dig in all the way, though, Susan put her hand under his chin gently and raised his face to look at her. His chin began to tremble.

"I can't do this without you, so let's get going." She spoke firmly, but Paul heard a quaver in her voice. And Jack must have too, because he suddenly folded, rather than make her fall to pieces.

He could have stood up to the firmness, Paul thought, *But not to the quaver.* A tear rolled down Jack's cheek, and he squinched his eyes shut. But he nodded. *He thinks it's on him to keep her going. He's worried sick for her. Brave boy.* Paul thought.

Susan turned back to the kitchen to pick up the bag of sandwiches. Still, Jack didn't move from his chair, and continued to cry, as silently as he could manage. After a few moments, Jack looked Paul up and down. Paul caught his eye. "This is hard," Paul said. "And I wouldn't want to go either. But it's the best way we can help her, isn't it?"

Jack met Paul's glance, surprised. Jack sat there, just looking, still not knowing how to feel.

"Let's move it," Susan said from the kitchen. "Now." Then, after a second, "Chop, chop!"

*J*ack climbed onto the booster seat in the back as Susan strapped him in.

"You drive," his mom said to Paul, handing him her keys. "I'll sit in the back with Jack."

Jack gave her a look. She hadn't done this since he was a baby. He told her she didn't have to sit in the back with him. He was big enough now.

"But I will, anyway." Susan gave him a peck on the cheek.

Jack was glad she was with him, strange as it was. He sat quietly and watched her as Paul slipped into the driver's seat and backed the car out of the driveway. Soon they were racing through San Bernardino.

"Read to me," Jack said. He rummaged in the backpack Susan had brought to the car for the bag of sandwiches and the thermos. Finally, he pulled out a copy of *The Lion, the Witch, and the Wardrobe.* There was a bookmark a few pages in. Seeing it, Susan shuddered.

"Tom had just started that," his mom said to Paul, as if it were a

86

neutral fact. "He read a lot to Jack." But reading that book was clearly too much for her right now. "He was so good at it," she said, as if the issue were that she didn't do it well enough. "I can still hear him reading it if I let myself." She put the book back in the backpack. Jack was disappointed and turned to look out the window.

His mom kissed Jack on the temple and held him in her arms. He still didn't look at her. He was hurt, and he wanted her to know it. Then she stroked his hair until he melted for her and turned to receive her kiss on his forehead. After a while, she took a cassette recorder out of the backpack.

"It's hard to read in the car," she said, as if that had been the issue. "Maybe you would like some music, Jack?"

Jack didn't say no, but he didn't know what he wanted. She continued to stroke his hair. He put his thumb in his mouth and looked away from her, out the window.

The cassette in the machine was an album of songs for children. After a few minutes, she clicked it on. The first song was "Autumn to May." His mother hoped he might sing it with her. He didn't feel like it. He didn't really want anything but to go back home and go to bed and never get out of bed again. But as she sang the song in his ear, he did, after a few lines, softly join in.

By the time they reached the end of the song, they had both fallen asleep.

13

*P*AUL COULD SEE SMALL RANCH BUILDINGS FROM THIRTY MILES away in the emptiness, and every few miles a dusty side road branched off, heading towards nothing. The route was treeless, a universe of death, a broad, barren plain bordered by rumpled brown hills, broken by an occasional cluster of red or orange heights, like something the sky had dropped there and forgotten about. The scattered sagebrush, dun and silver, not even appearing to be alive, clutched down everywhere into the sand. The sun blazed down on them, something unaccustomed to showing mercy.

At intervals, under a scattering of brush, willows, and cottonwoods, there would be a settlement with a gas station, widely spaced tin-roofed houses, and a handful of abandoned truck trailers. Randsburg. Johannesburg. Inyokern.

After Brady's, the brown ragged hills that fore-ran the distant Sierras began to draw closer to the road, and after that the bare hills moved in on both sides of them as they crossed the saddle into Inyo County. Past Olancha, as the hills rose ever steeper to the west, they saw the broad, white, ruined playa where once Owens Lake had been. Two rows of tall transmission towers marched alongside the highway, and off to the right they saw the rusted remains of a mill, the roof collapsed but the three silos still standing sentry beside it. A red watertank stood just at the edge of the highway, with a freshly painted sign "Gateway to the Eastern Sierra." Far off, beyond the playa, the Inyo Mountains wavered in the shimmer of heat.

Susan came out of her drowse. "Wait. We have to stop in Lone Pine first."

She said this as quietly as she could manage, so Paul almost whispered. "Okay."

She checked to see whether Jack was still asleep. "We have to stop at the coroner's office to identify the body," she said. "The D.A. asked me to."

"They really need that?" Paul looked at her through the rearview mirror.

"Jane Davenport—that's her name—will want to cross every t and dot every i. She thinks I won't be happy until I drink that man's blood. Or maybe until she does." In her anger, Susan had allowed herself to raise her voice. Then she caught herself. But she could not keep the anger down. "That's how she came off on the phone. Because it's her ticket, my grief. It makes me ashamed of grieving. She's going to make sure that that James Cole, that's his name, by the way, is never in a position to hurt anyone again, she says. I don't want to think about what she means by that. But Inyo County will be safe as safe can be, if it's up to her. And then she gets to go to Congress."

Jack stirred a bit, hearing his mother's feeling.

"I'll sit with Jack while you're in there."

"Yes. He shouldn't go in with me."

Jack stirred again, not asleep but not quite awake.

As they climbed the gentle rise out of the lakebed at about 10:30 am, they passed a sign at a cluster of buildings that said "Lone Pine Smokehouse." Paul looked back to see whether Susan had noticed it. She nodded at him. "I saw it too. It must have been somewhere around here."

"What must have been around here?" Jack asked.

"Nothing." Susan looked out the window.

Jack looked at her. She had dug in her heels about something, and Paul saw that posture had made Jack wary. Susan meant business, and she wasn't going to be drawn into anything she didn't want to be drawn into.

"Go back to sleep. I'll wake you when we get there," his mother said.

Jack closed his eyes, but Paul could tell he did not sleep.

Beyond, at the head of the rise, they could see another cluster of trees. On the right, in the shade, there was an RV park for tourists. On the left, in the brush, was a scattering of trailers. A gravel road branched off there, heading up into the mountains, disappearing behind a hill after a few hundred yards. Susan and Paul looked at it, then at each other. They did not know whether this was the spot that Corbin had been forced off the road. But they both felt sure of it. Neither said anything about it. Then Paul saw that it was where he had stopped to cry the previous day.

The coroner's office, which did double duty as a funeral home, was a well-kept, two-story stucco building, gathered around a flagstone courtyard over which a U.S. and a State of California flag flew, with a Spanish-style terracotta roof, and tall, well-manicured bushes around its foundation. Paul found the sight of the building reassuring, having expected it to be a grim, shabby site that reflected the chaos and darkness of the unnatural death that brought them there.

The coroner was a tall, burly man with a gray buzzcut and a closely trimmed mustache and goatee, rather like a Kentucky Colonel. He had aviator glasses that glittered on his face in the sun, and he wore a bolo tie under his blue laboratory coat. He was friendly in a rural way. He introduced himself as Dr. Michael Celio.

Susan was greeting Dr. Celio as Paul lifted a sleeping Jack out of the car. Paul instantly saw on Susan's face that he had made a mistake. It would have been better to have Paul and Jack wait in the car while Susan went into the morgue to identify her husband's body. But Susan, in her exhaustion, had not warned Paul about what to do, and Paul did not have the experience as a parent to know better. Now it would be much harder to keep from Jack why they had stopped at this strange place. But had Jack awakened while Susan was not in the car, Paul reflected, there might have been trouble too, and too many things to explain away. Paul braced himself for the consequences of his blunder.

"Maybe you and the boy can go up the block for an ice cream," Celio said, intuiting the situation. But by then they had all already stepped into his office.

"Is my father here?" Jack said suddenly, clearly, as if he had just become much older. Susan and the coroner looked at Jack, the coroner keeping his face carefully neutral. But Paul could only watch Susan. He was at a loss.

"I heard you in the car. I want to see him too."

The coroner looked at Susan in alarm.

"No, you don't want that," his mother said. "It will hurt you forever."

"I know he's here. I want to see him," Jack insisted.

Paul could hear that it hurt Jack to stand up to his mother. Jack's job was to help her, to protect her. But Paul saw desperation on Jack's face; he might have no other chance to be with his father. Jack's eyes began to well.

"Please," Jack begged.

She didn't answer.

"Please."

"I'm supposed to protect you, so when I tell you no, I mean it," Susan replied.

Jack locked his knees as if to brace himself against her pressure. Then, as Jack stood there stiffly, his face working, she knelt in front of him, holding out her arms to take him in. But he wrenched himself away from her.

"Jack," Susan said as her son stood his ground for another second. "I wouldn't do this if it weren't right for you."

But rather than give in to her he turned, threw himself onto the coroner's couch, and wept bitterly. Before his mother could react, he had already begun to stifle his tears, pushing his face into the back of the couch. Paul just stood there staring. Susan sat down next to Jack and tried to put her arms around him, but he shrugged her off. She stroked his back until he had cried himself out.

"You won't want to see him like this. Because you'll keep seeing it when you don't want to," Susan said.

Jack didn't listen to this.

"Believe me, I know what I'm talking about," his mother insisted.

Finally, Jack brought his wet, red face out of the back of the couch and just looked at her, blinking away his tears, his breath trembly.

"We'll see him again at the wake," she said. "It will be better than this. I promise."

Jack stopped resisting and allowed her to hold him. But Paul saw Jack didn't buy what she had said. After a few moments, he began to breathe more evenly. Then, again, he put his thumb into his mouth, closed his eyes, and pressed against her.

91

"I guess I'm ready," she said, after a few moments. "Are you okay here, Paul?"

Paul couldn't quite speak, but he nodded at her. She detached herself from Jack, who sat by himself on the couch, too numb to move, still sucking his thumb.

"Then let's go do our business," she said to the coroner, and they left the room, closing the door carefully behind them.

Paul sat beside Jack on the office couch for a couple of minutes, not knowing what to do.

"I know that hurts," he finally said. "But she really is trying to protect you."

Jack wasn't quite ready to concede this. He took his thumb from his mouth, and knotted his fingers together, as if to keep from sucking his thumb again.

"And I know you are trying to protect her too," Paul added.

Jack was surprised by this comment and looked up at Paul's face.

"Because I want to too," Paul went on, "and I don't know how either."

He looked at Paul for a long minute. "All right," he said at last, and leaned against Paul's shoulder. Paul was surprised by this and put his arm around him.

After a few minutes of feeling the boy leaning against him, hearing him breathe, Paul fished out *Frog and Toad Are Friends* from the backpack.

"Shall I read this to you?" Paul learned later that Corbin had read this book to Jack over and over again, during Susan's intern year, when she was often away.

"Let me try it myself," Jack said, again sounding a little older than he was. And he carefully worked his way through "Tear Water Tea," filling in from memory the words he couldn't sound out.

Later, when they were driving back to Riverside, while Jack dozed, Susan described her conversation with the coroner to Paul. Corbin had been badly cut up, with many defensive wounds on his forearms, and a slash on his cheek. He had certainly, the coroner said, tried to resist his attacker.

Susan said she didn't know what to make of this fact. Corbin had been too smart to fight with a mugger over a pocketful of change and credit cards, or even over a car. "The coroner did his best to be kind to me," she told Paul, "But he shouldn't have implied that Tom was a fool. I saw that he knew that as soon as it slipped out. He wanted to take it back, but by then it was too late."

"He mustn't have many murders out here," Paul said. But he had a further thought, one that he did not share with Susan. He remembered how recklessly Corbin had behaved with the Tribal Police back at Pyramid Lake. And he remembered how Corbin had almost pushed the policeman to put him in jail and said that that would be better than going home. Corbin had been in a mood for the whole visit. Was he so divided about leaving Susan for Rachel that he would seize any expedient to keep from having to do it? Paul wondered. But he knew this was a question he would never be able to answer. And he knew he should never raise it with Susan. Not in a million years. *Poor Tom.* Whom he had loved but had not helped. *Poor Tom.* For the first time, Paul's grief overpowered his anger.

14

$\mathcal{T}$HE DRIVE FROM LONE PINE TO INDEPENDENCE TOOK ABOUT twenty minutes. Off to the right, the green, tree-marked thread of the Owens River ran down the center of the valley, now grassland speckled with cottonwood trees, and the Inyo mountains were a corrugated pastel wall far across to the east. Steep Sierra foothills edged up to them on the left, and they crossed the great Los Angeles Aqueduct, its geometric severity a contrast to the loose meandering of the river whose life it drained. The Sierras began to crowd the road, tall, white, and green, a snowy rampart, the border of a different world from the valley. They passed the barren, unmarked site of the Manzanar detention center, where thousands of Japanese Americans had been confined during the Second World War. Just as the Sierra wall came close to the road, at the foot of Mount Williamson, they came to the outskirts of Independence.

The courthouse was a limestone building in a grassy yard with a tall cedar; four Ionic columns held up a pediment in the central section, a raised portico giving the building something of the look of the White House. They parked under the cottonwoods alongside the building and climbed the broad stairs in front of the portico up to the main entrance, Paul holding Jack by the hand. A khaki-uniformed officer, wearing a pistol, greeted them at the front door and led them down a granite-floored hall to a conference room, where they were told to wait for the District Attorney.

Jane Davenport was a blocky, brisk woman in her middle 40s with short, chin-length black hair and unruly bangs. She wore a beige jacket with shoulder pads, which matched her skirt, and a white blouse with a high, frilly collar, rather more feminine than the suit, and rather more feminine than her demeanor as well.

As they sat around the wood-edged gray Formica table, she introduced herself to Paul and to Jack, but focused her attention entirely on

Susan. Paul fished out two pencils and pads from Susan's backpack, one for Susan's notes, and one for Jack and himself to draw on, after which he and Jack retreated to the far corner of the table to draw together.

Jack and Paul took turns drawing something, and challenging the other to guess what they had drawn. Most of what Jack drew were fanciful creatures with made-up polysyllabic names, so this was a contest he easily won. Paul suspected drawing monsters been a frequent game between Jack and his father. Paul's monsters all looked rather like horned cattle.

After the D.A. had walked Susan through the whole process, Jane told Susan that she could wait in the room until the arraignment began. Or she might want to go to lunch. There was a deli a block or two south on Edwards. "Just be sure to tell the officer at the front door that you should come back to this room."

"Thank you. We brought our lunches," Susan explained.

"You can wait here until then. It will be later than we thought. They probably won't be bringing the defendant over from Bakersfield until 4 pm. An officer will come get you when it is time for the arraignment. The child is not coming in, is he?"

Jack looked up from his drawing.

"No. My friend will sit with him," Susan said.

"There will be a bench in the hall. It won't take long."

*T*he bench was large enough for both of them, and perhaps for one more, and it was positioned just across the granite hall from the courtroom. When Susan disappeared behind the door, Paul led Jack back to the bench and sat beside him with Susan's backpack.

"*Frog and Toad*? or *Narnia*? Or maybe something else?" At this, Jack toppled over and sobbed. Jack had kept himself together for his mother since the coroner's office, but now that she was out of sight, he couldn't keep it up. Drawing his knees up to his chest, he curled up on the bench.

Paul knelt and pressed his face to Jack's wet cheek. "This is so hard, honey. I know it's so hard." He stroked Jack's shoulder. "So hard."

"I know the bad man's in there," Jack said through tears.

While the D.A. had been explaining to Susan how the arraignment would go, Paul had tried to distract Jack with their drawing because he knew Jack was trying to listen. He had not known how much Jack had heard.

Sucking his thumb, Jack began to whimper.

"Are you afraid he'll hurt your mom?"

"No," Jack was trying to control himself now, but the effort made him sound as if he were choking, and a tear or two ran down his face anyway. "It's because it's so hard for her."

Paul paused a second. "Yes. So hard for her. And you've been so brave for her all day."

Wiping his eyes, Jack sat up, trying to be that brave boy. Paul got up from the floor and sat at Jack's side. Jack nestled to him. "It's OK for me to be sad," Jack said. "I just don't want her to be."

Paul held him tight. "Me too."

"And she'll be sad if she sees that I am."

"We're all going to be sad for a while."

"Are you sad too?" Jack asked.

"Oh, my God." This comment just slipped out of him. But how he felt about Corbin was too complicated for him to explain.

Jack laid his head on Paul's shoulder.

"I know it hurts even more when you can't help her," Paul said.

Jack nodded, gulping.

"But you are helping her," Paul went on. "Just being here helps her." Paul wondered whether Jack would believe this. Was Paul himself really helping her?

Paul held on for another minute. Jack shifted to sit in Paul's lap, and Paul held him for a very long time. He kissed the top of Jack's head.

They sat there together in the empty hall until the door of the courtroom opened. Susan was almost the first person out the door. She was stricken, pale and faint as if she had just been rescued from death by force. She saw red-eyed Jack sitting in Paul's lap on the bench and knelt down in front of them both.

Jack leaned out, put both arms around his mother's neck, buried his face in her cheek, and cried.

"Jack, baby," she whispered, in his ear. "It's all right." She stroked his back. "Everything will be all right."

Jack sniffled. "Are you all right?"

At this question, she pulled back for a second to look at him.

"Yes," she said, gravely. He was still looking at her. She held his gaze as if she thought it might make him believe her.

"Really?"

"Really." She held him close again and rocked him from side to side, so she wouldn't have to answer another question.

Paul awkwardly stroked Jack's hair too. *You can only take so much truth at a time.*

"Let's just wait here a few minutes while everyone goes away," she said, after a moment.

Paul felt the pressure of somebody's gaze, somebody who had just come out of the courtroom and was standing in front of the closing door. At first, he saw a dark dress and thought it was someone who had noticed the boy crying, someone who might be pausing, wondering whether to express concern or sympathy for the crying boy with the two adults holding him.

Then he noticed it was Rachel Lake, looking hard at Susan, appraising her, obviously her first sight of her lover's wife. Paul saw that she still had that cold, slender, gracile beauty that turned men's heads and made them stop where they stood. With a life of its own, her glossy hair still fell thickly over her shoulders. Her pale face had hardened, as if beyond feeling or suffering, but her dark eyes still blazed with that suggestion of flame seen through ice they had always had. Her lips were a defiant red, lips you had better be ready for. Paul felt a tightening in his chest, as if he had just come face to face with a loaded gun.

There was a note of pity in her face. But there was also a note of contempt, the kind of contempt you feel in the presence of a someone who just can't manage. Susan was facing Jack and could not notice her, and Jack's face was buried in Susan's cheek, so he didn't notice Rachel either.

Rachel had trained her gaze on Susan for two or three full seconds before she noticed that Bishop was with her. A glance of recognition passed between them. They looked at each other, neutrally, not betraying to anyone else that they had seen each other. But each knew the other had guessed everything that mattered.

Rachel raised a finger to her lips and shook her head. Then Bishop looked away and heard the heels of her pumps clicking down the hall.

15

SUSAN TIDIED UP AS THEY FINISHED THE LAST OF THEIR SAND-
wiches in the car, parked under the cottonwoods alongside the courthouse. The shadows cast by the Sierras were already lengthening, and it
took them a long time to feel ready for the journey back to Riverside.

Finally, Susan asked Jack whether he needed to go to the bathroom
in the courthouse before they set out. Jack did not want to go back into
that building ever again. Susan kissed his forehead and brushed the hair
out of his eyes before buckling him in beside her in the back seat. Then
she closed the backpack to put it on the floor at Jack's feet.

She saw Paul glance discreetly at her over the seat back as he turned
to back the car out of its space. But he needn't have worried about her,
she told herself; just as it had been that morning, the fuss of getting ready
was welcome to her. It gave her something else to think about for a while.

Then, just as Paul put the car in gear and turned south onto Edwards,
abruptly, before Susan could tense to bear it, all the weight came on to her
and pushed her under. Deep in a cold sea under a night sky, Tom waited
for her. Down and down, she plunged to him. As she let the weight force
her through the suffocating water, she clutched her desire to her, like a
held breath, like a last thought. *Take me, Tom. I'm ready to go where you
are. Let me lie with you again.* She reached out her arms, feeling for him
in the murk. But her arms remained empty. *Don't leave me here. Please
don't leave me here.*

"Did you see him? The man who killed Dad?" Jack asked.

Susan opened her eyes and looked at Jack from far away, as though
through a thick pane of glass. She had to pick life up where she had
left off, but it was a strange life to her now, and for a long moment she
couldn't find her place. She was back in the car again, and Paul had barely
steered Susan's Dart out of Independence.

Jack was still waiting for her to answer his question.

"Yes, I saw him." Susan knew Jack wanted more than this. But she left it there.

"Did he see you?" Jack asked.

"He was looking down at the floor the whole time."

"Were you scared?" Jack persisted.

She was weary. But she had to answer. He needed an answer. And she had to live, although she didn't want to. "No. I wasn't scared. I was sad."

"But was he angry?"

"No, he was sad too. He was very sad. And very afraid."

"Is he sorry about what he did?"

"I think he knows he will go to jail for a long, long time."

Jack looked out the window. Finally, he said, "That's not sorry."

"No. It's not. He was sorry for himself."

"You said he'll go to jail for a long time. Will he get out of jail?"

Susan didn't have the energy to lie. "In many years, he might get parole."

"What's parole?"

"It's when they decide that you have been in jail for a long enough time."

Again, Jack looked out the window for a minute. "Will he want to come kill you then?"

Susan saw Paul turn to cast a worried glance at her. But she avoided his gaze. She leaned her cheek against the top of Jack's head. "Oh, baby." She held him to her.

"I'll keep him away," Jack said.

Susan kissed Jack on the forehead. But that wasn't an answer. She felt as if she had just run out of answers. "I think his killing days are over for good, now."

"Why do you think that, Mommy?"

She looked him closely in the eye. "Because he seemed so sad."

"Too sad to hurt anyone?"

"Sad enough that he's given up. He's given up everything. There's not enough left in him to hurt anyone." She wondered whether Jack would understand what it is to just give up.

"But I'm still afraid of him. Are you?"

"No, I'm not afraid of him." Shifting her gaze from Jack, she looked out over his head at nothing.

"Is that because you are braver than he is?"

Again, she saw Paul cast her a worried look. But she didn't look at him. And she didn't look at Jack.

"No, it's because I'm too tired to be afraid. I'm just tired. I'm so, so tired."

This admission put a stop to Jack's questions, and he turned away from her to the window.

She knew that it wasn't that he was satisfied. And it wasn't that he was no longer afraid. It was because he had heard in her voice that at that moment she didn't care whether she lived or died. Susan knew that, having that knowledge, Jack wouldn't push her, because it would hurt her too much to be pushed. She knew he had been watching over her, shielding her, fearing for her, every waking minute for months. So of course, he knew, he must know, everything she felt, despite everything she had done to keep it from him. But now she was too weary to keep from him even the worst of it. *I never thought I'd just let him hurt like this.*

Suddenly she shut her eyes tight, pressing her fist to her mouth, hoping Jack wasn't looking. *All he has in this world now is me. And I have nothing to give him.* The moment wouldn't pass. *Help me, Tom. Help me to know what to do. If you ever needed me and I left you hanging, forgive me. I really need your help now.*

She had always talked with him when he wasn't there, in the quiet colloquy of intimate absence. And she had relied on him in those moments, more than when he was actually there to take her in his arms because the imaginary Tom, Tom as (she believed) he wanted to be, loved her more simply than the actual Tom did. But this time she had been talking to nobody. Tom had nothing to tell her about how to live past his death.

Now again in the depths of the ocean, she tried to brace herself, thrashing against the bitter desire that still forced her downwards, her lungs bursting. She fought her way to the surface. And there was Jack, looking out the window. She took her fist out of her mouth. Nobody had seen what had happened to her. But before the relief, like a deep breath, could spread through her body, she had another thought: *Everything will happen anyway, no matter what I do. And I will be no help to Jack once it does.*

They drove in silence past Lone Pine again, and south into the drier parts of the Owens Valley. After a long time, Susan picked up her back-pack and rummaged through it for the cassette player. But as she took it out, she noticed that Jack, exhausted by the long day, and by his grief, and by the effort of trying to keep himself together for his mother, had fallen asleep.

16

THE MAIN THING SUSAN FELT AS SHE CAME OUT OF THE ARRAIGN-
ment was disappointment. She was disappointed first of all by the sight
of the murderer. He seemed too poor a creature to have killed Tom. She
rebuked herself for the naïveté of thinking the killer would have the dark
charisma of evil. It was silly, she thought, to imagine that evil has any
special meaning, any special access to the truth of how things are. *We
cook up a dramatic idea about what evil is because it's the only way we can
keep from seeing the fact that every pain we feel, every defeat we go through,
is so absolutely empty.*

She was also disappointed in herself, in her response to the occasion.
What will I do when it's Jack I have to save, not this nobody? And he was a
nobody to her. She had felt nothing for Tom's killer. And she had left
Jack to suffer for himself.

She spoke to Paul just over a whisper, trying not to wake Jack, "Do
you remember asking me why I wanted to look at Tom's murderer for
myself?"

"Yes, and I remember what you told me," Paul said.

Susan saw him raise his eyes to glance at her in the mirror, and she
looked away. *If he wants to help me, it's only because he doesn't understand
me.* "I couldn't do what I thought I had to do." She gazed at the darkening
Sierras. Leaving the slopes in shadow, the sun blazed behind the summits.
"I saw him shamble in, in shackles, led by an armed Deputy. And I saw
him slouch down at the defendant's table, hunched over, not meeting
anybody's gaze, drawn in on himself as if he wanted to make himself as
small as he could possibly be."

"He was ashamed of himself. And afraid for his future. At least as
much afraid as ashamed. Like you told Jack," Paul suggested.

"Yes, he was ashamed. He was like a beaten dog," she said. Susan saw
Paul steal another glance at her, discreetly checking, because the tang of

that last phrase had surprised him. But she gave him nothing.

The desert streamed past.

"I thought you hoped to feel something for him other than anger," Paul said. "And you did do that."

"I did keep from hating him. And I saw that he was pitiable. Pathetic, really. Someone who had never had a chance and had thrown away every chance he didn't have." She was still looking out the window, over Jack's sleeping head.

"I think I would call that exceedingly generous, given the circumstances," Paul said.

Susan wouldn't let him defend her. She shook her head, still not looking at him. "I felt pity for him. But I also saw his self-pity. And that closed the door for me. I felt pity for him, but I didn't feel one moment's compassion." She knew Paul would want to answer this, but she couldn't face him. She turned to look out the other window, across the valley at the Inyos, golden in the sunlight still pouring over them from the west. *And I didn't help Jack when he needed it, just now.*

With a flash of impatience, she turned back to Paul. *Don't you think I know what I've just done?* She didn't let herself say this. "I'm about to need everything I have. I'm disappointed that I didn't make it through the first step without faltering. There are a lot of steps to go, hard ones. Harder than this one I just bungled."

"Do you mean through the trial? I'll come back for that as many times as you need," Paul said.

That she had bungled anything, Susan was disappointed to see, was news to Paul. *He will just never see me clearly,* she thought. "No. There's something else." She could see he was startled by the impatience in her tone, so she met his gaze in the mirror.

"Tell me what it is, then," he said at last.

She had gone too far to put him off. She hadn't meant to tell him about any next step, only to wave off the excuse he was making for her. Now she had no choice but to burn her ships. But that inevitability, now that she had to face it, gave her a rush of relief, and, remembering how Paul had held Jack to him in the hallway when he needed it, how tender he had been with him, she suddenly saw her way clear before her. *He*

104

wants to take care of me. I don't want to know why. And I'm going to let him. "Do you remember I told you, when I called you the first time, when Tom was still just missing, that there was something important I had to tell Tom about?"

"I was surprised you would tell me something like that on first meeting me," Paul said.

"Somehow I knew I could trust you." She paused to let him take that in. "Can I trust you with this?" He brightened a bit as she held his gaze in the mirror. "I guess I don't have to ask," she said. Then she touched his shoulder lightly, over the seat back, a trace of a smile, for just a moment, on her face. "But you may get more than you bargained for."

A truck hurtled by, and Paul had to steady the wheel.

"Last week, while Tom was up in Reno, I had some tests at work, at my own hospital. They found that I'm sick, really really sick, with cancer. Melanoma."

"My God."

Except for her chief resident, she hadn't told anyone about this before. She knew how Paul would look at her when she told him. *I'm ready for it,* she thought. But suddenly she couldn't bear his gaze. She was surprised by her flinch, because she had decided to trust him, and she did trust him. But still, faced with his exclamation, she flinched. Because she knew what he felt, and she knew, to her shame, what, because she had to, she would do to him. *Everything will change for him now. There will be no going back.* "And I probably won't get better."

"My God."

"But there's a long-shot chance for me. And I'm going to take it."

"Yes."

"I'll need someone to stay with me, for the first night, after the treatment. Next Wednesday." This time she had braced herself for the moment she let him catch her eye.

"I'll come back for it. You don't have to worry. I'll see you through," Paul assured her.

"If I have a reaction, Jack will be scared. And he really has something to be scared of."

"I understand," Paul said.

She was still watching him, not sure he really understood. "I'm scared myself."

"Yes. Of course. How could you not be?"

"It's okay for Jack to know that I'm sick. He can hardly miss that, anyway. But I don't want him to know that I'm scared. That would be too much for him." She had kept her face completely straight through all of this, and she hoped that what she wanted Paul to see was all he noticed, her self-possession as she faced the music, her certainty about what he should do for Jack. *What will happen to Jack? He will have to watch me die. He will see it coming long before it happens, and through it all, however afraid he is, he will be trying to protect me when I should be protecting him. Then I will leave him alone in the world, in the care of strangers.* Then her thought ran ahead of her. *It would be better for Jack and me both to die right now, so we don't have to go through what's going to happen.* Drowning in that thought, she came to a halt. She was shocked by it, but she couldn't push it away. *If we were dead, I wouldn't feel this way. And we'd both be safe. If we could just do it without pain. And without being afraid.*

Paul was looking at her, still waiting for instructions, with no idea what she was thinking. When she didn't go on, Paul had to pick up the thread himself. "I promise," Paul said. "I'll do my best for him."

Looking at Paul, she took a breath. *How simply he said that.* He was waiting for her to answer. But she was still just looking at him. *And he will do his best. We will need every bit of it.* She came to herself. But what she had been thinking left a trace of fear and shame. She was still unnerved. Then as she watched Paul drive, something warm welled up from deep in her body and rushed out to every part of her. *My God. What is this?* She knew what it was, and that she had no right to it. *But just for this moment. When I need it. Please. I won't ask for more. Please. Just for this moment.*

"Thank you, Paul," she said. "I really didn't have anyone else I could ask." Paul had turned all his attention to the road, but she couldn't stop looking at him. She felt as though he had, just as she had given herself up to the strangling water, carried her unconscious body from a winter sea. Now he was trying to make her breathe. *He doesn't know how close I came. Or how much he just steadied me.* "I know I can't ask you for this."

"I want you to ask," Paul said.

At this reassurance, she managed to smile for him, a flash of relief and gratitude, through the rear-view mirror. *Thank you. Thank you. Thank you.* Suddenly she took a deep breath, as if coming to out of nothingness. *And bless you. Bless you for coming to me.* Then the fatigue rolled back over her. *What have I just done to him?*

"How long have you been sick?" Paul asked.

"Tom found the primary behind my knee in January," Susan said. The shadow the car was casting on the desert had begun to lengthen, and the sun, blazing over the Sierras so brightly that they seemed to be darkened clouds on the horizon, still cast a gold, late-afternoon light on the Inyo mountains across the valley.

As the color deepened, and Jack slept quietly in his seat, she told Paul some, but by no means all, of what had happened to her. She spoke softly, glad that it had become harder to see her in the dusk.

17

SUSAN REMEMBERED THAT DAY, A CALIFORNIA WINTER DAY, A
Thursday, because she had felt flurried and annoyed. Corbin had been
delayed picking up Jack at Shetland for the second time in a week, and
they'd had to call her at the hospital when they couldn't get him by phone.
She was mortified that they had made the Shetland staff wait for them to
pick up their son yet again. And she was also ashamed of the speeches to
him she began rehearsing as she waited, through supper and reading time,
for her husband to finally arrive. When Corbin got home, just as she was
finishing the dishes after putting Jack to bed—she was pretending not to
hear him coming in—he came softly up behind her at the sink and took
her in his arms, kissing her under the ear until she faced him to return his
kiss. She never could stay angry with him. Despite herself, she was stirred
top to bottom.

"You look sad," she said, drawing back her face. "What is it?"

"I'm not sad," he said, moving to kiss her again.

"Yes, you are," she said, evading his kiss. "You look like your best
friend in the world just died."

"I'm with that person now, and she's very much alive," he said, smiling.

Susan wasn't sure she believed his smile, but she was faint with desire
for him, and she let him kiss her and lead her from the room.

She and Corbin had lain together late that January Thursday evening
in a moment of post-coital tenderness. She had rolled over onto her
stomach. Corbin was massaging her shoulder and lifting her hair to kiss
the back of her neck. Then he began to spell out words on the smooth
skin of her back.

"Darling," he wrote.

"Mmm." she said.

"I love you," he wrote.

"I love you too," she said.

Since November, Tom had been especially tender with her in bed. Susan didn't want to know why, but of course she both knew and didn't know: *He feels he has to make something up to me. But he only feels he has to make something up to me because in the end it's me he loves.*

She wondered, as a thrill passed up and down her body, if he was feeling unfaithful to whomever it was he had sought refuge from by making love so gently to his wife. *Why not just enjoy him now?* She let herself go completely. She poured herself out for him, and he drank her to the lees.

Softly and slowly, with all four fingers just barely touching her, he traced a line from the nape of her neck, past her shoulders, down her spine, down over her buttocks and down the back of one thigh. When he reached the back of her knee, he kissed her softly there.

"Why are you doing that?" Susan asked vaguely.

"You have a birthmark here," he said, tenderly kissing her there again. "It's beautiful. Kind of a secret. A sexy secret."

Susan smiled, although she was facing away from him. "Am I full of sexy secrets?" she said, raising an eyebrow.

"Beautiful ones, in every shade from a dawn blush to midnight black."

She inhaled, then sighed.

Corbin went on: "They're all here, in this birthmark, every shade."

A thought crossed her mind: *Different shades in a birthmark? Oh, that's not good.* But she was already drifting off to sleep.

The next morning, before taking her shower, she looked at the mole carefully in the bathroom mirror. It was a little more than three quarters of an inch across, with scalloped edges, some parts of it black, and others tan and brown, almost in the shape of a little hand. *That will be a problem,* she thought. Later that morning, she smiled at Corbin as he got a cranky Jack to eat his cereal and comb his hair. As her husband lifted Jack to take him out to his car and drop him at Shetland winter vacation camp, Corbin said, "I may be a little late today," not saying the reason why. "You may have to have supper again without me."

"I'll pick up Jack at 5:30," Susan said. "It might be very busy today." When she arrived at the clinic, she asked her chief resident to have a look at the back of her knee. Her friend was concerned enough about it that she pulled strings over at Dermatology to have Susan examined, and in the early afternoon the dermatologist punched a disk the size of a quarter from the back of her knee, stitching up the wound neatly with dissolving thread.

"I've done this as carefully as I could, but I can't promise you that there won't be a scar," he said.

"It won't hurt my modeling career," Susan laughed. She turned her knee out to study the wound, turning it this way and that, as if showing off her legs. It was hard to think that something so small could be so full of threat.

It was probably a melanoma, she thought later as she dished out the mac and cheese and the frozen peas for Jack and herself. To Jack she said only that since Dad would be coming home late again that night, they would watch cartoons on the Betamax until reading time. She did not change out of her scrubs until she put on her pajamas after Jack's breathing had finally settled. She hoped to be asleep by the time Corbin came home. It would be one more night that she wouldn't have to tell him what she had been through, what they would both go through.

The biopsy came back positive as she knew it would. Her chief pulled strings again to get her a CAT scan, and an isotope scan, over the next few days, which was one of the perks of being a resident in an oncology clinic. She said nothing about what she was going through to Corbin. She was not sure why she did this, but she had an instinct about it.

She had what seemed to be good news from the CAT scan, which she kept to herself. On the evening of the isotope scan she would not allow Corbin to hold her because she was worried about the technetium that still might be in her system. *He will think I have something against him, that I'm onto him. He'll flog himself all night about it. But all I really want is him. I don't care about her. She won't take him from me. It's death, not whoever she is, who will come between us. Death is my secret lover, who will take me from him.*

When the isotope scan came back negative, she felt relieved, although she knew the episode might not really be over. She was, in any event, glad she had not turned her household upside down about it; since both scans were negative, she felt justified in not terrifying her son or worrying her husband needlessly, she told herself, then silently changed that "needlessly," to "prematurely."

On May the first, the Thursday of Corbin's reading in Reno, Susan had had another CAT scan. Going over the scans with her chief resident, Claire Wirthlin, on Friday morning, Susan could see two or three of the spots on her liver herself, but she didn't know how many more the radiologist would identify, nor how many more might be there, lurking beneath the threshold of the scan's resolution. She thought of her liver as a kind of petri dish, scattered with a galaxy of colonies. Except they weren't colonies of invading bacteria. They were fragments of her own flesh, turning against her.

Susan knew that Claire had been a paramedic in Long Beach for five years before medical school, and had seen everything. She had looked out for Susan since their intern year, and it had seemed natural to Susan to put herself into Claire's sturdy, square-cut hands. Susan was grateful that Claire had made sure that opportunities to gain experience—that Susan herself might not have been been assertive enough to put herself forward for—nevertheless came her way. Claire had even, just in February, arranged for Susan to assist on an open thoracotomy for a patient with suspected mesothelioma although it was early in her career for such an experience.

Susan did not have to be told that her situation was dire. Claire told Susan that they would be able to include her in the interferon study that was underway in that very clinic, for which their Program Director was the Principal Investigator. And while Susan was still assimilating this possibility, Claire had called him and arranged for Susan to have her first treatment on the 14th, slightly less than two weeks away.

Claire also told Susan that they would share out her shifts among the other residents until she had recovered from her first treatment and that she should take a few days at home to come to terms with her news, to prepare her family, and to begin to make plans for them in view of the likelihood of her early death.

Her mentor, now doctor, wanted to see Susan again on the following Friday, to begin the tests necessary to prepare her for her treatment the following week. Susan had wanted to work that week since she did not know when she would be well enough to pick up working again after her treatment, but Claire told Susan that she had nothing to prove and that there would be work for her to do after the treatment for as long as she was well enough to do it.

Susan wanted to be assured that she would be able to continue to work at her Residency as much as she could during her treatment. She didn't like the idea of making a complete transition from doctor to patient, from someone who healed to someone who was vulnerable.

Claire told Susan bluntly that there would be no way she could keep up a resident's schedule during treatment, but that she could keep her hand in as much as she was capable of doing. And if she had to step back entirely—Claire said this as if it were merely a possibility, but Susan knew what Claire really meant—she would keep Susan's position open for her until whenever she was well enough to take it up again. Susan knew that Claire knew it was unlikely that she would survive her disease in the long run. Susan knew as much herself. But she was glad that Claire had tried to humor her, even with something that both of them knew was probably only a fantasy.

At home, Susan went through the motions of getting Jack's supper— fish sticks, broccoli, rice—and reading to him from *Frog and Toad Are Friends* and *Where the Wild Things Are*, books he had outgrown because he had learned all the words , but still wanted to have read to him, particularly when he felt anxious. He was anxious, she knew, because he could not miss that she was worried. When she had picked him up at school, she had swept him up in her arms in the doorway and turned and turned with him, while the teacher at the door had grown more and more annoyed at the spectacle. Susan hadn't been ready to tell him what she knew. But how could he not know that something was the matter?

After dinner, Jack, sensing that something was on his mother's mind, hugged her and hugged her, and insisted that she read those books to him again and again, until she finally had to tell him firmly that reading time was over, and he really did have to go to bed. And then she burst into tears, something she had never done in front of Jack before. "It must unnerve you to see me cry," she said, holding him tightly. Jack was shocked and afraid, and Susan was ashamed and had to tell him that there really was something the matter. She and his father would figure out what to do about it when he got home, probably tomorrow. He was supposed to have gotten home that afternoon, but Susan had made up a story. Perhaps he had decided to visit with his friend in Reno for another day.

All evening, Susan lay sleepless, alone in the bed she shared with her husband, plotting out how much she would tell him about her condition. She wasn't certain she would even tell him that what she had was melanoma, for fear he might look it up. She would tell him that there was a clinical trial going on at her hospital, at Loma Linda, of a new thing called interferon, which was made made to ward off viral infections, and which just might set up the immune system against cancer. She decided not to tell him that early trials are always long shots, given mostly to terminal cases, and that what the investigators are really seeking to know is whether the treatment is too toxic to be safe to use.

But how she was going to break her news to Jack stopped her dead. She saw in her mind how stricken and afraid his face would become as she told him how it was with her, and with that vision before her she felt her eyes overflow. *I can't lie to him. My parents lied to me when my father was dying, and I can't lie to him that way. But I can't give him the whole truth either.* As she always did, she pressed her fist hopelessly to her mouth, but she could not stifle it down. *Dear God*, she thought, *I don't need the strength to go through what I'm about to go through. That I know how to do. But give me the words to break this to my son. Give me the strength to care for him as long as I can.*

Just then, Jack had come in the door and laid his face against her wet cheek.

18

*W*HEN, LONG AFTER DARK, THEY FINALLY ARRIVED BACK AT MAS-sachusetts Avenue, and Paul had lifted Jack, still asleep, out of his seat and carried him into his bedroom, and Susan had changed him into pajamas, so carefully that she did not wake him, Susan asked Paul whether he might like something to eat. She laid her hand on his shoulder, smiling. There wasn't much to have, she said, but she could put it together quickly. For a second, as she looked up at him, he looked into her bright face. *How lovely she is.*

Paul felt that his place was not in this house, in Tom Corbin's house. As gently as he could, he demurred. But Susan was disappointed as if he had laid a drawn sword down between them.

Friday morning, having packed up his satchel and his untouched final papers, he caught one embarrassed last glimpse of himself in the bathroom mirror at the Motel 6. *You didn't cross the line. But you are still a fool. Because you aren't anything unless she needs you. And you won't face why.*

*A*t seven on Saturday morning, while Paul was lying awake in his bed in Reno, still trying to sleep off the exhaustion of his trip before beginning a long weekend of grading, his phone rang.

"I saw you there." She didn't identify herself, but he knew who it was. "At the arraignment. Why do you think it was any business of yours to be there?"

Her whispery voice went right through him, as if her lips had brushed his ear, warm with her breath, her threat. He knew he should hang up, he absolutely knew it. And he knew he wouldn't. "Why were you there yourself? Were you looking for some confrontation with Susan?" He instantly saw he should have said "Tom's wife," not "Susan." But it was too late now. *Why should it matter to me,* he asked himself, *what Rachel, seeing me with Susan, had guessed about what I felt?* It did matter, though. And he knew she would know how to use it.

He felt a flash of shame before her. Every day, for almost a decade, he had worried about Rachel; every day, he had blamed himself for his failure of nerve in Gallup. And every day, he had flinched at what she had done after. With Corbin, he now knew. But what she had just guessed about him and Susan made him feel a newer, deeper kind of shame. Did she feel the same flash of shame, he asked himself, knowing what he had learned about her renewed affair with Corbin? *Rachel would never show shame before me,* he thought, *especially shame over anything she did with Corbin.* He was sure also that she would never concede that anything Paul had done had actually injured her, much less that he could judge her. And now she had him in a corner.

After nine years, Rachel had come back, ready to even the score with Corbin, and nothing was going to stop her. She had been prepared to trample Susan to get to Corbin who may have had it coming. But Susan didn't deserve any of it. Rachel had no right to hurt Susan. And no right to have contempt for her. Rachel had no fucking right to do anything to Susan. Paul suddenly felt ready to hurt Rachel for what she did to Susan. He didn't understand why.

"It was my future, not hers," Rachel said, coolly, "that Tom's murder foreclosed. As you know, I'm sure, because Tom told you what he was going to do. God knows why. I think I have more than enough right to mourn him." Rachel caught her breath for a second. Then, in her lingering whisper: "And I don't care that you don't think so."

She doesn't care what I think? Paul suddenly thought. *Then why did she call me? Why did she explain herself at all? That's why she's trying to bruise me, because she can't stand what I know about her, and she doesn't like being put on the defensive about taking Tom from Susan.* Rachel still had an unerring sense of where she could draw blood, as if she had taken Paul's measure in silent colloquy every day of those nine years. He was not surprised at how easily it came to her to wound him. But he, too, had taken her measure every day. And he was shocked at how easily it came to him to wound her.

"I could tell when I saw you in the courtroom hallway that you'd never laid eyes on Susan before. You were appraising her. Getting ready for something. What good would it possibly do you to harm her?" Paul asked.

"I was there for Tom. She isn't anything to me." Again, Rachel dropped to a whisper: "Though she seems to be something to you."

"It was cruel of you to be there at all. That was Susan's place," Paul said.

"I didn't do her any harm. She doesn't know me. She doesn't even know I exist." Rachel's voice was cold, angry, defensive.

"I'm going to keep it that way. She doesn't have to know about you."

Paul felt Rachel was stung by this. This took him by surprise: she wasn't used to being dismissed. And suddenly he knew just how to hurt her.

"Sure," she said, her voice, as her anger rose, a poisoned caress, "you'll keep her safe, all wrapped up snug in lies. Her future with him was over already. She just didn't know it. Because she didn't know the first thing about what he really was. Or she wouldn't always have been so quick to forgive him. But the whole world was always unreal with her, anyway, wasn't it? And I know you. You have a taste for the unreal. Or is it a distaste for the real?" Rachel sneered.

Paul knew she was just getting started. And he knew that nothing he could say could keep Susan safe from Corbin's mistress. Paul wondered how long it would be before he would fold.

"Don't tell me how pure she is, and how much better than me she is." Her whisper failed her, and her self-possession too. "Because I know she has some idea about what love is that nobody can live up to. It wore Tom out. Wore him out. It made him hate who he was and pretend to himself that he could be someone else," Rachel said.

"Some people would say that love helps people find the good in themselves," Paul replied.

"Some people would say love will do whatever it has to do to get the better of you. That's how she kept him in line. Forgiving him. Surely even you know that."

Suddenly, as Rachel's anger broke over him, he saw her face beneath him, straining towards the moment of sexual climax, her face flushed, her

116

breathing tight, her eyes locked on his. He tried to shake the image off, but it only became more intense the angrier she became.

"He wanted to do better by her," Paul said. "Susan knew that about him, despite everything he did to her. And Tom really did love her, no matter what he did, even with you. He told me that himself. She brought out the best in him." Hoping it would sting, Paul let that point sink in.

"If you can call what he did loving her. I know how he was." Then, with delicious malice, Rachel added, "And so does the whole fucking world except her. She didn't bring out any best in him. She just kept making excuses for him. At least I saw him as he really was. And that's what he wanted, and it's what I had to offer him, to be taken as he really was."

Paul hated himself, but his imagination continued to run riot, humiliating him worse than Rachel could ever have done. He felt Rachel tighten her legs around his hips and draw him into her. He knew he should have hung up the phone. But the more he tried to explain himself, the more helpless he became. Corbin wasn't the only one whom Rachel knew how to take as he really was. And she was enjoying it.

"Almost the only thing about Tom that I can still like him for," Paul said, "is the fact that, whatever he was, he was good enough to keep her love through all of it, because she knew he wanted to love her better. It's what he kept coming back to, the thought that someday he might get it all straight with her at last. But you were different from all those others, and you took any hope of doing that from him."

"So if what you love about her is that she never gave up on Tom, where does that leave you?" Evidently, this question wasn't quite enough. Rachel continued, "It leaves you just where you've always been from the beginning. Which is the only place you can stand to be." She didn't wait for him to reply before pressing on. "She could never make him into what he couldn't be anyway." She gave a quick laugh. "Don't you start singing me some aria about the redemptive power of love. You know you don't believe that yourself."

"You don't know what I believe." But Paul still couldn't get that image of Rachel out of his mind. She looked up at him, her eyes locked on his, her breath raspy, her mouth open in a tense O.

117

"Maybe you want to believe it," she said, "But you can't make yourself believe it just by telling yourself you do. She may be all sorts of pure, but you aren't. You know better. Anyway, you sure taught me better, and you were a pretty good teacher."

"I never taught you a thing. You were always ahead of me," Paul said.

"Maybe you want to try to believe it because Susan does, and you think it will help you score points with her," Rachel retorted.

"I'm not trying to score points with her. I'm just taking care of her."

All of a sudden, Rachel laughed, not an angry laugh, but a dismissive one, as if he had finally shown himself as the rube he was.

"Say the Rosary three times and put a dollar in the box," Rachel said. "If you still feel bad about what I did to you. Or maybe about what you did to me. Take your pick. I could tell at a glance when I saw you in Independence that you hadn't moved a single inch from where you got stuck years ago. But you're not going to fix that by letting Susan believe you're something you're not."

"I told you. I'm not asking anything from her. I'm just helping her," Paul explained, but it sounded like pleading.

"Sure," she said, her voice full of victory. "You are just trying to blacken Tom's reputation with her, so you can take his place."

"I haven't said a word to her about what Tom was planning to do with you." But Paul knew that the testier he became, the more ridiculous he sounded. He had to look out at the dead weeds in the courtyard to get back in control.

"You've kept that back as your last weapon, for when you get desperate, for when you've had enough of her fairy tales about him. Why Tom felt he had to ask you about leaving her for me is something I just don't understand," Rachel said.

Oh yes you do, Paul thought, but said nothing.

"Tom didn't owe anything to you about this," Rachel added.

That's not what he felt, Paul thought. *And you know exactly why.*

"You are taking some kind of sick revenge on him. Or maybe it's some kind of revenge on me."

"Why would I want revenge on you?" Paul asked. And then in his imagination, he watched her throw her head back, her mouth open, gasping, her eyes glittering, the crimson flush spreading down her throat and chest, her whole body tense. He was ashamed, but he could not push the image away.

"Because you know Tom took me from you. Back in Storrs," Rachel said coolly.

"I didn't know he did that until last week. I loved him too much to believe it."

"Bullshit," Rachel spat. "I told you all about it. Either you are an idiot, or you think I am."

What is she talking about? When did she tell me about her and Tom? he asked himself. He racked his brains to remember anything she had said on the subject. *Maybe it's that I should have known, that it would have been obvious to anyone but me.* No, it had to be more than that, but he was afraid to follow out the thought. *If she told me about it, I certainly wouldn't have forgotten about it. It would have been a relief just to know the truth.* However it was, he still felt like an idiot, and that was nothing new.

But either way it wasn't what she had done to him that made him feel like an idiot. She was wrong about that. It was what he had done to her when he received her anguished letter after their little excursion to Portland, when, believing that she was tempted by death, he had set out to come to her across the country to Riverside, as she had begged him to do, and got all the way to Gallup and turned back, something she didn't even know he had done. And he blamed himself for how cruelly he had broken with her afterwards, driven by a suspicion of her fidelity that he had not known then that he was right about. *If she betrayed me with Corbin,* he thought, *I abundantly had it coming.* But how he had betrayed her, so much more bitterly than how she had betrayed him, had not come clear for him until he had broken up with her, though his flinch in Gallup had taken place months before. He knew he was an idiot. But she had her own ideas about why he was an idiot. He couldn't say anything. He looked off into the kitchen, his shoulders tensed as if he were expecting her to hit him.

"Because you knew and didn't know what Tom and I were doing," she went on. "Because part of you couldn't face it, and kept on pretending you didn't know about it, though you did. And the rest of you was turned on by it, and couldn't admit it, so that part pretended you didn't know it too. Congratulations. Now you get to turn the tables. Except turning the tables on a dead man doesn't really count."

"I don't want revenge on Tom," Paul said. "I'm keeping him from breaking his wife's heart. He's beyond any harm I could do to him now, anyway."

"But you do covet his wife," Rachel said.

"I haven't said that," Paul replied.

"But you do. I know it."

"I'm not going to hurt her to make her love me."

"She's not going to give back to you what I took from you. She doesn't even have it to give. Why is she even worth it to you? Surely, you don't see anything in her. She doesn't live in any world that really exists. Who in his right mind could possibly want that?"

Why does this matter to her? he thought. But it obviously did. He didn't know what to say to her. Because everything she said about him was true: everything he felt for Susan had something to do with what he had done to Rachel, or with his rivalry over Rachel with Corbin. These facts gave Paul pause, but they didn't stop him.

Rachel was all wrong about Susan. Paul could have cut her short with a sentence, but it wasn't his sentence to use, and he couldn't bring himself to say it. But Rachel didn't really know Susan, and she didn't care about her. She was just using Susan to get to Paul. It was himself, not Susan, who was on Rachel's mind. And that was a subject she understood perfectly.

Paul couldn't let Susan go. He had to throw her at Rachel again. "She does know reality," he said at last, "She deals with dying people day in and day out. And she's a good person. Better than any of us." As soon as he had said this, he knew how lame it had to sound.

"She doesn't know, she doesn't really know, the first thing about love," Rachel argued.

"And what do you know about love?" Paul asked.

"I know you have to take love exactly for what it is, and not have any illusions about it. That's what I learned when you left me hanging in

Riverside all those years ago," she said.

Paul had nothing to say to that. But she still wasn't finished.

"That's what you're going to wind up teaching her yourself. Whether you want to or not. You think you're doing her such a kindness. But you're just playing on her vulnerability. Tom isn't even in his grave." Rachel gave a scornful little laugh. "And you think *I've* been bad to her. Wait till you see what *you* wind up doing."

"I don't think it's a bad thing for me to help her so long as I don't ask anything of her."

"You can't live up to her any more than Tom did. All you are doing is taking advantage of her grief. If you think that's a way to earn her love—"

"I'm not trying to earn her love. I'm trying to love her. Didn't you hear me?"

"I heard you. And you keep saying the same thing again and again, but I don't believe you. And you don't believe it either. Anyway, you tell me how good she is—"

"You don't have anything to say about whether she's good or not."

"I have a thing or two to say about you: if she's as good as you say, you can't earn her love in any way that would be worthy of her, if you are starting off with a lie, which you are, and with a pretense you can't keep up, which you also are. All you will do is harm her."

Paul had to take the receiver from his ear for a second because he felt as if Rachel had slapped him. "I would never harm her." He knew that if she heard the anger in his voice then she would know she had defeated him. But he couldn't keep it out.

"You'd never intend to harm her. But you will. You say you're not trying to make her love you. She will fall in love with you anyway, and you will break her heart. Because you can't help it. You will try not to, but you will. Only a fool would count on you. And she just might be fool enough to count on you."

Because you think she was fool enough to count on Tom, Paul thought. *Or is it because you were fool enough to count on me?* "All I am doing is trying to help her. She's in a bad spot."

"All you are doing is trying to make yourself necessary to her. Worse yet, you are making yourself necessary to her little boy. You are making him love you. That was obvious at a glance, and I didn't even know him. And that's not fair. You can't use a child's love that way. And when you break his heart that's going to be a worse thing than when you break hers."

Paul was really stung by this remark and couldn't think of an answer to her charge. It was false, false, false. He would never do something like that. Never. He couldn't find the words, though. But he didn't have to because Rachel hung up on him and left him gaping.

He stood there with the receiver still in his hand for two whole minutes. When he hung it up, he made himself a promise: *I will try to do this selflessly. I can keep Tom from breaking Susan's heart from beyond the grave. And Jack will need caring for, especially as his mother gets weaker. I can't keep her from death. But I can help her all the way there. And I will never let anything come up between us that might get out of hand.*

But as he hung up the receiver, he saw in his mind that Rachel was still looking up at him, breathing heavily, calm, exhausted, and triumphant.

19

*W*HEN ATHENEUM BOOKS PUBLISHED *AN OBOL FOR THE BOAT-*
man, in the last week of October, 1979, Helen Vendler remarked in *The*
New Yorker, in an issue that came out the very week that Iranian militants
seized the U.S. Embassy in Tehran, that it was strange that a publishing
house of such quality would print a volume of poems by someone whose
poetry seems to have never appeared in any periodical, major or minor,
before the publication of the book. Atheneum's willingness to take such a
risk, she added, was a testimonial to Paula Kyriakos's unashamed lyricism,
a feminine riposte to an age of spare masculine irony.

William Logan, in *Poetry*, complained that Kyriakos's poems, many
of which turned on mythology or on other poems about which they were
reflections, "smelt of the lamp." Logan went on to argue that there was
something received about all the poet's concerns and that Kyriakos's book
seemed like the art of a painter who worked only from photographs.

But Guy Musetti, writing in the Hartford *Courant*, wrote that the
author's indirectness and artifice made possible an expressive openness
that could not have been available to a poet whose poems were understood
as self-display. "If you ask me just to be myself, I freeze," he wrote, "but
if you ask me to play a role, I play it in a way that tells you who I am."

In one of the poems that Corbin, writing as Paula Kyriakos, had
included in *An Obol for the Boatman*, Katherine Woodcock, the recently
deceased wife John Milton had described seeing in a dream in his sonnet
"Methought I saw my Late Espoused Saint," retells the story of Milton's
dream from her own point of view. Milton's sonnet compares Katherine
to Alcestis who chose to die to spare her husband Admetus from death
and was herself rescued from death by Heracles—although at the price of
muteness. Milton does not rescue Katherine but rather he acknowledges
being rescued by her; her restoration to life, and to him, is a reward for
her courage and her generosity. However, just at the moment in the

dream when Katherine bends to enfold the poet in her arms, she vanishes. The poet may have imagined himself to be Admetus, whose wife was redeemed from death because of her steadfast love, but he, in fact, is more like Orpheus, whose failure to redeem his wife from death is also the failure of his love, and of his poetic power, which cannot transcend the boundary between life and death or between dream and waking.

Now Milton, who, despite his feeling for Katherine, has come down to us as a rather bad husband, had lost his sight before he ever met her, so he never in life had had what he experienced in the dream, "full sight" of his wife's countenance "without restraint" (phrases that capture the pathos of Milton's blindness, and also the pathos of his longing for her). And because Katherine is mute in the poem, the poet is in no position to recognize her from her voice, and only recognizes her from her face, which he had never actually seen in his waking life. Milton knows that the veiled, radiant woman who approached him was Katherine only in the impossible way one knows things in dreams. But he also knows, something he might have had reason to doubt, that Katherine loves him despite everything. When the dream breaks, day brings back the double night of the poet's blindness and his grief and, perhaps, the even deeper night of his marital guilt.

As Corbin wrote it, at the moment when Katherine, her face radiant with sweetness and goodness, returns to her husband from death, her grieving husband is astonished by her spontaneous delight at encountering him. He knows that she longs for him, but he also knows what kind of husband he was, and knows that if the sight of him brings her this flash of joy, it can only be because she is still vulnerable to him. He is certain that her love is wasted on him. If he loves her, he must free her of her love of him. Only then might he actually deserve her love, although the price of that deserving is separation. Noticing her husband's hesitation, Katherine reaches for him to break the impasse, to rescue him yet again through her selfless love, but her doing this breaks the boundary that only he can cross, so death reclaims her.

Corbin's poem combined several things William Logan had complained about—masking its feelings both in mythology and in literary history—but Susan heard in it something Corbin could never have said in his own voice, even to her. Especially to her.

There were other poems, narrated with graceful wistfulness, about what the reader was meant to assume was the poet's own life. In one poem, the poet learned to ride a bicycle under the trees of the Willamette Valley and learned that only by keeping in motion could she remain upright. In another poem, her father, whose refusal to face the fact of his imminent death from lung cancer was motivated by his desire to protect her, wound up leaving his little daughter more vulnerable to his death than he ever would have wanted her to be. But facing her father's death gave her a vocation as a cancer doctor, and a clear sense of the enemy with whom it would be her life's task to grapple and be repeatedly defeated by.

Later poems follow out the development of that vocation, as the poet undergoes her training as a medical doctor. One poem rendered how the poet and her lab partner in their college Biochemistry lab went to the Chemistry stockroom to get a Dewar flask of liquid nitrogen, which bubbled fiercely in the glass like something from the beginning of the universe, a result that left both girls so lost in wonder that much of the nitrogen had evaporated before they were able to return to the lab. In another poem, she peers through a microscope at a stained section of tissue, and the multicolored lattice of cell membranes seems to her to be the Rose Window of the cathedral of the body.

There was also a sequence of poems about the poet's small son, whose pure love the mother luxuriates in. But she knows that from the day he was brought home from the hospital, he has already, without his awareness, begun to withdraw into his own life. He has been preparing from the very beginning to survive in the world that will move on without the slightest change of course after her death, as it will later do after his own. Life closes up behind us like the sea behind a boat.

What drew the most comment, however, were two different sequences of erotic poems. One sequence began with a blunt account of the speaker's furtive abortion as a college student in the years before the *Roe* decision, a poem centering on her awareness of a dried bloodstain on the green tile of the grubby procedure room as the doctor begins to work. Further poems concerned her sexually violent later relationship with another man, from whom the speaker was never able to quite detach, despite seeing her situation clearly.

The more the speaker understands her relationship with her lover, the more she is entangled in it despite herself. She discovers that to see eros clearly is to understand how it transforms and repeals our wills so that we use our freedom only to give ourselves freely over to our obsessions. Eros fulfills and destroys identity in the same breath; it allows us to choose either meaning or living but not both, because the price of meaning is the willingness to sacrifice everything to it, even dignity, even life. The speaker survives her tormented relationship only by turning her back on eros by main force. But she survives in a diminished way; she is alive only in the way that those who have chosen mere empty life can be said to be alive since life is able to go on only once it has abandoned the pretense of standing for anything.

The other sequence saw the erotic life in a completely different way. When you love, you choose the one person you want to have with you when you each have to face the music. We have to love each other with everything we have while we can because we have to die, and that we have done our best for each other is our only testimony against death and the one thing death cannot take away. Love does not conquer death, but because of love death does not conquer everything.

The poet dwelled, in one of the sequence's signature poems, on the sweetness of yielding to sleep in her beloved's arms after a whole night of lovemaking, an experience she compared to an infant's falling asleep with repletion at her mother's breast, but also to the blissful and delicious surrender to nothingness, in which dissolution resolves not into death but into transfiguration.

The book seems not to have decided between these two views of erotic love. Is it an expression, as the later sequence implies, of tender longing through which lover and beloved help each other to redeem their common mortality, or is it instead a driven passion in whose power we transcend but also consume ourselves? Many critics understood that the poet sought to turn away from the idea of sex as a dark, transgressive adventure, but this turn was not generally taken to be entirely convincing, and William Logan and Louise Glück both described that turn as a failure of nerve.

An Obol for the Boatman was received as part of a wave of volumes of poetry in the late 1970s by women who were collectively working through new ways of thinking about what it was to be a woman, what her experience of love was, of the body, of abortion and then motherhood, of her calling to her profession, and of the natural world. Critics compared the book seriously, but not always completely favorably, to such volumes as Elizabeth Bishop's *Geography III*, to Mary Oliver's *Sleeping in the Forest*, to Louise Glück's *The House on Marshland,* and to Olga Broumas's *Soie Sauvage.* Some reviewers, however, complained that next to Rich's *The Dream of a Common Language, An Obol for the Boatman* seemed squishy and irresolute. However mixed the reviews, Corbin almost persuaded himself that the book proved him to be someone with a sympathetic insight into women's lives, an ally in their struggles, a better man than everybody said he was. He was sure somebody would give him credit for it some day, if ever the secret of the book came out. And that would really show some people.

20

OTHER THAN HARRY FORD, CORBIN'S EDITOR AT ATHENEUM, THE only person aware of the true authorship of *An Obol for the Boatman* was Susan. She knew that others, had they known the book's authorship, might have seen the book differently from how she did, perhaps as a practical joke at the expense of feminism, or as a masculine attempt to appropriate feminine experience. But she saw it as a sign of her husband's longing to escape the constraints of a public identity, and for that matter a private history, in which he felt increasingly imprisoned. She felt this way because she knew that Paula Kyriakos was Corbin's (idealized) vision of Susan herself and that most of the incidents of Kyriakos's life had been drawn from her life. Corbin's book was his offering to his wife despite everything he had ever done to her.

Susan knew also what part of his private history her husband was trying to put behind him: it was no secret to her that her husband was sexually reckless, and heedless of consequences, at least for other people—there never were consequences for him—but she balked at the thought that his continuing affairs with other women showed that he was merely selfish. There was, she tried to believe, "just too much life in him for him to contain himself, and that kept getting him in trouble." But she knew better than this, really.

Corbin had told her once how he saw it, but Susan did not believe him: he was just fallen human flesh, he had said, and couldn't offer excuses for what he did, but did not need to offer excuses either, since human beings are what they are. Besides, all the women he slept with knew already what he was, knew from the beginning how much or how little they could expect from him, and got from the experience only what they had all along expected from it. Sometimes, Susan thought, he succeeded in believing that, usually when he was charming some girl into bed. But by the next morning he would see himself, Susan knew, exactly as his colleagues at Riverside saw him, as someone who did whatever he pleased, so long as somebody else paid the price, and would continue to do so for so long as he could get away with it.

Susan knew from repeated experience that her husband was ashamed of his infidelities once they were over though the shame did not change him. Other people might have wondered whether the shame merely served to spice up the pleasure of the affair or to spice up the pleasure of the reconciliation after, but Susan always rejected these ideas. She understood from the strain of self-contempt she had seen in him from the beginning of their relationship—and, in a way she found difficult to acknowledge, had always been drawn to—that her husband knew that sooner or later that shame would catch up with him. He knew himself, he told her during one of their first nights together, and he was disappointed how little difference that self-knowledge had made. He was waiting to pay the reckoning he knew was coming, wondering whether he would be able to pay it when he had to.

How, Susan asked herself, did he imagine love would punish him? By making him understand, when it was too late to make a difference, that he had never experienced it because he had never made himself worthy of it? Or would the reckoning come by making him actually experience love in all its dark power? This thought made her feel something she did not want to name but which shook her from head to toe. She knew she would wait for that reckoning with him. However it came, Susan knew he would need her then.

Behind her husband's guilt and shame, Susan guessed, had to be a woman in his past Corbin had told Susan nothing about, a woman her husband could neither face nor forget. Susan was sure that Corbin's thought was always going back to that woman, unable to ask for forgiveness and unable to forgive. And unable as well to give up desiring her.

From the first moment, he had made clear the kind of man he was, and Susan had, she thought, entered the relationship with completely open eyes. Whether he had done this to foreclose her ability to criticize him later for betraying her in bed, or because he knew it would fascinate her and draw her on, Susan didn't know. But she could never bring herself to believe that his love for her wasn't real. She was his, absolutely, and she was certain that ultimately the day would come when they would love each other more simply and he would be hers absolutely too. Then what he had done with so many women whose names he quickly forgot wouldn't matter. She had a calling about him; she would pull him from the brink even if she risked falling over it herself. To Corbin's dying day a casual look at Susan over his shoulder as he passed out the door or his hand brushing her knee as she backed the car into the street would always drive her so wild she could barely wait for the sun to go down. And she knew how she made him tremble from head to foot. She was sure she would vanquish that unknown woman in his past.

She could never see her love for him as wasted either. Because she knew he'd staked a lot of hope on her, hope about himself as a husband, hope about himself as a father, hope about himself as anything but the priapic caricature he had been afraid of becoming. That hope, whatever came of it, was a gift he had accepted from her, since none of those things he hoped for were anything he might have imagined for himself had she never loved him.

Did that hope mean anything? Was it only a pretense, an evasion of a reckoning with himself? Susan could not be sure either way, because she knew her husband himself was not sure. He did not want to want what he wanted, but he wanted it anyway, and every promise he made to himself divided him from himself, so that what he wanted to be and what he actually was faced off against each other. In that contest *what he was* always had the claim to be closer to the truth about him than *what he wanted to be* was, and so he treated every promise about himself as if it were rooted in a lie, a worse lie than any of his other lies were since that lie was sugar-coated with wishful thinking and unreality. What better argument does *akrasia* have, Susan thought, than the demand that you face up honestly to what you are? *Better to be truly bad than to put up a pretense of goodness.* But Susan knew that even being honest with yourself about how bad you are is almost always just another round of performance for a spectator you can't really hope to fool.

Still, Susan could never see Tom just as someone who had lied to himself as badly as he had lied to her. Because she could not think that the deepest truth about him was what was worst about him, what he couldn't live down and couldn't get past; for her the deepest truth about him was the struggle he could never win but never give up either. *Would it make a difference* she sometimes asked herself, *If he knew I knew this about him?* But the answer was always no, because she also knew he felt he didn't deserve the forgiveness she was always ready to give him; accepting forgiveness would always seem to him either like an excuse or like a manipulative bargain he tried to make with God. She knew that sometimes he seemed to see himself from far away, as if he were someone else, someone he watched with bitter detachment, a disappointed spectator.

When the time came when the unending disappointed back and forth between himself and himself that Susan knew kept running in the back of her husband's mind would make him too sick of himself to go on, she would still be there. Susan was certain that she would know how to make him hers again, because however often he had broken her heart, however often he had carelessly showered humiliation on her that she kept to herself, however often he had relied upon the forgiveness he told her came too easily to her—but which she gave him again and again until he began to treat his contrition and her forgiveness as if it were to him only a part of the sexual dance between them—she was, she knew, she absolutely knew, still the only woman he had made to suffer whose suffering weighed with him, the only woman he had promised himself never to discard. The only woman, that is, except for that one to whom he owed something beyond his ability to pay. *But that was in another country.*

*T*here was a reason Susan thought this way about her husband. Like so many other girls before and after, she had herself been swept off her feet by Corbin, at a poetry reading under a tent on the lawn of the Riverside Art Museum in August 1973. This was just after Corbin had arrived for his first visiting appointment at Riverside, after rocketing to fame the previous December when Atheneum published *Lament of Saint Stephen*, a prophesy directed against the masters of war, informed at once by liberation theology and by mysticism, by Dorothy Day and by Thomas Merton, and by Pablo Neruda and *The Dark Night of the Soul*.

131

Corbin had written that book while he was still a graduate student at the University of Connecticut.

Susan, who had graduated from Harvey Mudd College the previous year, and had just completed her first year at the Loma Linda University School of Medicine, had found herself in Corbin's bed, in the little house on Massachusetts Avenue he had just bought, by the end of that evening.

Like so many other young women Susan had been captivated by how the poet's religious commitments, not only from Day and Merton but also from Daniel Berrigan and Dietrich Bonhoeffer, had borne fruit in political ideals. And, as with so many other young women, the tender Mariolatry of the last poem he read, the sonnet "Lullabye," persuaded her to see him not only as the special ally of women but as someone uniquely suited to sympathize individually with Susan herself, as if he had always had her number.

Before the first morning had passed, Corbin had invited her to live with him. It wasn't, she knew almost by instinct, what he usually did with girls he took home after readings, as it was obvious to her he was in the habit of doing. There was something about her, he had said, that made her hard to let go of. It was difficult for him to explain, and his request was clearly as strange to him as it was to her. She had no idea why she had a hold on him; indeed, she did not even understand that she had a hold on him at all, and she would not have tried to make something of that hold even had she understood it. But over those first few weeks Susan learned that she was not the only one who made a leap in the dark that night. Somehow, although it made no sense to her, he was hers absolutely.

But what could possibly have mattered so much about me, Susan had wondered. She had no notion why she might be special to him. But she had stayed on with him, letting go of her apartment on Linden Avenue. Her living with Corbin had become a fact of life, and, for Corbin's colleagues at Riverside, a source of scandal.

About ten months later, in June 1974 on the day of Jack's birth, as, flushed and exhausted and exhilarated, Susan sat with Corbin in the delivery room with their new baby in her arms, he told her that over that first night he had glimpsed in her a seriousness about life that brought him up short, something that made her matter but would hurt her too

132

unless he cared for her.

As he sat in the chair beside the disordered hospital bed, stroking her damp, limp hair, she raised herself on one elbow, pale and bone-tired, and, struggling up, took the wrinkled body of her infant in her arms. The baby lay there, fitfully twitching, bewildered, his eyes unfocused, until she steered his pale mouth to her nipple. "Oh, but he's lovely," she said, smiling up at her husband.

When Corbin smiled back at her a look passed between them, and Susan instantly understood what it meant. It wasn't just that he was happy in the love of his wife and in the promise of his child, although he was. It was that this was a scene he had been waiting for, had been preparing for even before he met her. Because it was a scene from the poem among his own poems in which he was most invested, the poem that had also most transported Susan herself at the reading where she first saw Tom read. Her child too had ridden at her heart, dreaming in the wordless rush of her pulse. Her child too clung to her, vulnerable, precious, speechless, bewildered, loving. And she too had given to Tom what she had given her child, that love that only mortals can give each other, that love that at once faces down and looks past mortality.

Corbin told Susan about the moment after that first poetry reading in August when who she really was had become clear to him. Corbin's new colleagues had taken him (and, at his insistence, Susan too, who had come up to him at the end of the reading to ask him to sign her copy of *Lament of Saint Stephen*) for drinks after the poetry reading at Duke's Bar and Grill near the university. They had had more than one round, and it was hard to hear each other over all of the inebriated students and over the Dodgers game on the television over the bar.

A waiter, clearing away their third round of drinks, had dropped an entire tray of dirty glasses. In the embarrassed silence that followed, Corbin had caught Susan's eye and, apropos of nothing, asked her what she did with her life. She didn't answer that she was a medical student. She answered that she had the same kind of feeling about cancer that Captain Ahab had had about the white whale and that she was going to chase it down wherever she might find it. This she had said looking Corbin gravely in the eye, as if she had been suddenly restored to sobriety.

Then, perhaps thinking she had no right to such gravity, particularly in a group of people among whom she was so obviously out of place, she added, with a had-one-too-many grin that didn't quite conceal the fact that she really meant it, that she intended "to chase it round Good Hope, and round the Horn, and round the Norway Maelstrom, and round perdition's flames before I give it up." Susan had had enough to drink that night that she didn't remember saying this and hadn't noticed the effect it had had on Corbin until he told her about it on the day of Jack's birth.

Later, she understood that Corbin's colleagues at Riverside drew their own conclusions about her from this drunken little speech and never changed their view of her. And she knew that Corbin's colleagues, watching him seduce this slender, bright-eyed, too credulous girl on almost their first meeting with him, had drawn their own conclusions about him too. That's why Susan kept clear of them all.

But Corbin knew, he told her that morning in the maternity ward, that she hadn't been joking about what she wanted to do with her life, and he was brought up short by the flash of intensity she had shown to a man who had only wanted to take her to bed. Pure rank lust was the only motive he would have acknowledged at the time, but it wasn't his only motive; it wasn't even his principal motive. To everyone but Corbin what Susan had said was just a drunken sally in a loud bar full of students. And, ten months later, in the rumpled hospital room, hearing Corbin's story about that moment, Susan wondered, as her wrinkled, red-faced newborn took his first pull at her nipple, whether it had been anything more than that even to herself.

Although everyone else at that table had been embarrassed by her drunken proclamation, Corbin had seen in her a quixotic, single-handed rush against death. She had struck him, he told her, as brave, but as hopelessly brave, and his rush of admiration for her included a touch of pity too, as if it would be up to him to keep her from suffering the worst of what that bravery would cost her. It had never occurred to him before that he was capable of a thought like this one. He could scarcely believe what he was thinking. But he had already crossed the Rubicon. And now, as she looked up at him from the hospital bed as he told this story,

Corbin didn't have to ask her whether she believed he meant what he had said to himself ten months before. Like so many men who delegate their emotional lives to the women they loved, he would experience his own deepest and best feelings only vicariously through her.

When she drew off her clothes that first night to stand small and pale and virginal before him in the little bedroom on Massachusetts Avenue, turning around slowly in a pirouette before him with her arms raised above her head, it was, she knew (and now, having read his last book, she saw he knew this too) an act at once of daring and of faith. She had known from the beginning that he was not safe to love. But she gave herself completely to him, knowing that she had moved him despite himself to promise to keep her safe, safe even from him, and all because of something she had not even noticed about herself. At that moment, he could only stare, stupidly good. He was someone into whose hands she had placed, as a kind of spectacular gift, not just her body but her future, something nobody could ask for and only she could give. And he would carry it with him forever, as if it were his secret, not just hers.

Corbin had asked her, as they lay together on the morning after their first night in the bedroom of his house on Massachusetts Avenue in August 1973, to tell him how she came to her calling. Nestled in his arms, Susan told the story of her own first brush with death, the death of her father when she was eight. She understood later that the story came to have a talismanic meaning for him, as if it explained not only Susan's calling but his own, his calling with her anyway. And it was this story, which, to his own astonishment, moved him to ask her to live with him.

Whenever Susan tried to summon up the memory of her father, Fred Meredith, she told Corbin, it occurred to her that she had no memory of a time when he was healthy. But her mother, Sarah, had never told her what the matter was or, indeed, conceded that anything was the matter at all. "Your father is resting today," was what her mother said. Susan heard him coughing late at night, coughing so loud it awakened her in her room across the hall.

"Surely you must have guessed," Corbin said, caressing her cheek, "That he was dying."

"I knew and didn't know," she said, turning to him. "But I thought I could save him if I loved him enough."

"If only love really did have that power," he said, kissing her softly on her forehead.

"Don't be so quick to give up about it," she said, lifting her head to return his kiss.

"You see?" she said, with a mocking smile.

"I do. But please go on with your story."

One Sunday, her father sat in the Morris chair in the parlor and clenched his unlit pipe in his teeth so vigorously that Susan thought the harder you bit your pipe the better you must be feeling. But he wasn't well enough to go to work on Monday. "His allergies are very bad this spring," her mom told her. "He has been putting in too many hours at the agency." He sold auto insurance from a little office in Corvallis, Oregon.

Once, Susan found a handkerchief on the bathroom sink with a knot of bloody phlegm in it. "I just cut myself shaving, honey," her father told her. Then he took her on his knee to ride horsey, but while she was screaming with laughter, he ran out of breath and had to stop. "Whoa," he said, "that was some stampede." He held her close, coughing, pretending, she later understood, that it was only the desire to hold her close for a second that had stopped the game.

When he was very sick, her father sent her and her mother to the movies. Sarah said it was so Susan's father could do his lessons for the correspondence law school course he had begun taking as soon as he was diagnosed. Taking that course was, Susan now understood, his way of shaking his fist at death. He was almost finished, Sarah said, as if that explained how often she had to take Susan out of the house. When they returned from the movies there was no sign that a doctor had visited the house, and Fred was always in bed, with his textbook open on his lap.

"He wanted to keep you in the dark about death, didn't he?" Corbin asked. Susan's head lay on his shoulder as she felt his chest rise and fall with his breath, and he ran his fingers through the tangles of her love-disordered hair.

"He loved me enough to want to deceive me, and I loved him enough to let him believe he had."

"Brave little girl."

At the end of his last summer, as Susan and Sarah were coming home from the movies—they saw *South Pacific*—her mother told her that they might move to San Diego before winter. It was a beautiful city where it was always summer. There was lots to do. And they have the greatest zoo in the world.

"What does Dad think about it?" Susan asked.

"He thinks he'll breathe easier there. Everything will be easier there." Sarah said this as if she really believed it.

Just a few weeks after raising the idea of moving to San Diego, Sarah took Susan to her friend Marcia Thurston's house to spend the night. Susan had not been much for sleepovers, but her mother thought it was a good idea. A very good idea. Just after Sarah left, as Susan and her friend were setting up a big dollhouse, Marcia's mother came into the room and hugged Susan very hard, then slipped silently out of the room. "I don't know why my mother did that," Marcia said. Susan had noticed that Marcia's mother, particularly over the last few weeks, had, when she thought Susan wasn't looking, darted her a look of hopeless worry and tenderness, but she had not brought herself to tell Susan what was on her mind.

Susan had difficulty sleeping that night and watched the circle of galloping mustangs cast on the ceiling by the magic lantern nightlight Marcia had on her nightstand. Very late, she fell into a heavy sleep. In later years, she wondered whether her father died while she was watching the swirl of horses or whether he had waited until she slept.

Foolish Sarah had assumed that Marcia's mother had explained to Susan why she was spending the night at Marcia's house, but Mrs. Thurston never got further than the long, puzzling hug. Arriving back at home midway through the next morning, a Saturday, Susan bounded up the front steps and found red-eyed Sarah in the front hall. She clenched a handkerchief in both hands. "Your father is ready for you, upstairs," she said. Susan rushed up to the bedroom where she thought her father would be expecting her.

He was lying on the bed, still in his pajamas, with his head thrown back, and his mouth wide open. The skin of his face had drained away from his nose, which seemed larger and sharper than it had ever been in life. His face was unshaven—until the end he had been always very particular about being freshly shaved—and his pajama shirt was open, his skin already as grey as wet clay, but his chest hairs bristled, as if still charged with life. Her mother had not even been able to arrange the body in a more dignified way before sending Susan up to the room. After a moment, Susan ran out of the room, down the stairs, and out the front door. She didn't know what to say. But she had to be alone for a while.

Corbin lifted her head from his shoulder, held her face between his hands, and looked into her eyes. "If I could go back and change that, I would," he said.

She smiled at him, not quite believing him. "I thought you said love didn't have the power to change anything."

"It doesn't have to change anything to mean everything."

She broke his gaze and rolled onto her back, watching the thin white curtains at the window shift brilliantly in the slight breeze. It was already hot, and she slid the sheet off her body to feel the cool of the air on her damp skin. As Tom waited for her to go on, she reached over with one hand and played with the hair on his chest. She had to think about what he had said.

At her father's funeral, she heard his partner in the agency say, "Fred Meredith was a man who made plans. And it would be a much better world if more of those plans had worked out." Sarah Meredith was also a woman with plans, but, because she was a woman with no particular skills except that of tending to her dream-imprisoned husband, her plans fared no better than his. For some years, they imposed on the charity of her sisters. Sarah and her daughter spent almost two years with one sister, whose husband managed a grass-seed ranch in La Grande, then almost two years with another, whose husband ran a grocery store in Grant's Pass. For a while, Sarah was the cashier in the store.

Each sister asked, "Sarah, what are you going to do to get on in life?"

Every time she answered, "I'm going to marry a rich husband."

But there never was a rich husband although she had many male friends who gave her things. Eventually, her sisters tired of making loans to her that they knew she could never repay and of her succession of male friends.

Susan and her mother did actually get to San Diego where Sarah was a maid at a motel near the airport. The manager had given them a room. Sometimes, when the money was shortest, her mother made Susan skip school to pick oranges even though she was underage. When Susan came home, the manager was sometimes sitting on Sarah's couch and smoking a cigarette.

"And while all this was happening," Tom sighed, "I was in college, studying poetry."

"Why do you blame yourself about that? The fact that you had an easier life than I did didn't make mine one bit harder," Susan said.

Although she had tumbled her clothes at the foot of the bed, she had neatly placed the books she had with her at the reading, the copy of *Lament of Saint Stephen* she had him sign, and a heavy, bright orange textbook, *The Basic Science of Oncology*, on his bedside table. Corbin turned his head to peer at the books, and said aloud the author's name, "Lea Harrington."

"Not quite the author you are," Susan said, kissing him.

Susan had attracted the attention of her teachers in California. Through their influence, when she graduated from high school in 1968 she had won not only a college scholarship from the Rotary Club, but a stipend to help pay her expenses while she was at Harvey Mudd College. She took a job waiting tables in a bar and grill in Claremont to pay her own expenses and used the stipend to buy her mother a five year old Corvair. It was a chance for her to be a better daughter to the mother she had never quite been aware—until much later—that she had judged.

Before her second year was out, however, she learned that her mother had turned the car over at high speed and broken her neck. Alcohol was not involved, the coroner said. But he charitably supposed that she had fallen asleep at the wheel. Being three months pregnant had probably interfered with her sleep. Susan had to ask the county to arrange for a cremation, and she scattered the ashes in the eucalyptus grove in Presidio Park. She thought about contacting her aunts with news of her mother's death, but never did so. She left her mother's belongings in the motel.

Facing the motel manager again was too much for her.

Neither of her parents had ever used the word, but by the time Susan had finished her first year at Harvey Mudd College, she had come to the conclusion that what her father had died from—and what, by setting her adrift, had put her mother on her own path to death—was lung cancer, a disease she decided she would spend her life fighting.

When Corbin retold the story of her father's death in *An Obol for the Boatman*, Susan knew what its meaning had always been for him. He never wrote directly about their courtship, but this was his courtship poem, and in all the ups and downs of their relationship, even in the face of his many infidelities, Susan never lost sight of how his investment in this story explained his tenderness for her. She did not mention this poem when she told Paul that what her husband had written in *An Obol for the Boatman* showed that he had "known her down to the ground," but it was what she had been thinking about.

What did Susan make of the poem about the abortion? It wasn't her story—her first night with Corbin was her first sexual experience—but she could not make up her mind whether it was about some earlier passage in his life that Corbin regretted or about the future he came close to forcing on her. The darker sexual passages puzzled her, too, because what they described had never been their sexual life. But she knew he had that darkness in him. That darkness had drawn her to him in the first place, and it had given her a task, a task she had a misplaced confidence about her ability to carry out; she was not wrong, however, to see *An Obol for the Boatman* as testimony of her husband's love of her, even if she overestimated what that love could do.

21

*T*HERE WAS ONE MORE READER WHO DIVINED WHO THE AUTHOR of *An Obol for the Boatman* really was. Corbin was in his office late on a Thursday afternoon in mid-November of 1979 when the phone interrupted him at his grading.

"Who gave you the right to tell my story?"

Corbin had been half-expecting this call from her. But he didn't have a good answer ready for this question. While he tried to think, she played the card she had come to play.

"I'm in Riverside. I just drove here from Reseda after I got out of work. And I have to see you. I'm at the pay phone by the main desk of the Rivera Library. Come there right now if you don't want me to storm your office."

He had, after all, imagined that his book might provoke Rachel into getting in touch with him. When he actually heard her voice he was surprised at how much he was on fire to see her again. It was as if, without exactly choosing to, he had written that book for just this eventuality. But now that she had confronted him, for the first time he felt a little afraid of her.

Tom had played out the scene in his imagination several ways. But in the moment his self-possession left him. He had to think about where he might meet her, somewhere where he was certain nobody he knew would ever be, but also somewhere close enough he could get there soon. He could not clear his mind. He left his office in such a hurry that he did not call Susan to tell her he might be late. He did not even warn her that she would have to be picking up Jack after school.

When he turned into the restaurant parking lot, Rachel was already standing outside of her mustard-yellow Vega, tapping her feet, looking sharply at him through his windshield, her eyes squinting in the late afternoon glare. Before he had even turned off the ignition, she had seated herself in his passenger seat. Just as she was turning to give him her look, she paused to flip the hair out of her eyes, tucking it on both sides behind her ears.

It was that nervous hair flip, the gesture she had always made when she was trying to control herself, that made him decide to fall back on the old disarming stand-bys: *How are you? You look nice. It's good to see you. Really. Where are you living, and what are you doing?* But she was already wound up and wasn't going to be diverted. He didn't end up saying any of those things.

"I saw that line about the blood smear on the green tile," she said, without so much as a hello, her voice a fierce whisper, as though they might be overheard, although they were alone. It went right through him like a shiver. "And I knew you were telling my story. I didn't even know you knew it. You sure didn't hear it from me."

"How did you know I'm the one who told that story?"

"I notice you don't deny that it's your book. So how did I penetrate the mystery that baffled *The New Yorker*? Because, you slippery fuck, I already knew that the only person who was supposed to know that story besides me was Paul Bishop."

"Why didn't you think he wrote it?"

"He wouldn't have had the chutzpah to make up a female persona to tell his story through. And he couldn't have told that story to the world without worrying about how I'd feel about it. So he must have told the story to you, since chutzpah is your department and worrying about how I might feel about anything is not. I knew he just wouldn't have the stuff to keep that story to himself, no matter what he promised me. So who else would he tell the story to but you, his great confidant, his wingman, his loyal ally?"

"Don't get self-righteous. It was you who was dating him."

"Dating? That's one word for it," the angrier she became, the more furtive and conspiratorial she sounded. Corbin couldn't help it: he was stirred by it. "When you think of what you and I had been doing—do you want to call that 'dating' too?—his making that little confession to you seems rather pathetic, doesn't it? Didn't just hearing it from him make you feel strange? No, not you. Even though you knew the real story and he didn't. You wouldn't feel strange even telling the whole thing in print. So it had to be you. And besides that there's all that sexual stuff about me in there that Bishop wouldn't know. Stuff that's not in his line anyway."

Rachel, who had been a sexual novice at the time she and Bishop became lovers, still had not been the rank beginner Bishop was. Corbin knew that what he did to her shocked her, but it also showed her that she hadn't really known what sex was about before. Cautious, uncertain Bishop had not had a chance. She had told Corbin that she regretted that she had crossed a line there was no crossing back. But she told him as well that regret was pointless because it couldn't change what she knew she was, what Corbin had taught her she was.

"I recognized all that as your style," she went on. "I remember your style. Sometimes I still think about it."

Rachel gave him an impenetrable smile, part suggestion, part menace. She still had her regal posture and her glossy cascade of hair despite the neutral way she was dressed.

"Paul did tell me about your expedition to Portland."

"Was that tactful phrase yours or his?" Rachel looked at him directly. He knew he should not look away.

After a few seconds, Corbin said, "To do him justice, Paul held it back a very long time. He only told me weeks after he had failed his exams, and you had dropped from sight. But you should have told it to me yourself. I shouldn't have had to learn it from Paul. You owed that to me."

She scoffed, shaking her head. "At least Paul tried to do his best for me, as I knew he would, and as I knew you wouldn't. And what good would it have done me had I come out to you about it anyway?"

"If that child was mine, I had a right to know about it," Corbin said.

"I don't owe you shit. And you'd have wanted me to do exactly what I did, anyway." Then she laughed. "Paul thought a lot of you. Did you know that? I'd have been sunk with him if he knew the whole story. But you, God, he thought so much of you that he might have forgiven you even if you told him everything. I call that desperate, myself."

Why is she so hard on him? Corbin thought. *We were the ones who did him wrong. All he did was never imagine we would hurt him. She*

143

can't stand what she did to him, and she blames him for it. But she still can't stop thinking about him.

"Anyway," she smiled, "I'm glad I didn't put you to the test. I'm pretty sure you would have let me down. It's hard to imagine you not using what you know."

"I think your secret is still safe even if Paul reads the book."

Her smile became a little harder. "You don't think he'll recognize the little detail he gave you about the blood smear on the tile?"

"He'll know that poem is about you. But so what? After all, he knows that story already because he was there. And he told me himself the whole story about your trip to Portland, or what he thought was the whole story, because he didn't know what you and I had been doing. So when he sees the poem, he will know I wrote it. That is, if he doesn't think you wrote it. Give yourself some credit: so much of that book is from you that he might just guess that you were Paula Kyriakos, not me. I just don't see why his calling back to mind a story he already knows bothers you. You're not still carrying any torch for him. You weren't carrying a torch for him even then, as I know better than anyone. Even if you did try to go back to him. Because your going back to him didn't mean anything. It was no more than guilt." Tom scoffed.

"It's just like you to use a phrase like 'no more than guilt,'" Rachel shook her head and laughed, a conspiratorial laugh more than a bitter one.

"And besides," Tom went on, ignoring her remark, "the sexual stuff in the book all happens long after the abortion, not before it, and with some other guy she meets much later. It would be different if I had put in the book how it actually was."

"He just didn't know you well enough to know what you were capable of. I really don't care what he knows now, anyway. What does it matter what he thinks of me?" Rachel asked.

Corbin, as he always did, scented the lie as soon as it was uttered, and could not resist twisting the knife. "How do you know he doesn't already know the real story?"

But to his surprise, Rachel laughed. "Because I know you'd never have the courage to come clean with him. He loved and admired you, and you wouldn't have wanted to change that. Even if he would have forgiven you. I bet you haven't told him about it even now. I see you're not at all ashamed to be who you really are in front of me. But that's something you still can't be in front of him. You still don't want him to think ill of you."

What Paul thought did matter to him. Tom didn't like to hear her throw it in his face. But it did matter. Tom wasn't proud of what he had done to his friend. And he still didn't want Paul to know about it.

Rachel watched him, enjoying herself now. "I don't see what you get from writing this book," she said, "I could name quite a few venal things you might want to use your poetry to do. Sleeping with bright-eyed girls after poetry readings, for instance. But pulling the wool over the eyes of a lot of reviewers isn't one of those things I could see you wanting to do. For one thing, doing that isn't really worth anything. And when it all comes out, which it's bound to do sooner or later anyway, nobody will think you had any motive beyond finding some totally new way to be a jerk. But they all think you're a jerk already, so nobody will be surprised. So why do it at all?"

It was hard for him to reply to this. What he had to say had the disadvantage of sounding ridiculous, despite having the advantage of being true. "I just had to step outside myself. I had to get away from my own bullshit. And to do that I had to get myself out of the way."

"Tom Corbin the apostle of Negative Capability? Oh, please. 'The poet has as much delight in conceiving an Iago as an Imogen. What shocks the virtuous Philosopher, delights the chameleon Poet.' " Rachel recited the passage from Keats in a mocking, singsong voice. "Shakespeare could do that. That's why we have so little idea what he was like as a man because he could give himself to any kind of character. Maybe Keats himself could do that too. He sure wanted to. Maybe Browning also. Though, whenever I read Browning, I still hear him saying 'Just listen to me as I pull this one off!' behind all his characters. But Tom Corbin? Tom Corbin is a known quantity, and he has spent a lot of years and a lot of effort making that quantity known." Rachel could barely keep from laughing in his face. But he meant what he said even though he knew she would never believe him.

"That's just what the problem is. 'That which we are we are.' But I'm tired of being that person."

"I'm so full of pity for you."

"I wasn't trying for pity. I meant that I'm sick of everything I do, and I have debts to pay."

"To all those poets you climbed over on the ladder to the top?" Rachel asked.

"I was talking about my debt as a man."

"Stop the sentence there before you say something stupid. Remember who you are talking to."

"I know I've behaved badly with you. If I'm going to understand it at all, I have to see myself without excuses," Tom said.

"So that's why there's all that kinky stuff about what you did to me? Because you wanted to know what it felt like to, let me use the discreet phrase, to be fucked by you?"

"I'm not sure I would have put it that literally."

"But in those poems about me anyway it was exactly what you were thinking."

"Okay, but not only with you. You're not the only woman in the book."

"Yes. I read all the other stuff. The mushy stuff about Little Miss Pure-Heart who is so brave and loves everyone."

Corbin was offended, but somehow could not rise to the bait. He knew he should respond to this. But he couldn't. He couldn't even bring Susan up, much less defend her. All he could try to do was to look away from Rachel. But he couldn't manage even that.

"I'm sure your wife was impressed that you wrote so sweetly from her point of view," Rachel said, coldly, "I hope she rewarded you where it matters. But don't expect me to believe any of that, because you don't believe it yourself. You just want to."

A station wagon pulled into the space beside them, a woman at the wheel, her impatient teenage daughter in the passenger seat. The woman looked over at Rachel, as if waiting for Rachel to get out of her car before she would open her own door. After it became clear to the woman that the couple in the next car were not about to get out, she still sat there, watching Rachel and Corbin argue.

Rachel sensed that she was being watched and turned to glare at the woman until the woman looked down. Collecting herself, the woman and her daughter got out of their car and went into the restaurant, the girl complaining that her mother had embarrassed her. Rachel watched them all the way to the door.

Turning back to Corbin, Rachel looked at him, appraising. "So you want to know what I felt when I was in bed with you?"

She looked at him very directly.

"Yes. I guess I do."

At this she slapped him across the face, not hard enough to really hurt him, but hard enough to show that she meant business. Then, before the expression on his face had quite completed its change from anticipation to surprise, she kissed him very hard, pressing him to her, gripping the back of his head with both hands until he responded to her.

They spent the early part of that evening at the Thunderbird Lodge, a few blocks further down University Avenue, an Art Deco motel that had once been considered elegant. Although its best days were past, it still had the attractive feature of having its parking in an interior court that was not visible from the street.

Rachel fell into the habit of calling Corbin to her every few days. But only one more time did she agree to meet him in the faded Art Deco Museum of the Thunderbird Lodge. It was important to her that he come to her, in Reseda, an hour and a half away, and Corbin had to use all of his ingenuity to invent pretexts for missing office hours, rearranging Jack's pickup at school, or explaining arrivals home that were so late that Jack had had to go to bed without his story. The effort was exhausting, and Corbin usually arrived home from these adventures feeling spent and depressed.

Rachel was very reluctant to tell him much about what her life had been since she had left Storrs. She was also reluctant to give him any detail about her present life, even to tell him what she did for a living. She told him, in what must have been for him rather a reversal of roles, that he was not to seek to know her, nor to seek to have any relationship with

147

her beyond the sexual relationship they had already begun. Of the rest of her life, a life separated from that life in every way, he was to know nothing and to ask nothing. The veil of anonymity she drew between them, however, was transparent from her side, since, she said, his career was an open book to her, and she already knew more about him personally than anyone else, his wife included, and that she knew him better than she wanted to.

On his first tryst with her at her apartment, in late November, she had told him to arrive in Reseda some time after three, which he surmised must be when she left her own work. He would make the one hundred and fifty mile round trip in the Firebird he had recently bought because he thought he didn't have to be a family man at every instant, and they had the Dart for family stuff. The Firebird's throaty sound, when he pressed the accelerator, thrilled him, and the feeling of being thrown back into his seat that would shortly follow satisfied his sense of what it was to feel power at your disposal. Cruising along the base of the mountains that surrounded the bowl of Los Angeles County, he felt as though he were driving the banked curves of a great raceway. The road seemed to be a kind of sluice, bordered on both sides by walls, through which he caught fleeting glimpses of the densely packed houses, the shopping malls, the warehouses and factories. At Encino, he steered off the Ventura Freeway onto White Oak Avenue and made his way north on that broad, busy street until he crossed the concrete trough of the Los Angeles River and made his left onto Victory Boulevard, a street crowded with almost identical compact houses that had been built to hold the children who were being begotten, in stupendous numbers, by the returning veterans of the Second World War.

Coming up to a little park, he turned right onto Reseda Boulevard and pulled over to an unmetered space at parkside where, through the trees, he could see a baseball diamond set in a bezel of dead grass. He looked across the street at Rachel's building while making his mind up whether to enter. It was a modest, but well-maintained, two-story apartment building of dark yellow cinderblock with a broad slanting overhanging cornice of terra-cotta roof tiles running across the front and sides. It was divided into segments by wide, arched brick columns in a still darker yellow, each with an ornamental light fixture. The foundations were thickly planted, and there was a cluster of yuccas on each side of the front walk. It seemed perfectly ordinary, so unlike the place where he imagined the woman who had made love to him so fiercely in the seedy motel before might live.

He took the wallet from his pocket and removed the photos he carried of Susan and of Jack, putting them in the glove compartment of his Firebird. He knew Rachel would want to see a photo of Susan, but he couldn't bear the idea. And he was afraid he might even take the picture out and show it to her, if she pressed him, because he knew she knew how to get her way. On the day they first went to the Thunderbird Lodge, he had allowed Rachel to jeer at Susan. He was ashamed that he didn't stop her, but he knew he wouldn't stop her were she to do it again. That seemed to him a worse betrayal of Susan even than sleeping with Rachel. But he wouldn't show her Susan's picture.

Rachel buzzed him in without speaking on the intercom, and he found his way up to her apartment on the second floor. She said nothing to him when he opened the door, which she had left open for him, although she was not standing behind it. She kept him waiting even as he stepped inside. It was a bare, severe, white-painted room with a beige carpet. It was small, almost empty, with a threadbare couch and coffee table and a portable television on a stand. There was nothing decorative anywhere, no pictures, no ornaments, almost nothing personal, except a small pile of books on the coffee table, among which he noticed *An Obol for the Boatman*, with the back cover torn off. He closed the door behind him. It was not a place where somebody lived. It was a place where somebody waited out their life.

"Well," she said, not asking a question, looking him in the face.
Well.

One Thursday evening in January, after he had arrived home past Jack's bedtime, he kissed Susan behind the ear, and she tousled his hair. She told him, returning his kiss, that he looked as if his best friend in the world had just died. But he just kissed her again, then led her into the bedroom, where he tried to prove to himself that he was not really the person he had just been all afternoon. Afterwards, as he held her in his arms as she began to drowse, he told her in all honesty that she had never seemed so beautiful to him as at that moment. She rolled onto her stomach, and he traced loving words on her back. He traced a soft line along her spine with his fingertips, and down the back of one thigh. Behind the back of her knee he found a birthmark, in the shape of a small hand. This he softly kissed, with especial tenderness, as if it were the sign of how much it was Susan he loved the most, after all. He was about to add that he loved her more deeply than ever, but as he began to form the words, he heard the even breathing of her sleep.

22

$\mathcal{A}$FTER RACHEL RETURNED, IN LATE MARCH OF 1971, DEFEATED, from the University of Connecticut, to the home of her sympathetic but puzzled parents on trim, cedar-lined Larchwood Place in Riverside, she picked up where she had left off at the end of December, sleeping into the afternoon every day, wandering the nave of the St. Francis de Sales church, returning to eat dinner from trays in the living room as she and her parents watched Walter Cronkite deliver the news, as William Calley was convicted of the murders of twenty-two civilians in Vietnam, as five hundred thousand people marched in Washington D.C. against the Vietnam War, and as the Supreme Court ruled that the *New York Times* should be allowed to publish the Pentagon Papers.

Her coldness to her parents gave them no opening, and she volunteered nothing about why she had left graduate school; her parents only very timidly raised the question of her future plans, and she responded blankly to the question, as if it were such an impertinence that only by keeping silent could she preserve her dignity.

Once she indiscreetly told her mother she had spent the afternoon at St. Francis de Sales. Her mother found this encouraging. "Have you spoken with Father Ronan? He has always seemed to me to be a kind man."

"No, mother, I go there to think and to be by myself."

After dinner, Rachel retreated to her childhood bedroom, where her Raggedy Ann doll still sat on the shelf waiting for her, and the poster of Paul McCartney still made dewy eyes at her from the back of her closet door. On the white enamel-painted child's desk, the books she had loved in junior high school still stood in order: *A Wrinkle in Time*, *The Outsiders*, *The Diary of a Young Girl*, *The Martian Chronicles*, *Death Be Not Proud*, *A Wizard of Earthsea*.

She had left all of her college books, and all of her graduate school books, behind in her room in the house on Hanks Hill Road. One of the girls she had lived with wrote her a few weeks after Rachel had dropped out to ask her what she wanted them to do with the books, her typewriter, and the clothing she had left behind. She never replied to the letter. At length, the girl sent her a share of the security deposit they had put down, which Rachel had never bothered to ask for.

After her parents were safely asleep, Rachel took out of her purse the half-pint bottle of California brandy she bought each day, which seemed less desperate to her than gin, and drank it in small sips over the course of the night. She carefully rationed each sip so as not to become fully drunk, but she never let a night go by without drinking the bottle to the bottom and replacing it in her purse, to discard in a street trashcan on the campus of Riverside City College the next morning on her way to her usual rounds at St. Francis de Sales.

After she had finished her brandy, she wrote, as she often did, for a few hours in a wire-bound notebook she kept in the drawer of her childhood desk. The next morning, she always carefully tore up the pages she had written the night before, putting them in her purse, to deposit in the trash can with the empty bottle.

She wondered how, now that she was again living on the charity of her parents, among all the reminders of her adolescence, she was different from the teenager she had been when she last lived in that room. The humiliation was the same as it had ever been. But now there was the brandy, which she toyed with all of her night hours, flirting with the loss of control she knew she could never recover from if she so much as once gave way to it.

In high school, she had scorned alcohol, and all of the frivolous people who thought it gave them an excuse for doing all the things they had wanted all along to do but had lacked the nerve to attempt. Those were her mother's vices, not hers.

In July, she began to bring home a second bottle every day. Again, she never drank it quickly enough to feel really drunk, but having the second bottle made it possible for her to keep at it later into the night. And it made writing in the spiral-bound notebook easier. At the end of the month, she put down the notebook and began writing letters on the best sky-blue stationery she could find from the University Bookstore. Sometimes these letters became very long, and sometimes she worked on them for several nights, crossing out some passages and recopying them in her best handwriting. These were almost always letters to Corbin, whom she had desired, and lied to, and broken with, and been betrayed by, and blamed, and still desired. But she also wrote shorter letters to Bishop. She told herself she no longer desired him, but she knew she had betrayed him. Indeed, she imagined herself as prisoner of that betrayal. It never occurred to her to see him as the prisoner of his own betrayal of her. Mostly, because it was easier than facing what she had done to him or facing what she really felt about him, she thought of Bishop with contempt, saving her authentic rage and her best eloquence for Corbin. But with every letter, after she had sealed it in the matching rag paper envelopes from the stationery box, she stopped herself when the address she was writing was half completed, and, as she had with the notes before, tore the letter up into small pieces and put it in her purse to take to the public trash can.

In the second week of August, she opened the medicine cabinet in her parents' pink tile bathroom, and took out the bottle of Sominex her parents kept there.

I'm not a very good person, am I? she said silently to her reflection. *I'm not somebody I'd ever want to know.*

After midnight, she swallowed all of the pills with the brandy—not taking small sips this time. After half an hour, she threw up on the brightly flowered throw rug in her bedroom. Before morning came, she had gathered up the rug and thrown it in the trash can behind the house. While her parents still slept, she went back to the bathroom to rinse out her mouth and to wash her face. She looked at her reflection in the bathroom mirror, blurred by the steam from the tap.

What kind of idiot, she said to her reflection, *tries to kill herself with Sominex?*

The next week she arranged to take a course on Wordsworth, Coleridge, and Blake as a special student at UC Riverside. It was an undergraduate course, but her thought was that the way back into academia for her would have to begin with some baby steps.

She had planned to seat herself inconspicuously at the back of a large lecture hall—in the safety of vicarious experience. But it turned out to be a seminar in which everybody sat around a large table, and Professor Coppersmith was in the habit of working around the table, encouraging, as he said, students to put in their oar when their turn came around. Even more mortifying, he was especially delighted to have an older and better-read student in his seminar. He fell into the habit of relying upon her to give new turns to the class discussions.

When a student would express a half-formed thought about "Tintern Abbey," for instance, he would look at Rachel and ask her whether there was something she might bring out more fully in what Jeremy had just said. And when he asked the class some large, fraught question— "How is 'seeing a world in a grain of sand' in Blake like or unlike those moments in Wordsworth in which he senses 'something far more deeply interfused'?"—he was grateful that she understood that he was not looking for a canned answer, an answer which most of the other students were racking their brains to guess, but for her to weigh the possibilities thoughtfully. Back at UConn she might have been glad of the attention, and relished the opportunity to hold her own in a back and forth with the professor, a back and forth of which the other students would mostly have been resentful spectators. But here and now, it all struck her as ridiculous.

She came to realize that she had not entered the class to advance herself as a student but to lick her wounds anonymously in the presence of poetry, to submerge her private grief for a moment in the grief each of the poets was working through. The poems were something she wanted to sip carefully, in the middle of the night, all by herself, until she had drained them or they had drained her. Nothing struck her as sadder than those moments in which Wordsworth insists that he has come out of a dark experience, chastened, subdued, even rebuked, but also newly alive to the still sad music of humanity. *We all have to keep telling ourselves things like that. It's what we have to do to talk ourselves into going on. But who really believes it when they say such a thing?* She could not honestly say whether what she wanted was to feel something intensely again or to put feeling away entirely and never have to dwell on it any more. Coleridge

154

had called what she was experiencing "dejection," which she recognized as a darkness the spirit comes to recognize and depend on, a special friend who finally will do you harm in a way you had not conceived of yourself as vulnerable to being harmed.

By the end of October, she had stopped attending class although she still left her parents' house every day and spent the class hours as she had done the previous summer—haunting the quiet pews of St. Francis de Sales. She realized that the gravitational pull poetry had for her was a dark one, something like the gravitational pull that eros had. It was like an overripe fruit that she could not eat without smearing it all over her face, a fruit she sucked out of the peel like a heavily scented nectar, sweet, dreamy, intoxicating, and famishing her more and more with every bite she took.

She had to put a stop to this. She went to the bathroom, stood before the mirror, and clenched her fists at her side until the tension went straight up her throat into her jaw. *I won't let anyone make me feel that way again,* she thought, not talking about poetry.

If she had said what she said to the world, it would have been a defiant proclamation. If she had said it to Corbin, it might have been a rebuke, but she didn't know whether he would feel the force of that rebuke. If she had said it to herself, it would have been a promise, something she felt absolutely certain she would be able to keep for the rest of her days. But as she said it to herself, she realized, and this made her feel a flash of shame, that she also felt regret and desire.

*N*ow that it was clear to her that there was no going back to graduate school, she had to face the fact that she had no idea what she wanted to do. But she had also reached the point at which hanging around at her parents' house was no longer tolerable either, even if she punctuated her days with loitering at St. Francis de Sales and medicated her evenings with brandy. She decided to take the qualifying test to be a substitute teacher in the Riverside district, which at least would get her out of the house regularly. Once the January term began, she could find work at one elementary school or another whenever she wanted to. Sometimes, the teacher she was replacing had left worksheets for her to do or instructions about books to read aloud and discuss. But just as often, she was left to show a film on the 16mm projector or to have the students sit quietly and read. Occasionally, when the teacher she was replacing knew she would be out for a few days, lesson plans would have been left for her, ready to use.

It was mortifying to her to go to the Magnolia school, which she had herself attended. She was glad when she discovered that none of the women who had taught her years before still worked there, so none of them would have to be disappointed in her. But it still seemed to her every time she was assigned there that she had to have some reckoning with her younger self, whom she imagined would see through her immediately, with the scorn that had always come so naturally to her.

I always knew how to hurt people, didn't I? But I'm still that girl. I just became the kind of person she was always mean to. Which served her right.

She was depressed by how much more cheerful and lively both the students and the buildings were at the highly rated schools, like the Franklin or the Lake Matthews schools, relative to the dreary architecture and hair-trigger discipline of weaker schools like the Shetland School where she felt the district had already written off most of the students as hopeless cases. But at none of these schools did she ever seek to do more than to hold the fort for the absent teacher, and from one day to another the students she taught were a blur to her, which suited her perfectly.

As soon as her parents learned of her plan to be a substitute teacher, they bought her a yellow Vega so that she could travel to her daily assignments. She fell into the habit of driving aimlessly out into the desert after class each day to postpone another long evening at home. She did not pay attention to where she went on these drives; the point was to listen to the rumble of the motor rather than to the ongoing monologue in her head and to concentrate on steering the car rather than on steering her life.

After school on the Monday before Thanksgiving of 1972, Rachel found herself driving just before sunset in the desert, much further from home than she usually went. She had driven I-15 in a daydream to Barstow and had turned back there. She planned on taking the old Route 66 back as far as Victorville for a change of pace. At Helendale, she turned off the road to fill her tank. As she pulled in to the little market at the crossroads, she saw the lights flash on and the gates begin to drop at the level crossing on the Santa Fe tracks, perhaps a hundred yards away. She threw the car back into gear and sped around the gate, coming to a stop on the tracks, gripping the wheel, looking straight ahead, not looking at the oncoming train, lest she should lose her nerve. Her arms tightened. She clenched her teeth and felt a rush of joy as the train's horn began to wail for the crossing. *Now,* she thought, *finally.* She heard the train's brakes begin to squeal as the horn kept on screaming, a clamorous, angry duet. Then, without choosing to, she stamped the accelerator to the floor and cleared the crossing when the train was perhaps ten yards away, and then, slamming on her brakes, fishtailed the car until she was facing back the way she came at the other side of the crossing. She heard the doppler shift of the horn as the engine blasted past, the panicked engineer continuing to pull the horn for another ten seconds.

Coward she said, *I knew you couldn't do it.* She hit the side of her head with her fist as hard as she could. *I knew it! I knew you'd never do it!* She hit the side of her head twice more. Then a car came up behind her, and she pulled onto the shoulder to let it pass. But the driver came to a stop beside her and rolled down his window.

"Are you all right?"

She glared at him, not rolling down her window. "Just go on, will you?"

He looked at her a second, wondering what to do, as she continued to glare at him.

She rolled down her window. "You heard me, didn't you? Just go on."

He looked at her for another long second, but then he did what she had told him.

Now you know you'll never get it done, she told herself, still idling on the shoulder. *You'll scare people, like mother did. You'll pity yourself, like mother does, and make everyone miserable.* She looked at herself coldly in the rearview mirror. *And none of it will matter at all, because you will go on. But only because you don't know what else to do but go on.* It had gotten dark enough for her to switch on the headlights. *"A thousand thousand slimy things live on, and so do I."*

She did live on. By and by, she even got the habit of living again. Her shame about being someone who had foolishly played chicken with death, but lost her courage, began to subside. Facing down death began to seem no longer to be the only way she could prove to herself that she was in earnest about anything. Suicide, she concluded, was the last resort of forsaken maidens and other helpless creatures. It was something for dramatic posers who had miscalculated how far they could go or who had imagined that they could achieve some final satisfaction by making someone else feel guilt they could never live down.

Who would have felt guilt if she had died, anyway? Corbin wouldn't have even known about it. Her parents would have thought it was something they had done when the more painful truth of it was that they didn't come into it at all. But the train engineer would have seen that collision in his dreams every night. And she knew herself to have been selfish and small to have used his guilt to solve her problem. She was ashamed that she could not picture him even though she had almost changed his life. *Suicide is for contemptible people,* she told herself. There are better ways to make the people who have it coming to them suffer for what they did. And in the meantime, she had also learned how to make herself suffer what she, no less than they, had had coming to her.

*B*y the spring, she was ready to take another try as a special student at Riverside, this time taking an undergraduate course in the Education department, to make a case for admission to the teaching certification program at Riverside in the fall. Her parents—who continued to put a roof over her head and food on her plate as well as pay the tuition for the courses she took, although she had less and less to say to them—were discreetly relieved to see her taking this initiative. Better anything than just hanging around the house.

By May, she had begun to toy with the idea of not merely getting a certification to teach school in California, but of studying for the Master of Arts in Teaching degree. In early August, walking through campus on her way home from a summer class on *Pedagogy of the Oppressed,* she noticed a poster announcing a poetry reading at the Riverside Art

Museum by the newly appointed visiting poet Thomas Corbin, whose book *Lament of Saint Stephen* had appeared the previous winter.

Seeing his name on the poster, along with a photograph of him making a fiery gesture in front of a microphone—in which he bore an unmistakable resemblance to Che Guevara—she waited for the anger to flash up in her like a natural gas explosion in an abandoned house. But what she felt was intense curiosity. She didn't have to talk to him. She would hang back at the edges of the crowd and maybe just get a glimpse of him then slip away. But she had to see him, to see whether, after the last two years, after what had passed between them, his face had been marked as her own had been. Did he still have that angry political commitment, coupled with an irony at the expense of his own idealism, that she had been drawn by three years before? She just had to know. She was sure she could keep the whole experience at arm's length. But she had to know.

She did attend the reading although she stood so far away that she could only catch glimpses of him in the interstices of the crowd. But the voice she heard, slightly overdriven by the PA system, was the same voice she heard when she called his image up alone in her room after her parents had gone to sleep, and it awakened her as it always had. It also stirred her physically, and she had to do something about it. Something might happen between them. And then she would leave him. And it would serve him right.

First I'll fuck him. Then I'll break his heart.

At the end of the reading, Rachel found herself pushing her way to the front of the crowd. She edged several listeners aside with more force than she was aware of using as she worked her way in Corbin's direction. One of these was a large, elderly, red-faced priest, who, preoccupied with wiping his glasses with his handkerchief, had not noticed that she was trying to get by him. The priest was so startled when she squeezed past him that he dropped his glasses to the ground. Rachel wasn't sorry.

As she approached the front of the crowd, she noticed that Corbin was intensely engaged in conversation with a slight, thin girl with a blonde ponytail. From where Rachel stood, she seemed barely old enough to be of legal age, but she knew the girl had to be older than that. She was short, very short. She'd always be a girl, never a woman. She had given him her copy of his book to sign, and she could barely contain her rapture. But she was leaning so as to prop a large orange book on her hip. Rachel had to see what this girl was carrying: *The Basic Science of Oncology*. Rachel had to suppress a laugh. *She won't be his type.* Rachel thought, *Except in bed. They are all his type there.*

Corbin hadn't noticed Rachel, so engrossed he was with the little blonde. *More cute than beautiful,* she thought. *Full of virgin fancies. Will be boring at thirty-five, with school-age kids.* But her eyes were shining, and she seemed so thrilled to have the poet's complete attention that Rachel almost thought the girl was going to jump up and down in excitement. With her bright, eager face, the girl seemed to be giving him her breathless little smile as if it were the costliest gift she had. And Corbin was returning her gaze with focused attention. *My God,* Rachel thought. *That's what he takes seriously?* She decided that Corbin had never looked more vulpine.

She pushed her way back through the crowd as rudely as she had pushed her way to its front as if she had just discovered in herself a distaste for crowds. Everyone she nudged out of her way seemed to have a bad smell. Then she reached the sidewalk. As far as she knew, she was safe. Corbin had been too wrapped up in that little blonde to notice that she was there.

Within ten days of that day, she had discovered that she could enroll in an accelerated teacher preparation course, beginning the next month, at California State University at Northridge and had moved out of her parents' house with as little explanation as she had given them when she moved into it. Bringing a few of her belongings to the new apartment her parents had paid the first month's rent for on Reseda Boulevard in Reseda, she set up her apartment in the most monastic way she could think of, with a second-hand couch, a coffee table to eat on, and a portable TV on a cart at the end of the room. In the bedroom, she put a twin bed mattress directly on the floor. The austerity of the apartment would be her freedom, her drawing a line between herself and everything she had wanted and suffered for. She would practice isolation as if it were an art. She would renounce, but she would not repent. She would shape a habit of life as rigorous and as chaste as possible. She hoped and expected never to have a sexual thought again.

After a year of accelerated study, she had emerged in the spring of 1974 with a teaching certificate. As she had done during her time in Riverside, she spent her free hours (the ongoing financial support of her parents had given her many of them) haunting the precincts of a neighboring Catholic Church, St. Teresa of Avila, just over the Ventura Freeway in Encino, attending Mass daily, but never taking communion, never making confession. To do either of these things seemed to her a form of cheating, a form of breaking the discipline she had imposed on herself.

If she was a believer, which she denied, she was one who despite herself believed and trembled. She used her unbelief as a way of denying herself consolations she had not earned. She treated her alienation from the resources of faith as a kind of penance, and her renunciation, even of the consolations of religion, began to take on for her a kind of religious force, the stern rule of a negative monastic sect.

By the summer of 1974, she had settled on the idea of teaching in a parochial school as a career appropriate to her design of self-control. She had noticed that the two priests at St. Teresa of Avila had grown accustomed to the sight of her, sitting quietly in the pews at early Mass every day. Perhaps they imagined they knew something about her, a sinner borne down by grief, perhaps by death, which her severe manner and her austere clothing would have given them reason to believe her to be. Nevertheless, although she never seemed to miss a day, her very posture made it clear that she did not want to be known.

In the beginning of December 1979, a few weeks into her renewed affair with Corbin, when her prohibition about his knowing anything about her that did not take place in the bedroom had begun to relax, he asked her why, since she was so obviously not a believer, she seemed in every other way to be Catholic. They were seated on her ruinous couch and still, for the moment, fully dressed.

"With Catholicism, I am a sinner, but without it I am simply a neurotic. As a sinner, I live in a world with meaning although I am on the wrong side of that meaning. But as a neurotic, I live in a world that doesn't mean anything at all."

Corbin gave a little smile. "Why not just say that your neurosis makes good use of your Catholicism? It's a convenient cover for your doing what you want to do anyway."

Rachel took a second to respond, gathering her forces. "That's just like you to say, Tom. But if you really believed it, you wouldn't be here."

"What do you think my being here means?"

"It means that you are like me. You tell yourself that you believe nothing and that everything is permitted to you. You think your cynicism frees you. But that freedom is so empty you could not bear it for one minute. If we know ourselves at all, we both know ourselves as sinners who will never be anything else. We, neither of us, face the choice of whether to be good or bad. We only have the choice of whether to be bad or to be nothing."

"That's not Catholicism. And I don't believe everything is permitted to me. I expect to pay for it."

"That's how you get away with everything. Because you think you'll have enough time for repentance between the stirrup and the ground. And you can't imagine that God won't be just as charmed by your little poem about the Virgin as all those girls were, the ones whom you talked into bed with it."

"You're sure that's all I meant by it?"

"Maybe that poem is what you wanted to believe about yourself, but it's not what you'll ever be. And you can't use it as a get out of jail card."

"No, I expect to pay. But I do hope to be redeemed in the end."

"Of course you do," Rachel said. "It's how you put up with yourself when you can't face who you are. And don't tell me that you do face who you are, because I see through it and I'm sure God does too."

Corbin thought about this. "I would have thought the whole point of Catholicism was redemption."

"Redemption." Rachel practically spat the word. "That's just a way of evading sin, not atoning for it. The only things that make me what I am are the ways I've gone wrong. Get rid of the wrong and you get rid of me. At least I don't lie to myself the way you do. I'm Catholic only in my own way. I belong to a church of one. A church that I am on the wrong side of. But without it, I am still only your plaything. Your cast-off plaything."

Of course, the priests and nuns at St. Teresa had no idea about her.

They must have felt, when Rachel approached the nun from the Sisters of the Immaculate Heart of Mary who served as the principal of the parochial school and applied to teach the fifth grade, that she was at least already somebody with an investment in the community. And so, in the fall of 1974, finally making her own living and finally cutting her ties with her parents, whom she stopped visiting even on Christmas and Thanksgiving, Rachel joined the seven other lay teachers and two nuns who were the faculty of the St. Teresa of Avila Elementary School.

All the other faculty saw of her private cult of renunciation was that she dressed a little more severely than the dress code for lay faculty required and that she did not allow herself to be known. With the other faculty, she behaved with the arctic reserve she might have used had her vows required her to give up social trivia as rigorously as they required her to give up the idea of redemption.

In taking this stance, she was distinctly out of touch not only theologically but culturally with the actual parish, which had thought of itself as convivial and welcoming, especially to the Spanish-speaking Catholics who were an increasing presence in the region. The junior priest, Father Alvarado, who had just finished seminary and had arrived at St. Teresa bursting with the ideas and cultural mindset that had swept through the Church in the immediate aftermath of the second Vatican council, played the guitar and spoke both Spanish and Tagalog fluently. The senior priest, Father LaTour, was a severe Quebecois of the old school. Between the two of them, there would be something for everyone in their increasing and increasingly complex parish.

The lay faculty, all of them women, ranging in age from their early twenties to their middle fifties, were very friendly with each other, and three of them had attended elementary school at St. Teresa. Every Friday, they got together for modest drinks and Cuban dinners at the Versailles restaurant a few blocks down Ventura Boulevard. Rachel went with them for the first week and ate a modest plate of Ropa Vieja and plantain fritters, but drank not even a single glass of sangria. She took just enough part in the conversation to avoid being thought of as rude, but did not really open herself to the other faculty any more than she had to. It could not be said that she never attended a similar event again, because not going to dinner at all with the other teachers would have made her more conspicuous than going to dinner with them only a few times a year. Once Rachel overheard the young kindergarten teacher complain to the Principal that she was haughty and snobbish, but the Principal took the view that Rachel was a wounded bird and that it would not do to press her very hard.

Her students, she knew, did not think she was a wounded bird, and indeed were frequently terrified of her, although she never bullied them, and never showed temper in front of her class, unlike even some more popular teachers. In fact, she was patient and forbearing with her students, thoroughly prepared for every class, and even a fair grader. But she never showed warmth towards her students, even those who sought to cultivate her favor by answering questions readily in class or by staying after class to wash the blackboards. Through the open windows, Rachel heard them on the playground. The children said she was always angry at something and that they wanted to make sure that it would never be at them.

23

*L*YING IN BED WITH RACHEL ONE LATE THURSDAY AFTERNOON IN early January of 1980 as the time for picking up Jack at his after-school came and went without his even telling Susan that it would be her who would have to pick him up, Corbin told himself that only in the last few weeks had he begun to discover what love really was. He had learned that love demanded everything; that love humbled pride; that it fulfilled and destroyed him at the same moment. Loving Rachel was both his destiny and his fate; it was what he was made for, but it was also what he had coming to him, a fitting culmination to a life of pretense and the empty exploitation of women that pretense had bought him.

When Rachel had slapped him in the car in the restaurant parking lot, she had intended only to humiliate him, but she had also opened his eyes. He had always wanted to know reality although nothing he ever knew was real. This was the reality that Rachel had awakened him to: that everything he had been and done was nothing, that we are all nothing, that everything we call life is merely our daily little portion of death. To burn everything down was not just consummation but transcendence. With Rachel, he felt the promise of being able to push through life into something beyond life, something beyond mere flesh and its desires, something beyond mere feelings and the little mes and yous that have them. This is what love is, he thought, that feeling of being at the same time nothing and everything, that fact of being at the same time everything and nothing.

Rachel told Corbin that the only virtue she could claim for herself over the last few years was an unflinching honesty, and he knew that it was that honesty that gave her an erotic hold over him. He had always had the advantage in every relationship, even in his marriage with Susan, but he had from the very first moment lost the advantage in his relationship with Rachel, and that experience of losing control was frightening and thrilling. Whatever else he had gone on to do in life, he still knew what his role had been with Rachel, and however he might explain or extenuate himself to himself, he knew she knew differently, and he knew she would never let him evade what he really was. And indeed, that was one of the reasons he was drawn to her, because the debt to her he couldn't repay itself radiated sexual fascination for him, a reckoning with something that however dark was at least something undeniably true, true to what he finally was.

Rachel stirred awake, and, smiling to herself, climbed over him, straddling his hips with her knees. As she moved back and forth against him, she began to whisper to him.

It was to her, not to Susan, Rachel insisted, looking down into Corbin's aroused face with glittering eyes, that Corbin had always been unfaithful. "Even the first time you laid eyes on Susan, you chose her over me. The first kiss you gave Susan was something you owed to me. Every minute you have spent with Susan has been a separate act of betrayal of me."

He shifted beneath her, involuntarily responding to her, rocking with her as she rode him.

"But you didn't see that," Rachel went on, still in an angry whisper. "You were too shallow to see that. You forgot who you were. And you gave yourself to that slip, that waif, that never quite a woman. She heard you read, I'm sure. She looked up to you. And she was green enough to believe that your poems showed you'd be tender with her in bed. She could never really know you. But I was waiting for you, waiting until you came to yourself and came back to me. And you still have a price to pay. I didn't wait all those years just to start where we left off."

Corbin couldn't help himself, and had to say something. "Why do you have to speak about her that way? Susan doesn't deserve that."

"Why are you here if you are going to defend her?" She had not stopped rocking back and forth on him as she spoke.

"You're lucky to have me," she said, her breath quickening a little, "Otherwise you'd believe your own bullshit. And then where would you be? There'd just be no truth for you any more after that, and no reality, and no way back. That's what back in CCD they used to call a Sin Against

166

the Holy Spirit, the kind there's no forgiving."

He didn't know what to say. But he couldn't break off his gaze into her face, which had begun to flush. Suddenly, his thought turned to Susan, and as he looked up into Rachel's straining face, he felt himself to be something filthy. He would have to make this up to Susan when he got home. He would bring her to bed. And making love to Susan again, as he always had, would not scare him the way all this scared him.

Rachel put her hands on both sides of his face and held him firmly, so he had to look into her eyes. He turned his mind back to Rachel as she rode him. She wasn't going to leave his question unanswered.

"Why do I speak about her that way? Because it turns you on when I abuse her," she said, looking straight into his eyes, "And it turns you on when I tell you how bad you've been to her."

She placed her hands on his shoulders, pinning him to the bed with her weight. It was cruel of him to betray Susan in bed, she went on, but it was more cruel to get her hopes up about him, and more cruel still to keep up in her the illusion that she could do anything to change his nature.

And Susan's faith in him did him no favors because Susan was totally wrong about what it is to love somebody. She didn't love Corbin as he was, but only as he wanted to be, as if he could be someone for whom sex did not always bring with it the shadow of exploitation.

Still riding him, Rachel jeered at the idea that such a thing was even possible: "If she doesn't know that sex always involves exploitation, it's because she's the exploited one. And the reason she doesn't know that, is that being exploited is what she really wants. That's why she lets you trample her. Because she thinks it means something that you feel bad about how you treat her. And because she's let sex make a fool of her."

As he climaxed into her, she smiled to herself, then looked up at the ceiling. Corbin clinched his eyes shut, ashamed, but still shuddering.

By the middle of April, Rachel was pressing Corbin to come out to his wife about his ongoing affair. "You are not sparing her by lying to her," she said to him as he was hurrying into his clothes and rushing to safety. "You are only compounding the pain you are going to cause her later."

167

Corbin knew that at some point in the not very distant future he would give in to this pressure. Grasping at straws, Corbin argued that if Rachel had had a prior claim on him, then Paul Bishop, whom they had both treated shabbily, had a prior claim on her, and that both of them had unfinished business with him, unsettled obligations to him.

"You know what's happened to him, don't you?" Corbin was rapidly buttoning his shirt.

Rachel scoffed. "What hasn't happened to him would be more like it."

But Corbin would not be put off the track by this remark even when she raised the stakes with him.

Why would anything that became of Paul Bishop matter to him at all? Paul Bishop, Rachel jeered, who thought that the way to a woman's heart was by baking fruit pies for her. Paul Bishop, who felt he had to ask permission to hold a girl's hand. Paul Bishop who, in bed with a girl, behaved as if he were mortally afraid that she might break.

"You want to ask him for permission for us to love each other? Why don't you ask your mother, too, while you are at it?" This as Corbin was rushing out the door.

But Corbin, who had begun always to fold to her under pressure, stood his ground, because what he had done to Bishop years before was still a sore point with him. Bishop had been his friend; Bishop had looked up to him. All through the ups and downs of Bishop's relationship with Rachel Lake it was to Corbin Bishop had turned for help. And in the crisis over what Bishop had called her religious conversion, which is to say the crisis that followed Rachel's earlier betrayal of Bishop with Corbin and the abortion of the child she was not certain which of them had begotten, it was to Corbin that Bishop had turned for advice. It was Corbin who had accompanied him on his ill-fated pilgrimage, the journey that ended in the cathedral in Gallup, New Mexico, and Bishop had had no suspicion of the false position Corbin had been in the whole time. As Corbin's renewed relationship with Rachel took that deeper and darker turn that Corbin insisted on thinking of as a turn to love, to love as it actually was rather than love as we might wish it to be, his unfinished business with Paul Bishop began to weigh on him more and more heavily.

The subject of Bishop weighed on him so heavily that it even came up between him and his wife. Corbin did not give Susan any of the details, of course, but he did mention that something that had happened years ago between him and his friend had begun to bother him, to really bother him. Susan could not have helped but be aware that something had gone deeply amiss with her husband. So she suggested that if he really wanted to mend fences with his oldest friend he might find a way to give a poetry reading at his friend's university in Nevada, as a pretext for seeing him and setting whatever old ghosts were haunting him at rest.

The Chair in Reno clearly thought it was very odd to schedule a poetry reading of some importance in the last couple of days of the semester when the minds of even the best students would probably be on other things. But the offer seemed too good for him to pass up, and the expenses Corbin had proposed seemed so nominal, so unbelievably modest, that he agreed that taking up this offer would be a good thing to do even if the date would make attendance at the event thin.

"You actually want to drive up to Reno to ask Paul Bishop's permission to take up a life with me?" Rachel asked, that evening, in bed. "Do you also plan to come clean to him about what we did together all those years ago? Or do you think that asking this question of him won't set his memory working?"

24

*P*AUL'S PLAN WAS TO WORK STEADILY THROUGH THE WEEKEND at the seventy-five final papers he had to grade, to proctor the three sections of final exams he was planning to give on Monday, and to drive to Riverside again on Tuesday morning, so he would be ready to take Susan to her treatment at Loma Linda hospital on Wednesday morning, May 14.

Not knowing what to expect from Susan's treatments, whether he would be going back to Riverside every few weeks, or whether he would spend the entire summer there taking care of her, Paul had canceled his summer classes. His Writing Program Director was surprised by this request—he had always been among the most reliable of her instructors—but because he had been so reliable, she didn't raise an objection about it. Registration was still in flux anyway, and if she had to she could give his classes, even at the last minute, to other instructors who could use the extra money. Without the few thousand dollars his summer teaching would earn him, however, money would be tight for the next year. But he was used to a very small life, and living a smaller one did not scare him.

Late on Saturday morning, as he worked his way through his stack of papers on the Formica dinette table, he noted which students had done something in May they had not been capable of in January, and which students had coasted by, writing papers that never got beyond their first thoughts on the subject, or, worse yet, repeated in unconvincing tones the things they thought he believed.

He lost his focus almost as soon as he began, brooding over what Rachel had said to him in her angry phone call earlier that morning. Paul knew that Rachel, who had seen at a glance in the hallway in Independence how it was with him, believed that he had become what he became because of what she and Corbin had done to him long before. She had practically thrown it in his face: you won't get back what we took from you by falling in love with Susan, and if that's what's driving you, nothing good will come of it for either of you. Corbin must have felt the same way, or he would not have felt he had to ask Paul's permission to live with Rachel.

But they were wrong about this. What burdened him wasn't what Rachel and Corbin had done to him, which he hadn't known about at the time anyway, but his own failure of nerve as Rachel suffered alone through the aftermath of her abortion. He kept coming back to that moment when, as he rushed across the continent to her side after her pleading letter to him, he had stopped to follow the Stations of the Cross in the cathedral in Gallup and had faltered and turned back home. That moment had changed her as much as it had changed him. He was shocked by her, and he was shocked also by his response to her.

At the moment of his flinch in Gallup, he hadn't actually chosen to abandon Rachel because he didn't have it in him to choose any one direction over any other. He had merely lost his will to go on and had given up, and the act of giving up had itself confirmed the unfaced misgiving that had brought him to a halt in the first place. And now he knew, knew past unknowing, what he really was. Because when he read her letter, he had heard in it the whisper of death, of the suicide that was not yet a plan but was already a delicious temptation. He knew that whenever Rachel was by herself, death nuzzled softly, catlike, up against her body, always demanding to be stroked, always kissing her with finicking kisses, its warm breath brushing her face. Paul had not saved her, and if she had come through anyway, he still knew that he had left her to face that temptation alone. He had come home to Willimantic, and Rachel had come back to Storrs, and for a few months, they had both pretended that nothing had happened between them at the end of December. And indeed, nothing had happened, and that nothing stood immobile between them until their relationship collapsed that March.

He remembered how something had made him stop stock-still just as he came back into the sanctuary after the little wounded sparrow had come back to life and beaten that life out against the glass of the Rose Window. As he stared at Corbin kneeling by the dead bird, he had suddenly known that he would do nothing for Rachel, and that she was beyond his reach. A quiet, dull sound had filled his ears, the sound of nothing. This was death's world, he had thought, and the vault over his head was as dark as space, as empty as his heart. He had felt a chill go through him, and he couldn't move. He didn't want to move again. Every thought left him, every desire, and every hope. Whatever he had been didn't matter, and whatever he had wanted to be was unreal. Before he knew it, he had given himself up to the dull sound, and his will drained away, and he became a kind of nothing. After a few moments, it was as if he had never been human at all.

When the angry sexton pushed past him—shouting something he didn't make out—Bishop came to himself. Something had happened to him that he knew he would never get over.

And then he had left Rachel to live, or to die, he didn't know which. It no longer mattered which.

Now, sitting at his messy table in Reno years later, he knew also that under the right circumstances he was capable of doing to Susan what he had done to Rachel, just as Rachel had said on the phone. Rachel did not know when his nerve would fail, but she had no doubt it would, and when Susan would need him the most.

Suddenly, as he thought this, again he saw Rachel's face, flushed, straining, every muscle tense with sexual climax, just as he had imagined it when he had been talking with her on the phone that morning. This time he did not fight off the vision: *Is this how she looked when she was making love to Corbin? Or is it how she looked making love to me, but thinking at every moment about Corbin?* Those two thoughts chased each other in circles, each time giving him a jolt of anguish, but also, and this was mortifying, a little thrill of pleasure, until he had to put his head in his hands and close his eyes, brought to a standstill by shame and recognition.

What had stung him most in Rachel's call, more even than her claim that his attraction to Susan was posthumous revenge on Corbin, was her accusation that he was using Jack's affections to get to Susan. It was a lie! A lie! A lie! But she had gotten under his skin. That he might fail someone at the moment of truth was something he always knew he was capable of; that he might be using a little child instrumentally was another matter.

Was he really trying to make Jack depend on him? Or wasn't he just responding to the immediate emergency as anyone would have done? Yes, he did want Jack to like him, and to trust him. And in fact Jack did like him, and did trust him, as far as he could judge, anyway. Was that such a bad thing? If he had not wanted it so much, Paul could have been more certain of his answer.

What Jack was in for in the next few months weighed on him heavily, and how painful every aspect of his future would be hurt him more and more every time he allowed himself to think about it. Paul's impotent pity for Susan and Jack overwhelmed him with a sense of his moral incompetence, which by that afternoon had driven every other thought out of his mind, including that of his still largely ungraded paper set, which became yet one more of the many small things he didn't know how to manage, and evidence that he would never be able to manage the big things when it came to it.

He had assumed that Susan would call him between eight and nine that Saturday evening, after Jack had dropped off to sleep, if indeed sleep would be in the offing for him after the day Paul was certain Jack would have had. But at about seven, Paul could no longer contain himself and dialed her number himself. To his surprise, it was Jack who answered the phone.

"Hello, Paul," (he was no longer Mr. Bishop to Jack). "Do you want to speak to my mom? She's washing the dishes."

"I was going to ask her how you were doing, Jack. Would it be all right if I asked you that myself?"

"I'm all right." Jack paused for several seconds. Was he wondering whether it was just a polite question? Then he picked up the thread after all. "She's not all right, though." He said this in a tone designed not to be overheard easily. "She told me that she's really, really sick."

"She told me that too. You must be worried."

"Please don't tell her that."

"Of course, she already knows you are worried. She wants to face it with you."

"I can't make her get better."

"It helps her to know she can still be your mother, no matter what

173

happens."

"But she'll always be my mother."

"Yes. And that's just what she wants to be now."

"But all I do is worry about her."

"That's all I do too," Paul said.

Jack took this in.

"No. You help her," Jack said.

"And so do you. More than I do. Loving her helps her. And loving you helps her."

The line fell quiet as Jack thought about this.

"Okay."

Jack was going to soldier it through, whatever it took. And he counted on Paul to soldier it through with him.

Paul felt a wave of gratitude. "Yes. And we'll both help her as much as we can."

"Here's my mom."

After a second, Paul heard Susan's voice.

"I'm sorry, Paul. I was up to my elbows in a sink of greasy dishes. I had to dry my hands." She was brisk and bright, as if, just for that moment, the only thing on her mind had been the dishes.

"I'm sorry I jumped the gun. I was worried how today went."

"I'm very glad you called." He knew she wanted him to know that. She gave the pleasantry a little more emphasis than it required. But she wasn't going to answer his question. At least not while Jack was within earshot.

Paul pictured her at the phone, practical, cheerful, wrapping and un-wrapping the headset cord around her wrist as she talked, as in command of herself as she had been when he had watched her making sandwiches in her kitchen on Thursday, just as if she could keep it up forever.

"I know you can't tell me now how it's going. But I guess I already know."

"I couldn't hear exactly what he told you, over the running water. But I got the drift." She thought a second and lowered her voice. "I'm glad he told you himself what he's thinking. He keeps trying to keep me from worrying about him."

174

"He's a brave boy."

This comment gave her a second's pause.

"Yes, but he shouldn't have to be. It only makes it worse for him."

Paul felt a challenge in this, an occasion he had to rise to. She wasn't looking for assurance that all would be well because she knew better. What she wanted was for Paul to be ready for whatever was coming. Until they couldn't keep it up any longer, Susan knew they would all have to pretend. But that they were pretending was an open secret among all three.

"Will you still be able to take me to Loma Linda on Wednesday?"

"Yes. That's why I called. What time is your appointment?"

"Not till one. They'll want me to stay an hour or two after. It's a new medication, and I'm taking a huge dose. They want to be sure it will be okay."

Paul knew that Jack was hearing this information and that Susan was speaking circumspectly.

"I'll call Motel 6 and make another reservation."

"Nonsense. You should stay here. I may need you Wednesday night. If there's a reaction, that's when it will likely be. I'll put the fold-out cot in Tom's study. And stay Tuesday night too. I'm making dinner for you that night, and I'm not taking no for an answer."

"Sure. But don't go to any trouble."

"I'm not that good a cook," she said. Paul could tell she was smiling. She added, "So it's no trouble. It's just a lasagna."

She paused a second. "Excuse me while I close the door."

Then he heard her from a distance. "Jack, I might be a few minutes. You can turn on the Betamax if you want."

Then she was back. "I'm a bad parent," she laughed. "I keep telling myself not to put him in front of the TV, and then I have to."

"I can't imagine a better parent."

"I can," she laughed again. Then, calmly, "I just want to thank you for helping me so much."

She said this more gravely than she had to. It wasn't just a pleasantry. But exactly what Susan was getting at he didn't know. Paul could not figure out how to respond. In a way he didn't want to explain, he was

175

invested in seeing her through her treatment. But he heard in her voice that there was something at stake in it for her that she too didn't want to explain. Absently, he straightened the pile of ungraded papers in front of him and put it aside.

"I'm doing it for Tom," he said, plausibly.

"Whatever your reason is, I'm grateful to you. And you've gone way out of your way."

"My term is over. There's not much else I should be doing."

"When your term ends, do you always drive hundreds of miles to help people you've just met?"

"No. First time. But I'm very glad I'm doing this. I really can't explain why I want to help you with this."

"However it is, it's kind of you. And I'm very, very grateful. Astonished, really. But grateful first of all."

He heard in this that she knew he had a reason that he kept to himself. But she was grateful enough that she didn't worry about what that reason was. *But only because she doesn't know what it is*. He also heard in her voice something she too had wanted to tell him, but had hesitated to say.

25

*O*N FRIDAY MORNING, THE DAY AFTER THE ARRAIGNMENT, WHILE Paul was making his long drive back to Reno, Susan had gotten Jack up and dropped him off at kindergarten as if she were going to a normal day of work at the clinic. At the clinic, Claire brought Susan to an examining room and closed the door behind them. Susan sat on the paper cover of the examination table, her feet not reaching the step, her heels kicking softly against the metal of the table's end. She thought how strange it was to be sitting there, where patients sat, feeling vulnerable and naked even while fully clothed, rather than in the metal doctor's chair at the table's foot, her usual station, where the healthy person sat, the one with the authority. Claire pulled up that chair and looked her silently in the face for a few seconds, uncertain about where to begin.

Claire said that she had just the previous day learned about Corbin's murder, and had called but Susan had been already on her way up to Independence for the arraignment. How was she doing? Susan knew that Claire wasn't just talking about the murder. Susan found herself telling Claire that she had been able to manage so far by trying never to think more than a few days ahead, as if the question were only about how Susan had kept up with all there was for her to do. It was apparent to her that Claire didn't believe she was holding her own quite as well as she said she was, and indeed she wasn't, but Susan wasn't going to cry at the workplace, not with Claire, who was her ally, and her doctor, but also her boss. Only at home, and only after Jack was asleep, was it safe to cry. But even then Susan was afraid that if she ever completely gave way to her grief she would lose herself forever.

Claire asked Susan for details about how Jack was taking the news of his father's death, and the news of his mother's illness. Susan had to confess to her that she hadn't raised her illness with Jack yet, because he was still coming to terms with what had happened to his father. She

177

didn't like to be pressed about Jack's feelings, or even more to be pressed about her own feelings, as if she were some fragile creature. She was perfectly under control, she was sure. And she was sure at the same time that Claire would never believe that. But she promised Claire that she would break the news to Jack that night. She suppressed a little flash of annoyance with Claire, who assumed that Susan was hesitating to face her son. But Susan in fact was hesitating. *Claire is always the big sister,* Susan thought to herself.

Susan had promised herself to approach her upcoming treatment as a doctor rather than as a patient, as someone who practices "the sharp compassion of the healer's art," rather than as someone helplessly suffering. To see herself as the one who was mortally ill felt like running headlong into the path of an oncoming train. While Susan was trying to control herself, Claire was watching her kindly. Suddenly, noticing that kindness, Susan had to close her eyes to keep from bursting into tears, unable to face her chief resident's sympathy. *She knows what's going to happen to me,* Susan thought. She clenched her teeth and turned her face away, ashamed of herself. Then, as quickly as it had broken over her, the wave passed. Susan hoped she had not given herself away, but then she noticed that her fists were clenched at her sides, and that Claire had noticed it too. Claire took up her right hand and stroked it, and Susan let her. Claire looked at her warmly, but Susan was still afraid to meet her gaze or to concede how close a call she had just had.

Claire gave Susan a moment to catch her breath, and, recovering herself, Susan sat herself up straight, again holding her head as high as if she were a statue of an Egyptian queen. Claire went on to brief her about what to expect from next Wednesday's injection. There was no effective chemotherapy for melanoma, and metastatic patients like Susan were usually given only palliative treatment. Interferon was something about which very little was known. How effective it might be was a mystery, though it showed promise *in vitro*. Even how human patients would tolerate it was unknown. Susan should understand, Claire said, that it was unlikely that a treatment in such an early stage of development would actually save her life, but lessons would be learned from the course of her treatment that might save other people later. Susan should expect a very high but transient fever, first of all, and days of fatigue, with nausea, anorexia, abnormal blood counts, and possibly a host of other unanticipated side effects. The plan was to give her an injection of interferon every three weeks. Hearing the formal, clinical language that Claire, as a sign of professional respect, used with her helped her face the facts calmly, like something she was reading about rather than living, even though what Claire had said was in fact chilling.

Susan was not afraid of the side effects; they were an enemy she expected and knew how to fight, far different from the silent treason in her body, and far different from the mirror-house of despair and death in which she had lost herself in the Owens Valley the previous day. Next to fighting those things, the thought of fighting these side effects braced her up, like a soldier at last getting a clear sight of the enemy, like the horse in *Job*. Better even a losing fight for her life than passively drowning in this hopeless grief and fear.

Now at last I'll finally know what I am.

Susan saw that her response, that she was almost eager to try her strength against the side effects of her treatment, puzzled Claire. She often puzzled her chief resident, who, she knew, believed she understood what was best for Susan better than Susan did. Since their intern year Susan had liked Claire and trusted her, because Claire had made it her project to look out for her, and Susan knew she had reason to be grateful to her. But Claire also somehow knew, although Susan had never said a word about it, that Susan's marriage with Corbin was a problem. For this reason Susan did not always confide in her.

"I have to ask this, Susan, so please forgive me."

"Anything. I know what you have to do." But she couldn't help thinking: *Here comes the common sense. Brace yourself.*

"I don't think you can go through these treatments by yourself. I can organize the residents to look after you if you need it. Have you made plans?"

Susan smiled at her impenetrably. "Actually, yes, I have made plans. It's strange how it happened, but I did make plans." Susan saw that her mentor was surprised by this, but also, warned by that last sentence, a bit wary about those plans. Susan was so eager to show her that she was capable of making plans herself that she forgot to thank Claire for her foresight. "When my husband was murdered," Susan said, "his oldest friend got in touch with me."

"How well do you know him?"

"I only just met him."

"And you're sure he's up to this?"

"He doesn't think so, but I do." Susan spoke as though she had no idea that what she said was strange. She let her supervisor savor the strangeness of her answer, and Claire was at a loss to reply and could not keep that out of her face. Playing with her friend this way made Susan, for a moment, feel a little less powerless, especially since she knew that Claire had always felt that Susan had let her husband dominate her. So Susan let her be mystified for a few moments about Paul. It was hopeless to persuade her anyway. But Susan also didn't want to explain what Paul was to her, because she didn't want to face it herself.

But how stupid of me. She just has to love Paul. They have to work together. I have to make her love him. She took a breath and looked Claire straight in the face.

"Because I saw the kindness in him, Claire. Out of the blue, and I don't know why, he came down from Reno to take Jack and me up to Independence for the arraignment. I had to take Jack with me; he couldn't be without me, not then. Paul took care of us all day. And when Jack melted down I saw how good Paul really was."

With every sentence Susan felt herself in deeper trouble. How could she explain to a reasonable adult how seeing Paul's spontaneous kindness to Jack made her spill her guts to him about how sick she was? And how could she explain how, hearing from her about the desperate situation she was in, instantly Paul had decided to see her through to the end? She had needed help, and there he was. Claire would never understand it, because Susan didn't understand it. But Susan had no doubt about what she was doing.

"But why did he do this?" Claire said, "He doesn't know you. And you don't know him. And why should what you're going through matter to him so much that he'll drop everything and take care of you for months?"

180

She thinks that this is just typical of me. Susan who is a good person and a good doctor but always such a fool about men. What does she think I want from him? Or he from me?

"I think he was just called to do it." Susan said this as if it would settle the matter.

"Called to do it? I don't even know what that means." But Susan had given up expecting Claire to understand, and the fact that Claire didn't understand was only more proof to Susan that she was right to depend on Paul. Susan had foreclosed explaining herself to Claire because the reason for her faith in Paul was something she could barely face.

As we were driving back from Independence yesterday I gave in to despair, and he saved me without even knowing I was in trouble. Hearing her describe her illness, Paul had promised to do his best for her and for Jack, had promised it so easily and naturally and without the slightest hesitation that there was no doubting him. She had been foundering, and he pulled her to safety, just like that. *He's so good to us. I don't know why and I don't care why. Jack and I will both have more need of him. And I know he'll come through for us to the end, however little he thinks he can manage it.*

But this she did not tell Claire. And she tried not to think about it herself, because even the memory of that moment of despair scared her. *I'm never going to wish for death again. I have to live this life to the end. I'm just lucky he was there to catch me when I fell.* And she remembered how, as they sped through the desert at night, long after he thought she had fallen asleep next to Jack in the rear seat, she watched him calmly driving, the back of his head slightly moving back and forth as he steered the car, completely unaware of what he had done for her. *Let him never know how close I came. But let him keep holding me up. And thank God for him.*

Susan's strange phrase about Paul's being called to take care of her put an end to the conversation. Everything Susan had told Claire was true, but she knew it wouldn't persuade Claire because it was none of the things Susan had said, but how Paul had saved her at that moment she was afraid to tell Claire about, that had made up her mind about Paul. And that moment of despair still frightened her too. Paul did not have any idea that he had saved her. But he did want to help her; he needed to help her and she needed the help too much to ask why. Whatever his reasons might have been, and they must have had to do with his complicated relationship with Tom, Susan knew she was not mistaken about his kindness. She also knew very well what else she wanted from Paul, what she had no right to ask from him. And what Jack would need from him. She was ashamed of those things because she had nothing left in her to give him in return. So she told herself she didn't want anything from him but the help he had offered, until she almost believed what she was saying.

26

$\mathcal{P}$AUL ARRIVED AT MASSACHUSETTS AVENUE JUST AS SUSAN WAS about to put a very large lasagna, large enough to feed the three of them for several days, into the oven. She was proud of herself. She told him she had never thought of herself as much in the kitchen, and mostly cooked whatever she could throw together out of what she had in the refrigerator. Corbin had been the cook. Knowing that she might not be herself for several days, she had taken the afternoon off from her work at the hospital to prepare enough food to last.

All through the dinner, Susan smiled at him, and Paul knew that she was taking pleasure in the pleasure he took in the meal she had made for him. She was delighted when he asked for a second helping, and they all enjoyed the vanilla ice cream with strawberries. Paul wanted to do the dishes when dinner was done—the habit of doing the dishes when he was a dinner guest had begun with him in graduate school—but Susan insisted that Jack and she had a ritual about it and that Jack would be disappointed if he didn't at least do the drying. So Susan set up a sort of assembly line, in which Paul would wash a dish, Jack would dry it, and Susan would put it away in the cabinet. For an entire hour, they had all kept the thought of death at bay.

How lovely she is, Paul thought, his mind full of her. *Let me do something good for her. Let me just be with her. Let me be good enough to want nothing more than that.*

After dinner, Susan suggested that Paul read *The Lion, the Witch, and the Wardrobe* to them. She said that however the next few months would play out a great deal of that time would be spent by Paul reading to Jack, and she wanted Jack to understand that having Paul read to him was not a poor substitute for her reading to him. Her pretext was that Paul would be better than she was at "doing the voices," as Corbin had been. Paul wondered whether he was really any good at that. But he was glad to retrieve the book from Corbin's study, and as they sat together on the orange couch he was surprised by a flash of happiness.

"Should we start the book over, or do you remember what was going on from before?" he said.

"It's okay to start the book over," Jack said.

"He likes to hear things more than once anyway."

So Paul began reading the story, but had only gotten a few sentences in when Jack asked how the Pevensie children happened to come into the Professor's care, how they happened to be separated from their parents. Lewis wrote in an offhand way about their being evacuated from London during the Blitz, as if it were an experience that was so common as to be commonplace, an everyday inconvenience rather than a traumatic upheaval. Of course, these children were afraid, anxious for their parents, and worried about their world. But they seemed not to say one word about it to each other. Paul found himself explaining what the Blitz was, and how children had to be rushed from London to the homes of distant strangers to be safe from the air raids.

"If the Blitz were to happen here, where would we go?"

"Somewhere safe, I'm sure."

"But I doubt there'd be a magic wardrobe there," Susan added.

"They never seem to mention the Blitz again," Paul said, "or even the Second World War, the worst days of which were going on just when that novel is set."

"Because it was something everyone was going through," Susan said. "It must have seemed selfish to foreground it. As if it would have made their own sufferings seem more important than everyone else's."

Paul read on, reading Lucy's foray into the back of the wardrobe, how she came out into the snow of Narnia and encountered the faun Tumnus at the lamppost.

"What did you think of Tumnus, Jack?" Paul asked.

"He might have been scary."

"Because he has goat legs and horns?"

"Yeah. But he was nice."

"People with umbrellas don't often seem scary." Susan said. "If anything, they seem fussy."

184

"Yes, that's it! Fussy is just what he is," Paul said. "And he says all these fussy things. I don't know anyone who says, 'Goodness gracious me!' "

"He's got good snacks, though," Jack said. "But watch out for what's coming."

And Paul read on, about how Tumnus burst into tears and told Lucy that he had been ordered by the White Witch, on pain of torture, to trap any humans he met and to deliver them to her. He hadn't been able to bring himself to betray her when it came to it and helped Lucy find her way back to the lamppost and to the wardrobe. But it had been a near thing. And in helping her escape, he had put himself in lasting danger because the cruel power, and the eyes and ears, of the White Witch, were everywhere.

"And you were telling me that World War II wasn't in this book," Susan said.

"I guess Lewis wanted us to know what it would be like to live under a tyranny. And that even nice British eccentrics who carry umbrellas and serve tea and cake would be hard-pressed not to collaborate with the dictators about turning strangers and fugitives over to the secret police."

"More reading, less talking," said Jack.

And Paul read the next chapter, where Edmund, who hadn't believed a word Lucy had said about there being another world at the back of the wardrobe, himself entered Narnia, and himself encountered the White Witch, who was proud, and cold, and beautiful, and completely in command at every moment, in her great white sleigh drawn by white reindeer and driven by a dwarf. Part way into the chapter, as Edmund found himself increasingly under the sway of the White Witch, warmed by her magic drink, and eating pieces of Turkish delight that only increased his hunger, Paul noticed that silent tears were rolling down Jack's face.

"Jack, what is it?"

"It's nothing, Paul. I'm okay." He wiped his face and pretended to smile.

"This is about as far as we got last time, where the White Witch gets control over Edmund," Susan said. "Tom read that part just the night before he went to Reno." Jack had climbed into his mother's lap.

Paul looked at Jack. "Is it too much? I'm so sorry."

"No," Jack said, "I spoiled it. I'm sorry. I was happy. Then it was strange to feel happy."

"Oh, baby," Susan said, stroking his hair, "Even when you are sad, you can be happy for a little while. It doesn't mean you aren't sad. I miss him too. And we didn't miss him any less when we were reading." She kissed him softly.

"I know that." He was still trying to smile. Paul felt helpless. *I'm an intruder here, stepping on the grief they have to work out with each other. I don't have a right to be here.*

Paul wondered whether it was for his father or for his mother that Jack was crying. Jack hadn't sobbed, and he wasn't sobbing now. But his eyes were still welling, and he was fighting to control his feelings. *Jack doesn't want her to know what he's feeling. So it must be her Jack is crying for.* All he could do was look at Jack. And worry about him. Paul watched and worried.

Then Jack noticed him looking at him. "I'm ready for you to read again," Jack said, after a few moments. But he obviously wasn't. *He's afraid and grieving, but in the middle of all that he's worried about whether he's hurting my feelings.* Paul didn't know how to respond, but he met Jack's look. Somehow what Jack saw on Paul's face settled him, and the boy gave Paul a look of recognition. From this look Paul understood that he had done something for Jack but he had no idea what it had been.

Susan was rocking Jack in her lap. "We'll all be mixed up for a long time, honey. We won't know whether to be happy or sad. I'll be feeling it just the same way you do." After a few minutes, he put his thumb in his mouth. And Susan held his head to her shoulder and stroked him.

She rocked Jack for quite a while, but that was as far as they read that night. But as Susan carried him off to bed, she flashed Paul a look of thanks over Jack's shoulder, and Paul wondered what he had done that she was thanking him for.

"It's good to have you here," Susan said, as they sat in the living room after Susan had put Jack to bed. "It's hard to face these things by yourself."

Susan began to tell him a story. In February, under Claire's supervision, she had performed her first thoracotomy, open chest surgery on a man in his forties who was thought to have mesothelioma. But when Susan had opened him, it was clear from the first moment that the man's case was hopeless. Susan had been upset that she had put the man through the brutal procedure for nothing. Claire had always told her that many of her patients would die and that she could not help any of them unless she held her own feelings at arm's length. Susan understood this fact in general, but that day she found it impossible to do. She kept her feelings under rein for the rest of the day, but when Tom came home that night, after Jack was asleep, she burst into tears.

Tom had held her and comforted her. Hearing her story, he had kissed her on the eyelids and told her that it was not her fault that her patient would die. His condition had been beyond help before she got there. She had used all her skill to help him, Tom had said, and that hadn't been able to save him because nobody could have saved him. But she had also heard him and comforted him and helped him come to terms with what was going to happen. She had not just taken care of him, Tom said, kissing her wet eyelids, but she had cared for him. "It mattered that it was you who took care of him," Tom said. He held her closely, and breathed into her ear. "You saw him as he was," he said softly, "not just as the face of his disease." Then she had put her arms around his neck, and he carried her to bed.

*P*aul wondered why Susan had told this story. She had said that it was because she was experiencing the difference between being a doctor and being a patient. But there was more to it than that. *She wants me to know that Tom loved her,* he thought, *because she knows that most people don't believe he did.* Paul was the one person, Susan must have believed, who would understand how she felt about Tom, who would know that the biggest decision she had ever made was not just a mistake.

And, listening to her, Paul believed her, despite everything else he knew about Tom. It wasn't just that she had loved Tom through it all. It was that whatever else he did Tom had loved her enough to want to find his way back to her, although he never did. Tom had been tender with her when she was at her most vulnerable, and Paul could not doubt that

Tom, at that moment, had meant what he said.

This story took place in February, Paul thought, *when Tom's affair with Rachel had been going on for three months.* Tom had probably made love to Rachel that very afternoon. Susan's cancer had already appeared, but she had still believed she could spare her family from knowledge about it. What did Tom really feel? How did he hope to set his life in order? *How can I ever make sense of him?* Paul wondered. He would never make sense of either of them—Susan or Tom. But he wouldn't give up on them either.

Watching him as he thought, Susan blushed. "I think I've said too much," she said.

"No. You should feel free. You can count on me."

She smiled at him and turned to go to her room.

"I'm glad that it's you taking care of me," she said, looking back over her shoulder at him as she left the room.

27

$\mathcal{B}$Y THE TIME PAUL WOKE UP—HE HAD BEEN NERVOUS ABOUT sleeping in Corbin's house, but he had also been exhausted—Susan was already frying eggs in the kitchen. Still in pajamas, he sat with Jack at the dinette.

"Over easy or sunny side up?"

"You choose."

"I never cook breakfast. But I thought today we'd need it."

Jack, however, a creature of habit, had stuck to his bowl of cereal.

"Paul, I'd like you to come with me when we drop Jack off at the Shetland school. You may have to do this by yourself tomorrow, and I want you to know the way. It's not far, but it's on the other side of Watkins, and you might find it tricky to get there."

"Are you going to the hospital to work today?" Jack said.

She was still at the stove, fiddling with the edges of the eggs with the spatula, not yet looking at Jack. But Paul saw that she had heard what Jack's question had really meant. Her eyes were puffy with sleeplessness. She set her teeth on her lower lip, then spoke firmly, looking at the skillet.

"No, Jack, I'm going to see my own doctor while you are at school. They are testing a new shot on me, and it might make me very sick tonight. That's why Paul is here, in case we need his help."

Wondering how he was taking this information, Paul glanced at Jack.

Susan flipped the eggs onto the plates with the toast and brought them to the dinette table where Paul had sat down with Jack. But Susan didn't sit down. Jack looked up at her, and Paul looked at Jack. It took her a second.

"I might have a fever tonight. That's why I want Paul to stay to help take care of us." She was controlling herself as she looked at Jack, and he noticed it. "I'm sure we can handle it. And I don't want you to be afraid about it. It's something I know will happen, and they wouldn't be giving me this medicine if they didn't think it would do me good." She said this a little more sharply than she must have planned to. Neither Paul nor Susan touched their eggs. And Susan still didn't sit down.

Jack sat stiffly in his chair, watching her, his face working. Susan came over to him and put her hands on his shoulders. But she wasn't going to lie to him.

"Will this shot make you better?" Jack looked up at her.

"I hope so." She had stopped herself from adding *I don't really know* out loud, but Paul saw that Jack had heard it anyway. Those three words, and their silent qualification, were as much as she was willing to say.

Susan looked Jack in the face. She had been blunter than she had intended, but it was too late to call it back. Jack did not want to cry. "It may be a messy few days, but nothing is going to happen that Paul and I can't manage." Jack was still trying not to cry.

She stroked his cheek and tried to smile for him. "It's okay, baby." But he didn't smile back, and he didn't say anything. "It's okay." She was still stroking his cheek. "I'll feel better tomorrow."

Jack still just looked up at her, not believing her, fighting to control himself for her. It was obviously not just the next few days he was worried about. She ran her fingers through his hair. Again, she tried to smile for him.

"I still know how to take care of you, honey. Nothing about that is going to change."

Jack had to look away from her, down at his bowl, fighting for control, not wanting, Paul guessed, his mother to read his face: she had no honest answer to give him about whether she would get better, and Jack had seen it.

Susan knelt down by him and kissed him behind his ear. "Nothing makes me happier, no matter how I feel, than taking care of you. That's what will make me feel better. That's what will help me get through all this." She put her arms around him and rocked with him for a minute, stroking his back, pressing his face to her cheek. He kissed her and closed his eyes. "You'll let me do that, won't you?"

"All right." He said this as if it were a concession. But Paul knew he had already stopped believing she was going to get better.

190

28

$\mathcal{A}$T THE CLINIC, SUSAN KNEW CLAIRE WANTED TO EXAMINE HER privately before administering the shot, so she asked Paul to stay in the waiting room. He nodded calmly and brought *Being Here* out of his pocket. When Claire entered, she noticed him and smiled. Susan decided not to be defensive with her about his coming. *She may have doubts about him, but she knows we are all on the same side.*

Mollified by Claire's glance at Paul, Susan opened to her. It was easier to accept Claire's attempts to help if she weren't going to be skeptical of Paul in the way she had been skeptical of Tom. *It would be different if she knew how I actually feel about him.* But even how Claire felt about Paul did not seem strange. It just seemed normal that someone would be sitting in the waiting room for her, ready to take her home. *It doesn't have to be any more than that.* She had to make herself believe this part.

What Claire wanted, once they were in the examining room, away from Paul, was to know whether Susan had living relatives who might take care of Jack after her death. "It may seem early to think about this," said Claire, "but melanoma moves quickly, and if this treatment doesn't work you may have only two or three months to figure it out."

Susan told Claire she had cousins in Oregon whose castoff clothes she had worn growing up, and who had told her that she would have been trailer trash had her mother been able to afford a trailer. She hadn't seen them since her mother moved to San Diego when she was twelve. Susan explained, "Tom's mother died a few years ago, of lung cancer. His father is retired, but has emphysema. And he has it pretty badly. He's been in the hospital twice since Christmas. Tom and he were in touch, but they haven't been close. They fought over the Vietnam War and never quite made up."

"Have you contacted him recently?"

"Since Tom's death? Yes, I called him in Connecticut to break the news to him."

"That must have been horrible for him."

"It's hard to think of anything worse than outliving your children." *Except leaving them alone in the world when they are little,* Susan thought.

"I imagine he took it hard. I certainly would have."

"I thought a shared grief might draw us together. But there'd been too much between him and Tom for too long. He was wary with me. Maybe he thought I blamed him. Anyway, he didn't want to sort that out now."

"Because he doesn't quite trust you?"

"Mostly because he's the kind of guy who has to lick his wounds in private. But it's true that he doesn't quite trust me."

"Does he know you're sick?"

"No, I haven't told him. Somehow, I just couldn't do it yet."

"How is he with Jack?"

"He's been good enough. But he never thought I was right for Tom. His wife thought I had boxed Tom into marrying me."

"That's so fucking unfair."

Susan looked at her, as surprised as she was touched by what Claire had said. *Of course she's on my side. And she has to ask these things.* Susan decided to let down her guard, something she had rarely done with Claire, who hadn't much liked Tom. Susan began, "I've tried not to make too much of it. But it's always been an issue. The whole thing was too quick for them. Besides, they had money, and they knew I didn't."

"Do you think he could put all that aside for Jack's sake?"

"You mean after I die? Probably. But he's sick. Not dying yet, but too sick to count on. And I'm not easy with leaving my son to be raised by someone who didn't like me."

"It looks like you're going to have to mend fences with your father-in-law."

"I don't want to think about that yet."

"This isn't a time for pride. Otherwise, Jack goes into foster care."

"All right. I'll think about it." Susan had thought about it, but she wouldn't face what her thought had been. She was hoping the solution would happen by itself, without her. That would make it easy.

29

By the time they were ready to pick up *The Lion, the Witch, and the Wardrobe*, it was clear that Susan was beginning to fade. As a precaution, just in case fatigue from her treatment came on her suddenly, she changed into her nightgown immediately after dinner. When she sat on the couch, she drew her legs up beside her, so she was almost leaning against Paul as he read. Jack leaned up against him from the other side, so as Paul read, he seemed as much to be reading a bedtime story to her as to Jack. Susan smiled whenever Paul happened to catch her eye. She kept reaching behind Paul's back to tousle Jack's hair, which annoyed her son in the way he loved her to do.

Around midnight, Susan suddenly awoke, hearing herself cry out in her dream, "Now, Tom. Now. Please. *Please*." As she came to herself she heard Paul rushing to her room. By the time he got there she was fully awake, sitting upright. "My fever is coming up now. I've just had a strange dream."

"What should I do?"

"Get me some aspirin and some acetaminophen, too. I can take the maximum dose of both to knock the fever down. And get some ice and some washcloths. I'm just over 103 right now. Help me to cool down."

Susan didn't want to tell Paul about her dream. Wearing the clothes he had worn when she first saw him at the public reading at the Riverside Art Museum, Tom had come to her from the shadows. But there was something different about him. He seemed radiantly happy, happy as she had never seen him in life.

"Tell me how it is with you, Tom."

"You see how I am."

"Is it because I called you back that you are happy? Were you afraid I wouldn't call you back?"

"I always knew you would. It's because at last I can love you simply that I'm happy."

"Are you at peace now?" Susan asked.

"I don't know what it would be to be at peace."

"But do you see love more clearly?"

"I see only the things that are beyond me to change."

"But you said that now you can finally love me simply."

"I meant that I am past hurting you anymore."

"I've never given up on you. I will never stop wanting you."

"I couldn't have faced you. I had done too much to you."

"But now you do face me. Will I see you this way again, after everything is over?"

"You see me now. See me while you can."

She felt, through her entire body, the pang of hopeless desire. "I loved you so hard, Tom, so hard."

"I couldn't live up to that love."

"If I had loved you better, I would have made a way for you to come to me again. I loved you too greedily."

"It was me who had to find the way, and I didn't."

"I would have you over again, Tom, just as you were. Even now. Even with everything still wrong between us."

"I've given you a gift. I've set you free of me."

"I don't want to be free of you. Let me come where you are."

"I want you to live. You must do that without me."

"But it's you I want to live with."

And still in her dream, she rushed out of her bed to take him in her arms, and her arms closed on nothing. Then she was sitting up, shuddering as her fever continued to rise, with her tangled sheets and blanket thrown on the floor, and only Paul was there, asking how she was. And asking again.

When Paul came back from the medicine cabinet, she took the pills he had brought, and drank the glass of water in one swallow. "Get me another glass, please. I may be getting dehydrated."

Paul came back with a pitcher of water from the kitchen, a bowl of ice cubes, and some washcloths.

"Thank you. Help me cool down. I still haven't begun to sweat. I'll get hotter and hotter until I do. I felt like I was freezing. Now I'm burning up."

He folded some ice in a wet washcloth, and gingerly touched her forehead and wrists with it.

"No, you'll have to do something more drastic."

She took the icy washcloth from him and rubbed it vigorously over her face, over her throat, over her chest. Her hair was damp with ice water, and her eyes glittered. Her face was flushed.

"That's the way."

She gave him back the cloth. But he was still afraid of touching her too harshly.

"Don't be shy. I want you to do this. I have to cool down."

Still too gently, he swabbed her face, her throat, and her chest. "Yes. Thank you. Don't worry about getting my nightgown wet. I'll change out of it when the fever breaks."

"In the morning?"

"It might be a few hours."

"I'll keep watch. I'm wakeful anyway."

"I'm glad you're here. I'm going to lie down."

As he sat beside her on a kitchen chair, under the dim yellow light of the lamp on the end table, she lay on her stomach and closed her eyes. With the icy cloth he swabbed the back of her neck, and, lifting the collar of her nightgown, swabbed her shoulders and the upper part of her back.

After about thirty minutes she had cooled down enough to drift off to sleep. Paul drowsed in his chair, but he held one of her hands in both of his. But by three her fever was up again, this time to 105 degrees. Her eyes were unfocused. "You kept me from suffering your dying. But you also kept me from helping you and you had to suffer it by yourself. Why did you think that would make the pain of your death any less for me?"

Paul did not know what she was talking about. But he knew it wasn't about Corbin. He broke in. "Susan, tell me what to do." When she didn't respond he took her shoulders and looked directly into her face. "Susan, listen. Listen to me. Tell me what to do." She looked at him, blinking herself awake.

"Put cold water in the bathtub and put me in it." Paul ran to the bathroom and turned on the tap. While the tub filled he swabbed her face and shoulders with cold water. "I'm too weak to get up," she said. "You'll have to help me, please."

When the tub was filled, Paul said, "Lift your knees and your head a bit, if you can." He lifted her, still in her damp nightgown, in his arms like a bride. She shifted to cling to him with her arms around his neck. Even with the ice water on her skin she was hot to the touch. He felt her lips against his ear. "Thank you." Her breathing in his ear was labored. She pressed her cheek against his face and held on.

He lowered her carefully into the cold tub. As she unlocked her arms from around him, she kissed him softly on the cheek. "Thank you," she whispered again. He felt her warm breath. She smiled at him, and he didn't want to think about it. He felt a moment of danger.

She lay exhausted in her soaked nightgown in the cold water, her head thrown back over the edge of the tub. Paul scooped cold water with a glass from the tub, and poured it over her face and throat.

"Already a little better." Her eyes had cleared. "I'm sorry I lost control."

"Fortunately, you are very light," he said, responding to a different remark, one she hadn't made.

After a while, Susan began to feel cold, from the cold water this time rather than from the fever. "Can you bring me back to my bed? I'm still too weak to walk."

Paul pulled the drain plug of the tub, then gave her the bath towel from the rack. "Let me get you a clean nightgown. I don't want you to soak your bed. There's one in the dresser, right?"

As Paul came out of her room with the nightgown, he saw that Jack had come out of his room. Susan was still lying in the draining tub in her soaking nightgown when Jack came to the door.

"Mommy, why are you taking a bath in your pajamas?"

"I had a fever, Jack. Paul had to put me in the tub to cool me down." Jack didn't know what to say. Paul arrived with the dry nightgown and Susan took it.

"Were you afraid, Mommy? I came out in case you were afraid."

"No, Jack. I knew this was going to happen. I wasn't afraid."

"But I heard you cry."

"I had a fever, honey. I was afraid in my dream."

"Are you all right now?"

"I'm not all right yet. But I'm getting better."

"I'm right here if you are afraid."

"No, Jack, don't worry whether I'm afraid. I'm supposed to be doing the worrying for you."

"I'll be brave. I know how to be brave."

"Can you step out of the bathroom for a minute, Jack?" She gestured to the bathroom door with the dry nightgown in her hand. "I'm going to need some help getting back to bed, but I think I can pull this over my head by myself. You can help Paul put me back in bed."

As Susan was changing, Paul said, "I'm sorry you had to see that. But I think the worst is over for tonight. At least her fever is coming down, and she seems like herself again. Will you help me put your mother back to bed?"

Paul lifted her into his arms, again like a bride. Jack followed Paul into the bedroom.

When Paul had Susan settled back in her bed, he said, "Jack, will you be able to get back to sleep tonight? Or would you like to stay here?"

Susan said, "It will help me get back to sleep if you're here." She moved over to make room for Jack. She lay on her back, and Jack put his head on her shoulder. Paul sat on the little chair beside them, rubbing Jack's back until both Jack and Susan fell into an exhausted sleep. At seven Paul woke up, sprawled on the floor. It was time to get Jack ready for school. And time to let Susan rest.

As the end of the school day approached, Susan was still in heavy sleep, so Paul drove Susan's Dart to the Shetland school to pick up Jack, knowing that he would want to come home and resume his watch over his mother as soon as the last bell had rung. But Paul told him that it would probably be better for his mother if they could let her sleep for as long as they could. And he took Jack to the crowded playground. Jack wanted to be pushed on the swing, the higher the better. Paul finally understood what Jack wanted from him, which was that he hold the swing as high over his head as he could, and count down from ten, then run all the way through under the swing, pushing Jack as high as he could when he had run to the other side. "Blast off!" Jack shouted, for the moment beside himself with happiness. Jack wanted him to do it again and again. And they did do it again and again, until Paul was out of breath from running, and Jack was dizzy to the point of nausea from swinging. Exhausted, Paul sat with Jack on the edge of the sandbox, watching the other children climbing the monkey bars or going face first down the slide. Jack and Paul played on the swings and on the slide and on the seesaw until the parents of the other children began to appear to take them home for dinner.

When they got home, Susan was awake, but still in bed, not really wondering where they were, but wondering when they would arrive. Jack, rosy and dirty from the playground, sat on the edge of the bed to hug her as she struggled to get up, and held her tight, glad and relieved. Paul filled the tub for Jack to take a bath, and while he was bathing, heated up the last of the lasagna, which, however, only Jack and Paul ate.

30

*O*N FRIDAY MORNING, MAY 16TH, AFTER SUSAN HAD RELUCTANTLY decided to spend another day resting at home, and Paul had dropped Jack off at school, Susan received two telephone calls. The first was from Jane Davenport, the Inyo County District Attorney in Independence, who told her that the case against James Cole was ready to proceed to the next step, which was a preliminary hearing to be held at the courthouse in Independence at noon on Tuesday, the 20th of May. She warned Susan that if he made a plea bargain this hearing might be her only chance to hear what happened.

The thought of returning to Independence, the scene of her close call, still shook her. And she knew that Jane Davenport would still be wanting her to put on a show at the trial, if there was one, that she didn't want to be any part of, a show that would send the prosecutor to Congress. But what bothered Susan most was how empty she felt when she was faced with Tom's killer. Because she had not really seen him, as she thought Tom would have been able to do, and would have expected of her. She had thought of it as a test of her loyalty to Tom. But she had felt nothing for the pathetic figure in the dock at all. In her numbness, she felt as though the man had killed her just as much as he had killed Tom.

Susan sighed. *As if feeling a gush of compassion for the killer would have done anything for him anyway. Whatever treating him as human is, it has to be more than that, but what that more is I have no idea.*

The other call from was Michael Celio, the coroner from Inyo County, who told her that he was finally releasing Corbin's body to his family. Susan told him that she had arranged for the Preston and Simons mortuary to transport his body back to Riverside, and that she would make arrangements from there. It was good to be busy, even doing things like this. What it all meant seemed unreal to her in her fatigue anyway. Better even buying headstones than looking death in the face.

Paul drove her to Olivewood Cemetery, where she bought a double plot and two flat headstones. For Corbin, she had chosen the epitaph, "I must lie down where all the ladders start." For herself, she chose, "What if a laughing eye have looked into your face?"

They'll be filling in that date for me soon enough, she thought, *and then I'll lie down with Tom forever at last.* But she could not help but glance at Paul as she was thinking. He stood there mildly, ready for whatever she wanted him to do next. *He will do anything for me.* She felt a flash of shame. *What am I doing to him? What will become of him? Who will love him if I can't?* She turned away from Paul, afraid he might read her face. *It was you I wanted, Tom. But I couldn't keep you. And it's you I still want and can't have until I come here for you again.*

At the mortuary, Susan had told the director to preserve Corbin's body for the funeral. He asked her where she was planning to hold the service. He thought she might wish to have a memorial service at the college, perhaps in the University Theater. It might be possible to arrange a memorial service later, after things are more settled, and to have only a private service for those closest to the deceased now; it was up to her. Having a memorial service at the University Theater with all of the people who had been watching Corbin in action at Duke's Bar and Grill the night she met him struck Susan as the very last thing she wanted. They only thought they knew him, and the man they knew was not the man she loved. She didn't like what they thought about her either.

Corbin had been Catholic, Susan told the director, though not a very good one, and certainly not a very observant one, but she wanted him to have a Catholic funeral. She said this with a little more firmness than she was aware of, and the director involuntarily took a step back. She added that she was not Catholic herself—she had been raised as a generic liberal Protestant, but had not been inside a religious institution since she was twelve. Her mother had been religious before her father died and that had been enough for the both of them.

"We often deal with Father Ronan at St. Francis de Sales church, downtown," said the director, "Why don't you talk this over with him? I will call him and let him know you are coming."

200

*P*aul parked the Dart on 13th Street, in front of the broad steps that led up to the cool, white, Spanish-style church surrounded by courthouses and public buildings for the county and the city. But the office entrance turned out to be around the corner on Lime Street. Susan was feeling dizzy, and Paul took her arm to steady her. She had to stop halfway down the walk. Reeling, she suddenly turned in to him and clung to him, and for a minute or two he held her up while she rested her head against him. As he held her to him, he felt her breathing, slowly and deeply, until her vertigo cleared. The clean scent of her hair came over him, and he closed his eyes for a second. She sighed in his arms, her breath warm against his throat, her eyes closed. He rested his cheek against the top of her head. He felt a shudder go all the way down her. *How sweet to hold her like this.* Then, as soon as that thought was out, *Don't cross this line. It's not right for her.* But he continued to hold her. And she continued to hold him. After a few moments, she came to herself and looked into his face, her eyes glittering. She smiled at him and released her embrace, not saying anything. *That didn't really happen.* Paul thought. *It's just my foolishness.* But it had happened. She took his hand with both of hers and turned back towards the building. When they entered the office, she braced herself against his arm, and he put his hand on top of hers.

Susan wished to speak with Father Ronan by herself, so the administrator brought Paul to the bright, airy sanctuary where he sat in the calm and admired how the light fell through the windows.

Only as he sat down did he understand, although the name had rung a bell with him when the funeral director had mentioned it, that this was the church Rachel Lake had haunted during the weeks after their disastrous adventure in Portland, and that it was to this church that he had been bound during the failed pilgrimage that had ended with Corbin in Gallup almost ten years before.

He remembered finding a poem she had written during the last few weeks of their affair. Rachel had had meeting after meeting with Tom about it, and he had never been happy with it. Now Paul recognized where that poem had been set:

After the Fall

In the quiet church, before the hymn begins,
I watch the cool shaft slanting to the floor
From narrow windows, unseen high behind me.
Ceaselessly, the sparse dust tacks and wheels
Across the blaze whose shape it marks for me,
And winter daylight shimmers in the air:
Brief stars, brief voyagers from shade to shade,
Light falls and falls, and I am still alive.

Maybe Rachel had sat in the very pew he was sitting in, just inside the door, in the far back corner of the church. He wondered whether her furious thoughts ever gave her rest in that place, or whether its sacredness had only sharpened her suffering, indeed, whether she had come there not to feel solace but only to drink her alienation more deeply.

What he felt there was Rachel's bitter loneliness, and her sense, made sharper by his failure to respond to the anguished letter she had sent to him at his parents' house, that he had left her to face her demons by herself.

Had she ever really felt love? Certainly not for him. That was too stupid a notion to bear thinking about. He still couldn't imagine what she had seen in him. And whatever furtive adventure Rachel and Corbin had had together in graduate school certainly could not count as love either, not really. He wondered whether he really had the right to feel betrayed by her, so small did what he had given her seem in retrospect. Had he loved her? Had he loved anyone? He felt as though he had climbed a miles-high ladder to look down through the spheres on his past life, and he almost laughed to think how little all the pain he thought he had felt in that life had finally amounted to, even if it led on his part to living so narrowly as to disturb nobody and risk nothing. But he couldn't laugh when he thought of what had happened to Rachel, what she had become.

Had Rachel and Corbin loved each other later, when they renewed their affair? Corbin had told him in Reno that what was driving and tormenting him was love. And thinking back on it now Paul realized that although he had at the time scoffed at the idea that anything Corbin might have felt about anybody might fairly be called love, it was clear that Corbin was willing to turn his life upside down for it, willing even to outrage his usually flexible conscience on its behalf. That's what love for Rachel must have been like for Corbin, an experience of mystifying compulsion and abasement, overripe fruit you smear all over your face in the eating, only to be hungry for more. But what it had all been like on Rachel's side he did not know. He did know that over the years her nature had darkened, and her allure had darkened, in ways that frightened him. Maybe that was what love was for her, a way of surrendering one's self to one's own darkness: *Here is what I discover I am. I will not let myself be afraid of it. Let me be a loaded gun.*

He sat with this miserable thought for a minute. Then he thought *I don't want that kind of love. I don't think that's even what love is. If I love Susan, I have to want what's best for her,* which, he knew, was not himself.

What he had himself experienced over the last few weeks was something totally new to him. He was proud to have seen Susan through the night of her treatment. However strange it may have been to have committed himself so deeply to loving a woman whose deceased husband was not yet even in his grave, a woman whose love for that husband seemed still to be the central fact about her, nevertheless, if nothing beyond his taking care of her happened between them, if, after her death, he ended up going back to Reno and picking up exactly where he had left off, he would still think of himself as having lived a complete life. *I have at least known what it is to love.*

But then the thought of what would happen to Jack if Susan died brought him to a stop, unable to proceed, unable to stay where he was. Because he didn't have a right to make a plan for Jack.

31

*T*HE PRIEST, FATHER RONAN, SAT BEHIND A HEAVY WOODEN DESK that must have stood in that office since the Depression. On the desk stood a brass lamp with a green glass shade and an old-fashioned blotting pad with green paper. He sat heavily in an office chair with a broad wooden back, another relic from the prewar era. He was short of breath, and each damp inhalation required a moment's thought. His sad Bassett Hound glance was friendly, though Susan did not meet it.

Susan perched carefully on the small wooden chair across the desk, wearing the same dark dress she had worn to the arraignment. She kept her eyes down, looking at the swollen red hands he had folded on the desk. When he told her that he had read about her husband's murder in the newspaper, she stiffened. She wasn't prepared to hear condolences. Was he going to tell her that God understood what she felt and felt it with her? That there was a plan? She didn't want to hear about any plan.

But what he said was, "The randomness of it must weigh on you."

She took this in. "It's such a meaningless way to die. For a few dollars and a credit card. I'm at a loss about it."

He had to take in a deep breath before replying. "I don't think we'll ever know why things happen," he said. "Knowing that *why* wouldn't help us anyway. It would still hurt exactly the same way. And it would not seem one bit less cruel."

She didn't look up, but she was surprised.

"But there are still people we love in this world, so we have to find a way to keep living in it. Even if we don't want to," he added.

Only as he said this did she realize she had been holding her breath, every muscle clenched in resistance. Exhaling with relief, she looked up at him. "Yes, I guess so."

He took off his glasses and polished them with his handkerchief, his pale eyes watery and unfocused, his eyelids red. Finally, settling his glasses back on his face, he smiled at her. "We don't have to understand the world to love the people in it who need us. And whom we need, too. It's them we do this for."

Again, she took this comment in. "Yes, I know that my Jack will need this. It will help him live with what's happened. Maybe it will also make it easier for me to carry on. But I want it for Tom's sake too. And how can it help him? Do the people we've lost still *need* us?"

"Because that's what we come *here* for, to do some last something for them, something they still need? Is that what you mean?" he asked.

She just looked at him. She left him to answer his own question.

"I don't know," he said. "We need them to need something from us, though. It's how we come to peace with them. Especially when there were things left to settle. As there always are. But whether they really need anything we do for them, I just don't know."

Finally, she opened a smile for him. "Thank you for being honest with me. I wanted to give him this. He wouldn't have told me he wanted it. He didn't believe there was any way back from his regrets. He thought I forgave him too easily. But I did forgive him anyway. Now I can't give him anything but this."

"I don't think your love of him was a futile gift, even if he couldn't accept it."

"He told me once he wanted to love me more simply," she explained.

The priest smiled softly. "That's what grace is. It frees you from yourself. So you don't have to try to untangle love and wind up tangling it worse. That's what you wanted to give him." He paused. "You know, I did follow his poetry when he first came to Riverside. I even heard him read. Not my politics. But I remember his poem about Mary. It was the real thing."

"When was that?"

"Seven years ago, this summer, at the Riverside Art Museum."

"That was the day I met him. The day I fell in love with him."

"That's a romantic story."

Susan blushed. "Women were always falling in love with him at readings. I wasn't the last. But I was the one he kept coming back to. The one he wanted to get it right with, but never did."

"I don't know whether human love actually redeems anybody. However much we want it to." He paused.

"I loved him as he was. I still do," she said. "I knew what he was. He didn't have to become somebody else for me. Because I knew also what there was in him."

"Not everybody would have done what you did. Don't let anybody fault your love of him."

"I wish I had done better by him."

"It is hard to imagine a better gift than your forgiveness of him."

"Except that it did not hold him." She wasn't going to let him take her off the hook.

"You could not force him to accept your forgiveness. We are all still free. And the price of that is that we sometimes use our freedom badly."

"I just want somehow to tell him that I never doubted he loved me. Even when he couldn't stand what he kept doing, and did it anyway, he still loved me. I knew that. And he didn't know I knew that."

"It's your love of him that matters now, not his of you," the priest said, with an unaccustomed note of sternness. "And it's what you are doing now, not whatever he did then, that matters now."

After a moment, the priest asked, gently, "Have you given any thought to what you will do, I mean, with the rest of your life?"

She straightened herself, drawing herself up in her chair. "I have to make my son safe. He is about to turn six and imagines he can protect me." But then she came to a halt.

Father Ronan waited for her to complete her thought. Finally, he had to go on, himself. "I thought you were going to say that you were planning to bring your son up, to see him into adulthood. But that's not quite what you said."

Every muscle in her shoulders, in her throat, in her face, had tightened. But it was too late. Because his kindness had lowered her guard, what she had to say burst out of her anyway before she could stop it. "I won't be able to bring him up to adulthood. I'm very sick with cancer, and I don't know whether I will even be able to live out the summer." Then she caught herself, and again she didn't know how to go on. "I'm very sorry. I hadn't meant to tell you that." She said this with elaborate calm.

"I wanted to talk with you about Tom, not about me. And now I've put you in a false position. Because you will want to think about me, not about him. And that isn't what I came here to do."

He took her hand and looked at her softly, for a moment at a loss. She did not take her hand away, but she didn't return his look. "Are you being treated?" the priest asked.

"I'm a doctor. I'm getting the best treatment there is. But I know the odds. And I'm not going to complain about it either. I'm not going to chase rainbows. And I don't need prayers." She paused for a second, taken aback by her own rudeness. *Why did I say that? He doesn't mean me anything but well. But it was weak of me to tell him I'm sick, and it's too late to take it back.* She raised her face to look at him, fighting to be as stoical as her words had been. He was still looking at her kindly. After a second, she swallowed. "But I do need help bearing it."

"I don't think faith is anything other than what we do to bear a world we know we can't understand." He looked at her until she unclenched her shoulders.

"I am very grateful for your kindness. I really am. And I'm sorry I spoke so rudely."

He shifted in his seat to lean towards her. "Have you made any plans for your son?"

"Yes. No." She was stymied for a second. "I mean I don't have family, none that I have been in touch with since I was twelve. And I have an in-law who's ill and doesn't like me anyway. But I don't want Jack to go into foster care. I don't want strangers to raise him."

"So, what are your plans?"

"I only have a thought. I can't call it a plan. I can't say that, until this moment, I was even aware of it as a plan. But I did have a thought although I have tried not to think it. And I don't know whether it will work out. I don't know whether I even have a right to want it."

"Does it involve the gentleman I saw helping you up the walk?"

"Does it involve Paul? Why do you say that?"

"Because it is obvious, even at a glance, that he loves you. I saw how he caught you when you fainted just now."

She thought about how Paul had held her when she fainted on the walk. She wondered whether what the priest had noticed had been obvious to everyone in the world except to her. And she remembered how she had let herself feel in Paul's arms. It was something new to her. What had she felt? Was it just safety? Was it just support? No, it was not just those things, but those things were new to her too. She had to brace herself to face what it was because what she had felt was joy. As she sat there, an impenetrable look on her face, she let herself feel it again, let it run all the way through her body, knowing that soon she would have to tell herself that she didn't have a right to it. And then she would never let herself feel that way again. Had she given herself away to Paul too? If the priest saw it, surely Paul did. But Paul wouldn't want to face it any more than she did. She might still be safe.

The priest gave her a mild, guarded look. She saw that he had withheld the judgment that might have seemed so natural to anyone else, that it was strange that a woman whose sense of herself turned on her love of her deceased husband should, before that husband was even in his grave, already be thoroughly entangled with another man, and that it was stranger still that that other man could love her without her even being aware of it.

"He knows I'll never be available to him."

"Because you don't see any future with him?"

"I don't see any future at all for me."

"But that's not just because you are dying, is it?"

"No. It's because I only know myself as the woman who loved Tom Corbin. Who loved him completely, futilely. And who now has nothing to do on this earth but get ready to die." *If you ever want to live with yourself you have to stop thinking this way. You don't have a right to him. And you are backing him into something you don't have a right to ask for.* Another thought ambushed her before she could brace herself against it: *Better he had not saved you. Better you had given way to death than to do to him what you are doing.*

She shook off this thought. If Father Ronan had guessed what she was thinking, he did not show it.

"Does he accept that you will never be available to him?"

"I'm sure he does. That's why he has never been forward with me in any way. But I've seen what's in him. I saw him with Jack at the arraignment. And I saw him this week, as I went through my first treatment. He took care of me. And his kindness just wrenched me all the way through. If I were as good a person as he thinks I am, I would have loved him then. But there isn't enough left of me for him. Somebody should love him as he deserves to be loved."

He looked right at her, more directly than he had done before. "And you're sure, dying or not, that can't be you?"

She was shocked by this question. It took her a second to see that he meant it seriously. She felt a flash of anger. She stood up to storm out of the room. "If I do feel more for him than I acknowledge then I am in very bad trouble, and I am a very bad person because I am not free to have any feelings for him. If I were a decent person, I would have crushed those feelings out." She had to pause for breath. Then she sat back down. And what had been anger suddenly became sadness. "And worse than that, I seem to be backing him into taking care of Jack. I'm not warning him that he is getting in deep with Jack. Because I know they both feel for each other. If I were a decent person, I would have found a way to warn him about doing that. But I'm too desperate to be a decent person. I didn't plan for them to connect with each other so deeply. But I can't say I'm unhappy about it."

He was about to say something, but, looking at her for a long second, thought better of it. She heard it anyway: *And you tell me you don't love him?*

He looked at her calmly. "I don't know what advice to give you. But I'm not going to judge you. And I'm going to pray for you, if you'll allow me."

She realized that he thought he knew exactly what she would do in the end: let Paul love her. Then she would love him herself. And Susan was certain, absolutely certain, that the priest was wrong about that.

32

$\mathcal{T}$HE FUNERAL WAS ARRANGED FOR LATE MONDAY AFTERNOON AT St. Francis de Sales church, followed by a private burial at Olivewood cemetery. Susan asked Paul if he might be willing to stay at least until the funeral and the preliminary hearing were over. He could scarcely conceal his happiness about this request, and he worried whether Susan had seen that.

By the time they arrived back home from their visit to the church, Susan was again falling over with exhaustion. As Susan slept, Paul drove to Stater Brothers to buy groceries for the weekend, then set about grading papers at the kitchen table until it was time to pick up Jack at school.

It had been an unseasonably hot day, and the parks department came to the spray pool they operated at Fairmount Park and set it running, something they normally did not do until June. The spray pool was set up so that the sprinklers came on and off irregularly, sometimes at full force, sometimes at only a trickle. Most of the children there were fully clothed. The game was to stand in the middle of the asphalt spray area for as long as you could then escape from the soaking jets at the last second. Naturally, Jack got soaked. And, unable to resist, so did Paul.

"Mom will be really mad at us."

"Maybe not. My guess is that she thinks we need the fun."

"Then I'll tell her to be mad at you, not at me."

$\mathcal{W}$hen they finally arrived at home, Susan was awake, phoning Corbin's friends at the university to keep them apprised of the details of the memorial service. The freshman composition director offered to organize a buffet at the graduate student lounge, for mingling after the funeral and the burial service. She felt very grateful to him since, unlike many of the others, his sympathy for her had no trace of condescension.

Susan was proud of handling all of the details. It gave her the sense

210

that she was at least doing something, at least organizing something, at least in command of something, and not at the mercy of her grief or her illness. She was looking forward to picking up her practice again after the funeral although she knew she would not be able to keep a resident's schedule. For the moment, she was busy enough with the funeral that both Jack and Paul were able to change into dry clothes without her noticing.

Only after Paul and Jack were out of the room did she finally call her father-in-law in Whitneyville to arrange for his coming to the funeral. She knew Paul would have to drive to LAX to pick him up from his flight from JFK, since she couldn't do it physically, and the thought of explaining to the old man who Paul was brought her up short. She was afraid of Tom's father, and he was sure to get the wrong idea about it. The old man just couldn't stay in the house, which was also still upside down from her own illness, which she hadn't told him anything about either. But the phone was answered by the wife of the couple next door who had come over to feed the cat. Mr. Corbin was in St. Raphael's, she said. He had had an exacerbation the night before, and they had taken him by ambulance to St. Raphael's to get his breathing under control. He'd probably be there another two or three days while they checked out his lungs and his heart, so travel any time soon was out of the question.

Susan was able to talk to him at the hospital, but only for a few minutes, because he was still in intensive care. The attending gave her a rundown of her father-in-law's condition and allowed her to speak a few words with him, but he was exhausted, his mind was wandering, and he did not quite grasp that she was talking about whether or not he would be able to attend the funeral of his son.

While Susan was on the telephone, Paul enlisted Jack's help in preparing meatloaf for them to eat over the next few days with mashed potatoes and green beans. Jack really enjoyed the meal. "There's nothing like eating things you cooked yourself, is there?" Paul asked.

"I still don't really like green beans," Jack remarked.

"Wait till you grow up," Paul said, teasing him.

"I still won't like them." Jack was sure of this.

"As for me," Susan said, forcing herself to smile, "I like eating any meal I didn't have to cook."

"I'm glad you liked it," Paul laughed.

But in point of fact, Susan had only eaten a few bites. She was reluctant to tell either Paul or Jack this, but she was still feeling nauseated from her treatment. She hoped they had not noticed how little she had eaten. But when Susan looked up from moving the mashed potatoes around in small circles on her plate, she saw that Jack was watching her, as he always did.

As Paul read from *The Lion, The Witch, and the Wardrobe* on the couch that evening, Mr. and Mrs. Beaver were just figuring out the extent to which Edmund's defection to the White Witch had endangered them. They realized that they had let slip the prophecy that the four mortals would overthrow the White Witch, that Aslan, the great Lion, was on the move, and that, indeed, the children were expected to rendezvous with Aslan the next day at the Stone Table, upon which all of the secrets of the Deep Magic from Before Time were carved in glyphs none of them could read. They knew that within minutes the White Witch's servants would be surrounding them.

For Lewis, Paul thought, evil was not majestic darkness but the gradual wearing away of decency by its friction with resentment, narcissism, and self-pity. Englishmen needed not be that proud of themselves for not being Germans. Under the right circumstances, and with enough in the way of petty motivations, any of them could have followed Hitler too. The crimes the ruthless fanatics commanded could not have been committed without the help of a lot of ordinary people with no special talent or calling for evil.

Meanwhile, magic was afoot. The long winter of Narnia, the product of the Witch's spells, began to thaw, and Father Christmas (that's what they call Santa Claus in Britain, Paul explained), appeared and gave each child the weapon most appropriate for their use.

"Talk about a *deus-ex-machina*," Susan said. "Santa Claus saves the day? Please."

"What's that?" Jack couldn't understand why his mother was scoffing. Scoffing at Santa Claus was something about which Jack took a very dim view.

Susan said, "It's when the author uses magic powers to cheat his way out of the jam he's gotten his story into."

"Spoilsport," Paul said. Susan laughed and tweaked the end of his nose.

"Anyway," Paul said, "what is magic but imagination? And what's imagination but a way of calling up from yourself things you didn't know you were capable of?"

"I think I'd call that wishful thinking, not imagination. But I'm the scientist here, so you poets and fairy-tale readers will just have to excuse me for not taking your word about it."

"More reading please."

33

SUNDAY, AFTER LUNCH, PAUL ASKED SUSAN IF SHE WERE FEELING well enough for the three of them to take a little excursion to the University Botanical Garden, just at the other side of the campus. He had seen it on the map, and he thought the rose garden there might be in bloom. Susan was tired still, but the thought of spending an hour or two with green things that had nothing to do but drink in the sun and open themselves in bloom appealed to her. They could put Monday's funeral out of their minds for a day. It would be good to be with things that gave themselves completely over to the task of living.

They passed, near the entrance, the tall deodar cedars and the big western sycamore, with its leathery leaves the size of dinner plates, and made their way up the Alder Canyon, a vigorous stand of white alders at its mouth. The matilija poppies were in intense bloom on the slope of the canyon, and the hillside was alive with their spectacular, pure white flowers, each larger than you could spread your hand, with translucent but sturdy petals like white crepe paper, and a brilliant yellow ball of stamens and pistils in the center. Honeybees were hopping from bloom to bloom.

"They smell like apricots." Susan said, lifting a flower to Jack. "See?"

They doubled back near the top of the canyon and crossed along the slope of the chapparal region to the area where plants from the northern coast were growing. By the creekside, the low California fuchsia bore its crimson, tubular flowers. Susan saw a hummingbird probing one of the flowers, hovering furiously before it.

The rose garden, near the greenhouse, behind its phalanx of white cedars, was formal and orderly, unlike the more natural appearance of the rest of the park. They paused before each bush, comparing the fragrances. Jack suggested that they each pick a favorite. Jack's favorite was "Mr. Lincoln," whose blooms were dark, almost blood-purple. "You just picked that for the name," Susan said. Hers was "Chicago Peace," for its bright yellow petals with scarlet fringes. Paul's was "Herbert Hoover," a delicate pink rose with an especially sweet scent. "You didn't pick that one for the name," Susan said. "It probably smells better than President Hoover did, too."

By the time they reached the butterfly garden, Susan was tired. This frustrated her because she had always thought of herself as an athlete. She had been a long-distance runner in college, and she was hoping to be able to go back to work at the clinic by the middle of the coming week. She sat on the bench while Paul and Jack searched though the plants for butterflies. Jack brushed his fingers against the leaves of the Indian mallow. "They feel just like pajamas," he said.

She noticed that the Pink Breath of Heaven was just past its peak of bloom. "If I were a butterfly," Susan said from the bench, "I'd want to hang around a plant called Pink Breath of Heaven."

"Unfortunately, butterflies don't know about names." Paul relished the role reversal of playing the skeptic.

"I would, if I were a butterfly." Susan was not going to be so easily pulled out of her fantasy.

"I thought you were supposed to be a woman of science."

Through her fatigue, she smiled at Paul from the bench, brushing the damp hair back from her temples, then leaning back on her spread arms, her bright yellow sundress drawn about her like folded wings.

The verbenas lifted violet sprays in all directions, and butterflies flocked around them. Paul held his index finger next to one of the verbenas, and a yellow sulfur butterfly landed on it. He raised it carefully to show it to Jack. "I've made a friend, see?"

"How did you do that?"

"I saw a butterfly land on a flower. Then I held my finger very still next to the flower, and the butterfly just hopped over and landed on it. You have to be very patient."

"Let me try."

At first, Jack was too eager and scared the butterfly away.

"Slowly, Jack. Let them know they are safe with you."

After a few minutes, Jack too had a butterfly on his finger.

"Look, Mommy. It likes me."

"It's got good taste in friends," Susan said, smiling.

Jack and Paul turned back to the flowers.

As she sat, with her arms extended on both sides along the back of the bench, first one yellow sulfur butterfly, and then a second, and then a third, alighted on Susan's bare right arm. For an entire minute, they stayed there, opening and closing their wings. She watched them, quietly, holding her breath. Then she lay her head back and looked at the sky. *Let me not make more of this moment than it is. But let this moment last. Let me make this moment last.* She was smiling, but her eyes began to swim. *Please keep the future away as long you can. Let me love Paul. Let him know how much I love him. Let me live long enough to make him happy. Let him know that loving me wasn't a mistake. Please give us that long.* Tears ran down her face.

When she caught hold of herself, she brushed away her tears and saw Paul and Jack kneeling by the verbena bush, their backs to her. She was safe. They hadn't seen her, and they weren't looking at her now. She got on her feet with a little difficulty and went quietly over to them, standing over them as they looked at the flowers.

Paul looked up. "Ready to go?" he asked.

"I'll never be ready to go. But I guess it's time."

Jack stood up, brushed off the seat of his pants, and took her hand. And Paul smiled up at her and stood. "Ready when you are."

Smiling, she reached out with her other arm and took Paul by the hand. "Ready."

That night, in his little cot in Corbin's study, Paul replayed the scene in the butterfly garden, lost in the thought of how Susan had glanced at him by the verbenas. *How lovely she is.* The thought was like a coal in his mind, and he blew on it softly, to bring up the flame. *We have had our moment,* he thought. *It has to be right to love her. Because loving her has made me a different person.*

A warning light flashed in his mind. *She's thinks more of me than she's aware of.* And down that path, he knew, lay only confusion and heartbreak. He had no idea what to do about it.

How perfect, Rachel said in his mind. *How like you in every way.*

And, whispering in his ear so close he could almost feel the warmth of her breath. *And just what you wanted, though you said you didn't.*

34

On the day after the funeral, they set out early for the preliminary hearing in Independence. The accumulated fatigue and grief from Susan's first treatment, as well as from the funeral, made the prospect of facing Corbin's killer a more daunting one than it had been when they made the same drive to attend the arraignment. Nobody spoke very much on the long drive that morning. In fact, both Jack and Susan drowsed through much of it. Paul turned on the car radio while they slept. He listened to the news accounts of the aftermath of the eruption of Mt. St. Helens, which had exploded two days before, just as they were preparing their excursion to the Botanical Garden although none of them had any idea of it at the time.

Jack believed that he was better prepared this time for the long wait in the courtroom hallway and had asked Paul to bring along a checkers set for them to use while they waited. But when the moment came, he was too depressed to play and cried quietly in Paul's lap. Holding Jack's head against his shoulder and stroking his hair, Paul comforted him silently. Both of them knew that they would have to go through many more bad times and that they would likely be worse than they could prepare for.

When Jack's first flush of grief had passed, Paul suggested that they might need a walk outside. They went out to the lawn of the courthouse into the warm, clear, still weather, with the wall of the Sierras rising abruptly from the plain of the valley to their west. Jack held Paul's hand, and they walked slowly up Edwards Street, going nowhere in particular. But Paul was surprised by how beautiful the Sierras seemed to him. It was as if the mountains had just asked him to notice them; the mountains had been there before their grief and would be there still after they had all passed from the earth. In the late spring, their peaks were still snowy, but their slopes were mottled with the dark of the Jeffrey pines and the fresh new green of the aspens. They have seen grief like ours many times.

They aren't indifferent to it, but it doesn't change them. *We will be here.*
Take us as what we are. Be stayed by us. But don't look to us for sympathy.
Jack and Paul looked at them for a long time as the traffic ran past.

They passed the Winnedumah Hotel, whose paired stucco gables
and tile roof seemed to recall the Spanish missions. They passed the
administrative center and the Masonic Hall. At the end of the block, they
came to an ice cream shop. "I think we need this," Paul said.

"Won't Mommy want one, too?"

"If she feels like it when we come out, we'll have another. The more
ice cream she eats, the better."

Except for a few tactful bites of what Paul and Jack had cooked together every day, ice cream was about all Susan had been eating since her
treatment began.

"We'll just have to pretend we haven't had any already." Paul said this
as if they were conspiring to get a second serving, and Jack smiled at him,
as if sharing the joke.

Jack had a small chocolate cone, and Paul had a large peach one. They
walked with their cones to a small, grassy park in the next block, beyond
which the town seemed to end. They dawdled on the swings, idly pushing
back and forth with their feet. Jack looked over at him from his swing,
licking some of the melted ice cream from his fingers. "Thanks, Paul."

When Jack is an old man, Paul wondered, *and he looks back at this*
time of trouble, will he remember how we sat on these swings and had ice
cream? He couldn't help Jack at all, not really. He could not restore Jack's
father to life, whom Paul knew he bitterly mourned, although Jack kept
quiet about it, not wishing to burden his mother while she was sick. And
he couldn't save Susan's life for him either. He knew Jack had guessed
that she was dying. Susan hadn't told him that yet. But Jack had a way of
knowing things. Paul was glad anyway to have at least this little moment.
He knew he himself would need to remember it.

The hearing took longer than they had expected, and Susan emerged
from it disturbed and angry, although she did her best, with characteristic
unsuccess, to keep how upset she was from Jack. Once they got home,
Paul prepared a dinner of leftovers, which Susan picked at, followed by
ice cream. Jack and Paul looked at each other, but Susan was too fragile

for them to cajole into eating more. Because Susan felt too weary even to be read to that night the three of them watched old episodes of *The Muppet Show* until it was time for Jack to go to bed.

*L*ater that evening, as they sat in the living room together after Jack was asleep, Susan told Paul what had happened at the hearing.

Like the last time, James Cole had spent the whole time staring at a point on the floor a few feet in front of his table. His shoulders were tight, like someone expecting a beating.

"Did he pay attention to the prosecution's exhibits?" Paul asked. He was worried, Susan noticed, about how she was feeling.

"Not even once. I could barely look at them myself. But the pictures were so close-up that it was hard to focus on the fact that it was Tom's body. It all seemed very impersonal, like my anatomy text in med school."

As she said this, she was thinking, *Have I worn out being able to feel anything?* Because she knew that the slide of that stabbed torso and belly, those lacerated forearms, that slashed cheek, had been slides of Tom. But she had looked at them all as through a thick, mist-covered window. *I've already started to die: first my heart, later my body.*

She was not surprised that again she had felt nothing for the grizzled stranger at the defense table who, it seemed, had been called James Cole and who had murdered her husband. It didn't matter to him at all what she might have felt for him, and he was beyond her reach anyway, whatever she did, for him or against him. *So much for compassion and empathy.* He seemed even beyond the reach of the court. But that she could look so coldly at the slides of Tom's wounds shocked her. *Better that man had killed me instead. Then I would not have had to learn how small a thing my grief is.* She called up her thought of Jack, moaning a little in his sleep in the next room, and she knew that, somewhere deep in her, she was paralyzed by fear for him. But she seemed to see him from the bottom of a well, and even her fear for him seemed someone else's fear, someone she no longer was. *They are all beyond me now. I cannot help them at all. All I want is not to feel anything ever again. And maybe God will punish me by granting that wish.*

Paul touched the back of her hand. "You lost your thread. Are you okay?"

She looked at him for a second. *He is worried about me.* It was as if she had to remind herself about who he was. *But what good can that do me now? What good can I myself do for anybody now? It's a shame that he loves me. He will have to find his own way after it's over. And he'll have to find a better person to love.*

Paul was still looking at her. She knew she had to come to her senses. Because he was going to live. And the people who are going to live have to imagine they have a reason to keep on doing it. It would be cruel to deny them that. From a great distance away, she felt pity for Paul and for Jack. She had a secret, that death didn't mean anything at all, and she had to keep it from them because they couldn't bear knowing it.

She remembered how, as his testimony was ending, the coroner had turned his burly, kind face to her and shared a look, sorry for how his testimony had hurt her, unaware that there wasn't enough left of her to suffer about anything he had said. The memory of his hopeless kindness gave her a handhold, and she pulled herself back up from the bottom of the well. She owed it to him to pretend to go on living. She had to do the decent thing because he had been decent to her.

"The coroner was the man I met last time," Susan said, "still a diligent man who gets to the bottom of a lot of unpleasant things. He had to keep himself detached, of course. But I can't say I blamed him."

And how could I? Because I'm detached from everything now. Listen to me going on. Giving everyone their due. Answering their questions as if they mattered.

"Were there a lot of wounds?"

"More than I imagined. Many defensive wounds on his arms, on his shoulders. The one on his face I saw at the coroner's. Then the two wounds the coroner told me about, the one that brought him down, and the one that took his life."

She heard herself. She seemed to be listening to someone else, someone who was talking reasonably to someone who understood her. They were discussing something that had happened to happen. But not to her.

"Did the defense cross-examine him?" Paul asked.

"I thought they might. But they only asked a few questions. They did point out that the killer had bruises on his face and chest, and an abrasion where it seemed he had been thrown down in the gravel."

"We knew from what the coroner said that Tom put up a fight."

It began to occur to her that Paul had wanted something for her, not something from her. And here was the world. Paul was holding it out to her in his hands, for her to pick up again, like a book in which she'd lost her place. There was something she still could do in the world. He was sure of it, even if he didn't know what that thing was. And gradually she began to puzzle that something out.

"I think maybe they were trying to argue that he hadn't intended to kill Tom, only to rob him," she said, finally focusing on Paul, "but Tom put up a fight that made him fear for his life. You remember when we were last up there that even the coroner was unclear about whether Tom fought his killer because he knew he was going to try to kill him or whether he killed Tom because Tom put up a fight and the fight got out of hand."

"I don't see how that would get him off the hook," Paul said. "Even if you kill someone by accident while you are committing a dangerous crime, that's still felony murder, just as if you had planned to kill him from the beginning."

"Yes, I know that. I don't think they even had any serious hope of reducing the charge. I think they were just trying to get the death penalty off the table."

"But nobody has been executed in California for thirteen years."

"Yes, but Utah started executing people three years ago. And California may want to follow suit. And this killing looks a lot like those that Gary Gilmore did over in Utah. That's what the defense counsel seems mostly to have in mind."

"It'll be hard to build up public sympathy for him," Paul said.

"The state seems to think that having me drink James Cole's blood will make me feel all better. But I don't want the last thing I do to be to provide a pretext for sending somebody to the gas chamber to assuage my grief. And to send that Jane Davenport to Congress." Susan was surprised at how harsh her voice sounded.

"They'll want you to make a Victim Impact Statement."

"And I will. I'll use it to plead for that man's life. I might not be able to work up any compassion for him. But I certainly don't want him to be killed on my account."

She looked at Paul. *I promised myself I would never again let myself completely give way. But I did.* Then she saw that Paul, just as he had before, had not had the slightest notion about what he had just done for her.

Thank God for you, she said to him in her mind, thankful he could not hear her.

35

$\mathcal{T}$HE DAY AFTER THE PRELIMINARY HEARING, WEDNESDAY THE 21st, Paul drove Jack to school and Susan, who still seemed a little shaky to him, to the clinic for her first day of work since her treatment. Aware that he had run out of pretext for staying at Susan's house, Paul planned to drive back to Reno on Thursday morning (where he would finally turn in his grades), and promised to return before Susan's next interferon treatment, on the fourth of June. He didn't notice that Susan was disappointed to hear that he was leaving, so focused was he on not appearing to be pushing her to ask him to stay.

By late morning, he had finished both his final papers and his exams, and he put them into his satchel with his clothes to take back to Reno. In the early afternoon, he raked up from the yard several weeks' worth of miscellaneous flotsam that filled a large plastic bag. When he finished, he put it beside the house next to the trash cans.

Clipping the grass-catcher onto the back of the mower, he began to cut the side yard. He had only just reached the end of the yard furthest from the street when he heard a familiar voice from the end of the driveway.

"You are sure fucked up, aren't you?" Rachel remarked.

He left the lawnmower and crossed the yard to her, so they would not be overheard.

"Why are you here?" Paul asked.

"I might well ask you the same question."

But he wouldn't rise to that. "Susan isn't here. And I don't think you have anything to say to her."

Rachel laughed. "I'm the judge of that. But I'm here to talk to you, not to her."

"I don't have anything to say to you."

"But I have a few things to say to you."

"I won't see you here."

She flipped the hair out of her face with her finger and tucked it behind her ear, a gesture he could not help but recognize. He stared at her despite himself.

"Then you'd better come walk with me because what you have to hear is something I'm not leaving unsaid." This in her near-whisper. She didn't wait to see whether he would follow. Rachel led Bishop into the neighborhood of warehouses and factories beyond the Junior High School.

"I saw that you were at the funeral on Monday," he said, "in the back row, in the far corner."

"Did you tell Susan I was there?" She gave him a cold smile.

"Why would I do that?" Then he put together that she had just been baiting him.

"You had some nerve putting the funeral there."

"I didn't make the arrangements. And Susan didn't know that it was your church when she did."

She gave him a look. "And you let her pick that place?"

"How was I going to explain to her that she shouldn't? I don't want her to know that you even exist."

She scoffed. "Love is blind. Of course, you had to humor her in her fantasy about redeeming Tom."

"Just stay away from her. I'm going to keep Tom and you from taking from her the only thing she still relies on. You saw for yourself on Monday how she's tearing herself up with grief. And you want me to tell her that she didn't mean anything to the man she's grieving for?" Paul thought Rachel might look at him as he asked this question. He had stopped where he stood. But she didn't even turn her head.

It was useless. He couldn't just break the conversation off though he knew he should. He still felt he had to defend himself to Rachel. And he still had to defend Susan to her. He didn't know why. Meanwhile, as Rachel continued to walk, she looked up at Box Springs Mountain, completely calm, waiting for his anger to dissipate in the face of his instinctive shame before her. That shame would always keep him from holding his own with her.

"I'm not coming down here to throw Tom in her face," she said at last. "Neither of us can have him now anyway. And I at least knew what a bad idea it would have been to count on him."

"You didn't seem so self-possessed about it to me on Monday."

Rachel was taken aback by this statement. She had to regroup. She stopped and looked at Paul.

After a moment she said, "Do you think I'm not human? Of course I'm grieving for Tom. And despite what you think I've got no score to settle with Susan."

"That's why you always speak of her with such respect."

Rachel brushed this remark off. She was back in control over herself. "I didn't say she was right about life," she said, turning away from him again and walking ahead quickly. "I didn't say she had the slightest idea of who Tom really was. But she's a wounded animal now, just like me. And I'm not here to hurt her. I'm here to help her. By saving her from you."

Rachel had quickened her pace. Paul had to struggle to keep up. "I promised myself to leave her to Tom," he said to her retreating form.

"A likely story. But what good can possibly come of you backing her into loving you? I'm not here to tell her who I am or what Tom was planning to do. But I would do it if that were what it would take to put an end to this weird Sir Galahad fantasy of yours. The only thing I want is for people to be honest."

"Because you've always been so honest."

"Because I've always paid the price for it when I haven't been. A lesson you haven't learned yet. She'd be better off if she knew what Tom was. She's still all tangled up with him. And still all wrong about him."

"You're the expert on Tom, it appears."

"I wasn't the only one. I heard all the sarcastic things those guys from the university were saying about Saint Thomas of Riverside and all his women. Giving him a Catholic funeral seems pretty close to sacrilege to me."

"I wonder whether you and Susan are even grieving the same man."

"I wonder whether she is grieving a man who ever really existed. But she seems to be bent on wrecking her life for that fantasy, and you seem all hot to help her keep on doing it, you who knew Tom well enough to know better."

"She held out hope for him. She never gave it up."

"Yes, I know that. And he got all tied up in those hopes." Again, she stopped and brought her gaze to bear on him. He heard the pressure building in her voice: she was just getting started. "And sometimes it was worse than that. When he had crashed out of some sexual adventure, he had to find a way to get back in with her, and repentance was the way. It always worked, and he always knew it would work, and she was always ready for it to work. I don't call that repentance. And I don't call it forgiveness. I call that foreplay." This was more than she had set out to say.

He shook his head. "That's beneath even you."

She didn't argue; she had crossed a line, and he knew she knew it.

"I'm sure you saw, even you can't deny it," he went on, "how much he mattered to her."

"Yes, and you should free her of that. That was my point." Then, recovering herself, she continued walking, looking back over her shoulder, making him follow her. "It's no kindness to her to keep her from reality." She began to quicken her pace again.

"It's no kindness to take Tom from her." He was far enough behind that he had to raise his voice. "Right now, she needs to hold on to him as hard as she can."

Something in his tone made Rachel stop to face him. She waited for him to catch up to her.

"Why? What does she need him for? Surely not just to keep from going crazy with grief."

To her evident surprise, Paul came to a halt three steps short of her and collected himself. He could have answered her. Whatever Rachel had in mind, Paul could have stopped her cold with one sentence. But that Susan was dying was Susan's business to say, not his. And how Rachel might use the knowledge that Susan was sick against her was something Paul didn't want to think about. He left Rachel's question hanging in the air. He just looked at her.

"She loved him despite everything," he said at length, "It's what I love her for." He did believe that, but that wasn't what he had been about to say.

"How perfect." She turned away and continued to walk, continued to make him follow. "You know that she will never love you as long as all her thoughts are on Tom. But that's the thing you love about her. How pure and noble it all is. And how conveniently safe for you." He had to skip a step to keep pace with her.

"Whatever you think about me, I still know what she wants, and what she wants is Tom."

"You say she has been able to bear up through everything, through all the humiliations, and all the false repentances, because she has a picture in her mind of herself as Tom Corbin's faithful wife, and his would-be rescuer. If she loves you, she has to see that idea of herself as wrong, and she has to see everything she did while she thought of herself that way as an illusion and as a waste of life."

"Exactly. That's what I've been saying. That's what I'm saving her from."

"But it isn't what you mean. You want her. You do. But you can't face it. But face it or not, you'll still hurt her."

"I haven't hurt her, and I won't."

"Either she loves you, and her whole life is a lie. Or she doesn't love you, and she stays in her stalemate. Either way, she loses. You aren't going to be able to keep her from suffering. She has to choose which way of suffering is her way. You can't choose it for her. And if you use all your manipulative power to keep her from suffering you keep her from life."

"I don't want to manipulate her. I want to help her. I want to love her. It doesn't matter to me whether she loves me."

"Of course it doesn't. Because that's the only way you can stand it. It's all just too sick for words. And just what you always were."

He was at a loss for a few seconds, with the sentence he had been ready to say caught on a snag in his mind.

This pause made her stop again too, as if she knew she had again said more than she intended to.

There's some reason she's here, he thought, *a reason that she's not facing. Why does any of this matter to her? It's just too late to settle scores with me or with Tom. Or a score with Susan over Tom. And why does she have a score to settle with me over Susan?*

"You know," he said, still wondering what she was about, "when I first learned a few weeks ago about you and Tom, not what you were doing this year, but years ago, back in Storrs, when you and I were together, because I actually didn't know that story until Tom came to see me in Reno, and even then Tom didn't tell me about it in so many words..."

"Wait. What do you mean, you didn't know that story? What on earth are you talking about?" Rachel asked.

They looked at each other.

She thinks I knew it all along. Maybe I should have. Because she's right that I should have seen it.

"I mean I know, I really do know," Paul said, "that you didn't betray me back then just to humiliate me."

"Betray you," she scoffed at his melodramatic term.

Paul continued. "You chose Tom over me because you saw I would let you down in the end. Not because I was mean or selfish. Not because I wanted to. But because you think I can't face life for what it is."

"It's true you can't face life for what it is. Not that I ever had any faith in Tom. But I didn't expect any better from him. You must know all about him by now yourself. It was you I had the expectations about. Doing the right thing matters to you even if you don't know enough to know what the right thing is."

"And you think I love Susan because she can't face life for what it is either."

"That's also true. A second point for your team."

"And you think those things because I left you hanging in Riverside."

"Don't you dare pity me." She was suddenly angry. But she was also something else.

For a moment he couldn't sort out what it was. He had never seen her feeling vulnerable before. *But why would she be ashamed of what I did to her then? What does what happened then mean to her?*

"It wasn't that, as upset as I was, you didn't rush out across the continent because I needed you to," she said after she regained her composure. "That was a crazy thing for me to ask you to do, anyway, and maybe you were right not to do it." Bishop didn't understand why her anger had given way to woundedness. Why she seemed to want to let him off the hook about leaving her in the lurch when she was in trouble back then made no sense to him. Didn't she understand what he had done to her?

"I had your letter," he said, "I know what I heard in it. It was unmistakable, and I had to stop you from doing it. But I didn't."

"I would never have done anything like that," she snapped.

You mean, he thought, *because you're not a weakling like me.* Bishop didn't believe her because he knew she would never have been honest with him or anyone else about whether she had actually been in danger. But then he saw that despite herself the thought that he had been worried about her made her shift tack and soften towards him. *Even though I didn't save her from suicide.*

"It wasn't that you didn't come to me. It was that you didn't contact me at all." She was hurt, but, to his surprise, she was no longer angry.

Because she thinks I had a reason for what I did. She thinks I was right to hurt her.

She looked at him candidly. "If you had just said *Rachel, stop this foolishness about God and St. Francis de Sales,* I might even have been grateful for that, once I had thought about it. I would have taken it. Maybe it even would have knocked some sense back into me. But you didn't even do that."

Bishop didn't know where to begin. He couldn't answer her, so she went on.

"So I took what you did as a rebuke. I knew I had manipulated you when we were both at a weak moment. Because I knew you were vulnerable to me. But I had been dishonest with you. What you did wasn't just a rebuke of the foolishness I was saying, it was a rebuke of everything about me. As if nothing I ever did or said meant anything or ever would mean anything. And worse yet, I took it as something I had coming to me, because you were right about me. Because I'm a liar to the bottom. And you knew all about it."

What does she mean by that? But he was too full of the story he wanted to tell to be put off the track. "Tom never told you how close we came?"

"What are you talking about?" Rachel asked.

She was sure I was about to say something else. About something she did. Not about what I did. "Tom and I started to drive to California just after I got your letter."

"You actually started to drive to Riverside?"

"I got your letter on Christmas Eve. I couldn't leave my parents on Christmas. And I didn't have a car. (You remember why I sold it.) So Tom and I set out in his Nova. We left Willimantic on the 26th. We got most of the way across the country."

"You and Tom were driving together? You were both going to show up at my parents' house in Riverside? That certainly would have been awkward."

Now it was Bishop's turn to stare as he put together what Rachel had been saying. He had never been sure when Rachel's affair with Corbin had started. When he first guessed that it had happened at all, during his last conversation with Corbin in Reno, Paul had assumed that the affair had begun after her return from California in January, which would have been after the abortion and after he had failed to come to her.

But clearly Rachel's affair with Corbin had started much earlier than that. Certainly, it had started by September. Maybe as early as July, when Rachel had begun showing Corbin her poetry. Having both Tom and Paul show up at her parents' door unannounced would indeed have been beyond awkward. *Because that child she had been carrying may have been Tom's. But she didn't tell him about it. Because she didn't trust him. That's why she went to Portland with me, not with him. Which made me her patsy. But that's also why she wrote that long letter from California to me, not to him, because patsy or not I was the one she trusted, the one she wanted to be understood by. That's also why her letter never actually talked about her abortion, because that wasn't what was bothering her. It was her affair with Tom that was on her mind. Even though she couldn't come clean about it.* Rachel looked away, noticing that Bishop had just guessed something she thought he already knew. *This is what she thought I was talking about. This is why she thought I didn't come to her.*

"So Tom came along with me across the country" Paul said, "because he didn't know what you were going to say to me when you saw me. He

231

didn't know you had been pregnant. I sure hadn't told him about it, anyway, because I was ashamed of it, and I couldn't face what he'd think about it. I didn't tell him about it until after you'd dropped out of school. He was my friend."

Rachel raised her eyes to him. She had been brought to a standstill. And for her, he now realized, their story was not about his failure to rescue her when she needed it but about all the lies she had told him when they were lovers.

And that's why I turned back in Gallup. Because somehow I already knew about those lies. Or did I? Maybe that's just something convenient for me to believe. I'll never really know.

This thought brought him to a stop. But Rachel had caught hold of herself. And she still wanted to know something.

"Why didn't you tell me this story? I know why Tom didn't, but why didn't you?"

"Because I turned back. I didn't want you to know that. I knew what you would think."

"But I thought worse things when you didn't contact me at all."

"I was too humiliated to do anything but wait."

"So why did you turn back?"

"Tom had been riding me the whole time, how what you were asking was crazy, how I was a fool to put up with it, how you were jerking me around. He really didn't want me to get there, and now I see why."

"So what happened?" Rachel asked.

"Finally, I decided I just had to pray about what to do. And that was strange. I'm not the praying kind, as I'm sure you know. But in your letter, you seemed to have been putting things to prayer in a big way, so I felt I owed it to you to see if that might help me clarify my mind. We had gotten all the way to Gallup, New Mexico. I had looked in the AAA guide, and I knew there was a cathedral there. So I thought I would go there and ask God what to do."

"And what happened?"

"Nothing happened. God didn't speak to me. I saw that I was a complete fool to expect otherwise. And I just had to go home. So I did. And left you to do whatever it was you were going to do."

They looked at each other for half a minute.

"I didn't do it," Rachel said. "Whether I was thinking about it or not. And if I were, you couldn't have stopped me from doing it." She gave him a sad smile. "I tried it twice later, though." Only a few minutes before she had denied even thinking about it. Then she shook her head. "Now I'm sorry I put you through that. I didn't have the right to kill myself and pin my death on you, considering what I did to you. And only fools lay their deaths at other people's doors. I might not have known that then, but I do now." Then she laughed. "Anyway, God knows how I would have taken it if you had both showed up at my parents' house."

Bishop still didn't know what to say.

Finally, Rachel broke the impasse. "That really is such a sad story." Then she looked at him.

"Sadder in the long run for you than for me, it seems," Paul said.

"Still, a sad story for you too." She took a breath. "I've thought so many hard thoughts about you over the years. Now I regret that. Thinking those hard thoughts, I mean. Our relationship was over anyway, and there was no other way it could have gone other than the way it did go, though I struggled on with you into March."

Again, she laughed a little. "I don't know whether you know this, but I gave it up with Corbin as soon as I got back to Connecticut in January. Straight from the plane I went to your place looking for him to have it out with him. But you were there by yourself, so I made love to you instead. I actually thought I might patch it up with you."

So we each thought we had done something unforgivable to the other, Paul thought, *And we each thought it might just pass over, and we'd be all right if we could just pretend hard enough. We felt like idiots because we were.*

"I couldn't face you about Corbin and me, though," Rachel went on, apparently not noticing that Bishop's look had hardened. "And God only knows how long it would have been before he let something slip about it. You know he thought the world of you, and he couldn't stand that you might think ill of him. But it would have had to come out. I thought when you went back to your parents' house to cram for your orals that you had guessed how it was. So I wrote you another long letter

233

and confessed the whole thing and begged you to forgive me, but you didn't answer that. You just don't answer long letters from me."

So that's what was in the letter I threw away unread at my parents' house, he thought. *Would I have lived a different life if I had forgiven her then? Because I know I would have forgiven her if she had asked me to. Because I couldn't say no to her about anything. Would that have been enough?* He looked at her, trying to picture that unlived life, the different Rachel and the different Paul who would have lived it. *No. I had already crossed the Rubicon with her in Gallup, but I didn't know it. She isn't thinking about how I let her down. But that doesn't mean that I didn't do it. She wanted to come clean to me about what she did. But I never would have come clean to her about what I didn't do. Whatever she did with Tom, there was still no getting past what I did, myself. Because it showed me what I'd always be. If I had stayed with her, I would just have taken a longer route to the same place.* It was simpler for him to believe this point, and he tried to, but he was still looking softly at her because he couldn't help it. *Stop this.* Soon he was beyond stopping it. *Stop this now.* He met her gaze. And she met his. "You must have thought I hated you," he said.

"I knew you had reason to."

"It would never have occurred to me to hate you."

"I don't think you understand how it was even now. I never chose Tom over you. It was you who cared for me, and he didn't. And it was you I went to when I got into trouble, even when that trouble was something Tom and I had done to you. You think I could have asked Tom to take me to that place in Portland? I knew what he was by then."

She smiled at him, as if sharing a secret. But this was all news to him. He still couldn't imagine anyone preferring him over Corbin. Especially in bed.

"I always had thought of love as a dark adventure," she said, shaking her head, "a way of transcending ourselves in fire, and so did he, and the whole idea was all so stupid. I thought if I saw love that way I would strike through the mask of sentimentality and self-deceit and break into some truth, even if it was an unhappy truth, some truth that was worth every lie. But all I learned when I slept with Tom was that I was a different kind of person from what I thought I was, and there was no going back

234

to what I had been. He even changed what gave me pleasure, but I can't say any of it ever gave me the pleasure it promised."

Rachel again smiled at him, as if of course he would understand what it was that had changed what gave her pleasure.

"That's what I wrote to you, that it was always you who mattered to me, despite what I did, and that I hoped that maybe you could lead me back out of the mess I'd gotten into, because I couldn't get out of it myself. But when you didn't answer me, I knew what the only thing I would ever amount to was. And to learn that from you, even from you, you who I thought of all people could reach me, meant that I was just what Tom said we were, people who had trifled with love so much that love was wasted on us. Because we saw through it. And we saw through each other. And we saw through ourselves."

"I never got that letter. I was afraid of you. And I was afraid of what you would say. And that I'd just surrender. So I threw it away."

Rachel thought about that for a full minute.

"There wasn't really any way back for me, so maybe you did the right thing. Because if you had forgiven me, I'd have always been fooling myself about what I actually am deep down. Because I really am what Tom showed me I was. And I'd have gone on just to make you and everybody else more unhappy, as unhappy people always wind up doing. At least the way it actually turned out made me acknowledge the truth about me, that I have a taste for cruelty, and a vulnerability to it, that I just can't get rid of. I had to figure out some way of living with it since I couldn't change it."

"That's what made you drop out of grad school?"

"I was sure you knew about me, and that you were right about me, so I gave up everything and went home again to Riverside. I had some hard thoughts about you. Because you broke it off with me, which is not how I ever thought it would go. I've always been the one who does all the breaking off." She laughed a little at this thought before she went on, gravely. "I wound up blaming Tom for how it all turned out, but I knew it was as much my doing as his. I did have it coming. I knew that at least. And what you did to me that spring, I guess there isn't any point in going over that now." She shook her head, smiling. "But I would have thought about it differently had I known that you had actually set out to come to me in California. Even if you didn't make it. And I might have done many other things differently too."

"I'm sorry too," Paul said, "really sorry, if that means anything after all these years."

She reached out her hand and touched his cheek. He leaned his cheek into her palm and closed his eyes. After a few seconds, he took her hand in both of his and kissed her palm. She put her arms around him and kissed him gently. An electric pang of desire and regret rolled through him, and he returned her kiss. Then he came out of it.

He broke the embrace. "I can't do this to her."

"Paul."

"I'm sorry. I just can't." He began to back away.

"Why are you doing this? We've done nothing wrong."

"You haven't. But I have."

"You haven't either. It's still Tom that she really wants, not you. And he'll always be between you."

He turned his back on her.

"Oh, for God's sake, Paul. Don't be such a fool."

He walked a few steps away, conscious of trying to walk as slowly as he could. Then he found himself running.

36

$\mathcal{A}$s Susan and Jack arrived at the Shetland playground on Sunday afternoon, the new friend Susan had spent so much of Saturday in conversation with was already sitting on the park bench beyond the swings. She had introduced herself as Christine Shaw, and Susan, basking in the warm glow of the woman's fascination with her, had instantly felt as drawn to her as if each had been put on this earth for the other. It was a relief to have a friendly listener, because Susan had felt vulnerable since Paul had left in some kind of trouble on Thursday morning. This new friend had taken an interest in Susan but had said little about herself, not even explaining why a woman without children would be sitting by herself at a playground.

"I'd usually be pushing my Jack on the swings right now. See him over there in the cowboy shirt? He always wants to go too high," Susan said, as her friend gave a polite glance in Jack's direction. "But I've been so tired, so very tired, that I have to watch for now. At least he understands that I'm not up to it. And he's good enough not to make me feel guilty about it. But I do anyway, of course."

Hearing this commonplace mock-guilty parental chitchat, the woman had given Susan a grave look, and Susan, feeling that she had made a fool of herself, could not meet her gaze. Then, sensing Susan's embarrassment, Christine had caught herself and smiled. Relieved, Susan had felt something warm and rich rush over her, and she drank it in like a wilted plant. But she had learned her lesson.

Susan understood that beneath Christine's courtesy was an old suffering so familiar that she no longer seemed aware of it. This made her kindness to Susan, indeed her special consideration, stand out like a formal recognition. *She has suffered her way into gravity*, Susan thought. But the electricity of that grief was also somehow physical. Susan felt it in her throat, in her spine, in her knees. She could not stop looking at

Christine. Before Saturday afternoon was out the woman had recognized her as the widow of the professor at the university, the radical poet, who had been randomly murdered in the Owens Valley a few weeks before.

The woman was tall, and slender, and elegant, with a marble-pale face and a waterfall of glossy black hair. Her posture was erect and wary, her every gesture restrained and formal. But something was burning in her black eyes, like a flame behind a pane of ice. Susan felt, every time their eyes happened to meet, as if the woman had caressed Susan's hair or smoothed her fingers softly down Susan's face. *Oh, more of that, please,* Susan thought.

But there was also something Christine wanted to give Susan, something Christine had to whisper to her. And Susan wanted to hear it, wanted to be in on the secret. Susan could almost feel the warmth of Christine's breath on her ear.

When Sunday came, Susan was glad to pick up the conversation where they had left off. And she had carefully thought overnight about what to say.

Christine asked her how she was coping with her husband's death. Susan paused, wanting to get this right, because this woman knew something about grief that she didn't. And because it mattered intensely to her what her friend thought of her. The worst thing about grief, Susan finally said, is the unfinished business you may have had with someone you loved. There are always missed connections and mixed feelings, and now they'll be beyond you to sort out.

"Yes," Christine said, "I had unfinished business with someone too. But I was never able to grieve for him in public because my relationship with him was private, a secret." She smiled. "I sometimes felt that I should make it up to his widow. But I wondered what good that would do, since she didn't know about me. I had an idea about finding some common ground with her, since we had both loved him. But that was a fantasy."

"How lonely that must have been for you," Susan said while taking Christine's hand, holding it between both of her own, looking up into her face. Christine was taken aback, but Susan didn't notice. Susan thought her friend might go on with her story, but she didn't. It was Susan who had to pick up the thread because her friend was disconcerted and had looked off into the distance. "We are all fools about love, aren't we?" Susan said, casting a furtive look at Jack, who was out of hearing, "We want to be generous, and we want to be greedy. We want to give ourselves up to the person we love. And we want to bind him down as firmly as we can." She wanted her friend to understand that she knew this. But her friend did not turn to her.

Susan had always been reticent with Claire, who worried about her too much, and pried into her feelings too much. She had even been reticent with Father Ronan, until the dam broke. She had been open with Paul from the very first, so open that she had startled herself, but that was because of what they had both felt, she told herself, about Tom. But before this black-eyed woman she barely knew Susan lay herself down recklessly, wholeheartedly, as she had not done with anyone since the night Tom took her home after that first poetry reading seven years before. She didn't know why she did this, but she couldn't help it. And as she was doing this she was aware, as she had been that night with Tom, that her friend was not a person it would be safe to love, although that danger was itself part of the attraction, and gave an extra impetus to Susan's surrender to her. In front of her friend all of Susan's own grief and fear became transformed into need. And that need had become so urgent that the woman herself had had to step back in the face of its black blast.

"Maybe I was greedy like everyone else," Susan went on, "but if I wanted Tom all to myself I never did have him that way, although most of the women I shared him with didn't really matter very much to him." Susan broke off, waiting for a reply. But her friend made her wait. *That's what I need you to know about me,* Susan thought, as though she had given her friend a present. *Now tell me what you need me to know.*

"Did that make it easier or harder?" Christine turned and looked calmly into her face.

"That all those other women didn't really matter to him? I don't know the answer to that."

"Because either way poses a different kind of problem?"

Susan thought about this question. "Yes." Then she burst out, "But I don't care how hard it was to love him. Maybe that makes me a fool, but I wasn't going to stop loving him." Susan was very sure of this. But as she said it, the words felt to her like pleading.

Her friend merely glanced at her and looked away. "We don't matter to them as much as they do to us."

"I think I knew where I really stood," Susan said, brushing aside what her friend had said. "Every time I knew he'd come back to me in the end. But Tom was never at peace with himself and never allowed himself to be known. Even by me; especially by me. That's why he always went for women who couldn't ever actually know him."

Christine looked at her skeptically, and suddenly Susan felt naked under her gaze. Susan couldn't explain why, but she had to hear from her friend that she hadn't been a fool to love Corbin despite everything. Her friend left her hanging.

"I'm surprised that any man wants to be known by any woman," Christine remarked, "That's why they always want to be with women who ask so little of them. Or put up with so much from them."

Still holding Christine's hand, Susan looked down in front of her. It was urgent to persuade her skeptical friend that Tom had loved her. That loving him had not just been a mistake. She didn't know why. She traced a figure in the dust with the tip of her shoe, trying to catch hold of herself. But it didn't do her any good. *I'm in a state. What's happening to me?*

Gathering her forces, Susan caught a breath and looked her friend directly in the face, holding her gaze. "Maybe so. But there was still some hunger in him that made me wild for him right to the very end. That's why I can't complain about what he did. Because the thing that gave him that electric attraction for me was the very thing that kept driving him into the arms of other women."

Her friend shifted uneasily under all this. "Much joy it must have given him."

What did she mean by that? Susan thought. But she wasn't going to be turned aside. "I don't care who Tom slept with." Susan had shocked herself by saying this, but she couldn't stop herself now. "I wanted him as much the day he died as I did the day I met him and threw myself at him." She was sure that there was something that would weigh with her friend in this comment, something that felt like a sexual secret that she wanted her friend to know about her. She wanted that secret to bind them together forever. Hearing this urgency, her friend turned to face her. Christine looked Susan up and down for a long second. Susan flushed. *Keep looking at me that way, please.* "Those girls thought they loved him," Susan went on, finally feeling the warm current of the woman's full attention rushing over her body, "because they thought he had something they wanted. But you don't love someone because he *has* something, you love someone because he *wants* something. Because wanting something's how you know you're alive. That's why I had to have him. And that's why I didn't care about the other women." Susan paused. Finally, after her thoughts cleared, she went on, "It might have been different if it hadn't been certain to me that I meant more to him than they did. If there had been somebody he really gave himself deeply to...," she broke off again, "I'm not sure I could have borne it if that had happened."

Christine pulled her hand away, but continued to smile at Susan, although her smile became somehow brittle. What Susan had just said had made the woman shift in her seat, but Susan had no idea why. Whatever moment Susan had been waiting for between them had passed. Susan caught her breath and collected herself. Her friend waited for her to go on; her friend had something to say, but she wasn't ready to say it. Again, it was up to Susan to pick up the thread.

"His poetry took a turn last year," Susan said. "I'd never read anything like it before. It seemed like a breakthrough to me, but what do I know about poetry? He published it under another name, ultimately. But I knew from it how much he loved me. And I knew he wanted me to know it, despite everything." *I do have that,* she thought. The next thought took a second to arrive. *But that's all I have of him now.*

"Why didn't he publish it under his own name?" Christine asked.

"I think he was tired of the figure he had cut in the world. And maybe some of it was stuff he couldn't say straight out in his own voice. I don't think anyone else would have guessed that book was by him. I won't go into why."

"Did writing that book make him any happier?" Christine asked.

Something hung on the answer for her friend, but Susan couldn't place what it was. Feeling the challenge in the question, Susan first took in a breath. Then she looked toward the swings, but Jack wasn't there.

Susan stood up, but noticed Jack digging in the sandpit with the Peterson boy. "This is the strange part. I would have thought it would at least have changed our relationship. But shortly after the book came out, something came over him, something he never got out from under. Somehow, it was tied to the book, but I don't know how. He was absent, impatient, mysterious, even miserable. And sometimes he seemed so desperate. And desperate in bed. Especially desperate in bed."

"Like a man having an affair." Christine looked at her directly.

"It was different, darker. He was in a shadow."

"He was ashamed."

Susan didn't know whether her friend was scoffing, but she did know that her friend did not believe what Susan had said. Again, there was a challenge in her face. "Yes, he was ashamed. But he was often ashamed. It was more than that. It's as if he was ready to let go, ready to just glide all the way down."

"Down to what?" Christine asked.

"That's what I'll never know. My God, all I ever wanted was to love him."

Christine gave Susan a look. She was wondering something. Then she changed her tack.

"Do you blame yourself about that turn to the dark?"

"He always felt guilty about me, and I couldn't change that," Susan replied. "But this was different. He started to talk about a friend from graduate school, someone he had hurt. Somehow, whatever he had done to his friend had something to do with what had come over him. I thought he might feel better if he went to see him in Reno."

Christine shifted impatiently in her seat, and Susan saw a flash of distaste cross her expression before she could suppress it. Then, with studied cool: "Did seeing this friend solve your husband's problem?"

"Tom picked up the hitchhiker who killed him on the way home from Reno."

"Oh. What a waste. And now you'll never know."

"Know what?"

"Whether he would have stood by you."

Susan wondered what her friend had meant by that. More, appar-

242

ently, than that Corbin might have worked through his dark patch. Whatever she meant, she had turned Susan's thought in a different direction. Susan pushed through. "I'm sure he would have stood by me right now," Susan said. "And I really need him now. Because something's happened, something's been happening, that I need him to be with me to face. I wish I'd been up front about it with him from the beginning."

Christine's stiff, sympathetic expression did not change, but Susan sensed a tectonic shift in her attention. Susan's friend had been taken by surprise and had to take new bearings.

"What do you mean?"

"I had had a brush with cancer last winter, with melanoma, just when Tom started to take that dark turn. Funny, it was Tom who spotted the primary. He kissed it, on the back of my knee, one night back in January while we were lying in bed." Susan turned her knee out to show the scar, but somehow she felt as though she were asking her friend to admire her legs. Despite herself, Susan flushed, as if it were her friend, not Tom, who had, on the night her trouble began, kissed her so tenderly there, behind her knee. But something, some unease, perhaps a tremor of fear, Susan could not say which, passed across her friend's face. After a moment, controlling herself, her friend looked carefully at the scar. "I had it removed. When my scans came back clear, I decided not to tell him."

"But that wasn't the end of it, was it?" Christine asked.

"No. The Thursday he went up to Reno, I had more scans. And the cancer had come back."

"My God. I'm so sorry." Christine was at a loss for a second. And Susan saw her soften, as if she had let out a long breath. "Your husband died just when you needed him most."

"It isn't as though he had left me. He would have helped me face the music. Helped me to die, anyway."

For a brief moment, her strange friend looked at Susan with alarm. "Would he have? Are you sure?"

Susan was taken aback by her friend's response. Why was she afraid that Tom might not have risen to the occasion of Susan's illness? It wasn't an idle fear her friend had felt. The woman had meant what she said.

"That's when he was at his best," Susan said. "I still keep wanting to ask him things. I keep calling the answering machine in his office to hear his voice."

Christine didn't know what to say. She sat there at a loss.

Jack ran up. "Are you too tired, Mommy? Do you need to go home and rest?" He gave a hard look at Susan's friend.

"No, honey, I'm just fine," Susan said.

"You look tired," Jack answered.

"Are you Jack? I'm Christine."

Jack looked at her as if he didn't believe that that was actually her name. "Don't get her too tired." Jack let that command hang for a moment between him and the strange woman. Then Jack gave her another hard look, a suspicious look. After a few seconds, he ran back to the play structure.

"Where are you being treated?" Christine asked, after Jack was out of hearing.

"At Loma Linda. I work there myself. In the very clinic that's treating me." Susan told her how Paul, the friend her husband had gone to see, had taken her up to Independence to the arraignment of her husband's killer and had taken care of her son that day. He had volunteered to come back from Reno to see her through her treatments, and he had seen her and her son through some scary days.

"You must know what he wants," Christine said.

Susan had to give way and defend Paul. She wondered whether her friend would believe anything she said. She didn't know why, but she wanted her friend to love him. But then she wondered why anything about Paul's motives might matter to her. Had her friend seen through her? Had she guessed what Susan felt about Paul? Was she going to think less of her, already entangled with another man only a few days after her husband was buried?

"Paul's been good to me," Susan said, a little more firmly than she had intended to, "and he'll stand by me to the end. But he knows I'm not available to him. I'm Tom's wife. And I'm going to die that way, and sooner than anyone expected. He's never been forward with me at all. And I trust him completely." Drawn as she was to her friend, she did

244

not tell her about the moment in the car in Independence that made her trust Paul so completely. She was too ashamed of what Paul had saved her from. "But I do know what he feels," she went on, as if her thought had not been brought momentarily to a stop, "though he tries to keep it from me, and I'm ashamed of not putting him straight. I pretended to myself not to see it. Because I need him, and I can't get by any other way. I don't have the liberty of doubting his motives." But she couldn't meet her friend's gaze as she said this. She pretended to look for Jack on the play structure.

"Are you sure he'll see it through?" Christine leaned forward.

"Whatever his motives may be, his kindness to me is for real, and Jack loves him," Susan said, as if to close the door on the doubt about Paul. "I feel completely safe with him. I have to get ready to die. And I have to make plans for Jack."

"What are your plans for Jack?" The woman made a leap in the dark, putting together what Susan had edged up to but not quite said. "To give him to this Paul?"

This question took Susan completely by surprise. It was as if her friend were always one step ahead of her. "I don't have any right to ask Paul for that. But I'm sure he'll do it. I know I shouldn't use the feelings I've allowed Paul to develop for me to lead him on about Jack. I shouldn't even use those feelings to lead him on about helping me through my treatments. I don't want to just use him. But that's just what I'm doing."

"It seems to me like he's asking to be used." Christine said this as if Paul were about to receive a punishment he deserved.

Susan was mystified. "That doesn't make it right. I was trying just to let it happen naturally between him and Jack. But maybe it comes to the same thing as leading him on. Because I have nothing to give back to him." She paused for a second, gathering herself. "But that's all moot now."

"Wait. Why do you say that?"

"Because I'm afraid I have just scared him away somehow." For some unaccountable reason, the woman flashed Susan another look of alarm. "I told you how he saw me through my first treatment. I couldn't have gotten through it any other way. And neither could Jack. And Paul's kept on helping me. He helped me with Tom's funeral. He brought me back to Independence again this week for the preliminary hearing about Tom's murder. He's kept up Jack's spirits. He even raked up the lawn and cut the grass. He says he'll be back for my next treatment next month. But I saw when he left to go back up to Reno on Thursday that there was something the matter."

"Why would he go back to Reno?" Christine asked.

"He said from the beginning that he didn't want to be forward. That he didn't want to intrude."

"That's strange, for someone with feelings for you."

"Feelings he doesn't think he has a right to."

"I don't get it."

"As I said. I think I scared him off. I think I was forward with him. Sunday, when we went to the botanical garden. I didn't do anything, but I'm sure he saw what I was feeling."

"I would have thought that would have been what he wanted, for you to feel something for him. And doesn't that solve everything, anyway?"

"No. He's afraid."

"What, is he a mouse?" The woman shook her head, as if Paul's folly was just beyond belief.

"Not afraid of me. Not afraid of feelings for me. Afraid for me. Because I'm in a spot where I can't take any risks. Where I shouldn't do anything that might not be the right thing for me. Because I need to keep my head on straight to get ready to die. He's afraid I'll let myself do something with him I'll regret."

Christine had to think about this. She had been brought up short. Susan didn't understand why.

"If you had let your feelings go, would you have regretted it?"

"I don't know. I say that honestly. I really don't know." As Susan said this, she remembered that she had just told her friend that she was still Tom's wife and always will be. *And that's still true! It is!* Susan couldn't begin to sort out how she felt. But her friend did not even notice the contradiction; it was as if she had seen through Susan from the beginning.

"He's not afraid to love you, though he doesn't want you to know it. But he's afraid you might come to love him. Is he right? Have you come to love him?"

"A few days ago I could have denied it with a clear conscience. But now I can't." *In fact I did deny it,* she thought, remembering her hour with the priest, *but I was lying to myself.* "I don't even know whether it's the right thing or the wrong thing. I see only trouble either way."

"Trouble for you?"

"Trouble for him. Whatever tangles I get my feelings into, they'll all be over in a few months. But all I've got to give him for his love is my divided feelings. And grief and heartbreak. And he's so fragile and so doubting. All I want is for him to be happy, and I can't give him that. I do feel for him. And it would be so much better for him if he didn't feel anything for me."

"So where did you leave it?"

"He says he'll be back on the third for my next treatment on the fourth."

"That's only a little more than a week away."

"But Jack needs him now. And I do too." She hadn't planned to go this far, but it was too late now. Tears welled in her eyes, and, humiliated, she blinked them fiercely away, but couldn't hide them. "I told him when he left on Thursday that I was going to call him Saturday, last night. I wrote his number on the pad by the phone. But I didn't call it. I wasn't sure that I'd say the right thing if I did."

The woman gave Susan another long look, then brushed Susan's hair back with her fingers, and softly held her face between her palms, looking into her eyes.

"If he has any sense, he'll call you himself."

They sat together for a few more minutes, while Susan pulled herself together. Then Susan said that it was time for her to collect her son and begin thinking about making dinner. When her friend stood up from the bench, Susan hugged her tightly. The woman held her tenderly, and stroked her hair, pressing Susan's cheek against her shoulder.

"Baby, you have got one tough row to hoe. You hang on tight." The woman continued to hold Susan for several minutes and Susan relaxed in her arms. Finally, the woman kissed Susan on the forehead.

"Will I see you again?" Susan asked.

"Yes, I hope so. I'll look for you."

Susan watched her climb into a yellow Vega and drive off. She thought: *God knows why she came here yesterday. But today she drove here looking for me.*

37

SITTING THAT SUNDAY EVENING AT HIS DINETTE TABLE, WHICH was cluttered with two days of dirty dishes, Bishop could not tell which of the things he had done was worse, that he had let himself go with Rachel, or that he had fled Riverside when he knew that Susan needed him to be there.

He had stopped himself with Rachel, but not before he had responded to her kiss. Worse yet, her kiss had actually been tender and even chaste. It was he, feeling the familiar warmth of her body against him, who had given their embrace an erotic turn. And she had not even been attempting to seduce him; she was forgiving him for his failure of nerve in Gallup years before.

When he had first arrived back at Susan's home on Massachusetts Avenue, out of breath from his escape from his encounter among the warehouses with Rachel, his thought had been that he had to get away to collect his thoughts. He was glad that he was driving up to Reno anyway the next day, and the fact that he had already arranged to leave would make what he planned to do seem less like a chaotic retreat. He had half-persuaded himself that his flight back to Reno was necessary to protect Susan from what he had just learned about himself, that it was something he was doing in her interest. Only as he sat in his too-quiet dinette in Reno did it occur to him that the real harm he was doing to Susan was not whatever he had not quite done with Rachel but his guilty flight afterward. Rachel had been right about him. Whichever way he turned, he would do some harm to Susan, some harm he had never intended but could not avoid, some harm he would only deepen the more he tried to avoid doing it.

How he would face Susan when he returned to Riverside in a little more than a week, he did not know. He was committed to going; she would need him to be there when she had her next interferon treatment, and he knew that at the very least there would be a terrible bout of fever during the night after the treatment. But he wilted at the thought of facing her now that he had discovered how little integrity he had.

Why did he have to mix his selfishness into everything?

At just that moment, the telephone rang, and Bishop picked it up on the first ring.

"Is this Paul's house?"

"Oh Jack, I'm so glad to hear you."

"I know you're coming back next week. Can you come back now?"

"If your mother wants it, I can come back tomorrow."

"I'm sure she wants it. But she's sad."

Relieved as he was to hear from Jack, he still needed to hear from Susan.

"And I want you to come back too," Jack went on, while Paul was still thinking what to say.

"How did you know my number to call me?"

"My mother wrote it on the pad here. She had your card in her purse."

He paused a second. "I *know* my numbers," he said, as if daring Paul to be skeptical about it.

"She was going to call?"

"She sat here a long time last night. I wanted her to read to me. But she couldn't. Then she took out your card and copied the number. Then she copied another number. But she didn't call anybody."

"Another number?"

"Some lady she met at the playground yesterday. And she was there again this afternoon. Blah, blah, blah. She didn't even see how high I was swinging."

Paul could not help it. He guessed who the woman was. His heart sank as he surmised what had really happened. *So that was why Susan didn't call last night.*

"She didn't call anyone," Jack went on, "She just sat there looking at the phone, and I watched the Betamax until bedtime. So tonight I called you myself."

"Where is she now?"

"She was going to read *Frog and Toad* to me, and then she fell asleep."

"Was she up late last night?"

"We both were."

"Was she all right?"

"The fever didn't come back."

"Was she sad?"

"Not just sad. She felt all night like she had to throw up, but she didn't."

"Is she eating?"

"Not very much."

"That part must be the medicine."

"But maybe not all the sad part."

"No. Maybe not."

Paul thought for a second.

"Are you okay yourself, Jack?"

"Sort of."

Jack paused for a second. "I want to hear you read more of *Narnia*."

"I will."

"It will make my mother happy too."

"I hope so."

"I'm sure it will. That's why I'm asking you."

"All right."

"And there's another thing, too."

"Go ahead."

"I want you to teach me to swim."

"I was a lifeguard in high school. I can teach you to swim. If it's okay with your mother."

"Mommy can watch. She'll be proud of me."

"She would have wanted to do that herself if she were feeling better."

"She wants to see *you* do it. She wants to see you."

Paul imagined Susan beside him in the shallow end of an outdoor pool, in brilliant sunlight, smiling as Jack kicked through the water, pushing a kickboard and churning up bright fountains of water with his feet. He exchanged a glance with the imaginary Susan, laughing in the pool. He closed his eyes, full of her loveliness.

Then he heard her voice, in the distance, a little groggy.

"Jack, are you on the phone?"

"I'm talking to Paul."

"Oh! Paul called?"

"I called him."

"Is that all right with him?"

"Ask him yourself."

"Oh, Paul," Susan said, having taken the receiver, "I'm so sorry if Jack bothered you."

"I'm glad he called. I'm glad to hear you too." This was true, but saying it this way made him uncomfortable. He had waved off her apology. But he was the one with the apology to make, not her. He saw her smiling with nervous relief, her free hand playing with the ends of her hair as she leaned her head into the receiver. The image hurt him, but it also filled him with tenderness. *She deserves so much better.*

"I didn't want to be always butting in," she went on, "I didn't want to be taking over your life."

"He isn't bothering me at all. And neither are you. I'm just glad to hear your voice." That came out wrong too, as if she were the supplicant, and he the one with generous reassurance.

"I was going to call you yesterday." She paused. "But I lost my nerve. I was afraid of asking too much of you. I keep asking you for things. And you keep giving me things I don't have a right to ask for from you."

"I was afraid to call you too."

"Why on earth would you be afraid to call me?"

She really was surprised by this. And that surprised him.

Paul saw that whatever Rachel may have had in mind to do in that strange playground conversation with Susan she had so implausibly engineered, she had neither discredited him to Susan, nor told Susan what Corbin had been planning to do to her when he died. Paul could not figure why she had not done either thing. He decided to accept that gift from Rachel, although he did not have any idea what it meant. And he was ashamed that Susan somehow felt in the wrong. As if anything she was capable of doing could be wrong.

Oh, come on, said the imaginary Rachel. *She's afraid you might love her, when she can't love you back. She doesn't want to just use your love to get your help.*

But that's exactly what I want her to do.

Then she's afraid she might love you after all when she's still Tom's wife.

I'm not taking Tom from her.

That's not up to you.

This was too hard for him. And he had promised to take care of Susan during her treatment anyway, so he dropped the thought. He also decided for the moment to let what had gone on between himself and Rachel drop too; why hurt Susan more than she was already hurting? Honestly, he tried to tell himself, I'm not keeping this back just to cover my own shame. What good would it do Susan to tell her about that?

Sure, said the imaginary Rachel.

"I was afraid of asking too much of you too," Paul finally said, which was the truth, although not the whole truth.

"Aren't we a pair of complete idiots, both of us?" Susan's relief was a gift to him.

She laughed. "I guess Jack is the only one of all of us who actually knows what he wants. And has the sense to ask for it straight out."

"Please tell him how much it means to me that he called."

"It's funny. I was talking with a woman at the playground this afternoon—and yesterday too. I couldn't help it. I just spilled my guts to her." Susan couldn't stop herself. The whole story of her misadventure came tumbling out. She barely paused for breath. "I don't even know how she came to be at the playground; she doesn't have any children. But I've never met anybody like her. I knew she had just been through something—she didn't give me the details, but she seemed to have lost a man, a married man she was having an affair with whom she couldn't show grief for in public. She was very magnetic, and her grief was part of it; it colored everything about her, although she didn't say much more about it. It drew me to her. And she absolutely swept me away. I felt we understood each other completely from the very first word, as if we'd had all the same troubles. It was as if she already knew all about me. And she didn't even have to draw me out; I wanted her to know me, and I wanted to tell her everything, Tom's death, my cancer, all of it. I even told her I was worried that I'd somehow scared you away. And I didn't know what

I'd say to you to bring you back to me. But she told me you'd call. I don't know why she was so certain of it, but she was. It was as if she had been sent to tell me just what I most needed to hear. She did actually make me feel better. And here you are. So she was right."

Paul was ashamed of himself, after this firehose rush of confession from Susan. He hadn't confessed anything. And he still couldn't.

"But I didn't call," he said, "Jack called me."

"Thank God he did. And as I said, anyway, here you are. Will you come down tomorrow? Jack would like it. And so would I."

As soon as Paul got off the phone with Susan, Rachel called him.

"Before you hang up on me, just let me tell you that you have to call Susan right away."

"As it happens, I just got off the phone with her. But what is this to you? You wanted me to run back to Reno, and I did."

"You put me in a false position. I wouldn't have wanted you to run from her if I had known she was dying."

"How did you find that out?"

"I don't have to tell you that." Paul couldn't understand why, but there was the slightest hint of flirtation in her tone.

"I know anyway. You stalked her yesterday, and this afternoon too, at the playground. She didn't know who you were. But you knew how to get out of her what you wanted. And she let everything spill."

"You should have told me yourself that she was sick."

"It wasn't my story to tell."

"I'm not a monster, not the one you think I am, at least. I wouldn't have wanted to hurt her had I known that. I wasn't looking to hurt her anyway."

"Isn't that exactly what you sidled up to her to do?"

"I sidled up to her, as you say, to warn her about you. To tell her that your design on her is creepy. That she should watch her step with you."

"My design on her. I'm just trying to help her."

"Just trying to have her depend on you. So you can possess her for yourself."

"I'm not asking her for anything."

As he was tensing for battle, suddenly she laughed a disarming laugh.

254

"Do I believe that? I didn't believe it. Maybe I do believe it now." He could tell she was shaking her head. "But I don't know. Because it's not something any actual human being can do. You can't *just help* somebody you love. No matter how selfless you think you are, you just can't stop yourself from helping her in a manipulative way, because that's how it always is with love."

"Tell me everything else you know about love while you are at it."

"Oh, *love*, whatever that is. If *love* is the right word for whatever neurotic quest you seem to be on, to love without being loved back." Rachel paused, and he knew she had smiled. It wasn't just that she wasn't going to be drawn into a brawl. For all the ways she was poking at him, her tone was friendly and conspiratorial. Bishop could not understand why. "You are just strange enough to try such a thing, but not strange enough to actually pull it off. And anyway, you can't expect that she wouldn't sooner or later see what you feel for her." Rachel gave a cheerful scoff. "No human being could be that thick for very long."

Just as he had when Rachel had called him after the arraignment, and just as when Rachel had confronted him in person after the funeral, Paul knew from the first moment that he had to flee from her. Even hearing the tone she had just taken, cheerful, practical, ironic, knowing, the tone of a friendly co-conspirator rather than of a life-threatening temptation, he knew he would have to keep listening to her until he understood exactly what she had in mind to do to him.

He brushed her laugh aside. "I know she's not available to me. If she's seen through me, I hope she knows I know that. And that she can trust me to play by the rules."

"You 'know' it. But you haven't honestly accepted it. So you don't really know it. Besides, she likes you herself."

"That only makes it a bigger mess."

"She knows very well how much you have done for her. She told me how much it means to her."

"I never doubted that."

"And she's worried you may give up, may be spooked off. She told me that too."

"I promised to stick by her, and I've never wavered about that."

"But you were spooked off. You can't deny that. And that's the strange part. I went looking for you Wednesday precisely to spook you off, to show you to yourself as you really are."

"You won. That's why I'm sitting here in Reno."

"But then I changed my mind about spooking you off," she went on, as if she hadn't heard his tone, "because of what you told me about how you had set out for California all those years ago when I needed you to come to me. That put you in a different light for me. It didn't exactly get you off the moral hook with me, because after all you didn't make it to my door, and you went on to break up with me very badly."

She was teasing him. And he responded to her, although he felt ashamed of it.

Rachel continued. "Anyway, what you said made me see you differently. And in fact I felt something for you, maybe just pity, maybe a bit of regret, maybe even a bit of guilt, if you can believe that. I don't pretend to understand it, but life is strange. So I decided not to go after your weak spot. But then you yourself, all on your own, despite me, made exactly the point I had come to prove about you, just when I had decided not to make it."

He had to stop this. "Yes, that's exactly what I did. I admit it. I'm going back there tomorrow. I'm not waiting for her next treatment."

"That's why I'm calling you. To tell you to do just that."

"Thanks for making it so easy."

"Don't be a ninny. The question isn't whether you are among the pure of spirit. And it isn't as if she cares about anyone's purity. She was married to Tom, after all, and however stupid she was about him she did know what he was like, even if she always thought she could make him into something different. You just think about what she needs right now. You didn't cross any Rubicon with me. You had a moment of weakness. Stop trying to be different from everyone else in the world. And stop priding yourself about how different you are from Tom."

"Why are you telling me this? You were trying to discredit me to myself and you succeeded. I know I'm going to go back to Riverside. But I'm ashamed of myself. And I don't know how I'm going to face her."

"None of that matters. Your shame. Jesus Christ. And I'm sure despite the nonsense you just said that you actually do know what really matters. Which is what she's going through. So cut it out. Here's why I'm calling you. Because when I went there looking for her to find a way to warn her off you..."

"Without letting her guess who you were?"

"That wasn't hard. She never put her guard up. I would have found a way. I was just going to say some cynical true things about men, and let her draw her own conclusions. I wouldn't have had to tell her anything about me. Or let on anything I knew about her. It would have been easy."

"You made a strong impression on her. You could have had your way."

"She made a strong impression on me. Just as she did on you. Out of the blue, she had perfect faith in me. And I wanted to live up to it. If you can believe that, knowing me as you do."

"I had the same experience with her."

"Tom was stupid not to value her. There's something very serious about her. Something that makes me stare and leaves me open-mouthed. It made me want to do right by her. All at once, I wanted to draw her closer and hold her tight."

Suddenly Paul smiled. "You're in love with her yourself."

"I won't deny it. But I've done too many bad things to her for that, and there'd be too many things to explain. So the best thing I can do is to make sure you stick by her. It's also the only thing I can give her that she might really want, anyway. After what I did to her, I owe her something."

"If she has feelings for me," Paul said, "She's also ashamed of those feelings. They seem like infidelity to Tom. Loving me is a temptation she has to resist. And I want her to resist it. Particularly if it makes her ashamed. Because whatever Tom really was, she's going to need her idea of him to help her die."

"But all those ideas are wrong," Rachel exclaimed. "She needs to know what he was about to do to her. That would hurt her. But it would free her too."

"She already knows he was bad to her. She accepted that, in a way. But she doesn't know he was going to leave her for good. Knowing that would just hurt her at the worst time. She can't be herself without loving him. That's what I don't want to take from her."

"What she needs is you," Rachel said, "You're the one who should be with her when she has to face the music. And the only thing keeping her from seeing that is this fantasy about Tom. Tom who was in the act of leaving her for me when he died. Let her at least love somebody who loves her back as she deserves."

"Don't take Tom from her." Paul meant this to sound firm. But he knew that Rachel would take him to be pleading.

"I will if you don't keep your promise that you'll go back to Riverside tomorrow."

Rachel probably didn't mean this. But Paul didn't want to test her.

38

$\mathcal{T}$HAT MONDAY WAS MEMORIAL DAY. ALL THE WAY FROM RENO, Paul drove down the flag-bedecked main streets of desert towns. He arrived at Independence just as the ceremonies were beginning in front of the courthouse. A reviewing stand had been built in front of the steps with a lectern and a stand of flags. A handful of dignitaries sat at a table awaiting their turn to speak. Two sheriff's deputies, in dress uniforms, stood on either side of the flags. A small brass band, on the other side of the lectern, was puffing through *America the Beautiful* to a crowd of fewer than one hundred people when Paul pulled over at the intersection in the center of town. He cranked down his window to listen. Under other circumstances, he might have thought of it as quaint, a scene worthy of Norman Rockwell, but he could not bring himself to think of Independence as anything other than forlorn. When Corbin had passed through this same intersection, he was already, without knowing it, in his last half hour of life. But today the band was happy to be there, playing their glittering instruments in the sun, having their moment. The thought that anyone could be happy in Independence made him wistful. He helplessly wished them well.

And then the thought came to him of Susan, tired but happy, in her brilliant dress, standing over Jack and him as they kneeled where the sulphurs flitted among the clusters of verbenas in the butterfly garden. "Ready to go?" he had asked.

"I'll never be ready to go," she had said, "But I guess it's time." Her sentence wrung his heart. But he thought, *how lucky I was to have had that moment with her. How lucky I am to have known her.*

$\mathcal{W}$hen Paul arrived back at Susan's little house in Riverside, Susan did not allow Paul to feel ashamed or constrained with her. She was frankly and radiantly glad to see him. And she and Jack had cooked a big pot of chili, which was simmering on the stovetop when he arrived.

"I know you wanted to teach Jack how to make chili yourself," she laughed. "But I wanted to at least cook something with him while I have the energy. And I'm so glad about your coming here early that I just had to do something for you." Then she gave him her smile, the one she'd been saving for him all day.

Paul was more relieved than he could say. But he also felt a pang that he believed he concealed because she was nicer to him than he deserved. *Had she intuited how it was with him? Or was she just so glad to see him that whatever had happened, whatever he had done that had spooked him away, was suddenly something of no consequence?* However it was, he accepted her smile gratefully.

Paul noticed that she ate very little of the meal she and Jack had prepared. And he saw that Jack had noticed the same thing. "Don't you want more?" Jack said. "You should have more."

"I know it's delicious," she said. "But I can't eat more than a little just now."

"I didn't want you to miss out," Jack said.

"I'm enjoying it vicariously."

Jack looked at her.

"That means I'm enjoying how you like it," Susan explained.

"That's not the same as eating it." Jack wasn't going to let her off the hook, big word or no.

"Besides, I'm saving room for the ice cream."

Jack looked at her again.

"Yes, I *have* earned my dessert. I'm the one who gets to decide that." She tweaked his nose. "Jack believes in rules," she said to Paul.

"A good habit," Paul replied.

"A good habit in general," she said, going to the freezer, "but not for tonight. Tonight, we all get ice cream without having to earn it. Sometimes it's good not to have to earn everything."

Paul knew she was putting on a brave face for Jack. And Jack knew it too. But they both accepted her pretense, and not just because they were humoring her, but because they knew that if she were capable of going to such lengths for them, then she was still herself in the ways that most mattered, and conspiring to embrace her brave fiction was their way of returning the love that moved her so hopelessly to try to spare them what all three of them knew nothing on earth could spare them from.

After dinner, Paul picked up where he had left off in *Narnia* and read to the moment when Peter kills Fenris and Aslan rescues Edmund from the White Witch.

*P*aul was lying in the cot in what had been Corbin's study, reading *Scripts for the Pageant* when he heard a knock at the door. It was Susan, bone-tired, who had just finished putting Jack to sleep. She seemed even smaller in her nightgown, which shifted over her as she moved, as if she were a ghost in the wind. Her thinness hurt him, and he felt helpless about it.

"Are you still awake? Can I have a minute?"

Paul sat up and drew his legs down over the edge of the cot to face the door. Susan lingered in the doorway, not stepping fully into the room.

"I just wanted to tell you how glad I am that you've come back early."

"Jack called me. I couldn't say no. He's very persuasive."

"I'm glad to see you myself." She paused, and gave him a look. "Very glad."

Her look unsettled him. He didn't know what to make of it.

"You can count on me. And I'm glad I hurried back. My mind was here the whole time I was in Reno anyway. I should have known that was how it was going to be."

"I'm so grateful for you. I hope you know that."

"I know that without your telling me." But she hadn't just meant that she was grateful for his help.

She was still looking at him directly, making up her mind how to say it. "But I worry that I'm keeping you from your life."

"I wasn't doing anything in Reno that won't keep."

If he thought this would turn her aside, he was mistaken.

"And I think I've been asking too much of you."

"You haven't asked for anything I'm not eager to give you."

"But I haven't been able to give you anything in return."

"You have made me happy."

"I know you are happy here, with us. I couldn't help but see that."

He hoped she would smile as she said this. But she looked at him gravely.

"Yes, I am. I can't remember being happier."

"But you do know I'm going to die."

"I knew that as soon as you told me what you had."

"And you do know how bad the last part of it will be."

"I'm ready to keep figuring things out. As ready as I can be, anyway."

"That's brave of you. And I know you mean everything you say." For a brief moment, a smile of gratitude flickered across her face. But she owed it to him to go on to the end, though it took her another second to bring herself to do it. "I still worry that you want something you will never have."

"The only thing I want is to do exactly what I have been doing."

She shook her head, looking sadly at him. "I know there's more to it than that. I know you have feelings for me. How could I not notice something like that?"

He had been afraid of this moment. Her face was watchful and uncertain; he couldn't read in it how he should take what she said.

"I won't deny that I love you," he said, after a beat, "but I accept how things are. I understood that from the beginning."

How blunt his word *love* sounded to him. Had he really earned the right to use that word with her? He should have used a circumlocution as, out of tact, she just had done. It had never come easily to him to be honest under pressure. But he had said it now, and all he could do was wait for her reaction.

She did not shake her head, as he expected her to. Instead, she said, "How can I ask you to accept such an uneven bargain? It's just too selfish."

"I never think of you as selfish."

"But you know I can't keep up my end."

"I signed up for it. I'm ready for it. And you do keep up your end."

"I shouldn't take advantage of you just because you love me."

"You shouldn't punish yourself because I love you either. I know what next week will be like for you, and I can't imagine not helping you through it. But about us my eyes have always been completely open. I know that I don't have a right to love you."

"Of course, you have a right to love." This burst out of her so fiercely that he had to stare. "Even if it complicates everything. Nobody can tell you that you don't have a right to love."

He had to take a breath. Even she was surprised by what she had said. Hearing herself, she looked down. She was unsettled.

"That's kind of you to say," he said, "I promise not to presume on it. You don't have to worry about me."

Still not meeting his gaze, she fiddled with her nightgown. But after a moment, she gave him a sad smile. "That's easier said than done." Her eyes were shining.

"I'm not greedy about love. I'll never put you in a false position. I swear."

"But I'm already in a false position." Then she stopped short, and looked down again.

"Not with me. You're not in a false position with me."

"Yes, I am. Because I don't have a right to love you. And I do." She was still fiddling with her nightgown, twisting a fold of the cloth between thumb and forefinger, her eyes on the ground.

Paul had to take a breath. "You have a right to love, too," Paul said. "We don't have to destroy ourselves over it. It doesn't have to change anything. I don't want you to do anything you aren't ready to do."

She looked up at him, her eyes brimming. "I don't even know what I'm ready to do." She bit her lip for a moment, then plunged on. "I feel unfaithful to Tom. And unfaithful to you. You have to know you will never have me to yourself. And you have a right to have somebody to yourself."

"I know your situation. I'm not trying to change it."

She had to shift her gaze a little over his head. She couldn't look at him directly. "I knew, and I didn't know, what you were feeling long ago. Somehow you always know when someone loves you, even when they don't want you to know it. I also knew it would be complicated, more than I could handle. But I really had nowhere else to turn. Now I feel as though I've used you instrumentally because I needed everything you did for me. I feel ashamed of it."

"I am not selfish about love, and you are in no way exploiting me."

She still wouldn't meet his gaze. "The priest we visited, when we set up Tom's funeral, he saw your situation at a glance. He also said that I felt more for you than I acknowledged to myself. I brushed that off then. In fact, I got mad at him. But thinking back on our time in the butterfly garden last week I see that he was right." Then, finally, she looked him squarely in the face. "I'm ashamed I have so little to offer. My feelings are too mixed, and my time is too short. I don't want to hold you to an unfair bargain. I don't think there's enough left of me to ever make you happy."

"You have already made me happy."

She shook her head. "If you love me, you foreclose loving someone who can love you freely. Someone who can love you as everyone deserves to be loved."

"That isn't how love works. It's not like ordering something you like off a menu. You don't say *I reckoned up all her virtues and calculated that the circumstances for loving her were favorable*."

"But it's not something that just happens to you either, like being hit by lightning or catching an infection. Whatever love is, it involves wanting to do the best you can for the person you love. And I don't think I have that best to give. Not anymore."

She blinked away a tear and looked into his face. Controlling herself, she tried not to cry in front of him. "And the worst of it is that I know how good you are to me. More than that. How good you are. Though you won't believe there's much good in you. But I just don't have the power to do the same kind of good for you. And I'm sorry. I would do better by you if I could. But I know how it is. I think the only gift I would have to give you, the only thing I could do about loving you, would be to give you up to someone better for you."

Paul wanted to comfort her, wanted to rush across the room to her, but he knew Susan was ashamed she had given way to her feelings and for him to notice would humiliate her. All he could do was sit there. "Let's just think about what we have to do over the next few weeks."

"The next few weeks may be all there is."

"Then let's keep it as simple as we can."

"All right." She took a breath, and caught herself up. "But I want you to promise me something." Her tears had stopped, and she looked very seriously at him. There was to be no mistake that she meant what she said.

"Go ahead."

"I want you to promise that if there's anyone else you love that you won't give her up for me. I don't want to die knowing that among the last things I did was to break someone else's heart."

"That's an easy promise to keep."

But she wouldn't allow him to wave off what she said this way. "It would be easier for me if it were a hard one. Because then at least I would know you'll be all right in the end. That someone will love you."

"If I can make you easy, I will be all right in the end. Don't worry about me."

"Of course I'll worry about you." For the first time that night, she smiled at him. "But I'm more grateful than I can say that you came to me."

And with that, she slipped quietly out the door. Paul put out the desk lamp and lay in the half-dark of the room. The moon, just four days from full, shone down through the window. He could hear an occasional car pass on Massachusetts Avenue, and, faintly, from further away, the low continuous rush from the freeway.

39

PAUL AND SUSAN WORKED OUT A PLAN FOR THE WEEK UNTIL HER treatment. Susan would take Jack to the Shetland school in the morning on her way to Loma Linda, so at least that part of Jack's routine would not be disrupted. Paul would pick Jack up at school at the close of the normal school day and spend the afternoon with him. Since Jack had made a special point about it, Paul decided to take Jack to the Sippy Woodhead pool on University Avenue on Tuesday afternoon, the 26th, to give him his first lesson in swimming.

As they made their way from the parking lot across the little courtyard decorated with a tile compass rose, Paul lugging a canvas tote with their suits and towels and a kickboard, Jack asked whether they would have to change in front of everybody in the locker room.

"Does that make you nervous?" Paul asked.

"Everyone will look at me."

"I felt that way too. I bet everybody does."

"What did you do?" Jack asked.

They entered the locker room, which had the stale smell of chlorine, wet concrete, and musty benches.

"Here's what I did. I felt everybody must feel the same way. And we all seem to have agreed that we won't watch, and nobody will watch us."

Paul laughed. "Besides, it smells in here. Everybody wants to get out of here as fast as they can."

"Why don't you give me my suit right now, so I can hurry," Jack said.

Tom would have taught Jack to swim, had he lived. Paul thought. *He would have taught him all the things men teach their sons. All the things I never seem to have learned.* He wondered what kind of man he was, really. How would he teach Jack all those things he had never quite gotten down, all those things Tom seemed to have had as second nature? Wasn't he just a kind of second-rate substitute for Jack's actual father?

Jack was pulling his swimming trunks up onto his pale, pudgy body. *How will he manage all the growing up he has to do, without his father?* Paul thought. He knew that Jack was sensitive. As Jack struggled with his trunks, Paul thought he had never before felt Jack's vulnerability so deeply. *Bullies will be on to Jack the way they were on to me.* He wondered who would teach Jack how to manage those trials. Paul hadn't weathered them very well himself. But he had gotten through. He wondered whether Tom had had the first notion of what it was like to be bullied. *At least that's something I do know.*

Jack finished changing while Paul was still trying to tie the strings of his trunks. "I win!" he said, grinning. His eyes were bright with the triumph he expected Paul to kid him about and share with him.

"Be a gracious victor, Jack," Paul laughed. "You'll be an old guy like me some day."

Jack smiled up at Paul. *He's glad to be with me.* Paul thought. *Somehow he must think I'll do.*

Paul put Jack's towel around his neck, and put all of their clothes back in the tote. He led Jack out to the pool deck and put their stuff down on the benches at the shallow end of the pool. Then he took out a squeeze bottle of sunscreen and applied it all over Jack's body and then all over his own.

"What's that stuff? It feels like baby oil."

"It's sunscreen. Your mother would really want to be sure you wore this."

There was already a small crowd of parents and children at the pool, and the air was full of laughter and shouting in all of the languages of Southern California.

"Why don't the other kids wear it?"

"Your mother is a doctor, and she has a special reason to want you to be safe in the sun."

"What will the sun do?"

"Sunburn," Paul said, leaving the rest unsaid.

Paul led Jack to the ladder at the shallow end of the pool, but Jack preferred to jump in, so they jumped together.

"Geronimo!" Paul shouted.

"Why do you say that?"

"I don't know. It's what people say when they jump."

"Maybe it's for good luck."

"Maybe it's just so everyone will look," Paul said, "We'll stay at this end for now, so you can put your feet down. If you're ever scared or don't know what to do, you can just touch bottom."

"Okay, but I'm not scared." Jack was firm about this.

"First, a trick. If you know this one, you'll never drown."

"I'm ready."

"Just take a deep breath. Then put your face down in the water and let everything else go. You'll hang there like a jellyfish. Just hang there until you need to take a breath. Then take a breath and put your face back in the water. You can do that as long as you need to. As long as you just give yourself to the water, it will hold you up. They call this thing the jellyfish float, but my father called it the Dead Man's Float."

"It should be the Live Man's Float."

Over the afternoon, Paul taught Jack how to kick while holding on to the side of the pool. He taught him how to kick not just with his knees but with his whole leg, so "you don't undo your kick whenever you bend your knee." As soon as they progressed to the kickboard, Jack forgot this lesson as everyone does.

Jack spent most of the afternoon kicking around on the kickboard, first launching from the edge of the pool and kicking towards where Paul stood waiting for him. Paul kept backing up while Jack wasn't looking so that he would get all the way across the pool without knowing that that was his destination. "Stop cheating!" Jack said.

"Half of teaching is cheating."

Kicking up great fountains of brilliant water, Jack then splashed his way all over the shallow end of the pool. There was a crowd of children with their parents in the pool, diving and surfacing, playing Marco Polo, and bobbing in the water at tiptoe depth.

Paul thought how happy Jack looked, as happy as he had looked in that first picture of him that Corbin had showed him in Reno. So many moments over the last few weeks had been so dark, and darker ones were yet to come. *I wish that this boy will have more moments like this one, that*

268

whatever happens he will never lose sight of moments like this one. Paul thought about his daydream, about Susan in the pool. He wished Susan were there to share Jack's joy. He thought of all the moments with her boy she would miss. And, thinking of them, more quickly than he could have thought possible, his own joy was overtaken by misery.

"Paul, what's the matter?" he heard Jack saying.

"I was only wishing your mother were here to see you swim. I just thought of how she would like to see how happy you are right now."

"You're worried about her." Jack looked at him gravely.

"I'm worried sick about her." Paul replied, "I always am. We both are. But I'll protect her always, as best I can. And I'll protect you always, as best I can."

"She's going to die, isn't she?" Jack looked directly into Paul's face, expecting the truth from him. The truth he already somehow knew.

Paul took a very deep breath. "I don't know. She's taking some powerful medicine. If she were dying, I'm sure she'd want to tell you so herself. She wouldn't have left it to me to do. She still must think she has a chance."

"She's protecting me. And she's protecting you." Jack wasn't going to be evaded.

"We have to protect her, both of us."

"We can't really do anything."

"If it does her good to believe that we still have hope for her to live," Paul said, "we'll have to let her believe that."

"For now." Jack said.

"Yes, it's no good keeping up the lie forever." Paul conceded, "Soon enough, we too will have to come clean to her."

"When will that be?"

"When she knows that even without her to care for us, we will get by."

"But will we get by?" Jack did not say exactly what he was getting at, but Paul knew.

"Yes. I'll take care of you. I'll stay here and take care of you. I'll promise her that when the time comes. That will make it easier for her."

"Nothing will make it easier."

"No. But she will still want to be sure you are safe. And I'll keep you safe. I'll always keep you safe."

*A*t about the same time that afternoon, Claire Wirthlin asked Susan to perform a bone-marrow aspiration and biopsy on a nine-year-old boy whose pediatrician suspected he might have acute lymphocytic leukemia. Manuel had been reluctant to take the IV, although his mother had brought his bear, and had a whole candy shop in her purse to give him once he came to. Susan did not know how hard she could press him, but as she was strategizing, the IV nurse joked with Manuel that you should always leave it to the nurse, never to the doctor, to stick you with a needle, since they do it all day. The nurse shook his hand as if he were an adult, and introduced herself to him: Samantha Madden. Somehow, she gave a slight flirtatious edge to this promise of alliance that made Manuel feel a little older than he was, and he took the needle for her sake. Susan marveled at her trick and wondered whether she would have thought of it. Using the needle wasn't the only thing best left to Samantha.

After the aspiration was finished, Susan felt the need to sit down at her desk for a few minutes. As she was typing her notes on the case, she thought about Manuel's mother, whose first name she was embarrassed to have to look up again on the referral form. Manuel had been reluctant to allow the needle to be used on him. But his mother had thought to prepare for the visit. Even though Susan had rather placed her in the background, Susan knew that the visit may well have been a power struggle had Manuel's mother not been there. Manuel's mother had inconspicuously stood by her son, and brought candies, his stuffed bear, and her knowledge of how best to comfort him. It had been a mistake to put her in the background, Susan felt. She had been confident in her own ability to get through to the child, and it had worked, but it could easily have not worked, in which case she would have regretted not making a better ally of the mother. She was glad Samantha had been more acute about persuading Manuel than she had been, and had thought to bring out the big boy in him by flirting with him delicately. *I got away with the mistake this time. But I have to do better. Samantha saved me.*

Manuel was three years older than Jack, she thought. Who will be intervening for Jack when he's that age? It would have to be Paul, either that or some stranger appointed by the state. *I'm lucky to have him. It's wrong of me to use his love.*

She sat for half a minute, looking into space.

I should give myself to him. While I still can. It's unfair to him not to. And I should do it for Jack.

She thought a minute more.

The problem is, I do desire him. But to give myself to him seems to use him. To be something I do "for him." Worse yet, it's something I might do in order to saddle him with Jack. Or it's something I do that gets me free of Tom. I have too many reasons, and every one of them ulterior. You're not supposed to love someone for reasons.

She gathered up her papers with a show of briskness, as if what she had typed on them was what she had been thinking about.

What did Tom say to me in my dream? I wanted to love you simply. When was there ever anything simple about love?

"*Ah,*" Desire still cries, "*Give me some food!*"

40

EARLY ON FRIDAY EVENING, THE 30TH OF MAY, AFTER PAUL HAD picked up Susan at the clinic and Jack at the Shetland School, Paul was rooting in the refrigerator trying to put together a collection of leftovers for dinner while Susan was reading *My Father's Dragon* to Jack on the living room couch. Susan had begun to read more slowly and had finally dropped off to sleep in mid-sentence when Jack poked her. But after a few more sentences, she fell asleep again. As Paul was trying to decide whether there was enough American Chop Suey to go around, or whether he should fry up some hot dogs and make a salad (or maybe give Jack the hot dogs and share the American Chop Suey with Susan, if he could coax her into eating any of it), the doorbell rang. Claire Wirthlin was on the front porch, with a large pot of lentils with ham and kielbasa, which she had brought over from her own apartment in Loma Linda.

Claire explained that she had wanted to give Paul a break and had arranged for other residents to bring other meals on the coming Fridays. Her plan, she said, had merely been to drop off the dinner and leave for home, but Paul prevailed on her to join them to eat, and Susan roused herself to come to the dinette table while Paul and Jack set out the bowls, the silverware, and the glasses. While Susan picked at her food, Paul tried to cover for her, telling Jack that this had been one of his favorite meals as a graduate student, and he would teach him how to make it soon. He felt ridiculous, as if he were about to pretend that a spoon full of lentils was an airplane he would fly into the mouth of the reluctant Susan. She tried to rise to the occasion, knowing that Claire would want to know how she was eating. And she ate rather more than she usually did, but Claire wasn't fooled, and Paul and Jack both knew it. Susan did, however, manage a scoop of vanilla ice cream, over which Paul had sprinkled some of the strawberries he had sliced for the previous night's dessert.

After dinner, Claire insisted on helping Paul with the dishes (which was Jack's usual role), so Susan and Jack retreated to the living room with *My Father's Dragon*.

Once the water was safely running, Claire told Paul, almost under her breath, that Susan seemed to be fading tonight.

"She has good nights and bad," Paul said. "More bad ones recently." He handed her a drinking glass to dry and turned back to the sink.

"She's doing her best to keep up appearances," Claire said, as she put the glass into the cupboard.

"It's a show on your behalf," Paul said.

"She shouldn't have to do that for me," Claire replied.

"She thinks she's sparing us. Jack and I both know what the real story is."

"Jack too?" Claire asked.

Paul stopped and looked at her, a soapy bowl in his hand. "How could he not? He's a smart boy."

Claire put the bowl she was drying back on the counter to look at him. "He trusts you," she said.

"I owe him."

"You owe him?"

"He's the one with sense in this house." Paul finished the dish he had been rinsing and gave it to Claire. "I can't explain."

"I won't get it anyway. But I'm glad he trusts you. I guess I trust you, too. I wasn't sure about you."

"Neither was I."

Again, Claire stopped what she was doing and looked at him. "Thanks for being straight with me. I'll help you where you need it. Susan told me about you, but I had to see you for myself. And I see why Jack trusts you."

"He's counting on me."

"To keep things together while his mother dies?" Claire asked.

Paul paused for a beat, then plunged on. "And to keep things together after that," he said.

Claire looked at him and managed a half smile.

41

SUSAN AND PAUL BOTH BELIEVED THEY WERE BETTER PREPARED for her next interferon treatment than they had been prepared for her first one. The nausea she had felt after the first treatment had never completely gone away. Susan had started to lose weight after the first treatment, and had brought home a green booklet of high-calorie recipes for cancer patients from her clinic. All of the dishes were extremely simple to prepare, because the authors understood that the patient (or the patient's family) would not be in a position to cook anything more complex. Paul planned meals around the recipes in the book, and although he and Jack both ate them with relish, Susan only ate enough to be polite. With dramatic pantomime, she pretended to take great pleasure in what she did manage to eat. But Jack wasn't fooled by this in the least, although he kept telling her how proud he was of her eating, as if she were a reluctant child.

After dinner on the day of her second treatment, the trepidation everybody felt about the onset of Susan's fever made it impossible for them to concentrate on *The Lion, the Witch, and the Wardrobe*, and they knew that the next chapters would be very important ones, so they postponed them until the crisis of this treatment had passed. In its place, Susan herself, having finished *My Father's Dragon*, read aloud some favorite books from earlier in Jack's childhood, as she had always done when he was upset. So not only did *Frog and Toad Are Friends* make a reappearance, but also *Horton Hears a Who*, *Where the Wild Things Are*, *Make Way for Ducklings*, and even *Goodnight, Moon*. The last, a nostalgic favorite, Susan, already in her nightgown, read to Jack in his bed, and to her surprise the book worked its magic, and Jack fell asleep easily as Susan lay beside him and held him. Whether it was the comfort of Jack's bed, or the warm nostalgia of the book, or just the cumulative effect of weeks of exhaustion, Susan herself fell asleep next to Jack, and slept for an hour or two.

When she finally woke up, she came back out into the living room, where Paul was still trying to make his way through *Scripts for the Pageant.* Soon after, Susan, still sitting in the living room catching up on *The Journal of Clinical Oncology,* told Paul that she was suddenly feeling very cold, which meant that her temperature had begun to climb. She slipped into bed and asked Paul to bring down an extra comforter from the top shelf of the bedroom closet. (There it was, over the ranks of Corbin's carefully pressed shirts.)

As she huddled up on her side under the comforter, Paul pulled his chair up next to her bed. But soon she began to shiver, and after a few minutes she was shivering violently enough that Paul began to fear for her. Susan began to moan as she shivered.

"Can you hear me, Susan?"

"Yes. I'm just shivering, but I'm not delirious yet."

"Can I do something for you?"

"Get me some of the electrolytes from the fridge, in case I start to get dehydrated. Maybe I should take some aspirin now to try to get ahead of the fever."

Susan took the aspirin, but could only manage a few sips of liquid.

"Hold me please. Will that be okay? I'm so cold. So so cold."

She rolled over, so as to face away from him. Paul took off his shoes and climbed under the covers, still fully dressed, and held her to him. Her shivering did not abate, and she continued to moan.

"I'm so cold."

"I'm with you. I'll stay with you."

"I'm scared, Paul. I'm really scared."

He held her a little tighter. "I'll be here as long as you need me."

"I thought I wouldn't be afraid to die. I thought of death as something you just grit your teeth about and get through."

"I'm scared, too."

"When patients of mine have died, at some point a change came over them. Somehow, at the end, it seems harder to them to go on living than to die. All of the pain, the loss of bodily control, the loss of dignity, just wears them down. Death must feel like a relief."

"Is that a mercy, do you think?"

"I guess I'll find out."

"I hope that's a ways off."

"It's not, though."

He didn't know what to say. She rolled onto her back, to look into his face.

"I won't see Jack in the first-grade pageant. I won't see him in the fifth-grade choir. I won't see him learn to drive. I won't meet his first girlfriend. I won't see him off to college."

Paul brushed her forehead with his fingertips and stroked her hair.

"I'm so worried for him. Who will take care of him?"

"I will take care of him, Susan. If you want me to."

Susan lay quietly for a few moments, still shivering.

"I was afraid to ask for that," she said, "but it's what I've wanted. I know it's what Jack wants."

"It's what I want most, next to sharing him with you."

She tried to smile.

"Will you take him back to Reno?"

"Why should I take him back there? I wasn't living there. I was just camping."

Again, she paused for a beat.

"Will you stay here?"

"Jack will do better that way. I think I can find work here."

"Will your boss in Reno be upset?"

"I liked her. She was good to us. She'll be glad to put in a good word for me here."

"Do you know who to talk to about it?"

"Yes. I saw the writing program director from Riverside at Tom's funeral. Did you see him? Tall, bald-headed, with a moustache? Kind, serious, quiet. He's writing a book about Lincoln's speeches. I'd like working for him."

Still shivering, she held his face with both hands and looked at him.

"I'm sad I met you so late. In another life, we would have made each other happy."

"I hope I have made you happy, at least a little, in this one."

"If I could have had happiness again, I would have had it with you."

After about twenty minutes her shivering began to subside, and the siege of fever began in earnest. In the interval between chills and fever, Susan suddenly sat up and held out her arms, turning to Paul to embrace him. But the act of sitting up was too much for her queasy stomach.

"I'm so sorry Paul. I was trying to thank you, and now look what I've done. Go to the kitchen and bring back the dishpan."

He rushed back and held the dishpan against the side of the bed. And he brought a dishtowel to wipe up the vomit—there wasn't much, because Susan hadn't eaten much—from the floor. He thought it was lucky that he didn't have to change the sheets, at least not yet. Susan sat up quickly and put the dishpan in her lap. But she retched drily into it, not having anything more in her stomach to vomit. Paul went back to the kitchen, took the ice trays out of the freezer, and began to break up the cubes with a meat tenderizer.

As Paul was filling a mixing bowl with ice chips, Jack appeared at the kitchen door, awakened by Paul's hammering.

"I'm sorry I woke you up, honey," Paul said.

"I think she needs me."

"I'm sure she'd like you to get your sleep. But I'm glad for your help anyway."

"Have you had to put her in the tub yet?" Jack asked.

"Not yet, but probably later. I'm making ice-chips now, for her to chew. It might settle her stomach. If she can keep it down, I'm going to want her to drink some fluids."

"Is it better, now that you know what to do?"

"I feel less helpless." Paul said, "But whether I really know what to do I just don't know. I just do what she tells me. She's the doctor."

"Last time you helped her a lot." Jack wanted to buck up Paul's spirits. *It's my job to do that for him,* Paul thought. *He shouldn't have to do that for me.*

"And you helped too."

"Did I really?"

"Since you are up for the night, maybe, why don't you go in and lie with her? I think she'd like that. Maybe she can relax into sleep and sleep through the worst of it."

"All right."

"Tell her I'll be right in with the rest of the ice. And I'll bring some wet washcloths too."

*B*ut when Jack came into the bedroom, she was still sitting on the edge of the bed, retching dryly into the dishpan.

"Jack, you might not want to see me this way."

"I want to see you."

He stood next to her and held her heaving shoulders.

"Please don't let this be your memory of me."

"Maybe you'll feel better soon. We can do things."

Paul appeared at the door with the bowl of ice chips, and he and Jack sat on each side of Susan, who sat with her head bowed, still holding the dishpan on her lap. Paul and Jack took turns feeding her ice-chips, slowly, waiting for her to nod for another. After about half an hour she ceased to retch although she still felt queasy.

"Let me see if I can sip that." She took a large swallow from a glass he held out for her and threw it right up.

"Small sips," Paul said, "Every few minutes."

This pace worked better, but she was still always on the edge of vomiting.

"If I can't keep this down, you may have to take me to the ER for an IV." *I don't know whether I'll ever be able to come home again if you take me to the ER.* But she knew enough not to say this aloud.

"Let's see how your temperature is doing," Paul said.

It was just 103. They gradually got the upper hand over her vomiting, and she drank some liquids. Paul swabbed her face and throat and chest with an icy cloth. But by two, her fever had burst through, and Paul had to carry her to put her in a bathtub full of cold water again. By four, the fever had broken for the night, and everybody collapsed into sleep, Susan and Jack on the bed, and Paul on the floor.

Again, in Susan's dream, Corbin came to her, and told her that she had to let him die. But she coaxed him into her arms and lay with him all night in the darkness. *I will be lying with you again soon enough,* she said in her dream.

42

$\mathcal{W}$HEN, ON FRIDAY AFTERNOON, TWO DAYS AFTER SUSAN'S SEC-
ond interferon treatment, they arrived at the Shetland playground, with
a new green Huffy for Jack in tow, Susan took out a crescent wrench
from her purse and removed the pedals so that Jack could use the bike as
a glider and get the hang of starting the bike, balancing it, and leaning to
turn. For the first few minutes, she held on to the seat back and one of
the handlebars and pushed Jack forward. She trotted alongside him once
he had gotten the hang of gliding, but almost immediately found herself
out of breath and lightheaded. Paul supported her back to the bench,
where she caught her breath. But still she laughed, despite the wave of
fatigue, to see Jack turning in figure eights in the grass. She spread her
arms across the back of the bench and smiled at him, the sun in her face.

"I know how to do this now! Let's put the pedals on." Jack said, after
about twenty minutes, as he sped past.

Needing to rest a little more, Susan gave Paul the pedals and the
wrench.

As Susan watched Paul fiddling with the pedals about twenty feet
from the bench with Jack standing over him offering advice, she heard
a car pull into the parking lot behind her. She waited for it to pull into
a space, but the car continued to idle. Susan felt the prickle of being
watched. As she turned, she saw the driver of the yellow Vega suddenly
look away from her. The driver fixed her gaze on Paul and Jack. She
paused only long enough to register who they were, then put her car back
into gear and drove away.

She came here looking for me, Susan thought. *And she didn't want to
be seen by Paul. But the last time she saw me she was curious about him.*

Susan tried to shake off the thought and stood up by the bench. Paul
was just tightening the second pedal, but it took him a few seconds to
realize that he had to turn that one counter-clockwise to tighten it. By the

time he had the pedal adjusted, Susan had put her hand on his shoulder.

"I'll teach him to brake first," she said, "and then we'll teach him to pedal." When Paul stood back up and dusted the grass off his knees, Susan took his hand and looked up into his face as if it were he, not she, who needed to be steadied.

Saturday evening after dinner they all felt ready to return to *The Lion, The Witch, and the Wardrobe*. Paul picked up where they were in the story and read on to the scene of Aslan's death.

"If everybody forgives Edmund," Jack said, "then why does the witch still get to kill him?"

"He is really sorry, isn't he?" Susan added.

"He didn't set out to kill his siblings, just to show them a thing or two," Paul said. "But his ugly feelings stampeded him into things he hadn't planned to do, but couldn't keep from doing. He's humiliated because he did it all to himself. And he *is* sorry. But he's also sorry because he has to be. He knows he might not have been sorry at all had the White Witch really made him King of everything or had his revenge felt the way he thought it was going to feel."

"He is sorry for himself," Susan said, "but that doesn't mean he isn't sorry too."

"Everybody is too nice to say so, but they all have reason not to believe Edmund because he himself isn't sure whether he's sorry or just afraid. He himself sees through every apology he might make. Everyone sees through their own apologies if they have any honesty."

"All right, but why does Aslan have to die to get him off the hook?" Susan said. "How does Aslan dying make up for whether or not Edmund was actually sorry for what he did?"

"Let's get back to the story." Jack was tugging Susan's sleeve.

"Hold on, honey. Paul is about to turn into St. Paul and give us all a lecture about Original Sin and the Epistle to the Romans."

"That side of this book has always bothered me. I know Lewis wrote the whole story because he wanted to explain what St. Paul says in the Epistle to the Romans," Paul conceded.

"Could we get back to this book? Why do we keep talking about other books?" Jack asked.

"He's trying, but I'm not letting him," Susan said.

"Shhh," Jack replied.

"But it still feels like cheating to treat the story as only a spoonful of sugar to get a big dose of doctrine to go down," Paul added.

"That's a relief. I thought you had a whole lesson plan ready about it." Susan laughed.

"Whatever St. Paul says, Lewis still has to work out the logic of his own story from within the plot. I think the point is that you just can't save yourself from yourself. Especially when you've done something that gives everyone reason to never trust you again. And when you know you can't trust yourself either."

"That part I understand. But it still doesn't explain why Aslan has to die to fix it. I would think everybody's forgiving each other would be enough," Susan said. "I think you can always forgive people if you love them. And I thought forgiveness was the point."

"The other children can't just wish Edmund's betrayal away by being nice to him. Whenever I have asked myself, 'Do I really mean this?' a still small voice in the back of my mind always starts telling me that it sees through me. We see through ourselves when we say we're sorry. And we see through ourselves when we say we forgive," Paul said.

"How does Aslan dying prove that the other children mean it when they forgive him?" Susan asked.

"Aslan has to forgive Edmund too. And unlike the others, Aslan understands that Edmund really was willing, for a moment, to let the White Witch kill them all. It wasn't what he wanted, and it was never his plan, but he would have bent to the White Witch's pressure when it came to it, even if he would have regretted it miserably afterwards, the way so many people did about other awful things over the years this book was being written. So Aslan understands how hard it is to forgive, and his being willing to die for it shows how much it will take to actually do the forgiving. Without Aslan's death, they all might have been fooling themselves about whether they forgave Edmund, just as Edmund might have been fooling himself about being sorry," Paul explained.

"I thought St. Paul's point was that Christ paid the price we couldn't have paid on our own for what Adam and Eve did," Susan said.

"I think that's still mostly a way of saying how hard it is to turn the other cheek. You have to love your enemies without denying that they really have been enemies, and might still be enemies under the skin, because actual forgiveness costs even those who do the forgiving something that it might be beyond them to pay. Aslan has to die because forgiving really isn't in our power to do by ourselves, any more than being sorry is, because no human being can do anything that isn't double and doesn't take itself back in the doing. Besides, what better reason can there be to forgive people who hurt you than that God forgave you yourself when you didn't deserve it?" Paul asked.

"So you still think it all has to do with another book, but it's St. Luke's book rather than St. Paul's book," Susan laughed.

"I surrender." Paul laughed too. "But it's still a good thing to love your enemies."

"Yay," Jack cheered.

"Why do you think they have to wind up at home, Jack?" Paul asked.

"Because people would miss them while they were off in Narnia," Jack said. "They have to come home for them. And no time passed while they were away, so nobody had to miss them."

"Here's why everybody always has to come back home at the end of the adventure," said Susan, standing up. "Because at the end of the adventure, it's time for the people who are hearing the adventure being read to them to go to bed." But she knew that in Independence, that coming Monday, she would herself have to forgive an enemy. She also knew that at the end of her story, which she already understood would not be far off, she herself would not be coming home.

43

*T*HE TWELFTH OF JUNE, THURSDAY, THREE DAYS AFTER THEIR LAST trip to Independence, where James Cole, a repeat violent offender, had agreed to accept a twenty-five years to life sentence in exchange for the prosecutor taking the death penalty off the table, was both Jack's graduation from kindergarten and his sixth birthday.

Paul hoped the improvised party he arranged would take the bad taste of the plea bargain out of their mouths, and maybe also lift the ever-present shadow of Susan's illness for a few hours. He had invited all of Jack's classmates and their parents to come to the Shetland playground immediately after the graduation, where there would be cake and ice cream at the picnic tables beyond the trees, then a soccer game at the back part of the park, behind the trees that shaded the playground, near the fence by the railroad track.

Paul and Susan had bought the Smithsonian's *Children's Illustrated Encyclopedia of Dinosaurs* for Jack's birthday, and the question of which was Jack's favorite dinosaur—Triceratops—had already come up among them since dinosaurs were a topic of dinner conversation. So Paul had bought a plastic tablecloth with dinosaurs on it, and dinosaur plates and paper cups, and dinosaur party hats. Had there been dinosaur party favors or dinosaur noisemakers he would have bought them too. His imagination ran riot for a while on the subject of dinosaur balloons, dinosaur cake decorations, even dinosaur piñatas. He wondered whether there was something else from the Jurassic age he had forgotten.

Paul saved the largest of the frosting roses for Jack, but he also saved one for Susan, who did manage to eat some of the cake. They also had pink lemonade in the dinosaur paper cups. It was fortunate that so many of the parents had stayed, because Paul, who was new at this, had underestimated how difficult it would be to organize a soccer game for kindergarteners, many of whom had not played it before. What they wound up playing was a kids vs. adults game, which the kids who knew the game—three or four, whose parents had recently arrived from Mexico, had been playing since they could walk—played with a vengeance. The kids who did not know the game caught on quickly, having an opponent that was really worth beating. The improvised camaraderie of parents was new to Paul, and he was so caught up in the game that he almost didn't notice—and Jack didn't notice either—when Susan ran out of steam, slipped through the trees to the playground, and sat on her usual bench to catch her breath in privacy.

$\mathcal{A}$ familiar face was waiting for her there, a face Susan had half expected, and, indeed, she had wanted to see. She knew, after the glimpse she had caught of her the previous week, that she should be wary. But her friend did not notice Susan until she was almost on top of her. Susan was shocked at how faded she seemed, like the sun seen on the horizon through fog, a pale disk where the blaze had been. *This is how she looks when she is alone,* Susan thought. That dear-bought mastery over grief that gave her friend her charisma had ebbed from her, leaving only the grief behind. When they had last spoken, Susan had been so drawn to her that it almost didn't matter to her whether Christine meant her well or ill. The difference in her today made Susan feel a flash of pity, against her better judgment.

"I thought you might be here," Susan said, a little too brightly. Christine came to herself and smiled. "I was hoping to find you again, too." She stood up and hugged Susan closely.

Susan took in the fragrance of her friend's perfume and felt the warmth of her breath against her face. Despite herself, the electricity of Christine's embrace went to Susan's head.

"I have to sit down," Susan said at last. "I'm so exhausted I can barely keep upright. I'm sorry."

"Is that from your treatment? How did the last one go?" Christine asked, sitting down again at her side.

"Harder than last time. But here I am."

Christine looked at Susan, an unasked question on her face.

"I don't know whether it's working or not," Susan said. "I'll have some tests next month. I don't really want to talk about it."

"You're on my mind," the woman said. Then suddenly she brightened with undisguised pleasure. "And I'm glad you came."

"I glimpsed you in the lot a few days ago, but you drove off without parking your car." Susan looked closely at Christine as she said this, but her friend smiled confidentially, as if to dissipate the gravity of that look, and Susan had to return her smile.

"I saw you were with the friend you told me about and decided not to intrude on you. Where is Jack today?"

"It's his birthday. Paul and everyone from his birthday party are playing soccer just beyond the trees. I've just stopped to rest. I got so totally out of breath I felt dizzy, and I didn't want anyone to see how sick I was feeling. I'll have to go back to them in a few minutes, or they'll worry."

"I won't keep you, then. But I did want to ask how things had turned out."

Susan told her how, on the evening of their last conversation, completely on his own Jack had called Paul on the phone, and invited him to come back to Riverside the next day, and how Paul had seen Susan, so very gently, through her second treatment. He had even been teaching Jack to swim.

"I suppose that cleared up a lot of nonsense," Christine said. This came out a little more firmly than she had intended. Susan chose not to pick it up. But she didn't forget the note.

"Jack is very persuasive, as Paul says."

"I guessed that someone had broken the impasse when I saw your Paul with you the other day, fiddling around with Jack's bike. But I was hoping it was *you* that had done it." Again, she could not keep something out of her tone. She might have had more to say, but she didn't say it.

She turned her gaze on Susan again. "Has Paul leveled with you?" Christine asked.

"Yes and no." Susan found it too hard to explain just how things stood with Paul.

But her friend had to know. "What a strange man he is." Then she paused a second, to regroup, and to soften her tone. "It isn't as though you are hard to love. You deserve better."

"I *am* hard to love." Susan said.

"I can't think of anyone easier to love," Christine said, smiling.

Susan looked away. *I don't want to love him,* she thought, *but I can't help it.* She tried to throttle her thought with both hands, like a little gaping snake. *And right after I made him admit that he loved me, I told him that I'm not available to him. Then I told him that I loved him anyway.* She wondered whether her friend had read what she was thinking in her face. Susan held herself steady, still looking away, until the moment passed and she was safe again.

"It's like men to dither when they have something important to do with women," Susan's friend said at last.

You have something in mind here, and I don't know what it is. Susan thought. But she had something in mind of her own, and despite herself she relished springing the surprise on her mysterious friend.

"He's never dithered about whether he's going to help me through what I have to go through. And he's made the leap for Jack." Susan turned to meet her gaze.

"Made the leap for Jack?" It was hard for Susan's friend not to stare.

"Agreed to raise him when I die." Susan said this simply, as if she did not know how astonishing her friend would find what she said. "He was afraid I wouldn't ask. I'm seeing my lawyer next week to make it official. They're kind of alike, really. Both worriers. That's what must have come of Jack's spending his whole life worrying about the state of his parents' marriage. It's strange, but Jack is more like Paul than he is like Tom. They're on the same wavelength."

"That's strange," Christine said. "Paul's scared of his own shadow. He won't face up to loving you. But he's willing to lift a mountain if you need it moved."

"Something hurt Paul about love. Something Tom did. Or maybe the girl Tom took from him long ago that he never got over. He doesn't trust himself about love."

Christine didn't blink. "If he doesn't love you straight out, then he's a fool."

"Even I can see that he loves me. But he still doesn't think he has the

286

right to." Susan didn't add, *And I still won't let him do it. Because I also don't have the right to.*

Christine couldn't hide her exasperation. "How can you do anything that means anything if you don't trust yourself about love?"

Unexpectedly, Susan laughed. "Do you really trust yourself about love? Honestly? Do I? We're just better at keeping that doubt down than he is. But we find a way anyway, doubts and all. And he will too. He'll take care of Jack, just as he has taken care of me." *And Jack will love him more honestly than I've ever been able to.*

Christine paused, at a loss for once. She had to think about this remark. Finally, she smiled. "God bless him then, I guess. Because from what I know about him he's going to need all the divine assistance he can find." She shook her head, but she was still smiling.

"I have more faith in Paul than he does in himself," Susan said. "And more than you do."

"Faith in him or not, you are still keeping him at arm's length, aren't you?" Christine asked.

"I am. I don't know why, but I am. God knows I do love him. And I have only a few months to get it straight. But I just can't do it to Tom."

"Tom is dead."

This brought Susan up very short. But she suppressed the flash of anger she felt, because she thought she knew what her friend intended. *She thinks it will be good for me to love Paul. But why is she pushing me so hard about this? And why is she so hard on Paul, if that's what she thinks?*

"I didn't say that what I felt made any sense," Susan said, making a concession she didn't quite feel. "But I'm still Tom's wife. That is not about to change."

Susan saw that her friend was about to retort but then thought better of it. It took her friend a second to figure out what she wanted to say. Finally, her expression softened. "It's lucky then that that hasn't stopped Paul," Christine said. "It would have stopped most people. I'm glad for your sake he keeps at it." Then, as if releasing something she had held back, she smiled warmly at Susan, and Susan could not help relaxing her guard. She let that smile wash over her, luxuriating in it. *She thinks I'll love him in the end anyway, doesn't she? And that's what she seems to want.*

Still smiling, the woman put her palm on Susan's cheek, and Susan relaxed into her friend's touch. "Tom put you through hell. And now life has too. But you're a brave girl. It's no wonder Paul loves you. And Tom should have loved you better."

Susan didn't know what to say. She just looked at her friend. And her mysterious friend looked back into her eyes. She seemed to be holding up to her all of Paul's love to drink, as if it were hers to offer. *Can Wisdom be put in a silver rod? Or Love in a golden bowl?*

And suddenly Susan thought, as her friend searched her face, *Tom is no stranger to you. You understand him too well.* Almost at the same moment, Susan thought, *You also know Paul. When you saw Paul in the parking lot last week, you recognized him. And that's why you were so warm to me from the first moment. You were looking for me. But who are you? And what do you want?* As her friend softly took her palm from Susan's cheek Susan felt a flash of white-hot anger. She broke off the gaze Christine had been holding and looked down into her lap, withdrawing into herself, her face expressionless so that her friend could not read her. *Everything you have told me is a lie. And everything you have felt for me is a pretense. And everything I have felt for you is my own foolishness. Whatever you wanted, it can't be good, because you wouldn't have had to lie to me so much to get it if it were.*

Susan glanced at her friend. But her friend had closed her eyes, her face weary but at peace. *Something has happened to her. Something has taken the life out of her,* Susan thought. *I've never seen her at rest before. She has always seemed strong to me. But she's damaged. She's floundering.* Not opening her eyes, Christine reached for Susan's hand and held it in both of her own. *I should hate her but I can't do it.* Then Christine sighed, her eyes still closed. *She thinks she's at peace with me now, because she thinks she's given me Paul's love. And given me hers. She thinks that's saved her.* Susan turned this thought over and over.

As Christine sat Susan looked her up and down, wondering. Christine was older, and tougher, than the kind of woman Tom usually went in for, Susan thought. *That's why I didn't see it. It was fresh faced girls at poetry readings, the kind who couldn't tell the difference between being excited by poetry and being turned on by the poet, whom Tom always took to bed. He liked the kind of girl who would look up at him with bright eyes and think how lucky she was to be with him, just like I did, not grown women who had been scarred by love and survived it and knew how the world works.*

That's why you sought me out after he was killed. Because you were still obsessed with him so many years later. You must be the woman Tom took from Paul years ago, the one that wounded their friendship. That's how you know both of them. What happened between you made all three of you drop out of school. It broke and darkened you all. And none of you ever got over it.

That's why you are still so ambivalent about Paul. You think he's beneath you, because you threw him over for Tom, and he let Tom take you. But what he thinks still matters to you. And what you did to him still weighs on you. I think you still even feel for him, though you won't face it. That's why he's always in the back of your mind. And it's why you don't want to run into him yourself. You have too much between you.

And now Tom is dead and you wonder whether you even have the right to mourn him, though you've spent your whole adult life mourning him while he was still alive. And I'm the one person who would know what you are going through, the one person who mourns Tom as deeply as you do, but also the one person you can't be honest about it with. And maybe that's why you are so eager to see me and Paul sort it out. Paul is the only gift you can give me, the only way you can show what you feel for me. Because despite everything you've tried to do to me, you do feel for me. That's why you're so happy right now.

Coming to herself, Christine opened her eyes and looked Susan in the face. "Do you know what happened to your husband's killer? Did his case come up?"

Susan shook herself, turning a bit away from her friend's gaze. "There was a plea bargain. Paul and I went back to Independence for the hearing just this week."

"Did you go there to address the court?"

"I wrote a statement that I read into the record, a victim impact statement."

"God. How do you sum up what happened to you?"

Susan turned to look at her friend directly. "I didn't try. I just didn't want that Jane Davenport to make my husband's case the test case for restoring the death penalty. I could smell that that's what she wanted to do. Everything she said to me from the very beginning was about making that case. She didn't care for me at all, except as the victim whose grief she was planning to put to use to land herself a seat in Congress. I tried to feel something for the man, and I couldn't. I couldn't get past his self-pity. But I couldn't send him to the gas chamber for me. I've seen enough of dying this summer."

Her friend did not pause to take this in. "What did they give him?"

"They gave him twenty-five years to life."

"That doesn't sound like he got very much of a plea bargain."

"He was a two-time loser. They didn't have much latitude about what to offer him. But they took the gas chamber off the table. Which is what mattered to me."

"If it really was on the table to begin with."

"Maybe they just scared him into making a deal. They scared me into that deal, anyway."

"And then what?"

"Then he said something very strange before the judge handed down his sentence."

"Go on."

"He said, 'I know this won't do any good. But I want you to know this anyway. I never wanted to kill that man. I wanted his money. Cause I knew he had it. People like him always have it. And I wanted his god-damned too hot too pretty car. But I didn't want to kill him. I've never had to kill anybody before to take their stuff. But he fought me. And I thought he was going to get the knife away from me. He knocked me down, into the gravel. But I got up before he got onto me, and he didn't get my knife. He could have. I don't know why he didn't. It was close, anyway. Maybe he even let me get back up. Then I brought him down. And I was so mad because he was so God-damned foolish I stabbed him again once I had him down.' "

As Susan was saying these things, Christine's face grew more and more shocked. Suddenly, she said, "My God, am I really that vile?" Then she jumped up and ran away.

What did I just say? Susan thought, *And what just happened?*

And as she turned back to face the little woods at the end of the playground, Paul emerged from between the trees, just in time to see Rachel get into her car and speed away.

44

*T*HAT EVENING, AFTER JACK WAS ASLEEP, AS SUSAN SAT ON THE couch still leafing through *The Journal of Clinical Oncology*, Paul sat beside her, but he had not brought a book with him. A long moment passed, and Susan felt shaky. She felt she had kept something back from him that it would be awkward to explain.

"I thought I saw someone I recognized with you today, running from you," Paul finally said. "I thought she had seen me and had to run away."

Susan felt a flash of shame, as if behind Paul's back she'd allowed herself to go too far with her friend. And, she told herself, she really had felt too much for her. And told her too much. But Susan saw that taking her to task was not what was on Paul's mind; he was worried for her, as if she had been at risk. From his reaction, she knew she had been right about who her friend from the playground had been.

"No, she was running away because of something I said to her." She straightened herself in her seat as she said this, as if she were more sure of herself than she was, and more in control of what had happened. "But I don't know what it was I said that made her have to do that."

Then, with a rush of confidence that she thought would put her another few steps ahead of him, she added, "I have a guess about who she was, though. And I guessed she knew you and wouldn't want you to see her."

"She doesn't mean you well. I've been trying to protect you from her. I should have told you about her sooner."

Susan felt rebuked by this. *So he wasn't surprised to see her. And he knows what she planned to do.* "I seem that fragile to you? That much in need of protection?"

"You don't really know her."

"And she's dangerous?"

"Yes. But I couldn't figure out how to warn you about her without doing something that I knew would hurt you. I thought I could keep her away. I'm sorry I couldn't. I'd like to tell you the whole story."

I knew she was dangerous from the first moment I was drawn to her. That's why I was drawn to her.

What Paul said put her on edge, but she wanted to tell her story first. She had something to confess, and she couldn't let it wait. Whatever Paul was so uneasy about, whatever it was that he was in such a hurry to confess to her, it was hard for her to imagine that it would change her view of him. *He might be capable of doing something stupid,* she thought, *but he wasn't capable of doing something really wrong. And had Paul actually warned me about her, about how risky she was to know, how risky she was to love, would it have made any difference to me?* Susan did not even now regret meeting her, even though she knew she had been in over her head. But she knew her friend had approached her under a pretense and had ducked a thousand opportunities to come clean about who she was. "I don't know her name," Susan said, before Paul could speak, "though she gave me a name I don't think is hers. But I think I know now who she is. She's someone you loved back in grad school. Someone Tom took from you. Someone who loved Tom, and loves him still. Someone you dropped out of school over."

She felt a flash of triumph to have laid out before him how much she knew. *Even Paul has underestimated me because everybody does.*

"I didn't know Tom told you that story. And I didn't drop out. I failed out," Paul said.

"He didn't tell me the story. He did tell me that something he did to you years ago weighed on him. And because it was Tom, it wasn't hard to guess what it was."

"Rachel Lake is her name. That's who I saw running from you, whatever she called herself."

"She's a wreck. She's come to pieces since Tom died. I felt for her."

"Did she tell you that? That she was grieving for Tom?" Paul asked.

"No. She didn't tell me anything about herself. Though she did say she was still grieving for someone. I didn't know a thing about her, but I felt that grief. It swept me away. Because it felt like knowledge, secret knowledge. It didn't matter to me that it was strange for her to be there.

All I wanted was to sit there with her, to listen to her, to have her eyes on me. Maybe I should have been more wary about her. But I couldn't be. That grief under the surface was too powerful."

Unexpectedly, Paul smiled. "I can't blame you for feeling for her. That you can do that even for her is what's best about you."

He doesn't quite understand. He thinks all I felt for her was compassion. And he loves me too much to see me clearly. Please, please, please clear my path to love him as he deserves.

But Paul went on. "And I'm sure she also swept you away. I've been swept away by her. It's hard not to be. That's why she's so frightening."

Of course, he knows how she is. But she knew Paul had given her more than that. *He knows how hard it is to avoid getting wrapped up in her, and he doesn't blame me for it. Because he too has been wrapped up in her, and it still hurts him. She still has a hold over him.*

Susan told Paul how, under the spell of Rachel's sorrow, she had wanted to draw her friend to her by making one offering after another, by telling her everything: how something had darkened for her husband just after his most recent book came out; that somehow what had happened to Tom turned on what had passed between Tom and Paul years ago, which Susan assumed had to do with a girl; and how she had sent Tom to Reno to see if clearing the air with Paul might settle his mind.

"That's what Tom told you about why he had to see me? Because he had taken Rachel from me years ago and felt bad about it?"

She looked at him. *That was news to him; so Tom had some other reason.* She didn't know what to say. When she didn't answer, Paul asked another question.

"Hearing everything, she didn't tell you who she was?" Paul asked.

"No, and you don't have to tell me she had a design on me. I see that. I even felt that at the time. But I had to know her. And I had to open myself to her. There was something about her."

Paul nodded, but he seemed to be agreeing with more than what Susan had actually said.

"I told her about you too," Susan went on. "About everything you had done for me. I even told her what I felt for you. I don't know why, but I wanted her to love you."

"And what did she say about that?" he asked.

"She wondered what your motives were, but I told her I didn't care what your motives were. I needed your help and I was glad to have it." Susan paused for a second, hoping he would acknowledge her compliment. But he kept his face totally straight. *Because he himself doubts his motives. Even now.* She gave it another try, smiling at him. "I told her I couldn't doubt your motives anyway after the way you have been caring for Jack and me while I die. And that changed everything. I had been begging something from her. Then suddenly she was the needy one."

"She hadn't counted on learning that you were dying. That made whatever she had in mind to do look just too wicked to her to carry out," Paul said.

"No, it's more than that." She brushed off his suggestion. "She felt for me. I'm sure of it." She was prepared to face down Paul's skepticism.

But what Paul said was this: "Stranger things have happened. And anything can happen with her, so I don't doubt she did feel for you. But she's just as risky as a friend as she is as an enemy."

"If she had something in mind to do to hurt me, she didn't do it," Susan said. "And she could have. I told her everything. Even that I thought I had scared you away. And all she did was comfort me. She was sure you would be back, that you hadn't given up. She felt for me. You can't tell me she didn't care for me."

"Just after Jack called me and asked me to come back to Riverside early for your second treatment, Rachel called me too, out of the blue, to push me to do the same thing. She told me what she felt for you, and I believed her," Paul said.

"I thought you told me she wanted to hurt me," Susan replied.

"She usually called me to threaten you, or to threaten me away from you. But actually meeting you changed her, just as you said it did. But why was she there today? To see whether I really had come back?" Paul asked.

"No, she already knew that. She pulled her car into the parking lot while you were putting the pedals back on Jack's bike. She drove off as soon as she saw you were there."

"So why was she there today?"

"She wanted to see how it stood between us. She was impatient about it and talked to me like I was a child. I told her you had agreed to raise Jack when I die. And that made her change her tack. She had some trump card she was ready to play to make me take the leap. But just like the last time, she didn't play that card."

"What did she say when you told her about Jack and me?"

"It made her happy. It was the first time I'd ever seen her happy. And that's when I guessed who she was, because of how happy it made her. When I first met her, she told me she wanted to reconcile herself with her lover's widow. I should have put it together then, that she was an old lover of Tom's who couldn't let him go, but it wasn't until I saw that she was really invested in you and seemed to know more about you than she had occasion to know that I made the connections. I still don't know why it mattered so much to her to match you up with me. Maybe she felt she owed something to each of us, and she could settle it by bringing us together. Or maybe, if she felt for me, bringing you to me was the one thing she could do for me."

"But she still didn't tell you who she was, did she? Being happy that I was with you is not quite the same thing as coming clean to you."

"I think that's as close as she dares get. But here's where things took a strange turn. When I described what happened at the plea bargain hearing a few days ago, she lost control of herself. I don't know what it was about. I described how Tom had fought with his killer and what the killer told the court. And she seemed to get more and more upset as she heard it. I can't understand why. And then she said, 'My God, am I really that vile?' and ran away. I don't know what she heard in what I said."

Susan saw Paul's face change. "I think I know what she was thinking," he said.

Already alarmed, Susan looked at him.

"First, I have to tell you that she wasn't just an *old* girlfriend of Tom's. He had begun seeing her again last fall. Rachel saw something in Tom's last book and got in contact with him after many years. When he died, he was about to leave you for her. Since Tom died Rachel has been wanting to throw his affair with her in your face. She called me herself after she saw me with you at the arraignment to tell me that. I wanted to keep you from knowing what Tom was going to do. And I wanted to keep you from knowing that Rachel even existed. That's why I couldn't warn you about her."

Susan felt a flash of humiliation and anger, but she wasn't sure whether it was at Rachel, or at Tom, or at Paul. *Did everybody know what the story was but me? Wasn't anyone ever going to level with me?*

"How did you know this?" As far as she knew, she seemed in control of herself to Paul.

"Because Tom came up to Reno to tell it to me."

Susan completed his thought: *Which he had to do because it wasn't just one more fling like all the others. He meant it this time.*

She had to think for a minute. And again had to control herself. Finally, she said, "I thought it was to make up with you about taking Rachel from you years ago."

"I didn't even know he had done that. And he never did tell me about it. Though I did figure it out from what he told me."

"But why did he have to tell you about what he was doing with her now?" Susan asked.

"That's how I learned that he had taken Rachel from me before. Why else would he have thought I cared about what he did with Rachel now?"

"He felt he had to ask permission from you to leave me for her?" Susan was beginning to boil. *What did Tom really think of me? What do any of them think of me? Why can't any of them trust me with the truth? Why doesn't what I want matter to any of them?*

"Tom thought I'd be able to talk him out of what he was planning to do," Paul said. "That's why he came to see me in Reno. But, by the time he actually got to me, he had made up his mind, and there was no going back."

"But why was he doing this? I had no idea he wasn't happy with me." But then she thought, *That's not quite true. I knew I couldn't make him happy. But he cared for me. He never stopped caring for me. I do know that. Though it didn't stop him from leaving me. All his love for me ever did was torment him.* Her anger began to topple into despair.

"I'm not sure why he was leaving you. But I know he had been involved with Rachel since his last book came out. And that he wasn't happy with her at all. That even seemed to be the point. He wanted her to make him pay for something."

She bit back what she was about to say. But she had to go on: "But all I wanted to do was love him." *All I wanted was to love someone who could not allow himself to be loved, and who hated himself because he could not find the right way to love me. I thought I only wanted to make him happy. But what I wanted was to force him to be happy with me, and that's not happiness. Everything I felt for Tom was futile, and all I did was to make it worse for him. And that's all I'll do for Paul. I hope I die before I hurt him forever. Because that's all I seem to know how to do.* She saw that Paul wanted to take her hand. Paul wanted to comfort her. But he was afraid to. *If he loves me, he's as bad a fool as I am.*

"Tom knew that you loved him completely. He couldn't have missed it. And he wanted me to know about it. I saw it myself, how deeply you loved him, the first moment I ever saw you. And I'm absolutely sure he loved you too, despite everything, even as he was planning to leave you," Paul said.

But Susan had stopped listening to him. *Love doesn't save anyone! It never could! All we've ever done is lie to ourselves about it! All it does is get us in deeper trouble!* Then Susan looked at Paul and saw that he didn't think that way about love at all. She could not bring herself to tell him what she was thinking, even if it was the truth. It would hurt him too much. *It's because he loves me and thinks I've saved him from the impasse he was in. Paul thinks I've opened him to what love is, after he had given up about it. Because I loved Tom. Because he knew Tom loved me. What a strange reason to recover faith in love!*

Paul looked back at her anxiously, trying to read her thoughts, and noticing how he looked at her she softened towards him because she couldn't bring herself to take from him his hard-earned illusion.

He's happy that despite what he imagines about himself he's been able to give me everything he has. He's grateful to me about that, as if it's a gift I gave him, not one he gave me. But all I have to give him is my death. But then Susan thought: *And my son. Our son.*

Paul told Susan everything that had happened when Tom came to the reading in Reno. Then he told her, "I didn't want the last thing he did to you to be to break your heart. That's why I kept you in the dark about Rachel."

"But why did you do that for me? You didn't know me."

"When you called looking for Tom, I didn't tell you that he wasn't headed home to you. I hated lying to you, but I couldn't face what I had to say. You were in trouble, too. I didn't know you were sick, but I heard something in your voice, though you wouldn't say what it was about."

"But what was I to you? You didn't owe me anything."

"I asked myself that when I did it. Because it seemed so crazy even to me to jump in that way. And it meant I'd have to lie to you; I couldn't protect you without lying to you, but that lie would always be between us. But I had to do it. Because not doing it felt like choosing to have never been alive."

She held up her hand like a traffic policeman and looked at him until he stopped speaking and met her gaze. "If that lie brought you to me, I'm glad you told it." She stopped for a second to make sure he had understood what she said. "And I'm glad you called me, however crazy it seemed to you to do. I'm glad for everything you've done for me. And I don't care about any lie you told me about Rachel."

Even after all this time, Paul was surprised. *He thought if I ever really knew him, I would have to hate him,* Susan thought. They looked at each other for a long minute. *And even now he doesn't know the biggest thing he did for me. And never will.*

"I don't understand why Rachel wanted to hurt me," Susan said. "Hadn't she won? Wasn't she going to take Tom from me? And why was she beating up on you about it?"

"Because she knew she hadn't won. Tom never felt about her the way he did about you, even with all her power over him. What did he want from her anyway, except for her to punish him for how he had treated you? And she was angry to see me taking your side. She thought I was taking revenge on her and on Tom. Whenever she wasn't planning to hurt you about her affair with Tom, she was planning to warn you away from me."

Rachel still has feelings for Paul. If she can't have him, she'll make him hurt. Then Susan thought for another second. *And yet she gave him to me.*

"She was at Tom's funeral too. She took Tom's death hard. But she was watching you the whole time. She was enraged with you."

Susan stared.

"She's from Riverside. I don't think you knew that. And she's Catholic. Saint Francis de Sales was her parish growing up. She went to CCD there."

Susan said, "Lurking there during the funeral must have been agony for her."

"There's more to it than that. When we were students, she became pregnant and I took her for an abortion in Maine. After the abortion, Rachel went right home to her parents' house here in Riverside. And she haunted that church, St. Francis de Sales, every day."

"So that's why she was angry to see you at St. Francis de Sales. And with me."

"And the Wednesday after the funeral she came right to your driveway to have it out with me." Paul stopped short, looking down at the couch, plucking at the piping of the fabric.

After a second, Susan looked at him until he felt her eyes on him and had to meet her gaze. "Is that why you went back to Reno? Did she shame you into going back?" Susan asked.

"I was going back anyway because I had run out of pretext to stay. I had no right to be at your house. That was Tom's house, and you were Tom's wife, no matter how I felt about it. And I had to escape Rachel."

"And did you?"

"No and yes. I responded enough to her to feel ashamed of myself."

"How could you not be vulnerable to her?" Susan asked. "I myself was vulnerable to her. I'm still vulnerable to her. She almost swept me away this very afternoon. And I don't have the history with her that you do. I see that what she did explains why she sought me out while you were back in Reno. She wanted to discredit you."

"But then she changed her tack," Paul said. "She came to the playground at Shetland to warn you about me. But meeting you changed her mind. And she called me in Reno right after Jack and you did, and told me exactly that."

"She gave you her blessing?" Susan asked.

"No, not exactly. She threatened to tell you what I was trying to keep you from learning about Tom unless I went right back to Riverside. She said the only thing that was keeping you from loving me, since loving me suddenly was Rachel's idea about what you really needed, was an idealized notion about Tom that she could take from you. That was her idea of doing you a favor. But she probably did have in mind to do you a favor. And to hurt you at the same time."

"I think if she had told me Tom was leaving me for her, I would have told her Tom would ultimately come back to me."

"Because he'd want to take care of you?" Paul asked.

"No. Even if I were going to live. He couldn't face loving me. But it was me he really loved."

"Yes. And I hope too he would have come back even if you were going to live," Paul said.

But he doesn't think so, Susan thought. "We'll never know whether I was right," she said.

"So why do you think Rachel sought you out today?" Paul asked.

"I think she wanted to confess it all to me. And something happened between her and me that I don't understand. I don't know what it was in what I said that horrified her so. It's not something I would have wanted to do to her."

"Here's what I think," Paul said. "Tom did an unpredictable thing when he was with me in Reno. We got into a jam with the Tribal Police up at Pyramid Lake, and he practically provoked the policeman to arrest him. He was in a strange mood, and I didn't learn what it was all about until a couple of days later, when he told me what he planned to do with Rachel. He was tormenting himself about choosing between Rachel and you, and going to jail in Sutcliffe might have made that choice vanish, at least for a while, long enough for him to change his mind. When you told me what the coroner had said, the very first time we went up to Independence, I thought it was strange that Tom had resisted his killer the way he did. Tom knew well enough just to give muggers what they want. The thought crossed my mind that maybe he provoked his killer, with the idea that if he were to be killed, then he wouldn't have to choose, and wouldn't have to face the consequences of whatever choice he made. It took me a while to see that I was wrong."

"Tom provoked the robber? Because he couldn't face what he was doing to me?" Susan asked.

"Yes, I think that's what Rachel thinks."

"My God. But why isn't she right?" Susan did not want him to answer her because she was afraid she would not believe what he said. But she also had to hear it.

"Tom would have known how his killing himself would have harmed you. It doesn't make sense for him to kill himself to spare your feelings."

"But being killed by a drifter doesn't look like suicide. Tom could have wanted to fool me about it."

"He would have known you would see through it. And he knew how that would hurt you. Tom would never have wanted that."

"I still don't understand your logic."

While Paul was trying to figure out what to say, Susan burst in: "We have to go find Rachel before she kills herself."

"Why do you think she will do that?" Paul asked.

"Because whatever he felt for her, even if he loved her, he told you he didn't love her the way he loved me. She must know that by now."

45

$\mathcal{F}$IRST, PAUL AND SUSAN CALLED THE POLICE IN RESEDA TO ASK them to make a welfare check on Rachel. On the phone, they were ambiguous with the police about why they thought Rachel might be a suicide risk, but the dispatcher agreed to send a patrol car to visit her. Rather than waiting for the police to call them back after their visit, however, Susan and Paul set out for Reseda themselves as soon as they had gotten off the phone.

Susan was exhausted, and Jack was already asleep in his bed. They could not leave him alone in the house for the more than three hours their trip to Reseda and back would take, so they lifted him out of his bed and carried him to Susan's Dart as gently as they could, but he woke up in Paul's arms anyway while Susan was opening the rear door. She explained to him as they tucked his seat belt around him that they had to go help someone, and they couldn't leave him behind while they did so. Jack at first thought that the emergency might be about his mother's health and that they might be rushing her to the emergency room. But Susan was there herself, of course, and explained that it was her friend, the woman from the playground, who was in trouble. Jack was a little cranky about having to deal with her again, but Susan made it clear that she meant business and that he would have to go with them. Had Jack been fully awake he might not have accepted this situation. But Susan kissed him on the eyelids, as she always did when she wanted to bless his way back to sleep, and he relaxed against the seat back, his head canted to the left. Susan settled in the back seat with him, and before they had even left the city limits of Riverside, Jack had fallen back to sleep. Every now and again Jack moaned softly in his sleep, attempting to say something important that Susan could not make out.

It wasn't long before Susan's thoughts were drowned in the surf of the motor, and her own breath, deep and slow and even, came and went like the waves. Jack's head rolled over onto her shoulder, and he lay there as he had as an infant, drooling onto her blouse.

It was almost midnight by the time Paul parked Susan's Dart at Reseda Park, across the street from Rachel's apartment. They both knew that Rachel would never let Paul in the door, but she felt enough for Susan that there was a chance she would speak with her. When Susan climbed out of the car to ring the bell in the enclosed front hall of Rachel's building, Paul climbed into the back seat in case Jack woke up.

Susan had to ring repeatedly to bring Rachel to the buzzer. After almost ten minutes of ringing her doorbell, she heard Rachel's voice on the speaker.

"If you're the police, you've already been here, and I'm still alive. If you're not the police, go away."

"It's me. It's Susan Corbin. I was worried about you after this afternoon."

Susan was trying to keep her voice down, in case other tenants would hear. But Rachel's voice was loud, a sloppy voice, beyond shame about being overheard.

"I figured it was you who sent the police. They said some friend had called them. And I don't have any friends."

Susan asked herself whether Rachel was still groggy from sleep, or a little bit drunk.

"How did you know where to find me?" Rachel said, "How did you even know who I was?"

Susan answered as quietly as she could and hoped Rachel would take the cue about lowering her voice. "Paul saw you running away this afternoon."

"It figures. And he had to stick his nose in. I'm sure he's gloating about it now."

Susan told her how she had figured out who Rachel was herself, and how Paul had figured out what had upset her at Shetland Park that afternoon.

"He was always a figurer-outer. I hope he's proud of himself. I'm surprised he told you about what Tom and I were planning to do. I thought his whole reason for zeroing in on you was to keep you from finding that out. That's what he was always throwing at me, anyway, how he had to protect you from me. But now he's found a way to use it against me."

"He's not your enemy. He brought me here because I'm worried for you. And because he is."

"The police must have told you I'm okay by now. And nothing's changed since they were here except I've had a little more to drink. So you've wasted your time. Unless you want to rub it in some more."

Susan heard a voice from the second floor: "Shut up down there or I'm calling the cops! Jesus Christ! They've already been here once tonight."

Susan tried to whisper into the microphone. "Rachel, I didn't come here to yell at you about anything you did with Tom. We set out to come here right after I called the police. Because there's something else you have to know, something I had to tell you myself."

Rachel finally lowered her voice. "Isn't that just great. Why don't you go away and come back some better time? Some time when I'm fit to see you. If there will ever be such a time. I've had enough humiliation for one day."

"I've come all the way from Riverside in the middle of the night to talk to you. I wouldn't have done it if I didn't think I could do you good. I know what you did, all of it, and I also know you are suffering about it, and I've still come here for you. You have to know what that means. Please let me in."

Rachel didn't say another word, but she did press the buzzer and left the door to her apartment ajar. She had returned to her couch by the time Susan made her way, struggling a bit with the stairs, to her apartment. She did not get up when Susan knocked. "It's open," she said, as if to nobody.

It was an improvised room, at the same time empty and cluttered, and the sight of it brought Susan to a stop. Rachel slouched on the dust-colored sofa in her nightgown, but turned her head to gaze in her direction as Susan picked her way across the carpet. There was nowhere else to sit, so Susan stood there, unable to meet Rachel's eyes. After a moment, Susan looked away, at the TV on its little stand on the other side of the room. That again and again her husband had made love to Rachel on this lumpy couch made Susan feel a flash of pity.

Rachel had been drinking California brandy out of half pint bottles, as if the size of the bottles were a way of rationing how much she drank, even though she had several of them. She seemed to be nearly done with a third bottle, although how much of the brandy had still been in the first bottle when Rachel had begun drinking it earlier that evening was something Susan did not know.

"Please sit by me. I can't get up just now," Rachel said at last, indicating the seat next to her.

Susan perched on the edge of the cushion, as though she might fly away if Rachel made any sudden movement. She could smell the liquor on Rachel's breath.

"It's okay," Rachel said, looking at her. "I'm not going to bite you."

Susan sat there sheepishly, ashamed of her flinch.

"Is Paul waiting for you out in your car?"

"Paul drove me, yes. I don't have the stamina for long drives anymore."

"And he's part of this?"

"Part of what? He's worried for you too, if that's what you mean."

"Worried for me. He finally has me at a disadvantage."

"I don't think you understand him at all."

"It's been a while since I cared about understanding him."

Susan knew better than to believe her. "Stop beating up on him. You know I love him," Susan said.

"Yeah, I do know that. I knew it before you did."

"You should give him some credit for what he's done for me through all this. Never mind what he's just done for you. He deserves better from you."

Rachel paused, unused to such bluntness from Susan. "I know what he's done for you," Rachel said, "And I didn't think he had it in him. It still takes some getting used to. Paul as a lover. Paul as a saint. Now Paul as the savior of the wicked Rachel Lake." She said this last in a sing-song voice, like a wicked little nursery rhyme. She made a face. "Who'd a-thunk it?"

"You were just asking today how it stood between us," Susan said.

"And you didn't really answer," Rachel answered.

"The answer is that Tom is still between us. And I haven't gotten past that."

"You don't have much time to get past it. You'd better get down to business."

"He knows I feel for him."

Rachel gave her a crooked smile. "All right. Do it your way. It's the only way you can do it anyway. And where is your boy?"

"With Paul, in the car."

"You brought him to witness my fall from grace?"

"We couldn't leave him alone in the house."

"I'm glad I never had kids. Everything you do you have to do in front of them."

"I'm hoping that he sleeps through this."

"I was hoping you'd let me sleep through it too, so we're even."

"Are you angry that I had the police check on you?"

"No," she said, with a trace of annoyance. "I'm touched, I'm sure. It's just one more touching thing in a day full of touching moments. But you were right. I did plan to kill myself. But I couldn't figure out a good way of doing it. And then I lost my nerve, so I did what I usually do instead."

Susan looked at the mostly empty bottle in front of Rachel.

"Are you safe? Did you drink both of those bottles?"

"Oh, for Christ's sake. I'm not even that drunk."

Susan, a non-drinker although a doctor, had a hard time judging just how drunk Rachel really was.

"If I had been sober, I wouldn't have let you in anyway, so you should be thankful I'm a little drunk."

Susan didn't know where to begin.

"Whatever happened between you and Paul, he doesn't want you to tear yourself up."

"I don't want to hear about what Paul thinks," Rachel said, "I want to hear about what you think."

"I think you and Tom made each other miserable." Susan said this like a detective confronting a suspect in an interrogation room. "And I think that weighs on you, although it's partly what you wanted. Because it's what you thought you both had coming to you. But now that he's gone you wish it had been different. You wish things had turned out between you some better way."

"Maybe a step too far, but mostly right."

"And you thought to come between Paul and me too. Maybe because you and I were rivals about Tom, although I didn't even know it. Or maybe you had other reasons you won't face."

"Also, mostly right." Rachel smiled at her.

She's enjoying this. She's proud about how I'm talking to her. As if she didn't think I could do it before. Susan continued. "And you changed your mind when you learned I was sick. Because Paul, for whatever reasons he might have had, gave everything he had to take care of me."

"Right again," Rachel said. "But I also met you myself. And that made a difference too."

Susan felt a moment of awkwardness.

"And I thought Paul was the one thing I could give you," Rachel said. "The one thing I could give you that you might really want."

Susan felt even more awkward. Rachel was still giving her a drunken smile.

"But there was still Tom between us," Susan said, adding, because of Rachel's smile, an extra dash of gravity to her tone, "between you and me I mean. And you had to find out about Tom's killer. You had to know what the court was going to do with him. And because you had met me, you couldn't go up to Independence for the plea-bargain hearing yourself, the way you did for the arraignment, because I would have recognized you there, and put two and two together about who you are."

"If I had gone to the hearing, you would have figured out who I was. And if you had guessed who I was you wouldn't have wanted to see me again." Rachel was still giving her that crooked smile.

Susan again was brought to a full stop for a moment. "Anyway," Susan finally went on, "when you heard how Tom had fought with his killer you thought he chose to do that as a way of getting out of the choice between us. A kind of suicide by proxy. And you couldn't live with that, with the thought that you had a hand in killing him."

Rachel drew herself up straight at this remark, as if she were perfectly sober. "And you're telling me I was wrong about that? Tom was too smart to fight with a carjacker. I'm not wrong about that. And he let him get back up after he knocked him down."

"Tom would not have wanted to hurt me that way."

"He was willing to hurt you by leaving you for me." Rachel looked directly at Susan, testing her.

"We don't really know that. We know he wasn't sure what he was going to do, because he wouldn't have had to talk to Paul about it if he really were sure. And he died before he got to the turn in the road where he would have had to choose. Nobody knows what he would have done."

"What makes you think he might have come home to you that day?"

"I'm not sure. But I'm pretty sure he would have come back to me sooner or later."

"When he found out you were dying. Yes, I hope so. I even hope I would have sent him back to you myself. But I'm not sure about either of those things." Rachel gave Susan another smile, a sad one this time.

"He might have come back anyway. After a while. And I would have taken him back. No questions asked. As I always did."

"Yes, that's what he did when it was with all those bright young things he was always chasing after. He got tired of them and had to crawl back home. But it was different with me."

Susan took a breath. She felt a flash of fear about what Rachel might say next. "But you yourself," Susan said, "might have wanted him to come back to me too, in the long run."

"How do you know that?" Rachel asked.

Susan saw that Rachel really was puzzled by this remark. "I don't know that," Susan said. "I don't know that about the woman you were this winter. But I do know that about the woman you are now."

Rachel met her gaze and held it for a long moment. "But what makes you sure Tom didn't mean to die?" Rachel asked. "Just to be free of me. And to keep from doing to you what he was about to do. To free himself from me and to free you from him."

Susan thought for a second. "I already told you. Because he wouldn't want to hurt me that way."

"He couldn't hurt me without hurting you. Is that what you are saying? Since he didn't want to hurt you, he couldn't try to hurt me?" Rachel asked.

"I don't believe he killed himself over you," Susan repeated.

"Because I didn't mean enough to him?"

Susan was stung by the way Rachel smiled as she asked this question. But she took a breath and rose to the challenge Rachel had given.

"I don't know why Tom fought his killer. Maybe the carjacker's version is just something he made up to avoid the death penalty. We just don't know why that event took the turn it did. Just as we don't know which road Tom was going to take if he had lived."

"He might not have chosen to die," Rachel said, "but he still didn't choose to live, whether with you or with me. And he could have. If he could fight the killer, he could outrun him. Maybe he didn't know which way he wanted to go, and he knew that if he fought the carjacker he might not have to decide. He couldn't make a final choice between Rachel and Susan. And he couldn't make a final choice between living and dying. He didn't exactly choose to die. But he didn't love life enough to be careful with it."

There was half a minute's silence between them.

Then Rachel exhaled, slowly.

"Whatever he really intended to do, I don't know," Rachel said. "He didn't care how it turned out, one way or the other. Whether he lived or died. Whether he went with me or came home to you. But I put him in that spot, so I don't see any way that what he did didn't have to do with me. Of course, it was my doing, whichever way it went. But it means something to me that you were worried about me. So let me put you at ease about whether I'm going to kill myself over him. I think killing myself would be a pretty poor return for your coming here to talk me out of it. I couldn't have imagined you coming to me this way. I can't say I deserved it. But here you are, so I owe it to you to live, however little I deserve it. It would be the least I could do." Rachel was trying to smile.

"I had to do it," Susan said.

"You're the only person in the world who would think that. I wouldn't have." Rachel looked at her.

"I had to do it."

Rachel smiled. "You really are something. It's a shame our paths can't cross again."

"Nobody knows that our paths can't cross again."

"But whether they do or don't," Rachel said, "I'm glad they crossed tonight." Rachel gave her a long look.

Finally, Susan stood up. Rachel, too, got carefully onto her feet.

"Can I thank you?" Rachel opened her arms to take Susan in. Rachel held her close and kissed her very firmly on the lips. Susan did not know how to respond, but a warm flush spread through her entire body. After a few moments, Rachel broke off the kiss and leaned away from her, still holding her. "I took a liberty with you. I'm sorry," Rachel said.

"Don't worry about it," Susan responded as Rachel released her.

"I was thankful for you, and I let my feelings get the better of me." Rachel shook her head and tried to smile.

"You've had a hard night."

Rachel collapsed back onto the couch, unsteady on her feet. "I'm sorry. I can't even keep my balance. I feel ashamed for you to see me this way."

"You don't have to be ashamed with me." Susan looked down at her for a minute, unsure what to do. Somehow it seemed wrong to just walk out the door. She stroked Rachel's hair.

"At least let me get you settled before I go." Susan helped Rachel up and got her to bed. As Susan pulled up the covers, she saw that Rachel had already passed out. Susan kissed the little lost lamb softly on the temple, as she might have kissed Jack, and closed the door behind her as she left the room.

On her way out, she wrote on the little notepad by Rachel's phone, "We might not see each other again before I die. But whether we do or not, I want to tell you that I hope you find peace. Please don't feel badly about anything that's passed between us. I know where I have to go, and I'm ready to find my way there when the time comes. And I wish you only the best. Please look after Paul if you can. I hope he'll let you."

46

*T*WO DAYS AFTER HER THIRD INTERFERON TREATMENT ON THE 25th of June, Susan drove herself to the clinic at Loma Linda for a series of tests. The third treatment had gone very badly, the fever and nausea were worse. Over the last few days, she had felt persistent pain in her right hip. She also felt a little confused in her mind and emotionally volatile.

Susan had the CAT scan and the isotope scan scheduled after the third treatment to show whether the interferon had any effect. The news was rather bad. The tumors had grown only slowly, but they had not shrunk, which meant that the procedures would not be enough to save her life. The isotope scan detected new tumors that had begun to degrade her hip joint.

The isotope scan did not detect new tumors in her brain. But the Principal Investigator was certain that although they had not yet risen to the level where they could be detected, there must be new micro-metastases. There was also an alarming rise in the calcium in her blood, which might account for the confusion and nausea. There was no other line of effective treatment against melanoma, so all of the courses available to Susan were only palliative. The doctor prescribed her cimetidine for the nausea. He also planned a regimen to control the pain which he knew would shortly begin its inexorable rise, beginning with oxycodone for the early stages, then proceeding to methadone as the pain became more severe. Sooner or later, the pain would break through even the methadone, and they would have to manage her pain through the last stage with morphine.

Susan had known from the beginning that this was the likely course of events. But it was different to understand it in a theoretical way and to face it as an immediate prospect. She also knew she had a few weeks at best before the disease took away her autonomy, and then her dignity, until it would finally reduce her to something no longer even quite human, an inarticulate, only fleetingly conscious suffering creature unable even to respond to human voices, until finally the disease would finish its sport with her and let her drop.

She went to Claire Wirthlin and told her that she would be unable to return to her residency after that day. Claire knew what that meant and sat with Susan in her little office and told her how proud she was of how bravely she had kept at her work the whole time, and how many patients' lives she had touched while her own was in such danger. Susan was grateful for her kindness.

Once she got back to her car, she began to cry. After half an hour, she regained control of her feelings and carefully dried her tears with her handkerchief. She looked at herself in the rearview mirror and tried to decide whether it was obvious that she had been crying. It might be less obvious, she thought, by the time she had driven home to Riverside.

During the drive, she made some quick plans. To Jack and to Paul, she would give a last memory before her final slide down into nothing would visibly get underway—to Paul first, then to Jack the next day. Only after that, on Sunday, would she break the news to Jack. The thought of Jack and Paul's grief and suffering was more painful to her than the prospect of what she was going to go through.

After midnight that night, as Paul lay awake in the cot in the room that had been Corbin's study, she opened the door silently, slipping on bare white feet into the room, the hem of her nightgown brushing the cold floor. She climbed into the cot, releasing the loose gown from her shoulders, her arms thin and pale in the half-light. Paul held her softly, as she lay against his chest, listening to his heartbeat as his chest rose and fell with his breath. He stroked her hair down the back of her neck to her shoulders. Tentatively, he kissed the top of her head.

"Dear heart," she said.

She raised her face to him and kissed him on the lips, at first merely with tenderness, then more urgently. Uncertainly, he returned her kiss.

"We may not have another chance to do this. We'll regret it if we miss it," she said.

He kissed her again. She returned the kiss and held him tight.

"Please make love to me, Paul. I'm not going to break."

Later, as they lay on the little cot, Susan raised her head from Paul's shoulder, and looked at him. "I think it will be over in about six weeks. By Labor Day, for sure. I'm sorry I've left so much for you to clean up after that. It will all fall to you."

She hadn't meant to say this quite yet, but she couldn't help herself.

"Don't worry about that now."

"There are so many things I won't be able to do." She paused again. "I won't see Jack grow up."

"I'll take care of him, Susan."

"And I won't be able to keep up this life with you."

"I've had more of life than I thought I would." Paul said, "Whatever I did before wasn't life. This has been what life is. I don't regret it. I have had my life. I only wish you could have yours."

"I couldn't have asked you to do what you have done. It's been hard."

"It has been hard. But it's also been good. I'm glad I didn't miss out on it."

Susan thought about this sentiment. "I'm glad I didn't miss out too. It's easier for me to die knowing that I haven't missed out on everything."

"I wish there were more. More for us. More for you."

"So do I. But I've had the big things. I've saved lives. I've raised a child, partly."

"And done all that well."

"No, I haven't. But I've done what I could."

"There's not much you could have changed."

"And I've done the main thing. I've loved someone with all I have." She paused for a breath. "And I've been loved. Adored."

Paul looked at her.

She touched him on the end of his nose. "It's you I mean, silly."

"I should have been more honest about it," he said. "I should have told you straight out that I love you."

"I never doubted it."

314

47

SATURDAY WAS BRILLIANTLY CLEAR, AND, FOR THE LAST WEEKEND of June in the Inland Empire, cool and fresh as well. Susan suggested to Paul that they all walk to the top of Mt. Rubidoux, just west of the city.

"Are you sure you are up to that?" Paul asked. Susan had noticeably weakened over the course of June, and, because of the pain in her hip, had begun to use a cane when she walked outdoors. It would not have been under most circumstances a difficult walk, since the path was paved, and the whole thing was only about three miles long, with a very gradual climb around the brown, ragged hill, which rose in the middle of the plain next to the Santa Ana river, about eight hundred feet over the valley floor.

"I don't know, but we'll rest when we have to. I know there are benches on the way up, some of them even with shade. We might never have another chance, and I've always loved the view from up there. I'd like to see it one more time, and I want to show it to Jack while I can."

Susan had put on the bright yellow sundress that she had worn to the botanical garden and a broad straw hat with a yellow cloth band. She had let her hair out of the ponytail she usually wore. *This is what I will want him to remember about how I looked.* She smiled at him, seeing that he had noticed her hat.

The mountain abruptly rose out of the backyards of a leafy, suburban neighborhood. They parked in the large parking lot of Ryan Bonaminio Park, which, at ten in the morning, was already crowded. The trees in the parking lot were covered with brilliant white flowers, and children's teams were already playing at the two softball fields in the park. They went up what appeared to be an ordinary suburban street to the place where the trailhead came down into the neighborhood behind an apartment complex. There was already a parade of families around them as they turned up at the trailhead and passed through the pedestrian opening at the steel gate of the hiking path.

The hill itself was rumpled and bare and tan, with long, already dried grass bending among the boulders scattered on the slope. Because the sun was so bright, the grass looked golden, an almost transparent blond. Brushy trees dotted the slope with olive green. The three of them made their way up past the boulders. Even with her cane, Susan walked slowly. She put her other hand in the crook of Paul's elbow. When he put his other hand on top of hers, she thought how warm and soft it was. He caught her eye for a second and smiled.

As they crossed the eastern slope, they could look down into the backyards, into the swimming pools and swing sets, of the neighborhood that backed up to the mountain. They doubled back to the south, and passed beneath a jumbled cluster of boulders, and they could see the brown slopes of Box Springs Mountain behind the tall buildings of the city center. They crossed around to the west side of the ridge. Off in the distance, they could see Saddleback Mountain and to the north the Angeles National Forest with the white peak of Mount Baldy cropping up behind. Just before the little bridge they made a hairpin turn back across the ridge to the east side of the slope again, and after a few hundred yards they came to the Peace Tower, with its stone peak like a part of a Spanish castle, watching like a sentinel across the valley, and the Friendship Bridge, in its little cluster of trees. As they climbed, they could see, rising beyond Box Springs Mountain, the great rampart of Mt. San Gorgonio still mantled in snow.

With them, were dozens of families, taking the same walk, laughing and playing with each other. There were hundreds of people, moving up the gentle slope on the side of the mountain together, more like a procession than a crowd. Children were running, squabbling, singing. Their parents were holding hands and looking ahead. Around her Susan heard English, Spanish, Tagalog, Vietnamese, Cantonese: all the turbulent, effervescent vitality of southern California. *How sweet it is, this life I am about to leave*, she thought.

Finally, they came to the dozen stone terraces that led up to the Serra cross at the mountain's summit. They found the stairs at the end of the terraces and climbed to the cross itself. Beneath them was the whole valley.

Close by, but far below, were the tall buildings of the downtown. Susan saw the Community Hospital, the Courthouse, even the church where her husband's funeral had been held. The valley was lush with green although surrounded by dry mountains. She heard the traffic sounds, the restless bustle of the city below them. There was an ambulance siren, far off. *Someone is rushing to help*, Susan thought. *They are giving it everything they have. It means everything to get there in time.* She saw the traffic on the highway beyond the city center, and the cars on the streets closer in. *Everywhere I look people are busy with their lives. And they will be going on after I am gone. And all of them will someday be gone too, and others will be busy with their living after them. And all I can do is bless them all, those who knew me and those who never will, and those who are not yet born, and those who died long ago. They will never know how the thought of them has blessed me. And how I have blessed them, without their knowing. And some other person, maybe some other woman, someone who had the fortune to live to the end of her days, may stand here, dying too, years from now, and she will look out at this same scene and bless it as I am doing now. And I will be among those to receive her blessing.*

"Look, Jack," she said, pointing her cane, as if she had brought it for that purpose rather than to support her as she walked, "see the Carillon, straight out, over there. That's the university. And just south of that is the botanical garden, where we went a few weeks ago." Jack strained to look. "And up there, a little north, where you can't see it," she said, "is where we live."

Paul was watching Susan. He was quiet, at peace. Jack stood silently, looking out across the valley.

"Jack, what do you see?" Susan said.

"I see the world."

And there it was.

48

$\mathcal{A}$T THE BEGINNING OF SEPTEMBER, AT SUSAN'S SPARSELY AT-
tended funeral, which, because Father Ronan had been so kind to Susan,
Paul had organized at St. Francis de Sales church, Paul leaned with his
arm around Jack, who, wearing his first jacket and tie, sat as erect and
silent and grave as a soldier giving a salute; hearing a rustle behind him,
Paul turned and saw Rachel Lake, alone at the back of the church, by
the entrance, dressed in black, with a veil over her face, her head bowed
down. When she raised her head, she noticed that Paul had seen her, and
she walked quickly back to the door and out of the church.

$\mathcal{L}$ate in the morning of the day after Veterans Day, as Paul approached
the graves of Thomas and Susan Corbin, he noticed a woman standing
there, calmly looking down.

"You don't have to go away because I'm here. You have a right to
your grief too," he said.

Rachel turned around to face him. "Hello, Paul. I hope you are well."
She offered him her hand, and he took it.

"I hope the same for you." He noticed that she had laid her flowers
not on Corbin's grave, but on Susan's.

"I saw that you had been here before, a few weeks ago," he said,
looking at the flowers. "I come almost every day."

She looked at him. "Does it bother you that she is with him in death?"

"It was her loyalty in the face of everything that I loved her for."

"I can't bring myself to feel that way. I still think she defeated me. But
I know I shouldn't think that. I was cruel to her when she was vulnerable,
and I'm ashamed of it."

"I think she knew that love is cruel. She wasn't daunted by that. I
have to share her with Tom, and I don't regret it. You shouldn't regret
having to share him with her."

"I don't regret sharing Tom with her. And I don't regret sharing Susan with you. I regret that I treated her the way I did."

He looked at Corbin's grave. They were together again. Susan had brought Corbin back to her, and he would be with her now no matter what he had done to her. In all their time together, Susan had sought to love him, to forgive him, to redeem him. And, still loving her, in the despairing way he did everything, he had evaded her every time.

Susan had wanted to be a surgeon, had wanted, with her delicate knife, to detach the tumor from the body into which it had taken root, the body to which it was no stranger, no invader, the body of which it was a part, but a fatal part. But detaching the tumor was only possible where the disease had not already spread throughout the body. Paul wondered: does forgiveness drive out the hunger for the thing we need to be forgiven for? If it could not do that, Corbin had felt, then it could do nothing. But this is what Susan had never accepted. To forgive may be to love someone as they want to be, but that is not to refuse to love them as they actually are, too. Paul thought about what St. Paul had said about love, how it bears all things, believes all things, hopes all things, endures all things. It just can't be that that means nothing.

Would Corbin have found his own way back to her? Susan was sure he would have, and Paul had doubted it. But he knew that he would never really know the answer to that question because Corbin had been killed before he had come to the point in the road where he would have had to make a choice once and for all, if there ever really is such a point, beyond which there is no turning. Standing over her grave, Paul could not say for sure whether Susan was right about Corbin or not. And if he could not say that, then Corbin's story was still an unfinished one, and how it would end was still an open question. But that's what hope is, Paul thought, the unearned possibility that, whatever we know about ourselves, how our story will end is still an open question. And that's the gift love has to offer. It's the gift Susan had offered first to Corbin, then to Paul himself, then to Rachel, the gift of having a story that is not already over.

"I don't regret anything. And you shouldn't either," Paul said, finally turning to Rachel, finally answering her question, "I'm glad I met her.

319

What more can I ask out of life? After all, I've loved and I've been loved. And now I have a little boy to love and raise and be loved by."

"I have loved, and made a mess of it. And I have been loved, and made a mess of it," Rachel replied. "And I don't see that there is anything I can do about either thing now."

"Susan knew the whole story, and she forgave you. She knew all about it when she saved your life, and it didn't stop her."

Rachel smiled at him. "Tell me that you don't despise me."

"I might have despised you, but I don't now. I can't. She wouldn't have wanted me to, anyway. And we've both been through too much together for despising."

"I hope there will come some time, maybe years from now, when our paths can cross again." Again, she smiled at him.

"And when they do, we won't brood about what we did to each other." Paul squeezed her shoulder then walked back to his car. Later that afternoon, when school got out, Paul planned, as he so often did, to take Jack to the swings.

Acknowledgments

Chapter 7 appeared as "The Sparrow" in *Review Americana* vol. 19 issue 2 (2024).

I'd like to begin by thanking all the friends who listened as I thought through this book aloud, read drafts of it, and helped me shape it through their comments. Stephen Dowden read the first draft of every chapter as I wrote it, and was and is quite literally the reader I imagined myself writing for. Sharon O'Brien, Mike Howard, Amy Farrell, and John Bloom held my hand through the first few chapters at our informal writing group at Ferry Beach in Maine. Stephen Kendrick read the very rough first draft, and saw the possibilities in it despite its many flaws. My friends Matthew Abbate, Tim Peltason, Ernest Suarez, Jennifer Lewin, Jon Sudholt, Carolyn Ramm, George Franklin, William Flesch, and Laura Quinney read all or part of it, and they will each find moments in the book that arose from their comments and suggestions. My family was crucial too: Richard Burt, Frank Burt, Carol Burt, Denisa Burt, and most of all my wife Jo Anne Preston read through it, heard me go on endlessly about it, and helped me immensely with it. Stephen McCauley, Katrin Schumann, and Amaryah Orenstein read what I wrote with a professional eye. My developmental editor Jackie Cangro read the whole thing twice, and her detailed comments and encouragement helped me see the novel as a whole. I owe special gratitude to Prize Americana for selecting my book, and to Leslie Kreiner Wilson for editing it. It is difficult to put into words just how much gratitude I feel for the hard work she put into this book, from large scale issues such as the motivations of the characters and the logic of the point of view, to the fine details of word choice and punctuation. In fact, the single best sentence in this book was suggested by her.

About the Author

John Burt is Paul Prosswimmer Professor of American Literature at Brandeis University. His scholarly books include *Lincoln's Tragic Pragmatism* (2013) and *Robert Penn Warren and American Idealism* (1988). He is also the editor of *The Collected Poems of Robert Penn Warren* (1998), and *Robert Penn Warren's* Brother to Dragons: *A Parallel Text Critical Edition of the 1953 and 1979 versions* (forthcoming). In addition, he has published three volumes of poetry, *The Way Down* (1988), *Work without Hope* (1996) and *Victory* (2007).

Visit my website for more: https://johndaviesburt.com.